STAR TREK®

PANTHEON

STAR TREK®

PANTHEON

Michael Jan Friedman (signature)

Based on
Star Trek: The Next Generation®
created by Gene Roddenberry

A special signature edition of
Star Trek: The Next Generation—The Valiant
and *Star Trek: The Next Generation—Reunion*

POCKET BOOKS

New York   London   Toronto   Sydney   Singapore

POCKET BOOKS, a division of Simon & Schuster, Inc.
1230 Avenue of the Americas, New York, NY 10020

This book is published by Pocket Books, a division of
Simon & Schuster, Inc., under exclusive license from
Paramount Pictures.

ISBN: 0-7434-8511-4

First Pocket Books trade paperback edition September 2003

10 9 8 7 6 5 4 3 2 1

Library of Congress Cataloging-in-Publication data is available.

Manufactured in the United States of America

For information regarding special discounts for bulk purchases, please contact
Simon & Schuster Special Sales at 1-800-456-6798 or
business@simonandschuster.com

These titles were previously published individually by Pocket Books.

For Uncle Leslie, never forgotten

Introduction

I distinctly remember two things about the first-season *Star Trek: The Next Generation* episode "The Battle." One was that it featured a guy who had been my pal in second grade.

I noticed it the first time his face appeared on the screen. "My God," I said, "that's Douglas Warhit."

"Who?" asked my wife, who was five months pregnant at the time and understandably had other things on her mind.

"Douglas Warhit. We were pals in second grade. I haven't seen him in maybe twenty-five years."

My wife knew I never forgot a face (God's halfhearted way of balancing out my many failings), but this was different. This wasn't just a guy I had known a quarter of a century earlier. This was a guy I had known a quarter of a century earlier who was playing a Ferengi.

We're talking major makeup here—the ears, the nose, the forehead, the whole deal. And as far as I could recall, Douglas Warhit's teeth hadn't ever come to sharpened points. But I recognized him—in a couple of seconds, tops. It remains one of my most cherished accomplishments.

If I see you at a party, I'll probably tell you about it. At length.

The other thing I remember about "The Battle" was its revelation that, once upon a time, Picard had commanded another ship. Many years before he had even contemplated setting foot on the *Starship Enterprise,* he had worked with another crew entirely.

But in "The Battle," we didn't learn very much about that crew. They were left huddling in a dank, dark corner of the *Star Trek* universe, waiting to be discovered. And there's nothing I like better than shining light into dark corners.

As I write this, Picard's first crew has appeared not only in *Reunion* and *The Valiant* (the books that compose this volume), but also in several other novels, including *Requiem, The First Virtue,* and the four *Stargazer* titles published to date: *Gauntlet, Progenitor, Three,* and *Oblivion.*

I'm currently in the process of outlining the fifth and sixth books in the series, tentatively entitled *Enigma* and *Maker.* And Ben Zoma, the Asmunds, Simenon, Greyhorse, Vigo, and Pug, who started out as characters I thought I would use once and discard, have become like a family to me.

I hope you feel the same way.

And if you're out there, Douglas, I have to tell you something as a friend . . . get a dentist, dude. Pointed teeth just gross people out.

Michael Jan Friedman
Somewhere on Long Island
May 2003

PROLOGUE

United Space Probe Agency Starship
<u>S.S. Valiant</u>
2068

One

Carlos Tarasco of the *S.S. Valiant* stood in front of his captain's chair and eyed the phenomenon pictured on his viewscreen.

It was immense, he thought. No—it was *beyond* immense. It stretched across space without boundaries or limits, a blazing vermillion abyss without beginning or end.

"Amazing," said Gardenhire, his redheaded ops officer.

Tarasco grunted. "You can say that again."

Sommers, the curly-haired brunette who was sitting next to Gardenhire at the helm controls, cast a glance back at the captain. "You still want to go through it, sir?"

"Do we have a choice?" Tarasco asked her.

The helm officer recognized it as a rhetorical question and returned her attention to her monitors. With her slender fingers crawling across her control dials like an exotic variety of insect, she deployed additional power to the propulsion system.

"Ready when you are, sir."

Was he ready? The captain drew a deep breath.

The phenomenon had puzzled him ever since it came up on the viewscreen earlier that day. Their optical scanners registered what looked like the universe's biggest light show, but there was nothing there as far as their other instruments were concerned.

Unfortunately, it wasn't merely a matter of scientific curiosity. Tarasco and his crew of eighty-eight had set out from Earth years earlier, aiming to chart a stretch of space from their home system to the farthest reaches of the Milky Way galaxy—part of a sector that Terran astronomers had labeled the Alpha Quadrant.

They had almost completed their assignment when they encountered an unexpectedly powerful magnetic storm. At first, it seemed that they might be able to outrun the thing. Then they found out otherwise.

The storm caught them up and flung them light-years off course, well past what Tarasco's cartography team reckoned was the outer edge of the galaxy. If not for the readings their scanners took along the way, they wouldn't even have known which way was home.

But knowing the way was only half the battle. The storm had wrecked both their warp and nuclear impulse engines, forcing them to drift on emergency power until the crew could get them up and running.

Finally, after weeks of languishing under the glare of alien stars, Tarasco and his people got underway again. They knew that their trip back to Earth had been lengthened by nearly eleven months, but no one griped. They were just glad to be heading home.

And all had gone well from that point, the captain reflected. *Until now, that is.*

He couldn't be sure if the phenomenon had been there when the storm threw them so precipitously in the other direction, or if it had sprung up since that time. Certainly, their computer hadn't made any record of it.

One thing was for sure—they weren't going to get back to Earth without passing through the thing.

Tarasco glanced at Sommers. "Let's do it."

He could feel a subtle hum in the deck below his feet as the *Valiant* accelerated to the speed of light. The phenomenon loomed in front of them, a gargantuan, red maw opened wide to swallow them up.

"Still no sign of it on sensors," said Hollandsworth, his tall, dark-skinned science officer.

"Deflectors are registering something," reported Gardenhire. He turned to the captain. "A kind of pressure."

"So we're not just seeing things," Tarasco concluded. "I guess we can take some comfort in that."

"Maintain heading?" asked Sommers.

"Affirmative," said the captain.

The closer they got, the more tumultuous the phenomenon appeared. The ruby light within it began to writhe and shimmer, giving birth to monstrous caverns and towering eruptions.

It was beautiful in the way a stormy, windblown sea was beautiful. And like a stormy sea, it was frightening at the same time.

"All available power to the shields," Tarasco ordered.

"Aye, sir," said Gardenhire.

Suddenly, the ship jerked hard to starboard. Caught by surprise, the captain had to grab hold of his chair back for support. He turned to his operations officer, a question on his face.

"We're all right," Gardenhire reported dutifully. "Shields are holding fine, sir."

Tarasco turned back to the viewscreen. They seemed to be entering a deep, red-veined chasm, pulsating with forces that baffled him as much as they did his scanning devices. Before he knew it, the phenomenon wasn't just in front of them, it was all around.

He felt another jerk, even harder than the first. But a glance at Gardenhire told him that everything was still under control.

Behind the captain, the lift doors whispered open. He looked back and saw that his first officer had joined them. Commander Rashad was a wiry man with a neatly trimmed beard and a sarcastic wit.

"I hope I'm not too late," Rashad said darkly.

"Not at all," Tarasco told him. "The show's just starting."

"Good," said his exec. "I hate to miss anything."

The words had barely left his mouth when the lights on the bridge began to flicker. Everyone looked around, the captain included.

"What's happening?" he asked his ops officer.

"I'm not sure, sir," said Gardenhire, searching his control panel for a clue. "Something's interfering with our electroplasma flow."

Abruptly, the deck lurched beneath them, as if they were riding the crest of a gigantic wave. Hollandsworth's console exploded in a shower of sparks, sending him flying backward out of his seat.

Tarasco began to move to the science officer's side. However, Rashad beat him to it.

"Shields down forty-five percent!" Gardenhire announced.

Another console exploded—this time, an empty one. It contributed to the miasma of smoke collecting above them. And again, the ship bucked like an angry horse.

"The helm's not responding!" Sommers cried out.

Rashad depressed the comm pad at the corner of Hollandsworth's console. "Sickbay, this is Rashad. We need someone up here on the double. Lieutenant Hollandsworth has been—"

Before he could finish his sentence, the first officer seemed to light up from within, his body suffused with a smoldering, red glow. Then he fell to his knees beside the unconscious Hollandsworth.

"Amir!" Tarasco bellowed.

For a gut-wrenching moment, he thought Rashad had been seriously hurt. Then the man turned in response to the captain's cry and signaled with his hand that he was all right.

"Shields down eighty-six percent!" Gardenhire hollered. He turned to the captain, his eyes red from the smoke and full of dread. "Sir, we can't take much more of this!"

As if to prove his point, the *Valiant* staggered sharply to port, throwing Tarasco into the side of his center seat. He glared at the viewscreen, hating the idea that his choices had narrowed to one.

"All right!" he thundered over the din of hissing consoles and shuddering deckplates. "Get us out of here!"

There was only one way the helm officer could accomplish that: retreat. Wrestling the ship hard to starboard, she aimed for a patch of open space.

Under Sommers's expert hand, the *Valiant* climbed out of the scarlet abyss. At the last moment, the forces inside the phenomenon seemed to add to their momentum, spitting them out like a watermelon seed.

Tarasco had never been so glad to see the stars in his life. Trying not to breathe in the black fumes from Hollandsworth's console, he made his way to the science officer and dropped down beside him.

Hollandsworth's face and hands had been badly burned. He was making sounds of agony deep in his throat.

"Is he going to make it?" asked Rashad, who was sitting back on his haunches. He looked a little pale for his experience.

"I don't know," the captain told him.

Before he could try to help, the lift doors parted and a couple of medics emerged. One was a petite woman named Coquillette, the other a muscular man named Rudolph.

"We'll take it from here, sir," said Coquillette.

Tarasco backed off and let the medical personnel do their jobs. Then he did his. "Damage report!" he demanded of his ops officer.

"Shields down, sir," Gardenhire told him ruefully. "Scanners, communications, lasers . . . all off-line."

Beside him, Sommers pounded her fist on her console. "The main engines are shot. That last thrust burned out every last circuit."

"Switch life support to emergency backup," said the captain.

Without waiting for a response, he peered over Coquillette's shoulder to see how Hollandsworth was doing. The science officer's eyes were open, but he was trembling with pain.

"Easy now," Coquillette told Hollandsworth, and injected him with an anesthetic through the sleeve of his uniform.

Tarasco heaved a sigh. Then he turned back to Rashad. "Poor guy," he said, referring to the science officer.

But Rashad wasn't looking at the captain any longer. He was stretched out on his back, eyes staring at the ceiling, and Rudolph was trying to breathe air into his lungs.

Rashad wasn't responding. He just lay there, limp, like a machine drained of all its power.

Tarasco shook his head. "No . . ."

Just moments earlier, his first officer had assured him he was all right. He had even asked the captain about Hollandsworth. How could something have happened to him so quickly?

Then Tarasco remembered the way Rashad had lit up in the grip of the phenomenon, like a wax candle with a fierce, orange flame raging inside it. Clearly, they were dealing with matters beyond their understanding.

Tarasco watched helplessly as Rudolph labored to bring Rashad back to life, blowing into his mouth and pounding Rashad's chest with the heel of his hand. At the same time, Coquillette injected the first officer with a stimulant of some kind.

None of it helped.

"Let's get them to sickbay," a red-faced Rudolph said at last.

Numbly, the captain took hold of Rashad under his arms, though he knew his chief medical officer wouldn't be able to help the man either. On the other hand, Hollandsworth still had a chance to pull through.

He and Coquillette picked up the first officer, while Rudolph and Gardenhire hefted the lanky Hollandsworth. Then they squeezed into the still-open lift compartment and entered sickbay as their destination.

The air in the lift was close and foul with the stench of burned flesh. Fortunately, their destination was just a couple of decks up. As the doors slid apart, Tarasco and the others piled out with their burdens and made their way down the corridor.

In less than a minute, they reached sickbay. Its doors were wide open, giving them an unobstructed view of the facility's eight intensive care beds, which were arranged like the spokes of a wheel. Three of the beds were occupied, though metallic silver blankets had been pulled up ominously over the patients' faces.

Damn, thought the captain, his heart sinking in his chest. He had assumed the only casualties were those suffered on the bridge.

Gorvoy, the *Valiant*'s florid-faced chief medical officer, looked grim as he approached them and took a look. "Put them down here and here," he told Rudolph and Coquillette, pointing to a couple of empty beds, "and get up to deck seven. McMillan's got two more in engineering."

The medics did as they were told and took off, leaving Tarasco and Gardenhire to stand there as Gorvoy examined Hollandsworth with a handheld bioscanner. The physician consulted the device's tiny readout, crossed the octagonally shaped room and removed something from an open drawer. Then he came back to the semiconscious science officer.

"Hollandsworth will heal," he told the captain. "I wish I could say that for the others. Do me a favor and cover Rashad, will you?"

Tarasco gazed at his first officer, who was lying inert on his bed, his features slack and his eyes locked on eternity. Moving to the foot of the bed, the captain took the blanket there and unfolded it. Then he draped it over Rashad.

"Amir," he sighed, mourning his friend and colleague.

Gorvoy glanced at him as he applied a salve to Hollandsworth's burns. "He lit up like a lightning bug, right?"

Tarasco returned the glance. "The others, too?" he guessed.

"Uh huh. Kolodny, Rivers, Yoshii . . . all of them."

The captain considered the man-sized shapes beneath the metallic blankets. "But why them and not anyone else?"

"That's the question," the medical officer agreed. "Was Rashad near an open conduit or something?"

Tarasco thought about it. "No. He was near Hollandsworth's console, though. And it was shooting sparks."

It was possible the console had had something to do with it. However, the captain's gut told him otherwise. And judging by the expression on Gorvoy's face, the doctor didn't believe it was the console either.

Gardenhire was grimacing as he watched Gorvoy spread the salve. Tarasco put his hand on the ops officer's shoulder.

"Go on," he told Gardenhire. "Get back to the bridge. See if Sommers needs any help."

The redhead nodded. "Aye, sir," he said. With a last, sympathetic look at Hollandsworth, he left sickbay.

But Gardenhire wasn't gone long before Tarasco heard the sound of heavy footsteps coming from the corridor. Suddenly, another medical team burst into the room, carrying a young woman between them.

It was Zosky, the stellar physicist who had signed onto the mission at the last minute. She was a dead weight in the medics' arms as they followed Gorvoy's gesture and laid her on another bed.

My God, the captain thought . . . how many more? And what could have killed them, while so many others had been spared?

He watched as they laid Zosky down, as Gorvoy took a moment to examine her with his bioscanner . . . and as they pulled the blanket over her face. *Not the console,* part of him insisted.

The doctor eyed Tarasco. "Maybe you ought to get back to the bridge, too," he suggested.

The captain nodded. "Maybe."

He had started to leave sickbay when Coquillette and Rudolph came huffing in from the corridor. They were carrying yet another victim—a baby-faced engineer named Davidoff.

"McMillan said there were *two* of them," Gorvoy told them. "Where's the other one?"

As if in answer to his question, Chief Engineer McMillan came shuffling in with one of his men leaning on him for support. Tarasco recognized the injured man as Agnarsson, McMillan's first assistant.

Agnarsson was a big man, tall and broad-shouldered, with a strong jaw and a fierce blond mustache. But at the moment, he was weak as a kitten, fighting hard just to stay conscious. The captain helped McMillan get him to a bed and hoist him onto it.

"What's the matter with him?" Tarasco asked.

The chief engineer cursed beneath his breath. "He started to glow—he and Davidoff both. It was the damnedest thing."

The captain looked at him, his pulse starting to pound in his temples. "He was glowing? And he's still alive?"

"I'm fine," Agnarsson muttered, hanging his head and rubbing the back of his neck. "Just a little light-headed is all."

Then the big man picked up his head . . . and Tarasco's jaw fell. Agnarsson's eyes, normally a very ordinary shade of blue, were glowing with a luxuriant silver light.

Two

Captain's log, December 30th, 2069. Tomorrow will be New Year's Eve. We should be preparing our usual celebration, festooning the lounge and watching Sommers mix her killer punch. Unfortunately, with six of our comrades dead, no one feels much like celebrating. So instead of toasting 2070, we're delving under control consoles and wriggling through access tubes, trying to expedite the process of bringing basic systems back on-line. The problem is every time we think we've fixed something, a new trouble spot rears its ugly head. And even if we can solve all the little snags, we'll still be left with a great big one—the warp drive. Chief McMillan says it may be beyond repair this time. And if we're restricted to impulse power, none of us will live long enough to see Earth again.

Tarasco paused in his log entry, put down his microphone and looked around at his quarters. They were small, cramped—and yet palatial in comparison to those of the average crewman.

They hadn't seemed so bad when the captain first saw them. But back then, he was contemplating spending six or seven years in the place, at most. Now he was looking at living out his life there.

He recalled the story of Moses, the biblical patriarch who led his people through a wilderness for forty years and brought up a new generation in the process. But in the end, Moses was prohibited from entering the Promised Land with his charges.

Is that how it's going to be with me? Tarasco asked himself. *After all we've been through, am I going to be Moses? Have I already seen Earth for the last time?*

It was a depressing thought, to say the least. Putting it aside, the captain saved his entry, got up and left his quarters. After all, he was needed on the bridge.

Siregar stared at her fellow security officer as if he had sprouted another pair of ears. "You're kidding, right?"

Offenburger, a tall, blond man, pulled his head out from under a fire-damaged control panel. "Not at all. I'm telling you, his eyes were silver. And they were glowing."

"You *saw* him?" asked Siregar, her skepticism echoing through the *Valiant's* auxiliary control center.

"No," her colleague had to admit. "Not personally, I mean. But O'Shaugnessy and Maciello were in engineering when Agnarsson lit up, and they both told me the same thing. Silver and glowing."

Siregar grunted, then returned her attention to the exposed power coupling she had been working on. Normally, an engineer would have taken care of such repairs. However, with all the damage done by Big Red, the engineering staff couldn't handle everything.

Especially when they were missing two of their best men.

"At least Agnarsson's *alive*," she said.

"For now," Offenburger added cryptically.

Siregar looked at him. "What's *that* supposed to mean? Do they think he's going to die?"

"They don't know what to think," he told her. "They've never seen anyone with glowing eyes before."

"But is he going downhill?"

Offenburger shook his head. "I don't know . . . but I sure hope not. It'd be nice to see at least one of those guys pull through."

Siregar nodded. She hadn't been especially close to any of the victims, but she mourned their loss nonetheless. After she had spent years working alongside them, it would have been impossible not to.

"Yes," she agreed, "it would be nice."

Jack Gorvoy completed the last of his autopsy reports, sat back in his chair and heaved a sigh.

Six casualties, the doctor reflected, and each one showed the same characteristics. Severe damage to the victims' nervous systems, synapses ravaged up and down the line, cerebral cortices burned out as if someone had plunged live wires into them.

Yet none of the victims had suffered external injuries. There were no burns, no surface wounds—nothing to indicate that their bodies had been subjected to electromagnetic shocks.

With that in mind, the open-console theory didn't seem applicable. Besides, only Rashad and Davidoff had been in the vicinity of sparking control panels when they collapsed. Yoshii, Kolodny, Rivers, and Zosky had been in more secure sections of the ship.

It seemed the phenomenon had found a way to affect the victims' brains without intruding on any cells along the way. A scientific impossibility, as far as Gorvoy could tell. And yet, he couldn't think of another explanation for what had happened.

Which led to another question, perhaps bigger than the first. How was it that these six people had died when the majority of the crew had survived unscathed? What was different about them? the doctor asked himself. What was the common denominator?

He glanced in the direction of the intensive care unit, only a small slice of which was visible from his office. He could see Agnarsson, the only patient left to him now that Hollandsworth was well enough to return to his quarters. The engineer was sitting up in his bed, glancing at a printout of his DNA analysis.

Unlike the others who had burned with that strange light, Agnarsson didn't appear to have suffered any ill effects. Though his eyes had changed color, his vision was still perfect. In fact, the man claimed he felt better than ever before.

Under normal circumstances, Gorvoy would probably have discharged him and pronounced him fit for duty. But he couldn't—not when the engineer was their best shot at obtaining an understanding of their comrades' deaths, and by extension, the forces that comprised the space phenomenon.

Abruptly, the medical officer realized that Agnarsson was returning his scrutiny. Like a voyeur caught in the act, Gorvoy pretended to be busy with something else for a moment. When he looked up, his patient was gazing at the analysis again.

No doubt, he told himself, Agnarsson would prefer a novel to an analytical printout. Swiveling his chair around, he examined the lowest shelf of his bookcase, where he kept some of his favorites.

Picking a mystery, the doctor slipped it out of its place and walked it over to the intensive care unit. The engineer didn't look up from his printout as Gorvoy approached him.

"Here," said the doctor, offering his patient the book. "You might find this a bit more interesting."

Agnarsson continued to study the analysis. "Can I see some other printouts?" he asked.

Gorvoy shrugged. "I don't see why not. But if I may ask, what do you want them for?"

The engineer finally looked up at him, his eyes gleaming with silver light. "Just get them," he said softly but insistently, "and I'll show you."

As Captain Tarasco entered Gorvoy's office, he could see the doctor peering at his monitor screen. "You called?" he said.

The medical officer didn't look up. "I did indeed," he replied absently. "Have a seat."

"I'm a busy man," Tarasco ventured.

Gorvoy nodded. "I heard. McMillan says we'll be lucky to get the warp drive up and running this century."

"That estimate may be a little pessimistic," said the captain. *But not by much,* he added inwardly.

At last, the doctor looked up. "Take a look at this," he advised, swiveling his monitor around.

Tarasco examined the screen. It showed him a collection of bright green circles, some empty and some filled in, perhaps a hundred and twenty of them in all.

"I give up," he said. "What is it?"

"It's a DNA analysis," Gorvoy explained. "Those circles are traits. Sexual orientation, height, eye color, and so on."

The captain looked at him, still at a loss. "Is this supposed to mean something to me?"

"Agnarsson created it," said the doctor. "From memory."

Tarasco looked at the screen again, then at Gorvoy. "This is a joke, right?"

"It's not," said the doctor.

"But how could he have done this?"

"I wish I knew," Gorvoy told him. "About an hour ago, he said he was bored with lying in bed while I ran tests on him, so I gave him something to look at—his DNA analysis. He decided to play a game with himself, to see how much of it he could memorize."

"And he memorized *all* of it?" asked Tarasco, finding the doctor's claim difficult to believe.

Gorvoy smiled a thin smile. "All of *them.*"

With a touch of his pad, he brought up a different analysis on the monitor screen. Then another, and another still.

"Seven in all," Gorvoy said. "My analyses of the seven individuals who were afflicted with the glow effect."

The captain absorbed the information. "Obviously, this has something to do with his eyes."

"Obviously," the medical officer confirmed, "but only in that they appear to be symptoms of the same disease—if you even want to call it that. According to Agnarsson he's never felt better in his life, and my instruments back him up in that regard."

Tarasco frowned. "I'd like to see him . . . speak with him."

"Be my guest," Gorvoy told him.

The captain left the doctor's office and followed the radiating corridor that led to the center of sickbay, where the intensive care unit was located. Only one of the eight beds was occupied.

Tarasco could see that Agnarsson's eyes were closed. For a moment, he considered whether he should wake the engineer or wait to speak with him at a later time.

"There's no time like the present," Agnarsson said, speaking like a man still wrapped in sleep.

Then he turned to the captain and opened his eyes, fixing Tarasco with his strange, silver stare. He smiled as he propped himself up on an elbow. "My grandfather was the one who told me that."

The captain felt a chill climb the rungs of his spine. "What made you decide to say it now?"

Agnarsson shrugged. "I'm not certain, exactly. It just seemed to make sense at the moment."

Tarasco tried to accept that, but he had a feeling there was more to it than the engineer was saying. "The doctor tells me you've developed a knack for memorizing things."

"You mean the DNA analyses?" Agnarsson seemed to be staring at something a million kilometers distant. "To tell you the truth, it wasn't that hard. I just gazed at them for a while, and suddenly they were the most familiar things in the world to me."

"That's pretty amazing," the captain observed.

The engineer shrugged again. "I suppose you could say that. But do you know what's *really* amazing?"

Tarasco shook his head. "What?"

Agnarsson pointed past him. "That."

The captain felt a whisper of air on the back of his neck. Whirling in response, he saw something silvery sweeping toward him and put his arms up to protect himself from it.

Too late, he realized what it was—a metallic blanket from one of the other beds. As it sank to the floor like a puppet whose strings had been cut, the engineer laughed.

Tarasco turned to him, uncertain that he could wrap his mind around what Agnarsson had done—and even less certain of how the man had done it. "That wasn't funny," he said, not knowing what else to say.

The engineer bit his lip to keep from laughing some more. "Sorry, sir. I just thought . . . I don't know."

"That it might be interesting to float a blanket over and surprise me with it?" The captain couldn't believe he had said that.

Agnarsson met his scrutiny with his eerie, silver stare. "As I said before," he replied, "it seemed to make sense at the time."

"I see," said Tarasco, not seeing at all.

He was trying to effect a facade of confidence and calm, but he didn't feel those qualities on the inside. He had been prepared to find a lot of things in the vastness of space . . . people as strange as the dispassionate, pointed-eared Vulcans and even stranger.

But this . . . this was the stuff of fantasy.

"I'm not sure you *do* see," said Agnarsson. He laid down on his bed again, gazed at the ceiling and smiled an unearthly smile. "But that's all right, I suppose . . . for now."

The captain wanted to know what the engineer meant by that—and then again, maybe he didn't. Mumbling a few words of good-bye, he left Agnarsson lying there and left the intensive care unit.

He felt an urgent need to talk with Gorvoy.

Mary Anne Sommers was learning what it felt like to be sitting in the eye of a storm.

An even dozen of her fellow crewmen were laboring around her, punctuating their efforts with grunts, sighs, and colorful language. Some of them were trying to repair the control panels that had blown up. Others were removing and replacing burned-out sensor circuits with new ones.

The helm officer wished they could have replaced the warp drive that easily. Unfortunately, she mused, they didn't carry that spare part.

Sommers would have chipped in some elbow grease, except someone had to keep an eye on the *Valiant*'s progress. At impulse speed, it wasn't all that difficult, of course. But with their shields in such ragged condition, they didn't want to run into any surprises.

"Boy," said Gardenhire as he walked by with a circuit board, "some people have all the luck."

The helm officer begrudged him a smile. "Yes, I feel very lucky. I love being stranded a gazillion light-years from home."

"Hey," said the redhead, looking past her in the direction of the viewscreen, "watch where you're going."

Sommers turned and studied the starfield, with which she'd had ample opportunity to become familiar. To her surprise, Gardenhire was right. They were a half dozen degrees off course.

As she made the correction, she thought she saw something flicker on her monitor. But when she looked down, she didn't see anything—only the black of a system whose sensors were off-line.

"Uh, Mary Anne?" said the navigator.

The helm officer shot another glance at him. "What?"

Gardenhire pointed to the viewscreen with a freckled finger. "I think you may have overcompensated a bit. You're seven or eight degrees too far to starboard now."

Sommers examined the screen again. And to her surprise, her colleague was on the money. The *Valiant* had deviated from her course in the other direction.

Sommers didn't get it. Nonetheless, she made the necessary correction. "How's that?" she asked Gardenhire.

He leaned closer to her. "You celebrating New Year's a little early this year, Mary Anne?"

She looked back at the navigator, indignant. "No, I am *not* celebrating a little early this year. For your information, I think there's something wrong with the helm. Maybe you can look into it after you finish rebuilding the sensor system."

He chuckled drily. "No problem." Then he went back to his work.

Sommers harumphed. Of all the nerve, she thought. She checked the viewscreen again to make sure everything was all right—which it was. Then, purely out of force of habit, she glanced at her monitor.

And gasped.

"Something wrong?" inquired Gardenhire, who had stopped halfway to his assigned task.

The helm officer stared at her monitor, her blood pumping hard in her temples. There was nothing there, she assured herself. It's blank—completely and utterly blank.

"No," she said. "Everything's fine."

But she wasn't at all certain of that. A moment earlier, she thought she had seen a face on the monitor screen. A man's face, with curly blond hair and a thick mustache.

Agnarsson's face.

Captain Tarasco regarded the handful of staff officers he had summoned to the *Valiant*'s observation lounge. "I think you all know why we're here," he told them.

"We've heard the rumors," said Tactical Chief Womack, a sturdy looking woman with short, straw-colored hair.

"But rumors are all they've been," said Pelletier, the perpetually grim-faced head of security. "I'd like to hear some facts."

"A reasonable request," the captain noted. "Here's what we know. During our attempt to get through the phenomenon—Big Red, as some of us have taken to calling it—Agnarsson lit up and collapsed. But unlike the six who shared his experience, he survived."

"He *more* than survived," said Gorvoy, picking up the thread. "He became a superman. Without even trying, Agnarsson can absorb information at astounding rates of speed, pluck thoughts out of people's minds . . . even move objects through the air without touching them."

"According to Lieutenant Sommers," Tarasco remarked, "Agnarsson manipulated her helm controls from his bed in sickbay. And to add insult to injury, he projected his face onto her monitor."

Womack smiled an incredulous smile. "You're kidding."

"I'm not," the captain told her.

There was silence in the room for a moment. Then Pelletier spoke up. "You want a recommendation?"

"That's why I called this meeting," Tarasco replied.

"In that case," said the security chief, "I recommend you place Agnarsson in the brig and put a twenty-four hour watch on him. And if he tries anything like tugging on the helm again, you have him sedated."

"That sounds pretty harsh," McMillan observed, his eyes narrowing beneath his bushy, dark brows.

"We're out here by ourselves," Pelletier reminded them, "in the middle of nowhere, with no one to help us. We don't have the luxury of waiting until Agnarsson becomes a problem. We have to act now."

"I think you're forgetting something," said the engineer. "Geirrod Agnarsson is a person, just like the rest of us. He came out here of his own free will. He has *rights*."

"Believe me, Bill," the security chief responded soberly, "I'm not forgetting any of that. I'm just thinking about the welfare of the other eighty-one people on this ship."

"So it's a numbers game," McMillan deduced.

"It *has* to be," Pelletier insisted.

"If I can say something?" Hollandsworth cut in.

Tarasco nodded. "Go ahead."

The science officer looked around at his colleagues. "We're all assuming that Agnarsson is going to use his abilities to hurt us—to work against us. I'm here to suggest that he may decide to help us. In fact," he added, "I think he already has."

"What do you mean?" asked Womack.

"When I was lying in intensive care," said Hollandsworth, "recovering from my burns, I felt as if there were someone there with me—encouraging me, helping me to heal. At the time, I didn't know who it was, or even if the feeling was real. But now, I think it was Agnarsson."

The captain looked to Gorvoy. "Is that possible?"

The doctor regarded Hollandsworth. "He did recuperate a little faster than I had expected. But then, everyone's different."

"Then it *is* possible," Tarasco concluded.

Gorvoy shrugged. "Who knows? The man can read minds and move objects around. Maybe he can help people heal as well."

"Talk about your godlike beings," Womack breathed.

"He's no god," said the chief engineer, dismissing the idea with a wave of his hand. "He's just like you and me."

The security chief chuckled bitterly. "Except he can steer the ship just by thinking about it."

McMillan shot him a dirty look. "Imagine if it was you who had been altered. Would you want to be caged up like an animal? Especially when you hadn't done anything wrong?"

"This isn't about justice," Pelletier maintained. "It's not about right and wrong. It's about survival."

"And what's the point of surviving," McMillan asked him, "if we're to throw right and wrong away in the process?"

"Hundreds of years ago," said Hollandsworth, "people in Salem accused their neighbors of being monsters and murdered them, because they feared what they didn't understand." He looked around the room. "Is that what *we're* doing? Lashing out at our neighbor out of ignorance? And if I do that, who's the *real* monster here—him or me?"

"We're not lashing out at Agnarsson," Pelletier argued doggedly. "We're just talking about restraining him."

"For now," McMillan told him. "But what happens if your restraints don't work? Once you've taken that first step, it's a lot easier to take the next one, and the one after that."

"As someone once said," Hollandsworth added, "we've established the principle . . . now we're just haggling over the price."

Pelletier didn't answer them. Instead, he turned to Tarasco, his eyes as hard as stone. "What are you going to do, sir?"

The captain frowned as he thought about it. Coming into this meeting, his inclination had been in line with his security chief's—he had considered the idea of having Agnarsson watched closely and, if necessary, confined to his quarters. However, McMillan and Hollandsworth had made some good points in the man's behalf.

Agnarsson had been one of them, right from the get-go. He had risked as much as anyone to carry out the *Valiant*'s mission to the stars. And even if he hadn't, he was a human being. As McMillan had stated so eloquently, the man had rights.

"For the time being," Tarasco decided, "I'm just going to talk to Agnarsson— let him know he's treading on thin ice."

Pelletier didn't look happy. "And if he starts throwing people around instead of blankets?"

The captain looked him in the eye. "We'll cross that bridge when we come to it."

Three

Captain's log, supplemental. I have had another conversation with Geirrod Agnarsson. This time, I made it clear to him that I wouldn't tolerate his tampering with any of my ship's systems, or for that matter, frightening any of my crew. I also told him that he was to cooperate fully with Dr. Gorvoy in his efforts to explore Agnarsson's condition. Agnarsson seemed to understand the consequences of diverging from my orders and promised to follow them. For the time being, I'm willing to believe him.

Chantal Coquillette had heard the stories about Agnarsson's manipulation of the helm controls.

But when she entered the intensive care unit, he didn't look like a superman. He just looked like a normal human being, engrossed in one of Dr. Gorvoy's beloved mystery novels.

"How are you doing today?" the medic asked, her voice echoing from bulkhead to bulkhead, emphasizing the loneliness of the place.

Agnarsson looked up from his book. "Just fine."

The eyes, thought Coquillette. She had forgotten about his weird, silver eyes. But truthfully, even those weren't enough to make him seem like some alien entity, ready to tear the ship apart on a whim.

He still looked human. He still looked like the man who had helped bring their engines back when they were stranded.

"Can I get you anything?" she asked.

Agnarsson appeared to think about it for a moment. "I don't think so," he decided. "But thanks for asking."

The medic shrugged. "Don't mention it."

"I guess you're here for another scan," said the engineer, still intent on his mystery novel.

"You don't sound happy," Coquillette replied, removing her bioscanner from its loop on her belt. "I thought you *liked* me."

Agnarsson looked up again. This time, he smiled a little beneath his wild mustache. "I do. I just wish Doctor Gorvoy would let me out of here. I'm going a little stir crazy."

"Hang in there," the medic told him.

She wished she could tell him he would be released soon. However, it didn't look like that was going to take place—not until Gorvoy and his staff understood what had happened to him.

An hour earlier, the doctor had injected a drug into Agnarsson's bloodstream which would make his neural pathways easier to scan. Coquillette's was the second of three scheduled examinations. By the time they were completed, Gorvoy hoped to be able to come up with a hypothesis.

And if he couldn't do that? If the neural scan didn't shed any light on the mystery? The medical team would simply have to come up with another approach to the problem.

Coquillette played her bioscanner over Agnarsson from his feet to the crown of his head. She was almost finished when she noticed something. Agnarsson's hair . . . it had flecks of white in it.

She was sure they weren't there the last time she saw him . . . and that was just the day before. Besides, the engineer was a young man—thirty at the outside. How could his hair be losing its pigment already?

Unless whatever had altered him . . . was *still* altering him. It was a chilling thought—because if Agnarsson was changing on the outside, he might be changing on the inside as well. He might be getting *stronger.*

Fighting to remain calm, Coquillette checked her readout to make certain the requisite data had been recorded. Satisfied, she replaced the device on her belt.

"See you later," she told Agnarsson, hoping her anxiety didn't show, and started for the exit.

"You know," the engineer called after her unexpectedly, "you don't have to go. Not right away, I mean."

His voice sounded funny . . . louder, more expansive somehow. As if it were filling the entire intensive care unit . . . or maybe filling her head, Coquillette couldn't tell which.

He looked at her with those bizarre, silver orbs, not quite eyes anymore, and she felt panic. After all, if he could manipulate the *Valiant*'s helm controls, what might he not be able to do to a human being?

"Actually," she blurted, "I do."

And she left him there.

Jack Gorvoy was studying his monitor screen when Coquillette showed up at his door.

The woman looked pale, frightened. It got his attention immediately. After all, Coquillette was the steadiest officer he had.

"What is it?" he asked.

"It's *him*," Coquillette whispered, sneaking a glance back over her shoulder. "Agnarsson."

Gorvoy looked past the medic. From what he could see of his patient, the man was reading the book the doctor had given him—nothing more. Still, he didn't want to dismiss his officer's feelings out of hand.

"Close the door and sit down," Gorvoy said.

Coquillette did as she was told. Then she described the change she had seen in Agnarsson's hair color.

The doctor frowned. He had examined the engineer less than an hour ago, and he hadn't noticed any graying.

"I'm not imagining it," his officer insisted.

"I didn't say you were," he told her. "Can I see your bioscanner?"

Removing it from her belt, she handed it over to him. Gorvoy called up the scan Coquillette had just done on the device's readout. Then he called up the earlier scan on his computer screen.

"Well?" she asked.

I'll be damned, he thought. "You're right. Agnarsson's changed. And I'm not talking about his hair color."

Coquillette got up and circumnavigated his desk to get a look. "What else?" she demanded.

Gorvoy pointed to the screen. "The neural pathways in his cerebellum have re-shaped themselves. They're getting bigger."

She looked at him, her face as drawn and grim as he had ever seen it. "And his powers?"

"May be increasing," he said, completing her thought. He sat back in his chair and rubbed the bridge of his nose. "Congratulations. Your discovery puts mine to shame."

"Your discovery . . . ?" Coquillette wondered out loud.

Gorvoy nodded. "I figured out why Agnarsson and the others were affected by the phenomenon when no one else was . . . why Agnarsson, of all of them, survived and mutated."

Don't keep me in suspense, said a voice—a huge, throbbing presence that seemed to fill the doctor's skull.

Obviously, Coquillette had heard it too, because she whirled and looked back at their patient. Beyond the far end of the corridor, Agnarsson had tossed his blanket aside and was getting up out of his bed.

Gorvoy's mouth went dry. *I'll be glad to fill you in,* he thought quickly, knowing the engineer could "hear" him in the confines of his mind. *You don't have to leave intensive care.*

I've had enough of intensive care, Agnarsson replied, not bothering to conceal an undercurrent of resentment, *and I've had enough of people talking behind my back.*

The doctor glanced at Coquillette. "Leave," he said.

She shook her head. "Not if you're staying."

"Someone's got to tell Tarasco what's going on," he insisted.

Coquillette hesitated a moment longer. Then she opened the door, left Gorvoy's office and darted to her left down the hallway, heading for the exit from sickbay and the nearest turbolift.

In the meantime, Agnarsson had gotten out of bed and was headed toward Gorvoy's office. The medical officer rose from behind his desk and went to meet his patient halfway, thinking that would be the best way to make him forget about Coquillette.

It didn't take long for him to find out how wrong he was.

"Where is she?" Agnarsson demanded impatiently.

"She's got nothing to do with this," Gorvoy argued as they got closer to one another. "This is between you and me."

"That's what you'd *like* it to be," said the engineer. "But I'm tired of listening to you calling the shots—you and your friend, the captain. Now where *is* she?"

The doctor stopped in the middle of the corridor. "Why is Coquillette so important to you?"

Agnarsson's silver eyes narrowed. "She pretended to be nice to me, but I heard her talking to you. She's just like everyone else. She's scared of me." He laughed an ugly, bitter laugh. "And who can blame her?"

Only then did Gorvoy realize the extent of the transformation that had taken place. It wasn't just the engineer's hair and nervous system that were changing. It was his personality as well.

Quite literally, Agnarsson wasn't himself anymore. He was something else— something dark and dangerous, despite what McMillan and Hollandsworth had said about him. And the doctor would be damned if he would let such a thing walk the *Valiant* unchecked.

"Out of my way," Agnarsson snarled.

"We can help you," Gorvoy told him. "We can help you cope with what's happening to you. You just have to go back to intensive care."

The engineer lifted his chin in indignation. "You like it there so much? Why don't *you* go there?"

Before the doctor could do anything to stop him, Agnarsson grabbed him by the front of his uniform and sent him hurtling headlong toward intensive care. The last thing Gorvoy saw was the engineer's blanket-draped bed as it rushed up to meet him.

Then, mercifully, he lost consciousness.

Dan Pelletier hefted the laser in his hand as he made his way toward engineering . . . and hoped that he had guessed correctly.

As soon as he heard from the captain that Agnarsson might be getting belligerent, the security chief had led a team down to sickbay—and discovered Dr. Gorvoy slumped at the base of a biobed, bleeding freely from his nose and mouth. Pelletier wasn't a physician, but he knew a concussion and a set of broken ribs when he saw them.

At that point, Agnarsson had gone from being a misguided fellow crewman to a dangerous and potentially deadly fugitive. And when that fugitive could manipulate objects with the power of his mind, where was he most likely to go . . . other than a place where the slightest manipulation could place the ship in mortal jeopardy?

Especially when that place was where he had spent most of his waking hours over the last few years.

With that theory in his head, Pelletier had used the intercom to get Gorvoy some help and left a man there to look after him. Then he had taken Peavey and Marciulonis and headed for the engine room.

"Remember," he told his men, "fire only on my command. We don't want to blow the warp core with a stray shot."

"Acknowledged," said Peavey.

"Aye, sir," Marciulonis chimed in.

The doors to the engine room were open. Signaling for his officers to fan out on either side of him, Pelletier darted straight ahead, laser pistol at the ready.

When he got inside, he looked around quickly, hoping to find Agnarsson and take him down before the man realized he was there. But all the security chief saw were the surprised faces of McMillan and his engineers.

Agnarsson, it seemed, wasn't there.

Carlos Tarasco paced behind his center seat, wondering if Pelletier and his people had caught up with Agnarsson yet.

He saw now that the security chief had been right. Agnarsson was too dangerous to remain in a medical bed. He had to be incarcerated, for the good of everyone on the ship.

And even that might not be enough, the captain reflected. If the man's powers kept growing, if he became too big a threat, they might have to consider even stronger measures.

Is that how you treat a man who followed you out into space? someone asked, his voice echoing wildly in Tarasco's head.

The captain whirled and saw a strapping, blond figure standing at the threshold of the open lift compartment. Somehow, its doors had slid open without Tarasco's hearing them.

"Don't look so surprised," said Agnarsson, stepping out onto the bridge. "Pelletier's security teams were looking for me everywhere else. This was the only place I could go."

Knowing that the engineer could read his mind, Tarasco tried not to think about the weapons he had secured for himself and his bridge officers. He tried not to think of how those officers would be slipping the pistols from their belts to use them against the man who had been their comrade.

But he couldn't help it.

Agnarsson must have caught the captain's thought, because he whirled in Gardenhire's direction. The navigator had already drawn his laser and was aiming it at Agnarsson.

With a sweep of his arm, the engineer sent the weapon flying out of Gardenhire's grasp. But by then, Womack had drawn her laser as well—and while Agnarsson was disarming the navigator, Womack was pressing the trigger.

A bolt of blue laser energy speared the engineer in the shoulder, spinning him into the bulkhead beside the lift doors. Agnarsson lifted his hand to strike back at Womack, but a second beam caught him in the chest, knocking the wind out of him.

A beam from the barrel of Tarasco's pistol.

Fighting to stay conscious, Agnarsson glared at the captain with his gleaming silver eyes. *I won't forget this,* he thought, each word a reverberating torment in the confines of Tarasco's head.

Then Womack fired a second time and Agnarsson slumped to the deck, looking woozy and deflated.

Tarasco stayed alert, just in case his adversary wasn't as disabled as he looked.

But before he could even think about squeezing off another shot, he saw something happen to the engineer's eyes.

Miraculously, the silver glow in them faded. They became the blue of summer skies, the very human blue that Agnarsson had probably been born with.

For a fraction of a second, Tarasco wondered if they might have cured the engineer of his affliction—if all it had taken to drive the phenomenon's energies out of him was a good laser barrage.

Then the light in Agnarsson's eyes returned—and with it came a restoration of his incredible strength. He planted his hand against the bulkhead and tried to stagger to his feet, shrugging off the punishment his body had absorbed.

But Womack wouldn't have any of it—and neither would Gardenhire. They fired their laser pistols at the same time, knocking Agnarsson senseless. And when he crumpled this time, Tarasco was ready.

"Take him to the brig," he ordered.

Instantly, his officers moved to comply.

Four

Captain Tarasco was standing in the corridor outside the brig, watching Pelletier activate the force field that would keep the temporarily sedated Agnarsson under wraps, when Coquillette arrived.

"How's Gorvoy?" the captain asked.

"Sleeping," the medic told him, unable to keep from stealing a glance at Agnarsson. "But he'll be all right. He just needs a little rest."

Tarasco nodded. "I'm glad to hear it."

"Me too," said Coquillette. "I just hope he doesn't sleep too long. I don't think I could stand the suspense."

For a moment, the captain didn't know what she was talking about. After all, he had had plenty to think about in the last few minutes. Then he remembered. "That's right . . . Gorvoy's theory."

"It was more than a theory," the medic insisted. "He told me he had figured out why Agnarsson and the others were affected by the phenomenon . . . and also why Agnarsson was the only one who survived it."

"Did he give you any details?"

She shook her head ruefully. "He couldn't. Agnarsson overheard us at that point and interrupted."

Tarasco sighed. "I'd love to know what Gorvoy came up with."

"He might have made some notes," Coquillette suggested.

"Or crunched some numbers," the captain agreed. "Either way, there would be a record of it in the database."

He tapped a bulkhead pad to activate the intercom. "Tarasco to Gardenhire," he said into the grid below the pad.

"Gardenhire here. How's everything going down there, sir?"

"Agnarsson's under control," the captain assured him. "I've got a job for you, Lieutenant. I'd like you to see if you can find a file the doctor was working on when he was attacked. It had something to do with the victims of the phenomenon."

"Will do, sir," came Gardenhire's response. "I'll let you know as soon as I find something."

"Thanks," said Tarasco. "Captain out." He turned to Coquillette. "It shouldn't be long before we know something."

Coquillette glanced at Agnarsson again. The man hadn't stirred yet from his drug-induced stupor.

"Great," she said. "The sooner we know something about our friend there, the sooner we can help him."

Tarasco wished he could be as optimistic as the medic was.

Jack Gorvoy had treated any number of crew members in his sickbay since the day the *Valiant* left Earth.

However, he himself hadn't previously spent any time in one of his beds. And now that he *had* spent some time there, he didn't like it—especially after he heard what Tarasco had to tell him.

"The file was lost?" the doctor echoed, his voice still a little weak.

"It looks that way," said the captain. "And under the circumstances, I have to entertain the possibility that it wasn't a mechanical failure."

Gorvoy looked at him. "Agnarsson."

"Why not? If he can take over the helm, it's child's play to wipe out a little computer data."

"But why?" asked the medical officer. "He knew I'd be able to tell you about it as soon as I regained consciousness."

Tarasco smiled a sickly smile. "Maybe he didn't believe you were going to do that."

It wasn't a comforting thought. "Maybe," said Gorvoy.

"Or maybe he was just acting out of anger," the captain suggested, "throwing some kind of tantrum. Fortunately, it doesn't matter one way or the other. You *have* regained consciousness."

The doctor could still feel a dull ache where he had hit his head. "If you can call it that."

"So what did you come up with?" the other man asked.

Gorvoy frowned. "Extrasensory perception."

Tarasco looked at him. "That's it?"

"That's it. Mind you, not all of our seven casualties were tested for it, but three were—Agnarsson, Davidoff, and Kolodny. Davidoff and Kolodny scored pretty high . . . but Agnarsson? He was off the charts."

The captain shook his head. "You know what? It makes sense."

"That someone with a predisposition toward mental abilities would develop Agnarsson's brand of powers? I'd have to agree," said the doctor. "I just wish I had thought of the connection sooner."

"What about the rest of the crew?" asked Tarasco. "Are we going to have any delayed cases?"

"I don't think so," Gorvoy told him. "Of the thirty-eight whose records show they were tested, none showed any particular talent for ESP."

"Thank heavens for that, at least."

"You can say that again," said the medical officer. He searched the captain's eyes. "So what happens now?"

"That depends," Tarasco replied.

"On what?"

"Now that we know about Agnarsson's ESP, is there a chance that we can use that knowledge to change him back?"

"Honestly?" said Gorvoy. "I don't think so."

"Then you don't want to know what happens now."

Gorvoy was a physician. He had taken an oath not to hurt anyone. And yet, he couldn't argue with the captain's position.

"Hollandsworth was wrong," he found himself saying. "We weren't just lashing out at Agnarsson. He really *is* a monster."

Tarasco didn't say anything in response. Obviously, he wasn't especially comfortable with the task ahead of him. But who could be?

"Get some rest," he told the doctor.

"I'll try," said Gorvoy. But with what he had to think about, he didn't believe he would be very successful at it.

Security Chief Pelletier saw the engineer stir on the other side of the barrier. Glancing at his watch, he made note of the elapsed time.

An hour and eighteen minutes.

According to Rudolph, the drug he administered would have kept a normal man unconscious for seven or eight hours. Of course, Pelletier reflected bleakly, Agnarsson was anything *but* a normal man.

He glanced over his shoulder at Marciulonis. "Contact the captain," he said. "Let him know that Agnarsson's coming to."

"Aye, sir," Marciulonis replied, and tapped the bulkhead pad that activated the intercom system.

Pelletier turned back to the prisoner and saw that his eyes were open. What's more, they were staring in the security chief's direction.

"You're a fool if you think you can hold me," said Agnarsson.

"Then I'm a fool," Pelletier answered. "But if you were in my place, you'd be doing the same thing."

That made the engineer smile. "No," he said, his voice echoing, "that's not true at all. If I were in your place, I would have killed me some time ago . . . while I still had the chance."

The security chief didn't say that that was still the plan. He didn't even dare to think it.

"You're keeping something from me," Agnarsson observed. "Something you don't think I'll like."

There was no point in denying it—not when he was dealing with a telepath. So Pelletier remained silent.

"You can plot all you want," said the man with the silver eyes. "It won't do you any good. I'm getting stronger all the time."

Suddenly, Agnarsson took a step forward, as if to attack the security chief. As Pelletier jumped backward, fumbling at his hip for his pistol, the engineer laughed.

"Soon I'll be strong enough to grab you for real," he said.

And as if to prove his point, he extended his hand into the vertical plane of the electromagnetic field.

Sparks sputtered around Agnarsson's wrist, making him grimace with pain. But he didn't pull his hand back right away. He left it there, enduring what no mere human could have endured.

Finally, the prisoner staggered backward and cradled his hand. He looked weakened by the experience, even a little humbled. But then, Pelletier told himself, Agnarsson had been weakened before, and he had come back stronger than ever.

The engineer tilted his head, considering the security chief as if he had never noticed him before. "You know," he noted almost casually, "it's only a matter of time."

It was then that Pelletier noticed the patches of white at Agnarsson's temples. The man's appearance was changing again.

"I've notified the captain," Marciulonis told his superior. "He says he's almost finished."

Pelletier didn't take his eyes off the prisoner as he responded. He didn't put his pistol away either.

"Tell Captain Tarasco to hurry," said the security chief. "We may not have much more time."

Captain's log, supplemental. I'm sending out this message buoy despite my hope that we of the Valiant *will still make it back to Earth. The buoy contains all our computer data from the past several days, which will explain how we wound up in these unfortunate straits . . . and why I've opted for such a drastic response to them.*

Tarasco tapped a square, orange stud on his armrest, terminating his log entry. Then, glancing at Gardenhire, he nodded to show his ops officer that he had finished.

Gardenhire manipulated the controls on his panel. "Releasing the buoy," he announced gravely.

Tarasco turned back to his bridge's forward viewscreen. After a moment, he saw a small, gray object go spinning off into the void like a child's top. It had a squat, graceless body, three sturdy legs and a domed crown, and it would transmit a signal in the direction of Earth for hundreds of years if nothing happened to it.

The message buoy would tell the *Valiant*'s story. It would speak of the magnetic storm that had hurled them through space. It would describe the phenomenon they encountered at the galaxy's edge. And it would say how their first assistant engineer had mutated into a being capable of destroying the rest of the crew.

The buoy would also carry information about extrasensory perception, and how it related to Geirrod Agnarsson's transformation. It would warn other captains who intended to penetrate the barrier about the horrific consequences they might face.

The kind of consequences Tarasco was facing now.

Suddenly, his intercom grid came alive. "Chief Pelletier to Captain Tarasco," it sang.

"Tarasco here. What's the situation?"

"Not good, sir," said the security chief. "Agnarsson is having another go at the force field. He's been in contact with it for nearly a minute and he doesn't seem to have reached his limit yet."

The captain could hear the urgency in Pelletier's voice. No, he told himself, call it what it is. *The fear.*

For the last twenty minutes, while Tarasco was completing his preparation of the message buoy, Agnarsson had been trying to see how much punishment he could take. Each time he penetrated the barrier, it seemed, he was able to endure it a little longer than the previous time.

Eventually, he would be able to pass through it altogether. The captain didn't doubt that for a minute. In time, he reflected, Agnarsson would be unstoppable.

Tarasco desperately didn't want to destroy the engineer or anyone else. That was why he had taken so long to release the message buoy. It was why he was lingering here on the bridge, watching the buoy spin off into space for as long as possible.

But it was becoming increasingly obvious that he had to act. Agnarsson was a deadly threat to the life of every man and woman on the *Valiant*. The engineer had to be sacrificed, and soon . . . or the buoy would be all that was left of them.

And it wasn't just the crew that was at risk. If Agnarsson took control of the ship, he might be able to repair its crippled propulsion system. Then he would have access to every planet in the galaxy, including the ones that boasted sentient populations.

Including, ultimately, Earth.

Tarasco patted the laser pistol on his hip. He couldn't allow a monster to be unleashed on his homeworld. He had to put his dread aside and do something about it.

"I'm coming," he told Pelletier. "Tarasco out."

Slowly, feeling as if he were laden with weights, the captain turned to his helm officer. "Lieutenant Sommers," he said, "you've got the bridge."

The woman turned and looked at him, knowing full well what Pelletier's summons had been about. "Aye, sir."

Pushing himself up out of his center seat, the captain made his way to the lift at the rear of the bridge and tapped the touch-sensitive plate on the bulkhead. The doors slid aside for him and he entered the compartment, then punched in his destination.

It took slightly more than a minute for the lift to convey him to Deck Ten. The doors opened on arrival and he stepped out into the corridor.

The brig was just down the hall. Tarasco followed the bend of the passageway reluctantly. Along the way, it occurred to him that he would have to look Agnarsson in the eyes before he killed him.

It would hurt to do that, no question about it. But it wouldn't stop him. No matter what, he would press the trigger.

Of course, he could have ordered one of his crewmen to destroy the prisoner for him. But Tarasco wasn't the type to put that kind of burden on one of his people. If anyone was going to wake up screaming in the middle of the night, it was going to be him.

He was less than twenty meters from the brig when he realized that something was wrong. It was too quiet, the captain told himself. He couldn't even hear the buzz of Agnarsson's force field.

Drawing his laser pistol from its place in his belt, Tarasco held it before him and advanced more warily. After a few seconds, Pelletier's muscular body came into view. The security chief was sprawled across the floor, his neck bent at an impossible angle, a trickle of dark blood running from the corner of his open mouth.

The captain swore under his breath.

His teeth grinding with grief and anger, he paused to kneel at Pelletier's side and feel his neck for a pulse. There wasn't any. And the man's weapon was fully charged, meaning he hadn't even gotten a chance to fire it before Agnarsson got to him.

Tarasco got up and went on, sweat streaming down both sides of his face, his heart banging against his ribs so hard he thought they would break. At any moment, he thought, Agnarsson might reach out with his mind and strangle him to death.

But it didn't happen. The captain reached the brig unscathed.

It didn't take an expert to see that its force field had been deactivated or disabled. The room itself was empty. And the two security officers who had been helping to guard Agnarsson were laid out on the deck, their necks broken as badly as Pelletier's had been.

Tarasco cursed angrily under his breath and scanned the corridor in both directions. The monster was loose. He could be anywhere, preying on anyone at all. There was no time to waste.

Pressing the intercom pad next to the brig, the captain gained access to every member of his crew in every section of the ship. "Agnarsson has escaped the brig," he said, doing his best to keep his panic in check. "He's already killed three security officers. He is extremely dangerous and to be avoided at all costs. Repeat—"

You're next, Tarasco. The words echoed ominously in his brain, obliterating the possibility of any other thought. Tarasco scanned the corridor in either direction, but there was no one there. *After all, what do I need with a captain? Or a crew, for that matter?*

Tarasco swallowed back his fear. *Where are you?* he asked the engineer in the confines of his mind.

Not so far away, came the coy, almost childlike answer. *And getting closer all the time.*

Five

At the sound of his adversary's thought, the captain could feel a wetness between his shoulder blades. Following his instincts, he whirled—but the corridor was still empty behind him.

Then he spun the other way . . .

And there was Agnarsson, his eyes ablaze with silver light, a cruel smile on his otherwise expressionless face. He had always been a big man, but he seemed even bigger now, more imposing.

You can't kill me, the engineer insisted, his voice expanding to fill the hallway. *Much as you want to, you can't. But I can kill you.*

And he lifted his hand to carry out his threat.

However, Tarasco struck first. His pale blue laser beam slammed squarely into

Agnarsson's chest, forcing him back a couple of steps. The engineer's smile became a grimace as he pitted his mysterious power against the laser's electromagnetic fury.

At first, he merely stood his ground. Then little by little, with the beam's brilliance spattering against him, he did even better than that. He began to make his way forward again.

You can't stop me, Agnarsson told him, his voice echoing like thunder. *Nothing can stop me.* And he hurled a crackling bolt of livid pink energy at the captain.

Tarasco didn't have time to duck the discharge or get out of the way. All he could do was try to go limp as the engineer's power hammered him into the bulkhead behind him.

The next thing the captain knew, he was sitting with his back against the bulkhead, feeling as if he had broken every bone in his body. There was blood in his mouth and a wetness in the back of his head that could only have been more blood.

And it hurt like the devil to draw a breath. More than likely, he had cracked a couple of ribs.

Through tears of pain, he looked up at Agnarsson. The man was gazing at his victim triumphantly, in no apparent hurry to finish him off. Almost reluctantly, he lifted his hand.

But before he could accomplish anything with it, the corridor erupted with a blinding, blue light. It caught the engineer by surprise and sent him staggering into the bulkhead.

The captain squinted and was able to make out two high-intensity shafts. Lasers, he thought. On their highest settings. They seemed to be coming from the opposite end of the corridor.

Forcing his eyes to focus, Tarasco saw that two more of his security officers had arrived. Their laser barrage was pummeling Agnarsson without respite, forcing him to expend more and more of his newfound energy just to remain conscious.

The captain knew that this might be his last chance. Looking around for his laser pistol, he found it lying on the deck less than a meter away. Putting aside the pain that squeezed his midsection like a vise, he dragged himself over to the weapon and took hold of it.

When he looked up again, he saw Agnarsson fighting the security officers' lasers to a draw. It was difficult to predict which would give out first—the engineer's stamina or the pistols' batteries.

Tarasco made the question moot by adding his own beam to the equation. Skewered in the back with it, Agnarsson groaned and crumpled to his knees. Then he fell forward, momentarily unconscious.

The captain turned his beam off. So did his security officers, whom he recognized as Siregar and Offenburger. In the aftermath of the battle, they couldn't help glancing at the corpses of Pelletier and the others.

"Are you all right, sir?" asked Offenburger, a tall man with blond hair and light eyes.

Tarasco nodded, despite the punishment he had taken. "Fine, Marc." He managed to get to his feet, though it cost him a good deal of pain. "I need your help, both of you."

"What is it, sir?" asked Siregar, an attractive Asian woman.

"We need to get Agnarsson to the weapons room," the captain told them. "And I mean *now.*"

Their expressions told Tarasco that they didn't follow his thinking. But then, Pelletier had been the only security officer to whom the captain had revealed his intentions regarding the engineer.

Strictly speaking, he didn't owe either Offenburger or Siregar an explanation—but he gave them one anyway. "Agnarsson's become too dangerous. We have to get rid of him while we still can."

The security officers didn't seem pleased by the prospect of killing a fellow human being—a man with whom they had eaten and shared stories and braved the dangers of the void. However, they had seen the engineer's power, not to mention the bodies of their friends on the floor. They would do whatever Tarasco asked of them.

Kneeling at Agnarsson's side, the captain felt the man's neck for a pulse. It was faint, but the engineer was clearly still alive. And that wasn't the only thing Tarasco noticed.

Agnarsson's eyes, or what the captain could see of them through the engineer's half-closed lids, weren't glowing anymore. They had returned to normal again.

As before, Tarasco was tempted to believe that the crisis was over—that their laser barrage had somehow reversed whatever had gotten hold of the engineer, stripping him of his incredible powers. Then he considered the bodies of those Agnarsson had murdered with a gesture and knew he couldn't take any chances.

"Pick him up," the captain told Offenburger and Siregar. "I'll keep my laser trained on him in case he wakes."

Tucking their weapons into their belts, the officers did as they were asked. Offenburger inserted his hands under the engineer's arms and Siregar grabbed his legs. Then they began moving in the direction of the *Valiant*'s weapons room.

There were hatches that were closer to their location. Unfortunately, Tarasco mused, shoving Agnarsson out into space might not be enough. If the engineer was able to survive in the vacuum—and he might be—it was also possible that he could work his way back inside.

The weapons room was a deck above them, which meant they had to use a lift to get to it. It seemed to take forever for the compartment to reach them, and even longer for it to take them to their destination.

After that, they had to negotiate a long, curving corridor. It wasn't long before Offenburger and Siregar began showing the strain of their efforts. Agnarsson was no lightweight, after all. But eventually, Tarasco was able to guide them through the weapons room doors.

The place was dominated by a pair of missile launchers—dark, bulky titanium devices with long, cylindrical slots meant to shoot atomic projectiles through the void. They were empty at the moment, their payloads safely stowed in a series of obverse bulkhead compartments.

But at least one of them wouldn't be empty for long.

The captain pointed to it with his free hand. "Put him in," he told the security officers.

Siregar looked down at Agnarsson and winced at the idea. Offenburger hesitated as well.

"Sir," the security officer began in a plaintive voice, "there must be a better way to—"

"Do it," snapped Tarasco, his stomach clenching.

Offenburger bit back the rest of his protest. With obvious reluctance, he and Siregar placed the unconscious engineer in the open launch slot. Then they started to slide the missile door into place.

That was when Agnarsson woke up.

With a cry of rage, he sat up and slammed the missile door open again, filling the room with metallic echoes. Then he vaulted out of the slot and rounded on Offenburger and Siregar.

The captain wasn't about to let them get hurt—not when he had promised to protect them. Pressing the trigger on his laser pistol, he sent a blue beam slamming into the engineer's back.

It barely slowed Agnarrson down. He released a bolt of raw pink lightning at Offenburger, sending the blond man flying across the room. Then he did the same thing to Siregar.

Finally, he turned to Tarasco. *I told you,* he said in that strangely expansive voice of his, *you can't stop me, Captain—not any more than an amoeba can stop an elephant.*

And with that, he extended his hand toward Tarasco—not casually, as he had before, but with a certain resolve. The meaning of the gesture was clear. He intended to finish the captain off this time.

Tarasco fired at Agnarsson again, producing another stream of electromagnetic force. But the engineer wasn't daunted by it. He simply raised his chin and withstood the barrage, and retaliated with a spidery lightning flash of his own.

Fortunately, the captain was ready for it. Ignoring the crushing pain in his ribs, he ducked Agnarsson's attack and rolled to his right. Then he came up on one knee and fired again.

The engineer actually smiled. *I'm getting stronger with every passing second,* he observed. *You should have done something about me a long time ago. Now it's too late.*

Tarasco saw the wisdom in the remark. He *should* have done something a long time ago. He should have done the hard thing, the heartless thing, and destroyed Agnarsson as soon as he tampered with the ship.

But that didn't help him now. He had to find a way to slow the monster down, to give himself and his crew a fighting chance . . .

Suddenly, it came to him.

As the engineer raised his hand again, the captain fired his laser pistol—but not at Agnarsson, against whom it wouldn't have done any good. Instead, he trained his beam on the deck below Agnarsson's feet.

After all, this was the weapons room—and the *Valiant* boasted two kinds of weapons. One was atomic. The other was a laser cannon system supplied with power by heavy-duty conduits.

And as luck would have it, one of those conduits ran directly under the spot where Agnarsson was standing.

It took a moment for Tarasco's beam to punch through the deck plating. The tactic caught the engineer by surprise, causing him to stumble. But he didn't understand what his adversary was up to, or he would have removed himself from the room immediately.

As it was, he simply levitated himself above the ruined spot in the deck. *You're grasping at straws,* said Agnarsson, looking regal and supremely confident, his technical training obviously forgotten. *What'll you do next, Captain? Try to bring the ceiling down on my head?*

He had barely gotten the words out when Tarasco's beam found its unlikely target. Without warning, a gout of blue-white electroplasma rose up and engulfed the engineer.

Agnarsson writhed horribly in the clutches of the energy geyser. Finally, with a prolonged snarl, he hurled himself out of harm's way and landed on the deck with a thud.

However, the engineer's exposure to the deadly electroplasma had taken its toll. He was curled up in a fetal position, his clothes burned off, his skin and hair blackened and oozing with blood.

But his eyes still glowed with that eerie, silver light. And as Tarasco looked on, Agnarsson's flesh began to repair itself. Despite everything, he and his power had survived.

The captain bit his lip. It wouldn't be wise to try to launch the engineer into space a second time—not at the rate his strength was coming back. And he could think of only one other option.

Cradling his damaged ribs, he raced across the room to the intercom grid. Then he pressed the pad that activated it.

"This is Tarasco," he gasped. "All hands abandon ship immediately. Repeat, all hands abandon ship."

There was no time to elaborate, no time to explain. There was only enough time to issue the order and hope his people would follow it, because Agnarsson was already healed enough to focus his thoughts.

That was clever, the monster reflected through the haze of his pain. *But how many conduits can you open without destroying your ship?*

The captain didn't allow himself to think of the answer. Instead, he aimed his weapon at the deck below Agnarsson and fired again. This time it took a little longer for him to pierce the surface and reach the conduit, but the result was just as spectacular.

As the engineer was enveloped in the seething, blue-white flame, he screamed a high, thin scream. Then he lurched out of the plasma's embrace and fell to the deck, thin plumes of black smoke rising from him.

Tarasco's heart went out to the man. After all, Agnarsson hadn't asked for what had happened to him. He hadn't done anything to deserve it. In a sense, he was a victim as much as those security officers he had killed.

But as Pelletier had pointed out, this wasn't about right and wrong. This was about evolution. This was about survival.

And the captain would be damned if he was going to let his engineer shape the future of the human race.

As Agnarsson whimpered and clutched at himself with blackened, clawlike hands, Tarasco tried to rouse Siregar and Offenburger. Both of them were still alive, it turned out, though badly battered.

"Get out of here," he told them. "That's an order. Grab the nearest escape pod and get off the ship."

Offenburger glanced at the engineer, too dazed to fully grasp what was happening. "What about you, sir?" he asked the captain, his words slurred and difficult to understand.

"I'll follow when I'm certain Agnarsson can't come after us," Tarasco assured him. It was a lie, of course. He had no intention of following the security officers.

Siregar's eyes narrowed. Unlike Offenburger, she seemed to divine his intentions. "Let me stay and help," she suggested.

"No," the captain told her. "Now get going."

Siregar hesitated for a moment longer, loath to leave him there alone with Agnarsson. Then she put her arm around Offenburger and helped him stagger out of the weapons room.

Tarasco turned back to the engineer. To his amazement, the man was almost healed again, his skin raw but no longer charred. Agnarsson glowered at him with eyes that had known unbelievable pain.

You can't keep this up forever, the engineer told him. *Sooner or later, I'll destroy you.*

The captain's only response was to walk over to the launch console and punch in some commands. The first one armed the ship's atomic missiles, overriding the protocol that would have kept them from exploding inside the *Valiant.* The second command accessed the missiles' timers.

What are you doing? Agnarsson demanded.

"That's simple," Tarasco told him with an inner calm that surprised him. "I'm blowing up the ship."

You won't do that.

"Won't I?" asked the captain.

He estimated that it had been two minutes since he had given the order to abandon ship. By then, all surviving members of his crew should have cast off, with the possible exception of Offenburger and Siregar. And even they should have reached a pod.

With that in mind, he tapped in a detonation time. Then he took a moment to reassess Agnarsson's condition.

With an effort, the engineer had propped himself up on his elbow. Slowly, laboriously, he was reaching out in Tarasco's direction, no doubt intent on blasting him with another energy surge.

The captain didn't wait to see if Agnarsson had recovered enough to generate a charge. He simply fired at the deck below the man. As before, it took a few seconds to penetrate the plating and open the conduit.

A third time, the engineer was bathed in electrocharged fire. And a third time, he escaped its clutches to collapse on the deck, a crisped and bloody thing that barely resembled a man.

Tarasco almost allowed himself to believe that Agnarsson was dead—that he could deactivate the missiles and save his ship. Then the husk that had been the *Valiant*'s engineer began to stir again—began to roll over so it could see its tormentor.

Its eyes had the same startling silver cast to them. And they pulsated with hatred for the captain.

Damn you, Agnarsson rasped in Tarasco's brain, *you don't know what you're doing. I'm your future, your destiny . . .*

If the captain had needed a sign, he had gotten one. He didn't dare think about turning back.

So instead, he stood there and waited, counting down the seconds. He watched the engineer recuperate as he had before, but it didn't seem that Agnarsson was going to mend quickly enough to be a problem.

Tarasco's last thought was for his crew. Like Moses, he was going to be denied the Promised Land—but after all his people had been through, he hoped they, at least, would make it back to Earth alive.

PART ONE

United Federation of Planets Starship
U.S.S. Enterprise NCC-1701-D
2367

One

In the dream, he was on a crowded shuttlecraft.

They had left the *Stargazer* behind—a hulk, crippled in the encounter with the Ferengi at Maxia Zeta. Somewhere ahead—*weeks* ahead—was Starbase 81.

But there was no trace of the desperation they'd felt during the battle. No trace of the sorrow for lost comrades that had hung over them like a cloud.

Instead, there was an air of optimism. Of camaraderie, as there had been on the ship when it was whole. He looked around at the faces—familiar faces. Gilaad Ben Zoma, his first officer, dark and handsome, confident as ever. Idun Asmund, his helmsman, tall and pristinely beautiful as she bent over the shuttle's controls. "Pug" Joseph, his security chief, characteristically alert, ready for anything.

And another—a face that he was gladder to see than all the rest.

"Jack," he said.

Jack Crusher turned his way. He indicated their surroundings with a tilt of his head. "A little snug in here, isn't it, Jean-Luc?"

"That's all right. It won't be forever."

The other man quirked a smile, brushing aside a lock of dark brown hair. "I guess not. It'll only *seem* like forever."

It was so good to see Jack sitting there. So *very* good.

"You're out of your mind," someone rasped.

He turned and saw Phigus Simenon, his Gnalish head of engineering. As usual, Simenon was arguing some point of science or philosophy with Carter Greyhorse, the *Stargazer*'s towering chief medical officer.

"If it's by definition the smallest thing possible," the Gnalish went on, "how can there be anything smaller?" His ruby eyes were alive with cunning in his gray, serpentine visage.

"Easy," Greyhorse answered, the impassivity of his broad features belying the annoyance in his deep, cultured voice. "You take it and cut it in half." Easing his massive body back into his seat, he raised his arms. *"Voilà,* you've got something even smaller."

"Can't be," Simenon argued. "By definition, remember, it's the *smallest—*"

The Gnalish was interrupted by Cadwallader, their slender, girlish communications officer. She placed her freckled hands on the combatants' shoulders. "Could you keep it down a bit, fellas? Some of us are trying to sleep back here, y'know. Thanks *ever* so much."

Chuckling, the captain returned his attention to Jack. "What will you do when you get back? Take a leave for a while?"

His friend nodded. "I want to see Beverly. And my son. He's probably grown six inches since I last saw him." A pause. "Ever think about having a family, Captain?"

"You know me, Jack. I'd rather be boiled in oil than dandle a baby on my knee. Scares the—"

Suddenly, he remembered something. It chilled him, despite the closeness of the quarters. "Jack . . . you're not supposed to be here."

"No? You mean I should've taken one of the *other* shuttles?"

"No." He licked his lips. "I mean you're dead. You died some time ago—*long* before we lost the *Stargazer.*"

Jack shrugged. "I can go if you like—"

"No. Don't. I mean—"

But it was too late. His friend was moving away from him, losing himself in the crowd aft of the food processor.

"Don't go, Jack, it's all right. I didn't mean to send you away—"

That's when Jean-Luc Picard woke up.

The air in his cabin was cold on his skin. He wiped his brow and felt the perspiration there.

"Damn," he breathed. Just a dream.

Nothing like his tortured dreams of Maxia Zeta, inflicted a few years back by the Ferengi DaiMon Bok. No, this had been different, but in its own way just as frightening.

Nor did it take a ship's counselor to figure out why he'd happened to have the dream *now.*

Beverly Crusher was halfway across sickbay when she realized she had no idea where she was going.

Out of the corner of her eye, she saw Doctor Selar, her Vulcan colleague, watching her from her office. Crusher could feel an embarrassed blush climbing up her neck and into her face.

Think, Beverly, think. You were late for—

Suddenly, she snapped her fingers and started walking again. On the way, she glanced at Selar.

The Vulcan was still watching her. Crusher smiled.

Being Vulcan, Selar didn't smile back. She just returned her attention to her desk monitor.

Breezing into the examination area, Crusher saw that Burke was already waiting for her. She nodded by way of a greeting.

"How's it going?" he asked her.

"Not bad," she told him. "Care to lie down for a minute?"

Sitting down on the biobed, the security officer swung his legs up and leaned back until he was directly under the overhead sensor bank. As Crusher consulted the readings that were displayed at eye level, she found herself remembering again . . .

"Doctor Crusher?"

Snapping out of her reverie, she looked at Burke. "Mm?"

"I don't want to rush you, but I'm due to start a shift in ten minutes."

How long had she been staring at the bio-readings? She didn't dare ask.

The security officer smiled. "Listen, it's all right. I don't blame you for being a little distracted. Hell, even *I'm* excited about all those *Stargazer* people coming on board—and I don't even know any of them."

Crusher took a breath. "Actually, I don't know them either. Except one, of course. You can get up now—you're as fit as they come."

As Burke swiveled into a sitting position, he looked at her. "You don't know them? But I thought—"

He stopped himself short, realizing that he might be intruding, but the doctor supplied the rest: *I thought your husband served with them.*

"I heard about them," Crusher explained coolly. "But I never met them face to face."

Burke nodded. "Right. Well, thanks. See you in a few months."

"In a few months," she echoed, as he walked off toward the receiving area.

Leaning against the overhead sensor bank, she buried her face in the crook of her arm. *Damn,* she thought. Why did they have to pick *this* ship?

Will Riker sat down at his personal terminal, took a deep breath, and called up the ship's "visitor" file.

He had been looking forward to this for days. And not because one of his duties as first officer was to keep track of all personnel boarding and disembarking from the ship. The *Enterprise* was about to play host to Starfleet legends—*living* legends—and Riker wanted to know everything there was to know about them. The thousand and one other matters that had been cropping up and demanding his attention lately would just have to wait awhile.

Now, let's see, he told himself, scanning the list of names on the brief menu. The one he wanted to see first was at the bottom—of course. He called up the relevant subfile.

Name: Morgen. Affiliation: Starfleet. Rank: Captain. Homeworld: Daa'V.

The full details of Morgen's career in Starfleet since his graduation from the Academy twenty-one years before came up on-screen.

The record bore out what Riker had heard over the years about Captain Morgen of the *Excalibur.* That he was an even-handed leader. That he brought out the best in his people. That he was militarily brilliant, diplomatically adept, and personally charming.

Not unlike his mentor, Jean-Luc Picard.

Now Morgen was leaving the service that had benefited so much from his presence to discharge another set of responsibilities—as hereditary leader of the Daa'Vit. He was returning to the planet of his birth to assume the throne in the wake of his father's death.

And bringing with him an honor guard—seven Starfleet officers with whom he'd served on the deep-space exploration vessel *Stargazer.* It was a Daa'Vit custom for a returning prince to be surrounded by his closest companions. And despite the friendships Morgen had made on the *Excalibur,* he had selected his fellow officers on the *Stargazer* to stand by him at the coronation ceremony.

It was quite a tribute to those individuals. And to the esprit de corps that had characterized Picard's old ship.

Chief among the honor guardsmen was Picard himself, Morgen's first captain. The others comprised the remainder of the visitors' roster.

He returned to the menu. Some of the names were as familiar to Riker as Morgen's—Ben Zoma, for instance, the captain of the *Lexington,* and First Officer Asmund of the *Charleston.*

The others were somewhat less well known to him, but their names still seemed almost magical. Professor Phigus Simenon. Dr. Carter Greyhorse. Peter "Pug" Joseph. All of them had been part of the *Stargazer*'s historical mission—and, just as important, all had lived to tell the tale.

Riker leaned back in his chair and, not for the first time, wondered what it had been like to serve under the captain in those days—on a vessel like the *Stargazer,* whose mission carried her into uncharted space for years at a time. And beyond that, what it had meant to *lose* that ship, in the Federation's first fateful brush with the Ferengi.

With all of Picard's surviving officers scheduled to board the *Enterprise* over the next couple of days, the first officer would never have a better chance to find out.

Going to the top of the list this time, he called up another subfile.

Asmund, Idun . . .

Captain Mansfield of the *U.S.S. Charleston* sat on the edge of the *s'naiah*-wood desk. It was as uncomfortable as it looked, what with all the savage iconography carved into it. He frowned.

"Idun," he said, "if you'd like to talk about it . . ."

His first officer, who had been staring out the viewport, turned to face him. She was a handsome woman—he couldn't help but notice that. Tall and slim and blond, with eyes the elusive color of glacial ice. Deep, dark . . .

Enough of that, he told himself. *She's your exec, for godsakes. And even if she wasn't, what would she see in an old warhorse like you?*

For the four hundredth time, he put his libido aside. After all, there was something troubling her. If Asmund needed anyone, it wasn't a lover. It was a friend.

"I am all right," she told him evenly. But her eyes said that she was lying.

He sighed.

For six of the eleven years he'd been captain of this ship, Idun Asmund had been his second-in-command, and a damned good one at that. She'd never given him any reason to regret his having taken her aboard.

But he knew of the doubts people had had about her. After that terrible incident on the *Stargazer* . . . what was it? Two decades ago now? For a time, it had haunted her. Kept her from advancing through the ranks as quickly as she should have.

And her manner didn't help any. *Brusque. Icy,* even, some had said. But underneath, Mansfield had sensed a good officer. He'd taken a chance on her—and was glad of it ever since.

"I know you," he said. "You're nervous. And I think we both know why."

"No." She folded her arms across her chest. "I am surprised."

"That Morgen would want you to be with him at a time like this?"

"Yes. After what happened . . . I don't think he said two words to me. Then came Maxia Zeta and . . . well, frankly, I thought I'd never see him again."

"Maybe this is his way of making amends for all that. You and your sister were different people—vastly different, as it turns out. Can it be he's finally figured that out?"

Idun's eyes blazed momentarily. "He is Daa'Vit. When it comes to blood feuds . . ."

"He might not be the same person you knew back then," suggested Mansfield. He looked at her. "People can change a lot in thirteen years. Especially when they've spent half of them in a command chair." He cleared his throat. "Take me, for instance. I wasn't always an iron-willed dictator, you know."

Idun scowled. "He is Daa'Vit. That will not have changed."

"At least try and go in with an open mind," he pleaded. "Remember—you'll be seeing other familiar faces as well. Surely they didn't all treat you as Morgen did."

Idun thought about it. "No," she conceded. "Suppose there are *some* I would like to see again."

"There you go. That's the Idun Asmund that I know." He grunted. "And don't worry about us. We'll just go off and risk our lives somewhere while you take your grand paid vacation."

Her brows knit. "Captain, I can still decline this. Here *is* where my priorities lie."

"It was a *joke,* Idun. Just a joke."

She relaxed again. "Of course it was," she noted.

He chided himself for joking about duty with her. When one had been raised by Klingons, one didn't take such things lightly.

Pug Joseph was just where Erwin expected to find him—sitting by himself in the corner of the lounge. *He does too much of that lately,* the *Lexington*'s first officer told himself. *No wonder he's getting into trouble.*

As Erwin approached, Joseph turned around. His expression said that he wanted to be left alone. Then he saw who it was, and his features softened.

"Commander. To what do I owe this visit?" he asked, grinning.

The first officer turned his resolve up a notch. There was something about Joseph that made it very difficult to be stern with him. Maybe it was the man's resemblance to Erwin's brother's boy, who had died in a skirmish with the Tholians. After all, Joseph had the same close-cropped sandy hair, the same upturned nose. Or was it that no-nonsense attitude, a throwback to the first rough days of interstellar flight, that made him so endearing? The quality that, years earlier in his stint on the *Stargazer,* had earned Joseph the nickname "Pug"?

No matter. Erwin had promised himself he wasn't going to leave it alone this time. He wouldn't be doing anybody any good by ignoring the problem.

The first officer pulled up a seat and leaned close to Joseph. "I'll *tell* you what you owe this visit to. I just got a subspace message from my pal Marcus—on the *Fearless?"*

Joseph's grin started to fade. "Oh," he said.

"You know what Marcus told me," Erwin went on. "Don't you?"

The other man nodded. "Something about a little disagreement, I bet. One in which his man got the worst of it." The grin started to reassert itself. "You should've seen my right hook, Commander. I haven't lost a thing."

With an effort, Erwin frowned. "Fighting," he said, "at *your* age—and you a security chief, no less!" He shook his head disapprovingly. "It's a disgrace, Pug. It's got to stop."

Joseph looked at him. "You should've heard what he said about the *Lexington,* sir. About the captain. And about *you."*

Erwin stiffened. He came *that* close to asking what the man had said. But he restrained himself. "I don't care what anyone said about anyone else. We're supposed to be adults, responsible people—not children who start brawling at the drop of a hat."

The security chief sighed and looked away. "I hear you, Commander."

"That's not good enough," Erwin told him. "Look, you're an officer of this vessel. I want you to *act* like one." He leaned back and pulled down on the bottom of his tunic. "Is that clear?"

The security chief saw that Erwin wasn't kidding. "It's clear," he said.

"Good. And you needn't worry—the captain won't get wind of this. Just as he hasn't gotten wind of the other reports I've received." The first officer paused. "But it's the last time I cover up for you, understand? The last time."

Joseph seemed contrite. Reaching over the table that separated them, Erwin clapped him on the shoulder. Then he got up and made his way to the door.

It wasn't easy to keep from looking back, but he managed. As the lounge doors opened and he emerged into the corridor beyond, he breathed a sigh of relief.

He'd been pretty harsh—maybe harsher than necessary. But this time, Erwin was worried. Marcus had made it sound like more than a brief exchange of haymakers. Considerably more.

Of course, the message in the subspace packet couldn't actually come out and say anything; otherwise, it might have come to the attention of someone inclined to handle it more *officially*—someone like Captain Ben Zoma. But if Erwin read correctly between the lines, Joseph's opponent had taken a *vicious* beating. It was a miracle the man hadn't pressed charges.

The first officer shook his head. "Vicious" wasn't one of the words he'd ever associated with Pug Joseph. If things had gotten that far out of hand, his little reprimand had been long overdue.

He could only hope it would have the desired effect.

"I have the *Excalibur* on long-range sensor scan," reported Worf.

The captain couldn't help but notice the note of anticipation in the Klingon's voice. "Excellent, Lieutenant. Give them our position."

"Aye, sir."

Picard took in the bridge with a glance. Data was intent on his ops console; likewise, Wesley at conn. Everyone, it seemed, was going about his business with clockwork efficiency.

If they showed any emotion at all, it was excitement; they were upbeat about the imminent arrival of their captain's old comrades.

There was no trace of the trepidation Picard himself was feeling.

Fortunately, he had gotten quite good over the years at keeping his feelings under wraps. On the outside, he was his normal self—composed, focused, in charge. It was only on the inside that anything was amiss.

The dream of Jack Crusher still haunted him. *Still,* after all this time.

He remembered the lesson they taught at the Academy—the one that was supposed to put the loss of crewmen in perspective. It sounded as hollow now as it had then. *A starship captain makes a hundred decisions a day, and a goodly number of them involve the well-being of part or all of his crew. . . .*

For a while immediately afterward, Jack's death had cost him his confidence—caused him to second-guess himself. And for even longer, it had left a gaping pain of loss.

Because the victim of his decision wasn't just another crewman. He was a *friend.* And at that stage in his career, Picard had never before lost a friend.

Certainly, he had lost others since. Vigo and the others at Maxia Zeta. And Tasha—dear, fierce Tasha. But the first, as the expression went, was the worst.

Perhaps he should have expected this. With his *Stargazer* officers converging on the *Enterprise,* was it any wonder that Jack was on his mind? Or that his memories would manifest themselves in dreams?

And that was all right—as long as it didn't affect him the way it had once. As long as it didn't in any way jeopardize the safety of those for whom he was *now* responsible.

He resolved that it would *not.*

"Captain?"

He turned and looked up at Worf. "Lieutenant?"

"I have a response from the *Excalibur.* It seems that Captain Morgen would prefer to beam over without any preliminaries."

Picard smiled tautly, nodded to himself. "That sounds like Captain Morgen," he said. "Inform him that I will attend his arrival."

Worf took a moment to send the return message. "Done, sir," he said finally.

"Thank you, Mr. Worf."

Rising, the captain made for the turbolift.

Two

"Admiral?"

"Yes?"

"The *Charleston* has arrived, sir. Commander Asmund is beaming down now."

"Thank you, Mr. Marcos. Please see to her wants. I'll be by to meet her shortly."

Vice-Admiral Yuri Kuznetsov cursed softly under his breath as he pulled up his swim trunks. *Yet another of these* Stargazer *survivors,* he mused. And if she was anything like the first two, it was nothing to look forward to.

Look on the bright side, he instructed himself. *It's only for another couple of days. Then the* Enterprise *comes and takes them all away, and you never have to put up with them again.*

Truth be told, Dr. Greyhorse wasn't so bad. A little too serious for Kuznetsov's taste, a little too intellectual. Carrying on a conversation with him was like talking to a machine. But from what he understood, these were personality defects that ran rampant at Starfleet Medical. And if they were disingenuous, they were also tolerable.

It was the Gnalish, Simenon, that really jump-started Kuznetsov's reactors. Not only was he opinionated, self-centered, and domineering . . . he also brought out the worst in Dr. Greyhorse. Since their arrivals, which were almost simultaneous, the two had done nothing but butt heads on every subject in creation. No doubt, at some level they *enjoyed* their bickering. But listening to it was driving Kuznetsov up a wall—and then some.

He grabbed a towel, closed his locker, and padded barefoot across the synthetic tile floor. He could almost feel the temperature-controlled water leeching away his frustration.

It was his responsibility to entertain Greyhorse and the Gnalish—Starfleet Command had made that plain enough. They didn't want *anything* to go wrong with Captain Morgen's return to Daa'V. With the Romulans an active threat again, the Daa'Vit Confederacy was too valuable an ally to take chances with—and if the

Stargazer people were important to Morgen, that made them important to the brass back on Earth.

But it was 0600 hours—long before he was scheduled to go on duty. For a little while, anyway, he could relax.

As Kuznetsov approached the locker room exit, he had a premonition. A nagging *something* at the back of his consciousness.

In fifteen years of active service, he had learned never to ignore his feelings. So it was with some trepidation that he stepped forward, triggering the entry mechanism.

The doors slid apart silently. The pool sprawled before him, its blue depths lit from below.

And among the shifting light shadows floated Phigus Simenon, former chief engineer of the *Stargazer.* Noticing Kuznetsov's entrance, the Gnalish looked up, his slitted ruby eyes evincing amusement.

"Ah," he said. "Admiral. So good to see you." He raised his tail out of the water languidly, then let it submerge again. His scaly gray body gleamed in the bluish light. "Care to join me?"

My God, thought Kuznetsov. *Is there no escape?*

Morgen had served aboard the *Stargazer* for only nine years, but it seemed like much more. His presence was such that when Picard recalled his decades-long foray into deep space, he could swear that the Daa'Vit had been at his side from the first to the last.

Apparently, Morgen felt much the same way, or he would not have honored his *Stargazer* crewmates by asking them to be his honor guards.

But as the transporter platform became host to the Daa'Vit's reassembling molecules, Picard wondered how much Morgen had changed in other respects. After all, the last time he'd seen him, the Daa'Vit was still a junior-grade lieutenant. Now he was a captain—a peer. And more than that—Morgen was only days away from ruling one of the Federation's most powerful allies.

Then again, this prodigious fate had always been in the cards for the Daa'Vit. And he had never tried to gain special treatment because of it. Nor had he let it temper his sense of humor—a caustic wit that was apparently typical of his race.

Ensconced in a shaft of blue light, Morgen began to take on shape and substance. Picard recognized the features—long and angular, with jutting cheekbones and wide, deepset eyes. Fearsome-looking by human standards. And his protruding collar and hip bones only reinforced that impression.

Transporter Chief O'Brien made a final adjustment to his controls and completed the process. Morgen's eyes, a fiery yellow that contrasted with the green tint of his skin, came alive at the sight of Picard.

"Captain," he said.

"Ens—er, *Captain* Morgen." Picard frowned. "Forgive me. Old habits die hard."

"No need for apologies," said the Daa'Vit. As always, his tone was subdued, almost conspiratorial. "Not between you and me."

And in that moment, Picard realized that *nothing* had changed about Morgen—nothing significant, anyway. It was like old times again. True, this was not his ensign standing before him—but neither was it the head of a powerful empire. It was simply *Morgen.*

Stepping down off the platform, he extended his hand. Picard grasped it.

"This *is* how you humans greet one another—isn't it?"

"Yes," Picard smiled. "I am glad to see your years in Starfleet have produced *some* cultural improvements."

The Daa'Vit smiled back, obviously delighted. "Pitifully few, I'm afraid."

Picard chuckled. He was tempted to clap his former officer on the shoulder. "It *is* good to see you, Morgen."

The Daa'Vit looked around. "And where is the full-dress review appropriate for a guest of my stature?"

"Indeed," said Picard, "I have assembled my officers—though not here, and not in full dress. Rather, they await you in our Ten-Forward lounge—an environment I thought better suited to your . . . er, grave and formal demeanor."

Morgen looked at him askance. If he didn't know the Daa'Vit so well, he might have been alarmed by the intensity of the scrutiny. "Do I detect a note of sarcasm, Captain?"

Picard shrugged. "In all our years on the *Stargazer,* did you ever *once* know me to be sarcastic?"

"Come to think of it, no. But then, I wasn't wearing all those pips on my collar then—and you *were.*"

Picard grunted. "Strange. I don't believe I can remember that far back." He straightened his tunic and gestured in the direction of the exit. "Come. Let's see if we cannot refresh my memory in Ten-Forward. There are some people there who are eager to meet you."

Morgen inclined his head. "Agreed."

So much for melancholy, the captain told himself as they exited the transporter room with a nod to O'Brien. Seeing the Daa'Vit seemed to have cured him of it for the time being.

He was even starting to look *forward* to the remainder of this mission.

"Damn," said Geordi. "Seems like just a few years ago I was sitting in command class, listening to stories about the *Stargazer* and its valiant crew of deep-space explorers—and before you know it, they're going to be walking around in these very corridors, just like regular people. Hell, one of them's here already."

Walking beside him in the long, curving corridor, Worf scowled. "It is a problem," he rumbled.

Geordi looked at him. "A *problem?*" he echoed. "How so?"

His companion cleared his throat. "The dignitary we have taken aboard—Morgen. He is . . . Daa'Vit."

The Klingon appeared to think that that was explanation enough. But Geordi still didn't get it. He said so.

Worf's scowl deepened. He turned to the chief engineer without breaking stride.

"The Daa'Vit," the Klingon explained, "were the enemies of my people for more than three hundred years. We have licked each other's blood from our fingers."

Licked each other's . . . ? Geordi hoped that that was just a *figurative* description.

"Shortly after the Federation allied itself with the Empire, it entered into a similar arrangement with the Daa'Vit Confederacy. . . ."

The Klingon stopped himself as a couple of female ensigns approached from the opposite direction. The women nodded as they went by, and Geordi nodded back.

Not until the ensigns were well out of earshot did Worf continue—and then only in subdued tones. "The Empire had been wed to the Confederacy without its consent. Tempers ran high among my people."

Geordi could only imagine what *that* was like.

"In the end, however, the Romulan threat induced the Empire to keep its ally. And to tolerate its *ally's* ally." Worf grunted. "Since that time, no Klingon has attacked a Daa'Vit or vice versa. But then"—he paused significantly—"no Klingon has stood face-to-face with a Daa'Vit in that time."

Geordi was starting to see. "You're concerned that when you see our guest, your instincts will take over."

The Klingon looked at him. *"My* instincts?" He made a derogatory sound. "I am talking about *his* instincts."

Geordi smiled. "But Morgen was the captain of a Federation vessel for six years. Surely, he had dealings with the Klingons at *some* point."

"Possibly," conceded Worf. "But not *face-to-face."* He paused again. "You must understand—the Daa'Vit are a *barbaric* race."

The chief engineer found the choice of words interesting. If the Daa'Vit were barbaric by *Klingon* standards . . .

"There is no telling how he may react."

Geordi nodded. "And you can't exactly stay away from him. Not when it's your job to provide security for him."

"Precisely."

Geordi thought for a moment, his excitement about meeting the *Stargazer* crew pushed aside for a moment. "You know," he said finally, "maybe you *do* have a problem."

Riker looked around Ten-Forward and smiled. There was a feeling of history in the air.

Though their group was a small one, seated at a single unobtrusive table near one of the observation ports, it had drawn the attention of everyone in the room.

The reunion between Morgen and Captain Picard had not failed to live up to Riker's expectations. The Daa'Vit was every bit as charming as he had heard, and a hell of a raconteur to boot. The first officer—and everyone in the lounge, it seemed—couldn't help but be enthralled by him.

"Believe me," said Morgen, considering the glass of synthehol on the table before him, "I am far from eager to leave Starfleet. I have grown to love the starspanning life." He raised his eyes, glancing at Riker, Picard, and finally Troi before continuing. "But my father's passing has left a gap in the government that must be filled. As crown prince, it falls to me to fill it—and within the allotted time, as you are no doubt aware, or the throne will pass to someone else."

"Manelin was a good man," observed the captain. "I was sorry to hear of his death."

The Daa'Vit shrugged. "He was old. He was in pain. Better that he died when he did, with a few shreds of dignity left to him, than to drag it out any further."

It was a sobering thought. Riker saw Troi's brow crease slightly, no doubt in empathy with Morgen's discomfort.

"Of course," the Daa'Vit went on, "I don't wish to make it seem that I am complaining. If one must abandon a captaincy in Starfleet, ruling a confederacy of planets is not a bad alternative."

They all smiled. But Riker knew that Morgen's remark wasn't from the heart. He himself wouldn't have traded places with any monarch in the galaxy—and he was only a first officer.

"My only regret," said Morgen, "is that I could not approach Daa'V on the vessel I commanded. Now, *that* would have been *something.*"

The captain grunted. "Yes—something *dangerous.* I haven't forgotten your descriptions of Daa'Vit politics, my friend. Starfleet knew what it was doing when it offered you the *Enterprise* for your return."

Morgen smiled a thin smile. "Perhaps *some* Daa'Vit take their politics too seriously. I will concede that much. But the necessity of bringing a *Galaxy*-class vessel into play . . ."

"The Federation," said Riker, "values you too much to take any risks, sir."

The Daa'Vit eyed him. "Values me as *what?* A skilled officer in which it has a massive investment? Or the ruler of a confederacy whose friendship is strategically important?"

"Perhaps both," the first officer suggested.

"And does it really matter?" the captain asked, cutting into the subtly rising tension.

Morgen leaned back in his chair, his angular features softening again. "You're right. It *doesn't* matter. No doubt, I should be flattered that the flagship of the fleet has been deployed for my homecoming." He considered his glass from a fresh perspective. "And if nothing else," the Daa'Vit went on, "this gives me a chance to see old friends." He gazed meaningfully at Picard. "It will be a reunion of sorts, won't it? Who knows—maybe the last chance we'll all have to be together again."

The captain shrugged. "One never knows—though I would not be surprised." He met Morgen's gaze. "All the more reason to enjoy each other's company while we can."

The Daa'Vit nodded, turning to Riker. "A wise man, your captain."

Riker chuckled. "We like to think so."

Wesley Crusher made the necessary adjustments on his control panel, and the *Constitution*-class vessel *Lexington* jumped up two levels of magnification on the forward viewscreen. A moment later, the ship's image was supplanted by that of its commanding officer, a dark, lanky man with graying temples.

"This is Captain Gilaad Ben Zoma." He smiled. "You must be Commander Data. I have heard a lot about you—and not just from your captain."

Wesley turned in his seat to look back at the command center, where Data was seated in the captain's chair. The android seemed pleased by the recognition.

"I *am* Commander Data," he said. "It is my pleasure to invite you aboard the *Enterprise.*"

Wesley studied Ben Zoma carefully. Up until now, he had met only one person who'd served with his father aboard the *Stargazer*—Captain Picard. And the captain wasn't always the easiest person to strike up a conversation with.

But for the next few days, there would be *seven* other people who had worked alongside Jack Crusher—and Captain Ben Zoma, the man on the screen, was one of them.

Not that it was likely he'd have much of a chance to speak with any of the visitors. No doubt, they'd all want to reminisce about old times. Besides, these were important people. They probably wouldn't have much time for him . . .

"I accept your invitation," replied Ben Zoma. "There will be three of us altogether." The man had an infectious charm about him, an affability. "Oh, and Commander . . . If you will humor me, I would like to *surprise* Captain Picard. So it will not be necessary for you to alert him as to our arrival."

That caught the android off balance. "This is most irregular," he said.

"Granted," said the captain of the *Lexington*. "But I would appreciate it nonetheless." He paused. "Would you feel better if I couched my request in the form of an order? You can hardly disobey the instructions of a superior officer— providing you have no standing orders to the contrary."

Data took a moment to mull it over. "I have no *orders* as such, Captain. However—"

"Then it's settled."

The android was still perturbed—but he no longer had any choice in the matter. Ben Zoma had seen to that. "As you wish, Captain" was all he could get out.

Interesting guy, Wesley mused. A different style from Captain Picard's, for sure.

Wesley assumed the conversation was over, and was turning his attention back to his conn board, when he noticed Ben Zoma looking at *him.*

He returned the man's gaze—an eerie feeling, considering people on the viewscreen usually ignored anyone outside the command center. He'd almost forgotten he was even visible in some of these transmissions.

"And you," said Ben Zoma, "must be Wesley Crusher."

The ensign felt the heat of embarrassment climbing into his cheeks. He cursed inwardly.

"Aye, sir."

The captain of the *Lexington* nodded. "Without question, your father's son." The skin around his dark eyes crinkled. "I look forward to meeting you as well."

Wesley straightened eagerly. His heart was pounding in his chest, and all he could think of was to repeat his earlier response: "Aye, sir."

Then Ben Zoma's image blinked out, and once again the ensign found himself staring at the lines of the *Lexington*.

Riker happened to be facing the door, so he was the first to mark the trio of unfamiliar faces as they entered the lounge. He was on the verge of saying something about them when he observed the gesture of the dark-skinned man in the lead—a finger planted vertically across his lips.

Seeing the captain's pips on the man's collar, Riker kept his mouth shut. Nor did any of his companions take note as the newcomers wound their way among the intervening tables.

It wasn't long before the dark man was directly behind Picard and Morgen, a mischievous gleam in his eye. He paused there, savoring the moment. Finally, he spoke. "Damn. I'd heard the two of you had aged, but the stories didn't say just how much."

As recognition set in, Picard declined to turn around immediately. He looked at Morgen. "Just remember," he said, "it was *you* who invited him."

The Daa'Vit nodded. "In a moment of insanity," he said, straightfaced. "One that I am already beginning to regret."

"Liar," said Ben Zoma as they got up to face him. "You've missed me like crazy—both of you have."

He took their hands—first Picard's, then Morgen's. Riker found himself smiling.

"You haven't changed," observed Captain Picard. "Still the same old Gilaad Ben Zoma."

"*I* can attest to *that,*" said one of the other newcomers, stepping up alongside the dark man. A lieutenant commander, Riker noted, though she didn't look old enough to have come that far. Her freckles and tousled strawberry-blond hair gave her a girlish sort of appeal—but not the air of authority one generally associated with high rank. "That is, I *could* attest to it," she amended with a hint of an Australian accent, "if not for the fact that Captain Ben Zoma is my commanding officer."

"Cadwallader," said Picard. He took her hand. "Still keeping this madman in line, I trust?"

She nodded. "It's a tough job, but someone's got to do it."

"Don't make it sound like you do it alone," said the third arrival. A stocky, almost squarish man, he evidenced a slight limp as he came closer. "Security is something of an adventure on the *Lexington*—to say the least."

Riker tried to imagine the *Enterprise* officers talking about their captain that way. And to his face! But then, he knew from experience that not all ships were run the same way—and when formality was suspended to a degree, it didn't necessarily mean that the crew was any less efficient. It was just a matter of each captain's individual style and preference.

Apparently, however, Ben Zoma wasn't *quite* as liberal as first appearances indicated—because he stifled his companions with a glance. Then, turning back to his fellow captains, he said: "Don't listen to Commander Cadwallader—*or* Mr. Joseph. They've never had it so good in their lives."

Joseph—the stocky man—looked skeptical. The woman just smiled. And not a bad smile at that, Riker mused.

"I am glad you could come," Morgen said. "*All* of you."

"You couldn't have kept us away with phaser cannons," said Joseph.

"Please," said Picard, "pull up a chair, won't you? And I will try to forget that you bullied your way aboard behind my back."

Once they were all seated, Picard made the introductions. "Commander Riker here is my first officer. Troi is our ship's counselor."

"Something we could have used on the *Stargazer,*" Ben Zoma pointed out. He smiled at Troi. "Of course, someone of *your* beauty would be welcome anywhere."

The Betazoid took the compliment in stride. She smiled back.

"Captain Ben Zoma," Picard continued, "besides being one of the galaxy's great flatterers, was my first exec. We served together for twenty years, if you can bring yourselves to believe that."

The dark man shook his head. "I can scarcely believe it myself."

Picard indicated the woman who had come in with Ben Zoma. "Tricia Cadwallader. The best damned communications officer a captain ever had—back in the days when there *were* such things as communications officers. Today she's the second officer of the *Lexington.*"

Riker nodded by way of a greeting. It caught her eye, and for a moment she lingered on his gaze. Then she turned to Troi.

"Pleased to meet you," she said.

"Likewise," the ship's counselor replied.

"And last—but certainly not least—" Picard resumed, "Security Chief Peter Joseph—though we all know him as Pug."

The reasoning behind the nickname was self-evident. Joseph resembled nothing so much as a bulldog.

"The genuine article," the security chief quipped. "Accept no substitutions."

There was laughter all around at that, and when it quieted, Riker took the opportunity to raise his glass. "I'd like to propose a toast. To Captain Morgen. May his reign be a long and fruitful one."

There were sounds of agreement—not only from their own table, but from a number of others around them.

"And," added Morgen, "to the former officers of the *Stargazer*. May they never forget how fortunate they were to have served under the legendary Jean-Luc Picard."

As the others drank, Picard grunted. *"Legendary?"* he repeated. "I'm not *old* enough to be *legendary."*

As Troi approached the bar, Guinan shook her head in motherly fashion.

"You're a trouper," she told the empath.

Troi smiled. "What do you mean?"

"What do I *mean?* Counselor, you've spent the last five *hours* listening to *Stargazer* stories. And now that the *Lexington* contingent has joined us, you'll probably be in for *another* five hours' worth." Guinan grunted. "In my book, that's being a trouper."

"Oh, come on," Troi said. "I *like* listening to those old stories. Apart from their entertainment value, they give me insights into the captain that I've never had before. I can understand a little better how he became the person he is." She glanced at the table she'd just come from, where Ben Zoma was recalling some incident involving a shuttle and a pair of Grezalian ambassadors. "You know, it's funny. I get the feeling that Commander Riker and myself are being shown off in a way—almost as if we were his children." Troi paused thoughtfully. "Which is not so difficult to comprehend, I suppose. Captain Picard never had any offspring of his own. Why *shouldn't* he think of us as his children?"

"Actually," Guinan responded, "I think he considers you *all* his children—not only you and Commander Riker, but Morgen and the *Stargazer* people as well. And he's pleased that all his children are enjoying an opportunity to get to know one another." She shrugged. "It just seems a little barbaric for you to have to force yourself to stay awake."

"I am *not* forcing myself to stay awake," the empath protested. Then, noting the way Guinan's mouth was curling up at the corners, she added: "Besides, I can't let the older kids have *all* the fun."

Guinan looked past Troi. "Uh-oh. Don't look now, but one of the older kids is hitting the sack."

The counselor turned and saw Joseph getting up from his chair. He said something under his breath, got a round of laughter for his trouble, and gave the group an old-fashioned salute. Then he made his way to the exit.

When Troi turned back, she looked thoughtful.

"What?" probed Guinan.

The empath raised her eyes. "Mr. Joseph—Pug, they call him. He's not quite as

happy as the rest of them. Oh, he *seems* to be, on the outside. But inside, he's—"
She paused, trying to translate perceived emotion into words—not always an easy
task. "Bitter," she said finally.

"About what?" asked Guinan.

Troi shook her head. "I don't know. I'm not a telepath, remember? But I can
guess."

Guinan leaned forward over the bar. "I'm listening," she said.

"When the *Stargazer* set out," said the Betazoid, "Joseph was the chief of security. Cadwallader was a junior-grade communications officer, Morgen was an ensign, and Ben Zoma was the first officer. Obviously, they've all moved
up—Morgen and Ben Zoma to captaincies, and Cadwallader to lieutenant commander. But Pug is still security chief. No change in rank or function."

Guinan nodded. "No wonder he's bitter."

"And particularly so toward Cadwallader. From what I gather, he took her
under his wing when she joined the *Stargazer.* Treated her like a kid sister."

"And then she grew up and left him in the dust." She flicked her finger at a tiny
piece of napkin left on her bar. "But then, that must be fairly common in Starfleet.
Not everybody is moving-up material."

"No," said the counselor. "But that doesn't make it any easier on the ones who
are left behind."

"Mom?"

Beverly Crusher jumped at the sound. She looked up from her desk, saw that it
was only Wesley. Her heart pounding, she tried not to show how badly he'd startled her.

"Mom, are you feeling all right?" asked Wesley, entering her office. Unlike her,
he was still in uniform.

She smiled. "Of course I'm all right. Why shouldn't I be?"

He shrugged. "I heard that Captain Picard had assembled some of his officers
in Ten-Forward. You know—to meet the *Stargazer* people. And I knew you weren't
on duty, so . . . if you're feeling okay, why aren't you there? In Ten-Forward, I
mean, with everybody else?"

Crusher sat back in her chair. "That's a good question, Wes."

The boy—she would *always* think of him that way, she couldn't help it—regarded her with a lack of understanding. "I don't get it," he told her. "Don't you
want to see Dad's old friends?"

She shrugged. "Yes and no."

The lack of understanding deepened. "Why the *no* part?"

The doctor sighed. "This may sound strange, Wes, but I've come to terms with
what I knew of your father. With the Jack Crusher I knew. And *loved.*" Another
sigh. "I don't know if I want any *new* memories. Not if they're going to make me
start mourning him all over again."

Wesley started to say something, thought better of it. "Mom," he went on finally, "this isn't like you. You're not the kind of person who backs off from things."

"From most things, no." The doctor found she couldn't look at him, so she
looked at her desktop monitor instead. She didn't blame him for being surprised at
her. To tell the truth, she was surprised at herself. "From *this* thing . . . I don't
know. It's hard to explain."

Silence. An uncomfortable silence—for him, no doubt, as well as for her. But she didn't break it.

In the end, it was Wesley who took the initiative. "I suppose," he said, "you've got the right to do what you want." There was a hint of pain in his voice; maybe someone else wouldn't have noticed it, but *she* did. "If it doesn't bother Captain Picard, maybe it shouldn't bother me either. But I intend to get to know these people—that is, if they let me."

Her heart went out to him. "Wes . . ."

"I don't *have* your memories, Mom. I've got to find out all I can about him. And if it makes me start missing him again, then I'm willing to pay that price."

It hurt to hear him say that. "You do what you have to, Wes. Just forgive me if I don't feel the same way, all right?"

The pique cooled a little inside him. Not all at once, but it cooled.

Just like Jack. *Slow to hurt, slow to heal.* Wasn't that one of his favorite expressions?

"Look," said Wesley, "I didn't mean to say all that. Maybe it's not my place."

"You can say anything you want to me, Wes. *Anything.*"

"But it doesn't mean you'll agree with me."

"It's not a matter of agreement. It's . . ." She shook her head ruefully, at a loss for words.

He came around the desk and took her hand. She looked up at him.

"Try to understand," she said.

"I will," he assured her.

Then he left, and she drew up her knees and hugged them as hard as she could.

Three

"Thank you for having us," Asmund told Vice-Admiral Kuznetsov.

He smiled at her. "The pleasure was all mine, Commander."

Walking up ahead of them in the corridor, Simenon and Greyhorse were at it again, having found some new subject to work over. Kuznetsov never thought he would be saying this—not even to himself—but he had grown fond of the engineer and the doctor in comparison to the way he felt about Idun Asmund.

Not that she was rude, like Simenon. Nor was she annoyingly intellectual, like Greyhorse. Far from it—her comments were simple, down to earth. And certainly, she was wonderful to look at.

But, strange to say, she *scared* him—and had from the first time he met her. Of course, in the beginning, he couldn't understand why.

Then he'd inadvertently walked in on her exercise session. Exercise *indeed.* It looked for all the world as if she were fighting for her life—and enjoying every second of it.

"Sorry to interrupt, Commander. I didn't know you were in here."

"That's quite all right, sir. I was almost finished anyway."

She brushed aside a lock of blond hair, wet with perspiration. Breathed through her teeth, like . . . like what? An animal?

"Er . . . those knives . . . they're very unusual."

The blades were razor-sharp, the handles savagely carved. Made of some wood he'd never seen before—and the workmanship was so intricate, it looked like the things were writhing in her hands.

"Yes—they are unusual. They're Klingon-made."

"Oh. I see."

Later on, he'd taken a closer look at her file, and discovered why she had such an affinity for things Klingon. As children, she and her twin sister had been the only survivors of a Federation colony disaster on the planet Alpha Zion. As luck would have it, the Klingons intercepted the colony's distress calls and reached it before Starfleet could—no doubt hoping that there would be Federation technology there worth raiding.

Apparently, there wasn't. Just a couple of towheaded five-year-olds, sunken-cheeked and huddled against the elements.

Normally, it would have been unthinkable for a Klingon to take pity on a human. But after what the Asmund twins had gone through, it was obvious that they were made of sterner stuff than most Homo sapiens. Their courage was something the Klingons could not ignore—nor could they leave them there in the ruins, counting on Starfleet to arrive before the girls died of starvation or exposure.

The captain of the Klingon vessel packed the humans aboard his ship. He brought them back to his sister and her husband, who were childless, giving them the option of keeping them—or disposing of them as they saw fit.

They kept them—and raised them as Klingons. Apparently, the training took, if Asmund's exercise session was any indication.

Twice a survivor, Kuznetsov had mused upon finishing her file. First Alpha Zion, and then the *Stargazer.* Somehow, he wasn't surprised.

But something was still gnawing at him—still bothering him. What? For lack of any other options, he called up her *sister's* file—and realized where he had heard the name Asmund before.

How could he have forgotten? The incident had brought the Federation *this* close to losing the Daa'Vit as allies—maybe even starting a war.

Idun had never been linked with what her sister did. Her slate was clean.

But they were *twins.* Was it possible that she hadn't *known* about her sister's plan? Hadn't even suspected?

That question had kept Kuznetsov up late the last few nights. And given him another reason to be scared by her—though in some ways it was even less rational than the first.

Up ahead, Simenon and Greyhorse turned and entered the transporter room. A moment later he and Commander Asmund followed them in.

The transporter technician was waiting patiently for them. She smiled cordially at Kuznetsov; he smiled back.

He wondered if his relief was evident in his expression—though at this point, he hardly cared. The important thing was that he was getting rid of them—*all* of them.

Beverly Crusher had managed to keep to herself up until now, leaving little opportunity for her to run into the *Stargazer* people. But she was forced to abandon that policy when they reached Starbase 81.

After all, she had worked closely with Carter Greyhorse for most of the year she'd spent at Starfleet Medical. They'd become more than colleagues; they'd become friends. And he'd been sensitive enough not to bring up more than a passing reference to her late husband, once he realized she didn't want to talk about him.

So how could she snub him now by not attending his arrival? It would have been worse than bad manners. It would have been a breach of professional etiquette.

And if there was one thing of which she would *not* be found guilty, it was a lack of professionalism.

The doctor repeated that to herself as she stood beside Captain Picard and watched the last of their guests materialize. Under O'Brien's expert touch, the shafts of shimmering light coalesced into flesh and blood.

Greyhorse wasn't difficult to discern from the other two. His towering height, black eyes, and blunt Amerind features set him apart right away. And as if that weren't enough, the medical blue of his uniform stood out in stark contrast to the garb of his companions.

Crusher stepped forward. "Carter," she said, her smile coming naturally.

He clambered down from the platform and took her hand. She felt tiny beside him—she'd forgotten about that.

"Beverly. So good to see you." Greyhorse's voice was as dry as ever, but she knew him better than to be offended. Deep down, he was a warm, even affectionate person.

"Good to see you," she told him.

The captain was exchanging pleasantries with the others. After a moment or two, he turned to Crusher and touched her arm.

"Dr. Beverly Crusher, my chief medical officer . . . this is Commander Idun Asmund of the *Charleston*."

The blond woman had a small Starfleet-issue pack slung over one shoulder—a little unusual; ship's stores could reproduce any personal effect a passenger desired. But then, some effects were more personal than others.

Asmund extended her hand and they shook. She had quite a grip.

"And *this*," said Picard, indicating the third member of the party, "is Lieutenant Commander Phigus Simenon, once my chief engineer and currently an instructor at Starfleet Academy."

"And not dead *yet*," said the Gnalish, "contrary to popular belief—and the fervent hopes of my students." He smiled, his bright-red serpentine eyes slitting even more than usual as he extended his hands palms downward. His stooped posture made it necessary for him to crane his neck to look up at her—a gesture that would have been awkward, not to mention painful, for a human. Of course, Simenon was decidedly not human.

Crusher returned the greeting as best she could, extending her hands in the same manner. The Gnalish seemed to approve.

"Not only beautiful," he told the captain, "but respectful as well."

"I've been to your world," explained the doctor, taking the compliment in stride. "It was part of my training in xenobiology."

"I gathered as much," said Simenon.

"No doubt," said Picard, "you'll want to join the others. They're in our Ten-Forward lounge." He looked at Crusher. "In fact, one might say they're *commandeering* the lounge, and have done so for the last two days."

Greyhorse grunted. "Sounds about right," he remarked.

"To the lounge, then," said the Gnalish. "But only on one condition."

The captain became mock-serious. "And that is?"

"That afterward you take me to your engineering section. And leave me there with someone who knows a driver coil from a magnetic accelerator."

Picard nodded gravely. "I think we have *someone* like that. I'll see what I can do."

The Gnalish harumphed. "You mock me, Captain." He appealed to Crusher. "Imagine—ridiculing someone of *my* advanced years."

The doctor found herself smiling. Perhaps Wesley wasn't entirely wrong.

Both Simenon and Asmund had heard her last name, but neither had made the least mention of Jack. And Simenon seemed like the kind of person she'd like to know better.

She still wasn't about to invite them to her room for a party. Or, for that matter, join them in Ten-Forward. Not yet. But she made a promise to herself—and to Wes—that she'd be a little less of a hermit.

At tactical, Worf noted the intercom activity a fraction of a second before they heard the voice on the bridge.

"Lieutenant?"

It was O'Brien down in Transporter Room One.

Data sat up just a little bit straighter in the captain's chair. "Yes, Chief?"

O'Brien frowned. "Sorry to disturb you, sir. It's probably nothing, but . . . well, one of our guests—Commander Asmund—brought aboard some rather unusual cargo."

"Can you be more specific?" asked the android.

A pause. "Some kind of *knives,* sir. I can't tell you much more about them, except . . . I think they've got a sort of ceremonial look to them." Another pause. "I would've said something to the captain himself when he was here, but Commander Asmund *does* have top-security clearance, and I didn't want to embarrass anyone."

Worf grunted. Ceremonial knives? That *was* unusual.

Data rose and started to circumnavigate the command center. "Please make your scan available to the tactical station," he told O'Brien.

"Aye, sir," came the response.

A fraction of a second later, the image appeared on one of Worf's monitors. And a fraction of a second after that, Data was standing beside him, looking it over.

The android's brow creased ever so slightly. He turned to the Klingon. "You are the weapons expert, Lieutenant. Have you ever seen specimens of this sort?"

Indeed he had.

Worf nodded. "Mr. O'Brien is right. They are ceremonial knives." He frowned as his eyes traced the familiar serration pattern. *"Klingon* ceremonial knives. My brother showed me a pair just like them when he was on the ship."

Data nodded. "I see. Then that explains it."

Worf looked at him. "It *does?"*

"Certainly. They must have been a gift from her parents."

The security chief's confusion only deepened. "I do not understand," he confessed.

Data stared at him. Then comprehension dawned. "Did you not know that Commander Asmund was raised in the Klingon Empire?"

He might as well have told Worf that they were headed for the heart of a supernova. It took the Klingon a moment to recover.

"No," he said finally. "I did *not."*

But that would be rectified as soon as his shift on the bridge was over, and he had a chance to access the necessary information. Worf did not like mysteries—particularly when they hit so close to home.

Guinan was swabbing down her bar with a damp towel when Pug Joseph approached her, glass in hand. He smiled.

"We're keeping you busy, aren't we?"

It was an understatement. Now that the Gnalish and Dr. Greyhorse had arrived, the party was *really* in high gear—though the other newcomer, Commander Asmund, had declined to join them.

Guinan shrugged, returning the smile. "That's what I'm here for."

Joseph placed an elbow on the bar and leaned over in a conspiratorial sort of way. "Tell me," he said. "Do you have anything a mite stronger than this Ferengi bug-juice?"

She looked at him. "That's the first time I've ever heard synthehol referred to as Ferengi bug-juice. Very colorful." Her smile deepened. "In any case, the answer is no. I can offer you a beer, if you like. But the strongest drink we serve in Ten-Forward is synthehol. In fact, I'm a little surprised at the question. I thought synthehol was the strongest drink served in *all* ship's lounges."

"Well," said Joseph, "that's the way it's supposed to be—*officially,* that is. But, y'see, we bend the rules a little on the *Lexington.*" He indicated Ten-Forward with a tilt of his head. "Of course, we haven't got anything nearly this fancy on our ship. But we give a man freedom of choice—if you know what I mean."

Guinan nodded. "I know exactly what you mean, Mr. Joseph. But I'm afraid that doesn't change anything on *this* vessel. As long as I'm in charge of the Ten-Forward lounge, there will be nothing harder than synthehol served here. Keeps the repair bills down." She paused. "But how about an ice cream soda? I can whip up one of those in a flash—and no one has to be any the wiser."

Joseph scowled. "You're breaking my heart, you know that?" He held up his glass. "Look. I can go back to my quarters and fill this with the finest Maratekkan brandy." He jerked a thumb over his shoulder. "But that would mean I'd have to drink it all alone—when some of my closest friends in the world are sitting right there." He gave her his best cherubic look. "Now, normally, I could see your point. Hell—you don't want everybody drinking the good stuff, or what would happen in an emergency? But under the circumstances—these *special* circumstances—I think even the head of Starfleet would look the other way and pour me something interesting."

Guinan sighed. "You're a tough man to reason with, Mr. Joseph."

"That's what they tell me," he said.

"And I must say, you've got a point there. You *could* simply go to your cabin and drink anything you wanted."

"It takes an astute person to put matters in their proper perspective," he encouraged.

"But it strikes me that you might want a *real* drink a little too *much.*"

His expression hardened a little. "Eh? What d'you mean?"

Guinan resumed her swabbing of the bar. "Just this—that if I had a problem, I wouldn't keep it to myself. Especially when there's someone willing to hear about it. Maybe even help me with it."

"Are you saying that I'm an alcoholic?" His eyes blazed. "There are no such people anymore—haven't been for some time, in case you hadn't heard."

"They're rare, all right," she agreed. "But they do pop up occasionally. Even aboard starships."

Joseph's features went taut—so taut they looked painful. For a moment, Guinan had the uncomfortable feeling he was going to reach across the bar and grab her by the front of her garment.

But it never happened. Gradually, the fury in his eyes cooled.

"Thank you anyway," he told her, putting his glass down on the bar. "I guess I'll just have to seek my comfort somewhere else."

She watched thoughtfully as he left Ten-Forward.

Riker, like everyone else at the table, was listening to Ben Zoma's yarn.

"And then," said Ben Zoma, turning to Troi, "your captain here had the gall to ask the Clobatians if he could *drop them off* somewhere."

Troi smiled. "Did he really?"

Picard shrugged. "It seemed like the only humane thing to do. Without our help, they would have frozen to death."

Simenon snorted. "Naturally. You blew up their shuttlecraft."

"A last resort," countered Morgen. "As you well know, Phigus. If the Clobatians had returned to their mother ship before *we* returned to the *Stargazer . . ."*

"We never would have caught up with them," finished Cadwallader.

"Exactly right," said Greyhorse.

"And with the phasers they'd stolen," Riker added, "they would have held the key to our weapons technology."

Morgen nodded approvingly. "You have a better appreciation of the situation," he told the first officer, "than *some* of us who were *there."*

Picard grunted. "At least *someone* understands the subtleties of command."

Riker chuckled. "Thank you—both of you. But I'm afraid I'm going to have to take my appreciation and understanding and pack them off to the bridge right now. I believe Mr. Data's shift ends in a few minutes."

As he stood, Cadwallader got up as well. "That reminds me," she said. "I'm supposed to meet Lieutenant Worf—for a tour of the communications system."

"Communications?" echoed Greyhorse. "You're a second officer now. A generalist."

Cadwallader winked at him. "You know what they say, Doctor. Once a communications officer, always a communications officer." She looked at Riker. "You *did* say you were headed for the bridge? That's where my tour is supposed to begin."

"Then," said the first officer, "it would be my pleasure to show you the way."

Cadwallader inclined her head. "How gallant of you."

"Nice ship you've got here," Cadwallader remarked as she and Riker stepped out into the corridor.

He nodded. "Thank you." He paused, trying to be diplomatic. "Although to be honest, our communications system isn't a great deal more advanced than the *Lexington's.*"

She smiled. "I know. I get a kick out of *any* system. I wasn't entirely kidding when I said I was still a communications officer at heart."

A couple of security officers passed by, going the other way. Riker acknowledged them with a nod.

"You know," he said, "for a moment there, I thought you were going to say 'kid.' As in 'a kid at heart.' "

Cadwallader laughed. "That too. In fact, I'm sure most of them think of me that way—as 'the kid.' I was pretty young when I beamed aboard the *Stargazer.*"

He glanced at her. "I know. Nineteen, wasn't it?"

She grinned. "How did—oh. I guess you've been doing your homework."

Riker smiled back. "I guess I have. Let's see. Hometown: Sydney, Australia. Graduated from Starfleet Academy with honors. First assignment as ensign on the *Goddard.* After a year, you came to the *Stargazer,* where you served until the Maxia Zeta incident. Three years as lieutenant jay-gee on the *Victory,* and another three on the *Thomas Paine*—where you distinguished yourself by saving your captain's life on not one, but two occasions. When Captain Ben Zoma was given command of the *Lexington,* he offered you a promotion if you'd come aboard as his second officer."

She looked at him suspiciously. "You've got quite a memory, Commander."

"Will," he told her.

Cadwallader laughed. "All right. Will it is. But tell me—do you memorize all your visitors' bios the way you memorized mine?"

The turbolift was just ahead. As they approached, the doors opened to accommodate them. They stepped inside and the doors closed again.

"Main bridge," said Riker.

"You haven't answered my question," she told him.

He returned her gaze. "The truth?"

She thought about it for a moment. "No."

"In that case," he said, "yes, I *do* memorize them all that way."

She laughed. He found it infectious; a moment later he was laughing too.

"You're a very charming man," said Cadwallader.

"Some times more than others."

She eyed him. "Nonsense. I bet you were charming the day you were born." She looked at the ceiling. "Let's see . . . in Valdez, Alaska, wasn't it? Graduated from the Academy with *high* honors. Served as ensign on the *Zhukov,* lieutenant jay-gee, and later full lieutenant on the *Potemkin.* Three years as second officer on the *Yorktown* and two more as first officer on the *Hood.* Most recent assignment, of course, the *Enterprise*—where you've become known as one of the top officers in the fleet. Credited with almost single-handedly stopping the Borg invasion."

Riker's smile broadened moment by moment. "I guess," he said when she was finished, "I'm not the only one around here with a good memo—"

Before he could complete his sentence, the turbolift doors opened onto the bridge. Worf, Data, and half a dozen other officers were looking in their direction.

Riker cleared his throat. He considered Cadwallader, who obviously enjoyed having taken him by surprise.

"Carry on, Commander," he told her.

She nodded. "Aye, sir."

And as he made his way to the captain's chair, she headed for tactical—where Worf's replacement had already arrived.

Four

Geordi knew he was a little early for his engineers' meeting, but that was all right. It would give him a chance to get his thoughts in order.

The meetings were informal, and purposely held as far away from engineering as possible. Their original inspiration had been the incident with Broc—with Barclay. (Even now he had to be careful not to refer to the man by that silly nickname.) Geordi had realized that he didn't know some of his people as well as he should—hence, a weekly off-duty coffee get-together, which would give everybody the chance to let off steam without worrying about offending a superior officer. At the engineers' meetings, there was no such thing as rank—everybody was on an equal footing.

As the lounge doors opened, Geordi noticed that there was someone already inside—a tall, rather alluring-looking woman he was sure he'd never seen before, wearing a cranberry-red command tunic. She stood with her back to him, gazing out the observation port at the streaking stars.

One of the captain's friends, Geordi concluded. Entering the lounge quietly so as not to disturb her, he couldn't help but stare a little—and not just because she was one of the *Stargazer* people. He'd seldom seen a woman so well put together.

What's more, she was all by herself. Seems sort of lonely, he thought.

Or maybe not. Maybe she *wanted* a little solitude.

If he'd known in advance that she was here, he would have changed the location of the meeting. Lord knows, he told himself, there are plenty of other lounges on the *Enterprise.*

Geordi frowned. The least he could do was warn her that the lounge was about to be invaded. Coming a little closer, he cleared his throat. No reaction. Maybe she hadn't heard.

Walking the rest of the way across the room, he tapped her gently on the shoulder.

Before he knew what was happening, he found himself draped backward over her knee—looking up at her savagely clawed fingers as they hovered mere inches from his face. As he found her eyes, he saw a deadly hostility in them—a gleam that under other circumstances he might have called *murderous.*

Quickly, the hostility died. *"Qos,"* the woman breathed, mortified. Her cheeks burned a bright red.

Qos?

Lowering her hand, she helped Geordi get back on his feet. "I'm sorry," she said. "I didn't hear you come in. And—" She shook her head. "Please forgive me."

"Sure," he told her, grinning—trying to salvage what was left of his machismo. "No problem. I shouldn't have surprised you like that." Smoothing out his tunic, he held his arms out. "See? Good as new."

She didn't grin back. "There's no excuse for this. It's just that I was trained, early on, to—"

"It's all right," he assured her. "Really." He held out his hand. "Geordi La Forge, chief engineer."

She grasped it—more firmly than he expected. Though after what had just happened, he probably shouldn't have been surprised.

"Idun Asmund," she responded. "First officer of the *Charleston.* One of your captain's guests."

"I gathered as much," he told her. "You don't normally see too many command uniforms around here."

"No, I don't suppose you do."

Just then, Duffy and DiBiasi walked in. When they saw Geordi's companion, they stopped dead in their tracks. Apparently, she was every bit as striking as his VISOR had led him to believe.

"That's what I wanted to tell you," Geordi explained. "This place is about to become lousy with engineers. We're having a meeting, sort of—though you're invited to sit in if you'd like." He glanced at Duffy and DiBiasi. "I'm sure no one would mind."

"Thank you," said Asmund, "but no. I was just about to be going anyway," she lied.

Geordi shrugged. "Suit yourself. See you around, then."

She nodded. "Yes. See you around."

As she crossed the room, neither of the newcomers could take their eyes off her. "My God," said DiBiasi once she was gone. "Who *was* that, Commander?"

"No ranks here," said the engineering chief, "remember? And as for who she is . . . she's one of the *Stargazer* officers. You know, the bunch serving as Captain Morgen's honor guard."

Duffy grunted. "Some guys have all the luck."

"Hey," DiBiasi chimed in, "I thought all the captain's friends were in Ten-Forward. What's she doing *here?*"

Geordi shook his head. "I guess that's *her* business," he said. Suddenly, he saw those clawed fingers again—hovering like a hunting bird, ready to tear him apart. Shuddering, he put the image from his mind. "Come on. Let's get some coffee."

Beverly tucked one leg underneath her and sat down on her bed. Opening the box of audio modules, she picked one out at random.

How long had it been since she'd listened to Jack's old tapes? A year? Two? Had she played them at all since she'd come aboard the *Enterprise?*

She looked at the module in her hand. Reading the stardate, she decided that the message was about sixteen years old—which meant she would have received it on . . . where? Delos Four? Yes—Delos Four. Unbidden, memories flooded her mind like gentle rains.

Rain. She chuckled. It hadn't rained more than a dozen times during her entire internship in the Mariadth Valley, though the Delosians said that it rained there all the time. Of course, when one was as long-lived as the Delosians were, and used to places where it didn't rain at all, a dozen times in four years may have seemed like "all the time."

Her mentor, Dalen Quaice, had called Delos Four "the hottest, driest place in the galaxy." She could see him bent over a zaphlid-calf, inoculating it for scale-fever and complaining about the heat. "It's unbearable, Beverly. Have you ever been to Vulcan? No? Well, it's pretty dry there too. But this place makes a Vulcan desert look like a rain forest."

And without Jack it had seemed even drier, even more barren.

Taking a deep breath, Beverly slipped the tape into the mechanism next to her bed and waited for Jack's voice to emerge from the speakers. When it did, she was surprised at how young he sounded.

"Hi, honey. Greetings from the *Stargazer,* where we're wrapping up with the Mandrossa—*still.* It turns out that their negotiation protocols are a lot more complicated than those of other races we've encountered; even establishing an agenda for further contact has kept us here for weeks. In the end, though, I think it'll be worth it. The Mandrossa are way ahead of us in genetics, and we can teach them a few things about immunology. The way it looks, both parties will benefit from the relationship.

"Unfortunately, speaking of relationships, this puts off my shore leave awhile longer. But be patient. I can't wait to see you and little Wes. By my calculations, he ought to be about up to my waist now. Just big enough to swing my old baseball bat—you know, the one I got when I was a kid. Do you think I can teach him to hit in five days? I'm certainly going to try.

"As for you, my love . . . I have a little excursion in mind. You see, Pug Joseph was on Delos Four a while back, and he's been regaling me lately with stories about this place he rented in the mountains. Not necessarily the kind of stories you'd tell your grandmother, but then, that's Pug. Anyway, I did some research, and it appears his love nest is still around. What's more, it's supposed to be beautiful there. Seems like as good a way to get reacquainted as any—and Wes won't miss us overnight. Especially if he ends up getting a baby brother—or sister—out of the deal.

"Not too much else to tell you. Cad had a birthday, Morgen was promoted to lieutenant jay-gee and—oh, Greyhorse says he'll be glad to answer any questions you have about being a doctor aboard a starship. His main advice is to avoid any vessel that has a Gnalish aboard—his words, not mine.

"I guess that's it. Give my love to Wes and I'll see you soon, I hope. I mean, how much longer can these negotiations go on? We already hold the Federation record. Miss you."

Crusher took a deep breath, let it out. Stopping the tape, she had the mechanism eject it and replaced it in the box.

Then she began putting herself in a more professional frame of mind. She was due in sickbay in a few minutes.

Stopping at the entrance to the holodeck, Worf turned to the group that was trailing behind him.

"This," he said, "is a holographic environment simulator. Known in the vernacular as a holodeck."

The Klingon scowled. *Why,* he wondered, *has this task fallen to* me?

He had asked the captain the same question a couple of hours earlier.

Because, Mr. Worf, you have proven to be an expert guide. Commander Cadwallader said your tour of the communications system was nothing short of breathtaking.

Breathtaking *indeed.*

Worf considered his audience. Dr. Greyhorse and Morgen seemed interested. However, Ben Zoma was more intrigued by the shapely technician checking the disposal unit down the corridor.

The Klingon cleared his throat. It immediately had the desired effect, as Ben Zoma's attention was returned to him.

"Sorry," said the captain of the *Lexington.* "By all means, carry on, Lieutenant."

"We have four such facilities on the *Enterprise,*" continued Worf, as if he'd never stopped. "All four are on deck eleven. In addition, there are smaller versions—*personal* holodecks—scattered throughout the ship."

He tried to avoid the Daa'Vit's gaze—but it was not entirely possible. After all, he *was* standing square in the center of the group.

"I have a question," said Greyhorse.

Worf turned to him, relieved—even though he had to look up at the man, and he wasn't used to looking *up* at people. "Yes, Doctor."

"Is it true that the holodecks are used for exercise regimens? Jogging and so forth?"

The Klingon nodded. "They can be. Of course, the areas in the holodecks are finite. One cannot jog very far without reaching the wall. However—"

"However," Greyhorse interrupted, "the electromagnetic fields that make up the ground underfoot flow in a direction opposite that of the runner's progress—acting as a sort of treadmill, and giving the runner the illusion that he or she is moving forward."

The Klingon frowned. "More or less, yes." Obviously, the man was familiar with special field theory. But then, that was not surprising. He was a doctor, and doctors used force fields in any number of procedures.

"But," Greyhorse went on, "what happens if a second participant is placed in the holodeck—one who is stationary? Does the holodeck maintain the illusion of increasing distance between the stationary observer and the jogger? And if so, how is that accomplished?"

Worf grunted. "A good question," he conceded, despite the brusque manner in which it was posed. He approached the computer terminal built into the bulkhead. "And one that is best answered by a demonstration."

Seeking a relatively simple environment for purposes of demonstration, he called up the Ander's Planet program. Instantly, the doors opened on a barren but level stretch of terrain, ruddy with the orange light of twin suns.

"Follow me," he instructed, and entered. The others trailed along behind him, looking around and murmuring appreciatively.

"Ander's Planet," concluded Morgen, "in the Beta Sardonicus system. Correct?"

"Correct," said Worf without actually looking at the Daa'Vit. "I will need a volunteer—to serve as Dr. Greyhorse's jogger."

Ben Zoma raised his hand. "I'm your man. Neither my Daa'Vit friend nor the doctor have stayed in very good shape, I'm afraid. Old age robs some people of their motivation."

"And others of their sense," retorted Greyhorse.

Morgen laughed.

"Where do I begin?" asked Ben Zoma.

"Right where you are standing," said Worf. "But first, let me make an adjustment—so we can all be heard, no matter how far you go."

He looked up at the sky.

"Computer—amplify our voices so that we can be heard throughout the program."

"Done," said a pleasant female voice.

Worf turned to Ben Zoma. "All right," he said. "You may begin jogging. In any direction."

With a last look at Morgen and Greyhorse, Ben Zoma started off. Slowly, at little more than a brisk walk. And as if they were truly on Ander's Planet, he seemed to be getting a little farther away with each step.

Morgen said as much.

"Look back at us," Worf instructed Ben Zoma. "What do you see?"

His voice was like thunder. It seemed to reverberate to the heavens and back, godlike.

The captain of the *Lexington* looked back over his shoulder. "The distance between us is increasing."

"Fascinating," said Greyhorse.

"Actually," Worf told him, "it is quite simple. You see, the illusion created by the holodeck is made up of three components. One is the manipulation of electromagnetic fields you referred to a moment ago. Another is the creation of actual objects, using transporter-analog matter-conversion technology—though these objects must be simple and inanimate. Also, there are devices to simulate sound, smell, and taste, or alternately to dampen those senses. For example, when the illusory source of the stimulus is appearing to recede, like Captain Ben Zoma.

"But the fourth and most important component is visual—a stereoscopic image comprised of polarized interference patterns—"

"Emitted by omnidirectional holo diodes," contributed Greyhorse. "Millions of them, set into the walls."

"Yes," said the Klingon, again doing his best to ignore the interruption. Apparently, the doctor's expertise was not limited to field theory. "The patterns are programmed to intersect at the lens of the participant's eye. So whatever he or she sees appears to be three-dimensional. And as one moves around, the information emitted by the diodes changes, altering the view."

"All well and good, Mr. Worf," said the doctor. "But that doesn't explain how—"

"This is pretty impressive," called Ben Zoma, who now seemed to be twenty meters away. "I'm going to pick up the pace."

And pick up the pace he did. After a moment or two, he was sprinting—going all out. But it did not diminish the veracity of the illusion. From Worf's point of view, Ben Zoma's figure gradually dwindled.

"As I was saying," the Klingon continued, "the diodes dictate what one sees. Not only by creating pure images, but by altering the way one perceives other elements. The electromagnetic fields, for instance. The converted-matter objects. And, of course, *other participants.*"

Greyhorse grunted. "I see. The polarized interference patterns come together to act as a lens—making the moving participant appear farther away than he or she really is."

"Precisely, Doctor."

"And if we were to go running after him," said Morgen, "the treadmill effect would come into play for us too. So we could never close the gap between us unless we put in a lot more effort."

"Or he stopped and allowed us to catch up," suggested Greyhorse.

Worf confirmed it: "That is the general idea, yes."

By then, Ben Zoma must have tired of testing the holodeck's capacity for illusion, because he had turned around and was running back. To his credit, he had yet to break a sweat. His breathing had barely even accelerated.

"I understand," said Morgen, "that holodeck programs may be customized. Even created from scratch."

This time, he was addressing Worf directly. There was no way the Klingon could help but meet his eyes.

Worf could feel the instinctive reaction rising within him. It took an effort to stifle it—to keep it from being obvious.

"That is true," said the Klingon.

Morgen's eyes, bright yellow, narrowed the slightest bit. "Have *you* created programs, Mr. Worf?"

Inwardly writhing under the Daa'Vit's scrutiny, Worf nodded. "I have," he confirmed.

Morgen seemed about to ask something else. But it never came out. For a fraction of a second longer, he regarded the Klingon. Then Ben Zoma had returned from his run.

"Whew," he said, wiping his brow where a faint sheen of sweat had finally emerged. "Not a bad workout." He turned to Greyhorse. "So? Satisfied?"

The doctor looked around, nodded. "Yes," he said. *"Quite* satisfied." He turned to Worf. "Thank you for your patience, Lieutenant."

"It was my pleasure," said the Klingon. He looked up at the sky again. "Save program."

Abruptly, Ander's Planet vanished, leaving in its place the stark yellow-on-black grid of the unadorned holodeck. The visitors took it in, seemingly as intrigued by the naked space as by the illusion. Worf allowed them some time to look around.

Then he indicated the door with a gesture. "This way, gentlemen."

As he exited, he thought he could feel Morgen's eyes boring into his back.

What was the question the Daa'Vit had been about to pose?

In the cavernous engine room of the *Enterprise,* Geordi and Simenon stood side by side, gazing up at the mighty matter-antimatter core. On the catwalk above them, engineering personnel went through their daily diagnostic routine.

The Gnalish grunted. "You know," he said, "I've pictured this a thousand times in my head. Had to, in order to teach advanced propulsion at the Academy." He grunted again. "But seeing it up close . . . for *real*—it's so . . ."

"Impressive?" suggested Geordi.

"Disappointing," finished Simenon. He regarded the *Enterprise* 's chief engineer. "It doesn't look a whole lot different from the engine core on the *Stargazer.* Bigger, sure. But when you come down to it, a warp drive is still a warp drive."

Geordi took a second look at his engine room—the heart and soul of the ship, as far as he was concerned. "I guess," he said, "that depends on your point of view."

Just then, the turbolift doors slid apart and spewed out a familiar figure. Wesley crossed the deck as quickly as he could without actually running and came to a halt in front of the two engineers.

"You're out of breath, Ensign," observed Simenon.

"I'm . . . late . . . sir," explained Wesley. He turned to Geordi. "Sorry. Commander Data . . . asked me to make a course change . . . at the last minute and—"

The engineering chief put a reassuring hand on Wesley's shoulder. "That's all right," he said. "I'm notified about such things, remember? Besides, Professor Simenon just arrived himself."

The Gnalish looked at Wesley askance. "You're not in a hurry to meet *me,* are you?" He leered at Geordi. "Now, *that* would be a refreshing change—a young person actually *hurrying* to bask in my presence."

"Actually," said the chief engineer, "Ensign Crusher here *was* excited about meeting you. Weren't you, Wes?"

Wesley nodded. "I have an interest in warp engineering," he said, having finally caught his breath. "And with all the work you've done in that field . . ."

Simenon dismissed the idea with a wave of his scaly hand. "Nothing at all, compared to those who went before me. My real talent was *hands-on* engineering." He indicated Geordi with a tilt of his head. "What *this* young man does. What I *used* to do," he sighed.

The ensign smiled tentatively. He looked at the Gnalish. "You're kidding, sir—right? I mean, half the advances in the last ten years . . ."

Simenon snorted. "Overrated, I tell you." He turned to Geordi. "Listen to me, Commander La Forge, and listen well. Someday you're going to be faced with a choice like I had—a 'promotion,' they call it. For the good of the service." He poked a finger in Geordi's chest. "Don't do it. Manacle yourself to a monitor. Stow away. *Name of Scaraf*—steal a ship if you have to. You hear me?"

Geordi smiled. "I hear you. But somehow I don't think it's quite as bad as you make it out to be."

Simenon frowned. "No. You wouldn't, I suppose. Not until you've been there." He turned to Wesley. "And *you*—what do you *really* want from me?"

The ensign looked helpless for a moment. Then Simenon put him out of his misery. "You needn't explain," he said. "Even an old cog like myself can figure it out." He seemed to inspect Wesley with fresh interest. "Crusher. As in *Jack* Crusher. Your father, I gather?"

The young man nodded. "Yessir."

"You want to meet someone who served with him—yes? To learn a little more about him?"

Wesley nodded again. "Not that I'm not fascinated by your work," he amended quickly, "because I am. But I guess that's not *all* I'm interested in."

The Gnalish snorted again. "I'd be surprised," he confessed, "if it were any other way." He eyed the ensign. "Then again, I may not be the best person to ask. Certainly, I served with your father—but he was closer with some of the others. Captain Picard, for instance. And Vigo—though he can't help you much, having perished in that nasty business at Maxia Zeta." He paused to think for a moment. "Of course, there's Ben Zoma—he was your father's immediate superior. Cadwallader, I recall, used to trade research monographs with him. And he seemed to joke a lot with Pug Joseph . . ."

A resigned sort of look had come over Wesley's face. Geordi empathized with the young man's disappointment. Apparently, he'd really been looking forward to this opportunity to pump Simenon for some information.

The Gnalish must have noticed the look too, however. Because he stopped dead in his tracks and did an about-face. "On the other hand," he said, "I *do* remember a *few* things about your father. In fact, a particular incident comes to mind . . ."

Wesley smiled.

Without excusing himself, Geordi withdrew and headed for the nearest unoccupied workstation. He had a feeling that Simenon might be a little more open with the ensign if it was just the two of them.

Besides, he had *work* to do.

Five

"Strange," said Picard. "As I recall, Mr. Joseph was always quite punctual."

Standing on the other side of the battle bridge, Asmund shrugged. "Something must have held him up."

The captain frowned. "Apparently." He looked at his former helm officer, and gestured to the captain's chair. "Care for a seat?" he asked.

She shook her head. "No. Thank you." She looked around. "Actually, this reminds me more of the *Stargazer* than anything else."

Picard nodded, leaning back against one of the peripheral station consoles. "I have remarked on that myself, Idun. But then, that makes sense, doesn't it? When we separate the battle section from the primary hull, speed and efficiency are at a premium—just as they would be in a deep-space exploration vessel." He folded his arms across his chest. "There's no room here for the sort of luxury we enjoy on the main bridge."

Asmund went over to the conn position, leaned over the console, and looked at the empty viewscreen. "I like this better," she said. "Without the luxuries." She ran her fingers over the dormant control panels. "Yes. It feels more comfortable."

Picard watched her. It seemed that she belonged here—much as Worf had seemed to belong here, on those occasions when it had been necessary for him to man the battle bridge.

"And when you separate," said Asmund, "the battle section retains the full range of ship's capabilities? Weapons, propulsion, everything?"

"That's correct," said the captain. "The battle section is equipped with both impulse and warp drive engines, a shield generator, two photon torpedo launchers, and a complete spread of phaser banks."

"And the saucer section?"

"No warp drive. No photon torpedoes. But just about everything else." Picard sighed. "I wonder what Vigo would have said about all this."

Asmund looked back over her shoulder. "He would have wondered why you needed a primary hull in the first place."

The captain nodded. "Or, for that matter, living quarters." He smiled at his own joke.

Idun stared back at him, stony-faced as ever.

Picard looked at her. "Idun," he said. "I don't like to see you acting this way."

"Which way is that?" she asked softly, turning back to the console.

"Like an outsider," he said. "Apart from everyone else."

She sighed. "Captain . . . I *am* apart from everyone else."

He looked at her. "Why do you say that?"

Asmund stood up straight, returned his gaze. "You *know* why."

He smiled gently. "Idun, that was twenty years ago. No one holds that against you."

"That's what Captain Mansfield told me when I received Morgen's invitation. But he—you—you're wrong. Both of you."

"Morgen invited you to be part of his honor guard. Would he have done that if he intended to shun you?"

"Captain Mansfield said that too. But it's not just Morgen. Back at the starbase,

Greyhorse was . . . I don't know. *Different.* Not the way he used to be. Even Simenon was . . . distant. Aloof."

"Has it occurred to you that you haven't seen them in almost a dozen years? That they may have changed? That *you* may have changed?"

Asmund frowned. "It . . . occurred to me, yes."

"Nor are Simenon and Greyhorse our two most congenial former comrades. I would not use them as a barometer of how the rest of us feel about you."

She nodded. "Perhaps not." A pause. "With all due respect, Captain, I'd like to talk about something else."

Picard regarded her. He knew that Asmund, like Worf, could not be pushed. She would obey an order, if it came to that. She would go through the motions—but inside she would resist that much harder.

"As you wish," he said finally.

Just then the turbolift doors opened. Turning at the same time, they saw Joseph emerge from the lift.

He grinned sheepishly. "Hi. Sorry I'm late." He looked from one of them to the other. "I didn't miss anything, did I?"

The guided tour completed, Dr. Crusher sat down at her desk. She indicated the three cabins that comprised the ship's medical facilities.

"Well," she said, "that's what the well-dressed sickbay is wearing these days. What do you think?"

Greyhorse nodded. He seated himself across from her. "Very impressive, Beverly. Not as impressive as your holodecks, but impressive nonetheless." Picking up a tricorder lying on Crusher's desk, he put it through its paces. "A far cry from what we had to put up with on the *Stargazer.* We were lucky if both biobeds were functional at the same time."

She regarded him. "Tempted?"

He looked up from the tricorder. "I beg your pardon?"

"You know," she said. "To ship out again?"

Greyhorse chuckled dryly. "Beverly, there is no sickbay in existence that could tempt me to do that. Don't be deceived by the fact that I signed on with a deep-space exploration ship, where patient care was my first priority. I have always preferred things to people—which is why Starfleet Medical suits me so well. I would rather peer over my morning coffee at a computer monitor than have to deal with something that can talk back."

Crusher looked at him askance. "You mean you don't get even a little twinge now and then? A desire to push out the frontiers?"

"I *am* pushing out the frontiers. I would think you'd know that, considering you pushed them out *with* me for a year or so." He shook his head. "Truth be told, I should have been an engineer—like my father and brothers."

Now that she thought about it, Crusher remembered Greyhorse's saying something about a course in engineering at the Academy—just before he switched over to the medical curriculum, to avoid becoming "just another Greyhorse family robot."

"I don't know what kind of engineer you'd have made," she said. "But you're a damned fine doctor."

He put the tricorder down and met her gaze. "It is very kind of you to say so, Beverly." His eyes narrowed mischievously. "And, I might add, very discerning as well. Now, if you don't mind, could we take in some other part of your ship? I have this premonition that if I stay too long, I'm actually going to have to *treat* someone."

Normally, the gymnasium was quiet at this time of day—which was one of the reasons Riker chose this hour to work out. He was a social enough being in every other aspect of his life, but he'd learned something long ago: If you came to the gym to shoot the bull, all you'd end up exercising was your mouth.

Unfortunately, the gym wasn't as deserted as he would have preferred. As the doors to the room parted, he could hear the sound of heavy breathing, amplified by the echoing gym walls.

Entering, he saw that someone was on the horizontal bar—someone slender and female, her hair bound tightly behind her head, moving too quickly to be easily identified. For a moment Riker stood there, silently appreciating the grace with which each intricate maneuver was performed—not to mention the streamlined form that was doing the performing.

The gymnast, on the other hand, seemed not to have noticed his presence. Nor was that difficult to understand, given the concentration she must have had to apply.

This had to be someone new to the ship, he told himself. Nobody he knew was capable of *those* kinds of moves.

As he watched, the woman extended herself full-length, swung around the bar a couple of times, and then leapfrogged over it. The momentum she'd built up carried her almost half the length of the gym before she landed on a mat. A little stumble at the end marred what otherwise would have been a perfect routine.

Riker had already begun clapping before he realized whom he was clapping for. Then the gymnast turned around, a little startled—and he found himself staring at Tricia Cadwallader.

"Criminy!" she said, her hand resting on her breast. "You could have let me know you were there!"

He shrugged. "Sorry. I was too dazzled to think straight."

Cadwallader blushed through her light sprinkling of freckles. "I wasn't *that* good. You should have seen me back at the Academy."

Riker tried not to gape at the way she filled out her cutout tank suit. What was it about Starfleet uniforms that made women look like boys? "If I told you," he began, "that I can't imagine you performing any more beautifully *anywhere* . . . it would probably sound like a line, wouldn't it?"

She smiled as she thought about it. "I'm not sure. Why don't you try it?"

He nodded. "All right—I will." He approached her, taking her hand in his, and gazed into her deep green eyes. "I can't imagine you looking any more beautiful anywhere—not at the Academy or anywhere else." He hung on to her hand. It was soft and warm and just the slightest bit damp with perspiration. "How was that?"

Cadwallader's smile became a smirk. "Pretty good—except you got some of the words wrong. The first time, you said 'performing'—not 'looking.' "

Riker feigned confusion. "Did I? I guess it just came out that way."

She rolled her eyes. "Now, that," she said, taking her hand back with a flourish, "sounds like a line." Crossing the room, she headed for the towel rack.

"Listen," he called after her, "I wouldn't have to resort to such ploys if you'd have dinner with me." His voice echoed from wall to wall.

Cadwallader turned around. "Are you asking?"

Riker straightened. "I'm asking."

She chuckled. "All right, then. But not tonight. I have a prior engagement."

He watched her go to the rack and take down a towel. "Oh?"

"That's right," said Cadwallader, using the towel to dry her hair. "And so do you."

Riker didn't understand. It must have been evident in his expression, because she went on to explain.

"Captain Picard's feast," she said. "Hasn't he told you about it?"

Riker shook his head. "No, I don't believe he has."

Cadwallader shrugged. "It's at 1800 hours. I'm sure he wouldn't assemble all his officers and leave you out." She paused. "Would he?"

"I've been a little busy lately," he said, trying not to sound defensive. "There's probably a message waiting for me in my quarters."

She toweled off some more. "Mmm. Probably. Unless, of course, he means for you to take charge of the bridge then."

Riker couldn't help but smile at the way she was baiting him. "I suppose that *is* a possibility."

Slinging the towel over her shoulders, Cadwallader headed for the doors. As she passed him, she patted him on the shoulder in a comradely sort of way.

"It's all right," she said, tossing the remark at him offhandedly. "If you miss dinner tonight, you'll just be that much hungrier tomorrow."

Riker watched her go, his smile spreading. He had a feeling he'd be hungry tomorrow no matter *what*.

"And that," Simenon said, standing with Wesley in a corner of engineering, "is how your father and I held off a herd of charging thunalia on Beta Varius Four." He smiled in his lizardlike way, remembering. "If either one of us had panicked and made for the caves, the other would have been trampled—or skewered on the beasts' horns. And more than likely, both would have perished. But by standing back to back, we were able to keep them at bay with our phasers—at least until my transporter chief could beam us back up." The Gnalish nodded proudly. "What's more, we collected the data we went down for, as well as the tissue samples from which new thunalia could be cloned. And, in fact, *were* cloned. If you visit the preserves on Morrison's World, you'll see any number of thunalia roaming the plains—even though Beta Varius Four is now devoid of complex lifeforms."

Wesley shook his head. "That's great. That's really great. Mom never mentioned that story."

"Your mother may never have known about it," Simenon pointed out. "We were all restricted as to the frequency and duration of our subspace messages. After all, there were hundreds of us aboard the *Stargazer*—all yearning for families and friends—and the subspace equipment was occasionally needed for other matters, mission communications not the least of them. As I recall, your father always had this . . . well, *interrupted* look on his face after a packet went out. As though, given the chance, he would have said a lot more." He harrumphed. "Besides, I'm sure he had more personal things to discuss than an encounter with a few dozen predators. Bazzid's bones, we were risking our lives on a different planet each day." He straightened, realizing he might have gotten a little carried away. "Or so it seemed," he amended.

The ensign looked at him. He'd meant to say something about how terrific and how patient Simenon had been. But that's not what came out. What he said was: "Tell me how my father died."

That was the story he *really* wanted to hear—even if he hadn't admitted it to himself earlier. That was the hole inside him that truly needed filling.

Simenon sobered a bit at the request. "There's not much to tell," he said. He shrugged. "Besides, you must already know what happened."

"Only from my mom. And she didn't have much to go on. Just the official report from Starfleet, and whatever Captain Picard told her when he came to the house."

The Gnalish regarded him for a moment, his ruby eyes blinking. Wesley could plainly see the reticence in them. Nor was it difficult to understand.

It was one thing to have to dredge up the memory of a comrade's death. But to have to share it with that comrade's son . . .

"I'll tell you what," Simenon said finally. "Why don't I regale you with that story on another occasion? I *do* have that tour to take, you know." He smirked, abruptly himself again. "Though you're welcome to come along. I wouldn't mind hearing some more about all those contributions I've made to warp drive technology."

Wes smiled back, putting his feelings aside for the time being. "You can count on me, sir."

The Gnalish nodded. "Good. That's what I like about you, Ensign Crusher. You've got a healthy respect for your elders."

The door beeped. Worf turned at the sound.

He did not often entertain guests in his quarters. His preference for solitude was well known, not only among his friends but throughout the entire crew. After all, he was surrounded by humans and other races for most of the day; after hours, he needed time to just be himself. To just be *Klingon*.

Beep. He had not imagined it.

"Come," he said. The door opened.

If it had been Riker, or Geordi, or even Wesley, the Klingon would not have been all that surprised. They had been here before on one occasion or another.

It turned out to be none of them. In fact, his visitor was the *last* person on the entire ship that he had expected to come calling on him.

"Do you mind if I come in?" asked Morgen.

The Klingon had instinctively recoiled; he forced himself to relax. "Please," he said, expressing the rest of the invitation with a gesture.

His eyes never leaving Worf's, the Daa'Vit entered. Selecting a chair, he folded himself into it.

Worf sat down on the other end of the room. For a moment they just stared at each other.

"You must be wondering why I've come," said Morgen.

The Klingon nodded. "I confess to a certain curiosity."

Morgen grunted. "You Klingons have a way with words. From your lips, even a polite remark sounds like a challenge."

Worf shrugged. "Perhaps it is the way you *hear* it."

The Daa'Vit smiled. "Perhaps it *is*. But then—"

As before, in the holodeck, he seemed to stop himself. To regroup.

"How easy it is," said Morgen, "to get into a war of words." He leaned forward. "Especially when every part of me is repelled by you. Hateful of you."

Instinctively, Worf prepared himself for an assault—visually searching the Daa'Vit for concealed weapons, working out ways in which his posture made him vulnerable.

But in the next moment Morgen leaned back again. "Yet," he went on, "I am an officer in Starfleet—just as you are. We are sworn to stand side by side—not rend each other like beasts. If there is one thing I have learned in my time among humans, it is that prejudice—*any* prejudice—may be put aside."

Worf knew how hard it was for the Daa'Vit to express such sentiments. It gained Morgen a measure of respect in his eyes—if not affection.

The Klingon cleared his throat. "Permission to speak frankly, sir."

The Daa'Vit nodded. "Speak," he said.

Worf eyed his visitor. "I have not always found the same thing to be true. At least not in *my* case. Once, I was asked to save a Romulan's life through an act of brotherhood. I found I could not." He licked his lips. "And I am not sure the outcome would have been any different if the life in question were that of a Daa'Vit."

Morgen regarded him. "Honesty. I appreciate that." He paused. "Perhaps you misunderstand me, Worf. I am not suggesting we become *finna'calar.* What are the English words for it? Ah, yes—*blood brothers.* No, I am not suggesting that at all. But we need not be enemies either." He tilted his head. "You are a warrior. I am a warrior. Surely, there is a common ground on which we may meet."

Worf gathered himself, fighting his instincts. "I . . . would . . . *like* that," he got out.

The Daa'Vit smiled, though there was no humor in it. "Good. I may even have an idea in that regard."

"An idea?" echoed the Klingon.

"Yes. Do you recall what I asked you in the holodeck—if you had created any programs of your own?"

Worf began to see what Morgen was getting at. "Yes," he said. "I do recall. And I said that I *had* created some programs."

"Fit for a warrior, no doubt," said the Daa'Vit.

"I like to think so," replied the Klingon.

"It would be a novelty for a Daa'Vit and a Klingon to fight side by side—instead of against each other."

Worf couldn't help but smile at the thought. As ludicrous as it was . . . "More than a novelty," he decided. "It would be a challenge—one that could only bring honor to all involved." He omitted the last part of his thought: *if it works.*

Morgen nodded. "I agree. When?"

"Tomorrow at this time. I will be off duty."

"Done. Is there anything I should bring? A *ka'yun,* perhaps?"

"Nothing," said the Klingon. "The holodeck will provide weapons."

Gracefully, the Daa'Vit rose from his chair. "I look forward to it."

Worf rose too. "As do I."

Inclining his head to signify respect—another gesture that must not have been easy for him—Morgen took his leave of his new battle-partner.

And the Klingon, watching him go, decided he had much to think about.

Six

Picard stood, looking down the long table at his assembled officers—both past and present. He was glad to note that Idun Asmund was among them, seated between Ben Zoma and Cadwallader. And Beverly as well—though she had been reticent at first, she had apparently managed to overcome that without any encouragement from her captain. He raised his glass.

"A toast," he said. "To those who have served me in such exceptional fashion."

"Here, here," said Riker.

"*Jian dan'yu,*" agreed Morgen, voicing the Daa'Vit equivalent of Riker's acknowledgment.

Everyone murmured their approval and drank—just as their plates were removed and replaced with their main courses by a cadre of waiters. Under Guinan's supervision, of course.

The captain assessed his dinner as it was placed in front of him. The aroma was exquisite, tantalizing. "Manzakini Loraina," he said appreciatively. He looked up at Guinan. "An excellent choice."

Standing discreetly apart from the table, Guinan inclined her head. "I knew you'd like it, sir," she told him.

"This is an Emmonite dish, is it not?" asked Data.

"That's right," confirmed Troi, who was sitting next to him. "One of the *many* Emmonite dishes of which the captain is so fond." She looked at Picard and smiled.

"Nor am I the only aficionado of Emmonite cuisine," the captain reminded her. "It is served regularly at Starfleet headquarters."

"Is it true," asked Geordi, "that the Emmonites never heard of pasta before they joined the Federation?"

Picard nodded. "*Quite* true. As I understand it, the head of the Emmonite delegation dined at the home of Admiral Manelli—this being a good fifty years ago, of course, when Manelli was in charge of Starfleet. That night, the admiral's wife served linguini with white clam sauce, and the ambassador was so taken with it that he insisted on bringing the recipe back to his home planet."

"I heard he wanted to bring Mrs. Manelli back as well," said Ben Zoma.

Picard nodded. "He did. But that is another story."

Data consumed a forkful of the Manzakini, seemed to ponder the experience. He turned to Guinan. "Very authentic," he said. "My compliments to the chef."

Guinan inclined her head again. "Thank you. The food service units will be glad to hear that."

Joseph looked across the table at the android. "You *eat,* Mr. Data?"

Data nodded. "It is not necessary for my survival. However, I have found that in a situation such as this one, it is often distracting to others if I do *not* eat."

"Then you can actually *taste?*" asked Cadwallader.

"Yes," replied the android. "I have the requisite sensory apparatus. I can even analyze the ingredients. The only thing I cannot do is derive enjoyment from the sensation."

"Too bad," said Morgen. "But then, we all have our limitations."

"Pardon me," said the Gnalish, addressing Worf. "But your Manzakini Loraina looks a little different from mine. It seems to be *writhing.*"

"Worf is on a special diet," Geordi jested.

Picard gave his chief engineer a sidelong glance. "The lieutenant has a preference for *Klingon* preparations," he explained, "though he seldom gets them, except on special occasions. This qualifies as such an occasion."

The Klingon looked at Simenon as if he'd been challenged. "It is called blood pie." He pushed the plate toward the Gnalish. "Would you like to try some?"

Simenon swallowed. "No, my boy, I don't think so. I like my food to lie still on my plate. You know—to at least *pretend* it's not alive."

"Actually," said Greyhorse, "blood pie is quite nutritious." He looked around at the surprised expressions of his companions. "I didn't say I had eaten it. Just that it was good for you. That's not a crime, is it?"

Laughter. And from Simenon, a crackling that was as much for Greyhorse's benefit as anything else.

"I have eaten it," said Asmund rather abruptly.

The laughter died down.

"And?" asked Morgen.

Asmund regarded him evenly. "It is not as good as stewed *gagh.*"

"Gagh?" asked Geordi, mutilating the word in his attempt to pronounce it.

"Serpent worms," explained Riker. "I've had occasion to try them myself. They are quite . . . filling." He couldn't help but grimace a little at the memory.

"You don't appear to have enjoyed them, Commander," observed Cadwallader.

"It is," said Worf, "an acquired taste. Much like *chicken.*"

"Chicken," Simenon remarked, "doesn't try to eat *you* as you are eating *it.*"

Ben Zoma grunted. "Vigo used to love something called *sturrd.* It looked like a mound of sand with pieces of ground glass thrown in for good measure. And he would down it with half a gallon of maple syrup."

"It was *not* maple syrup," argued Joseph. "It only *looked* like maple syrup."

"Vigo," said Data, who had been taking in the conversation with equanimity. "He was one of your colleagues on the *Stargazer*—one who did not survive the battle at Maxia Zeta."

"That's right," said Greyhorse. "Unfortunately. Vigo was our weapons officer."

Morgen nodded. "And not just any weapons officer. He was the finest Starfleet has ever seen."

"I didn't know Starfleet *had* weapons officers," said Troi.

"Only the deep-space explorers," Picard expanded. "It was an experiment, really. A separation of the ship's defense functions from its security functions. But don't let the terminology deceive you—Vigo did a lot more than look after the weapons systems."

"That's right," said Ben Zoma. He turned to Dr. Crusher. "He also used to thrash your husband regularly at *sharash'di.*"

Beverly smiled. "I think I remember Jack telling me about that. Though as I recall, it wasn't just Jack he beat. It was *you* too. And a few others."

Ben Zoma laughed. "Now that you mention it, I guess I *was* one of the victims."

"And I as well," said Cadwallader.

"But Jack was Vigo's regular partner," recalled Joseph. "I think they used to play every chance they got. As if Jack couldn't accept defeat—couldn't accept the fact that there was something he couldn't do."

"Not that there was any shame in losing to Vigo," Cadwallader interjected. "He was uncanny. A master."

"Vigo lost only once," said Ben Zoma. He seemed to concentrate for a moment, then shook his head. "Though for the life of me, I can't remember who beat him."

"It was Gerda," said Asmund. "Gerda beat him."

Suddenly, there was silence in the room.

Asmund turned to Data before he could ask. "My twin sister," she explained. "The one who tried to kill Morgen."

Out of the corner of his eye, Picard saw Geordi exchange glances with Simenon. For once, the Gnalish had nothing clever to say.

Picard cleared his throat. The best thing, he decided, was to take the remark in stride. To act as if it were just part of the conversation, and not a complete bombshell.

But before he could open his mouth, Morgen beat him to it.

"What's that expression you humans have? 'Water under the bridge'?" He shrugged—a rather awkward gesture for a Daa'Vit. "As far as I'm concerned, the incident is forgotten." He looked at Asmund. "And forgiven."

The captain breathed a silent sigh of relief. Everyone at the table seemed to loosen up a little.

Everyone except Asmund. "*I* haven't forgotten it," she told Morgen. She looked around the table. "Sorry. I hadn't intended to put a damper on things." She got up. "Excuse me."

"Idun," Picard called.

She seemed not to hear him as she walked out of the room.

Ten-Forward was open around the clock. It had to be. The ship's officers and crew got off duty at various odd hours, depending on their section and individual responsibilities, and nearly everyone felt the urge to unwind in the lounge at one time or another.

And whenever anyone stopped in for a drink and some conversation, Guinan seemed to be there—standing at her usual place behind the bar, mixing drinks and distributing advice in small doses. Of course, that was only an appearance. Guinan slept like everybody else.

Well, perhaps not *exactly* like everybody else. But she slept. So it was unusual that she should have been around during the pre-"dawn" shift when Pug Joseph swaggered into the lounge.

He didn't look very healthy—or very happy. There were faint dark circles under his eyes and a pallor to his skin that told Guinan he'd been drinking more than synthehol. She smiled and prepared herself.

As she'd expected, he made his way to the farthest table from the bar—a small set-up for two right by an observation port. When he pulled out a chair, the legs clattered against the floor; as he lowered himself into it, he did so awkwardly. Then he slumped over the table, turning his head to the observation port—as if he preferred the company of the streaking stars to that of the crewmen who sat all around him.

Dunhill was the waiter assigned to that area. But before he went over to take Joseph's order, he cast a glance in Guinan's direction.

She shook her head slowly from side to side. Acknowledging her silent instructions, Dunhill waited on another table, ignoring the *Lexington*'s security chief. Somehow, though he wasn't looking in that direction, Joseph managed to notice. He turned, straightened, and glared at Guinan through narrowed bloodshot eyes.

Recognizing her cue, she wove her way among the tables, exchanging greetings with those she passed, until she reached the place where Joseph was sitting. He studied her sullenly.

She returned his hard gaze with a more pleasant one. "May I?" she asked, indicating the empty seat opposite him.

His nostrils flared. He shrugged.

Taking that as an affirmative response, she pulled out the chair and sat down. For a moment there was only silence between them—a silence strung so tight that it seemed liable to snap at any time.

Then she spoke. "You know," she said, "you're getting to be quite a regular around here. Aren't there any other parts of the ship you're interested in?"

He chuckled. The sound had an edge to it.

"Not that it's any of your business." He leaned forward, the pupils of his eyes larger and blacker than they had a right to be. "And if I were Morgen or Ben Zoma or—hell, *any* of the others—you wouldn't be mentioning that now, would you?"

"As a matter of fact," Guinan said, "I *would* be."

Joseph sneered, leaning back again. "In a pig's eye."

"I don't lie, Mr. Joseph."

"Uh-huh." He looked at her. "Where did you come from, anyway?"

"You mean what *race?*" she asked.

"That's right. What race."

"An old one," said Guinan. "Old enough to know alcoholism when we see it."

Joseph grunted. "Give me a break, all right? I can hold my liquor."

"No doubt," she answered, though she had lots of doubts. "The question is why you would *want* to."

His mouth twisted into something mean. "I love people like you," he told her. "Crusaders. They always think they know you—know all about you." His voice became menacing. "You don't know *anything* about me."

Guinan stood her ground. "I just might know more than you think."

"Like what?"

"Like you're bubbling over with hate. For others, to an extent—but most of all, for yourself. Because you don't like what you've become. Because you think it could've been different. And because you believe, in the secret center of yourself, that somehow it's all your fault." Seeing him shrink a little from her, she softened her voice. "And the alcohol is the only way you can keep the hate in check. It's the only way you can smile at people and not snarl at them, because if you let them see what's inside you, you know you're going to lose what precious little you *do* have."

Suddenly, Joseph's face was flushed. It took him a few seconds to respond, and when he did, his voice was little more than a rasp.

"You're crazy," he said.

She shook her head. "No. I just come from a very old race."

Gradually, Joseph's confusion dissipated. But it wasn't replaced by anger. Rather, the man seemed on the verge of tears.

"I'm as good as they are," he said. "I'm as good as *anyone.*"

"Of course you are," Guinan assured him. "But now you've got more than a couple of bad breaks to deal with. The *alcohol* has gotten in your way. Can't you see? It's like a jealous lover. It doesn't just console you—it makes sure you stay just where you are. Beaten. Bitter. If you really want to become the kind of person you *can* be, you're going to have to face this—and take care of it."

He looked at the stars again. His face, a portrait of a tortured soul, was reflected in the transparent barrier that separated them from the void. "I—I can't. I just *can't.*"

"You *can,*" she insisted. She sought his eyes, found them as he turned to her again. "I'll help. You hear me, Chief? I can help you."

For a brief moment it seemed Joseph was going to take the first step back. And then, with a pathos that tore at her inner being, he pounded on the tabletop. "No," he got out between clenched teeth. "No. You don't know what I—what it's like. Just—damn it, just leave me alone. You can *have* your stinking lounge."

Shooting to his feet, he glared at her one last time. Then, with all the dignity he could muster, he threaded his way among the tables and left.

Guinan was so busy watching him, she almost didn't see Dunhill's approach.

"Ma'am?" said the waiter.

"Yes, Dunhill?"

"Is everything all right?"

She sighed. "Not exactly." She looked up at him. "But thanks for asking."

The holodeck doors opened.

Morgen nodded approvingly. "I like it," he said.

Worf grunted. "I thought you would."

Before them loomed the remains of a ruined temple, neither distinctly Klingon nor distinctly anything else, but so barbaric-looking that only a Klingon could have invented them. The sky overhead was the color of molten lava; the ground was a dead gray, pocked with steaming, smoking holes.

God-statues stared at them, either from the heights to which they'd been erected or from out of the rubble into which they'd fallen. There were bird cries, savage and shrill, though the birds themselves—a carrion-eating variety—were not evident. Long snakelike things slithered over the crumbled stones, hissing as they went.

Worf indicated the weapons at their feet. Kneeling, the Daa'Vit picked up the one that was meant for him.

"A *ka'yun,*" said the Klingon.

Morgen inspected it appreciatively, testing its balance. He looked at Worf. "Very authentic."

The Klingon shrugged. "There were descriptions of it in the library computer. I merely drew on the data." He bent and picked up his own weapon, a long staff with a vicious hook at one end and a metal ball at the other.

"A *laks'mar,*" noted Morgen. He stiffened a little at the sight. "I am familiar with it. *We* are familiar with it."

Worf decided it would be wise to change the subject. "This program has two levels of difficulty. I have chosen the second," he said.

The Daa'Vit nodded his approval. "Let's begin."

O'Brien seldom took advantage of the holodecks. It wasn't that he had an aversion to them—just that he liked other sorts of recreation, chief among them being a good, steamy poker game.

Of course, it had been different when he'd first come on board. The holodecks had been a novelty then, and he'd vented his imagination in them. Once he'd constructed a pub in old Dublin, where he'd tossed a few down with his favorite author—a fellow by the name of James Joyce. Another time he'd had dinner with the Wee Folk under the Hill, and let their pipes charm him to sleep.

But after a while the novelty had worn off. The final straw had come when he found himself constructing *poker games* in the *holodecks*—and enjoying them less than the live games he played with the ship's officers.

When he visited Deck Eleven these days, it was strictly to visit a friend in his or her quarters, or to work up a sweat in the gym. And when he walked past the holodeck panels, it was usually without a second thought.

Except this time. On his way to Crewman Resnick's apartment, he'd seen Worf and Captain Morgen entering holodeck one. And he knew from speaking to Commander La Forge that Klingons and Daa'Vit didn't get along. Hell—Worf had been afraid it might come to blows. Or worse.

But if they didn't see eye to eye . . . what in blazes were they doing in the holodeck together?

In the end, it was more than curiosity that drove O'Brien to find an answer to that question. It was genuine concern for the Daa'Vit's welfare—not to mention Worf's. And if he didn't exactly feel right checking the computer panel to see what program they were using, he at least felt *justified*.

The panel readout indicated "Calisthenics—Lt. Worf. Level Two." When he saw that, O'Brien thought he understood what was going on.

Klingons were warriors. Daa'Vit were warriors. Yup—it all made sense.

Worf was trying to bridge the cultural gap between them. If they were human, they'd be playing billiards. Or Ping-Pong. But since they were who they were, they were mixing it up with alien monsters instead.

And Level Two—well, that didn't sound so good, but it didn't sound so bad either. After all, Commander Riker had once tried Level One—or so he'd said one night around the poker table.

O'Brien went to see his friend Resnick with a clear conscience. He'd done his part to ensure peace and tranquility on the *Enterprise*.

Responding to the Daa'Vit's request that they begin the exercise, Worf strode ahead into the most congested part of the ruins. Already, he could feel his instincts coming to the fore—his senses becoming sharper, the fire in his blood awakening.

Morgen followed, but at a distance of a couple of meters. A good idea, the Klingon remarked to himself. When things heated up, he didn't want them to become entangled with one another.

The birds shrieked, eager for freshly killed meat. The snake-things crawled. High above them, the heavens rumbled as if with an impending storm.

Movement. Worf saw it only out of the corner of his eye. His first impulse was to attack it, to draw it out.

But it was on the Daa'Vit's flank, not his. If they were to work together, they would have to trust each other. Trust each other's perceptions and abilities.

A moment later, Worf was glad that he had practiced restraint. For if he had gone after the first hidden assailant, he would have been too distracted to notice the second—a powerful, furred being that leapt down at him from one of the god-monuments.

He brought up his weapon just in time to absorb the force of the furred one's downstroke. Recovering, he launched an attack of his own, burying his hook deep in his enemy's shoulder. When the furred one tore it free, Worf used the other end to smash him in the face.

As the furred one sank to his knees, unconscious, Worf allowed himself a glimpse of Morgen's combat. The Daa'Vit was exchanging blows with a horned and hairless white giant modeled after the Kup'lceti of Alpha Malachon Four. No problem there, the Klingon decided.

And whirled in time to face another attacker, who had sprung from behind a ruined altar. This one was broader than the first, squatter, with a black-and-yellow hide and eyes like chips of obsidian. Shuffling to one side, Worf avoided his initial charge. Then, as they faced off again, he caught the being's mace on his staff.

For a moment they grappled, Worf snarling with effort as he tried to gain the upper hand. He could smell his opponent's fetid breath, hear the screams of the carrion birds drawn by the scent of blood. His pulse pounded in his ears, feeding the fires inside him.

Finally, with a mighty surge, the Klingon thrust his enemy back—in the process creating enough space between them to swing his weapon. The metal ball caught the being on the side of the head, spinning him around, sending him sprawling into one of the steaming hellpits. Roaring with pain, he struggled desperately to climb out of the hole. In the end, he failed.

Worf felt a cry of victory burst from his throat, piercing a roll of thunder overhead.

Coiling, wary of another enemy, he caught another glimpse of the Daa'Vit. Morgen was standing over not one opponent, but two—his angular face split by a huge grin, his sword dripping blood.

When he sensed Worf's scrutiny, he whirled and returned it. For a moment they stood there, each fighting the instinct to cut the other to pieces. Straining against themselves, measuring passion against intellect.

Then the battle fury subsided. The moment passed.

"Excellent," said the Daa'Vit. His yellow eyes glinted. "Better, in fact, than I had hoped."

Worf acknowledged the compliment with a nod.

Abruptly, the scene changed. The bodies of their enemies were gone—as if they had never been there at all.

Morgen looked at him. "Something else, Worf?"

The Klingon shook his head. This was not part of his program. It should have ended when they struck down the last attacker.

"Something is wrong," he said out loud.

He didn't have a chance to elaborate. The furred one was descending on him as before, whole again. As Worf leapt backward, a skull-faced warrior—a relic of past programs—advanced from another direction, making his way around a steaming hellhole. And a third opponent, a leathery-skinned, club-wielding Bandalik, was crawling toward him over a slab of stone.

It was happening too quickly. This wasn't Level Two. It was something more difficult.

But he hadn't *programmed* anything more difficult.

"What's going on?" asked Morgen, beset by a second group of antagonists.

"I don't know," said the Klingon. But he wasn't about to risk the Daa'Vit's well-being by subjecting him to a program too fierce for him. And possibly, Worf admitted, too fierce for him as well.

"Stop program," he called to the computer.

It had no effect. His enemies were still converging on him.

"Stop program," he called again.

Nothing.

Off to the side, Morgen cursed. Worf heard the clang of colliding blades, followed by a grunt and another clang.

The Klingon's lips pulled back in fury. This was no joke. Something had happened to the holodeck. It wasn't responding.

Even as he confronted that fact, Skullface swung his ax, meaning to separate Worf's head from his shoulders. The Klingon ducked, slammed his opponent with the ball end of his weapon—then whirled to strike at the oncoming Bandalik.

The blow landed; the Bandalik staggered back. However, the furred one was on top of him now, too close to defend against.

Worf's staff went up, though not in time to keep the furred one's blade from slashing his uniform shirt. There was a hot stab of pain—and the Klingon could feel something warm and wet trickling down the hard muscles of his solar plexus. It smelled like blood—*his* blood.

Hooking the furred one as he had before, he sent him sprawling. But before he could turn and face another adversary, something hit him in the back—hit him *hard*. Gritting his teeth against the pain, the Klingon did his best to keep his feet. But a second blow sent him spinning wildly.

The ground rushed up to meet him, and he found himself at the brink of a steaming hole. A moment later, Skullface was on top of him, bringing his ax up for the killing blow—and Worf had lost his staff when he fell. Still dazed, he forced himself to reach up and grab his enemy's arms.

It worked—but only for a moment. Then his enemy's superior leverage began to take its toll.

As he forced the ax blade down toward the Klingon's throat, Skullface grinned. Behind him, the furred one and the Bandalik looked on eagerly, waiting to finish Worf off if Skullface failed. . . .

Unfortunately for O'Brien, Resnick wasn't home. He called her on the ship's intercom.

"You *did* invite me over?" he asked. "I mean, I wasn't dreaming it, was I?"

Resnick cursed softly. "Sorry, Miles." She apologized profusely for having drawn an unexpected shift in security—and forgetting they were supposed to get together.

"I understand," he told her. "I guess I'll just have to find another way to pass the time."

Making his way back down the corridor, O'Brien passed by the holodecks again—and slowed down. He had nothing else to do, he thought; a visit with old James might hit the spot. As he stopped to see if holodeck one was still occupied, he noticed that Worf's program had escalated to Level Three.

"Hmm," he said out loud. Straightening, he touched his communicator insignia. "O'Brien to Commander Riker."

The response was barely a second in coming. "Riker here."

"O'Brien, sir. I know this is probably none of my business, but I saw Lieutenant Worf and Captain Morgen enter the holodeck together a few minutes ago—to participate in the lieutenant's 'calisthenics' program. And just now

I couldn't help but notice that the program had been bumped up to Level Three—"

"Level Three?" Riker exploded. "Turn it off, O'Brien! Turn the damned thing off!"

The transporter chief took a moment to recover from the force of Riker's reaction—but *only* a moment. Then he whirled and pressed the abort program area on the holodeck computer panel.

Nothing happened. According to the monitor, the program was still in progress.

"It's not working, Commander," said O'Brien. He tried to terminate the program a second time, but with no more success. "The program won't abort."

"Damn it," said the first officer. "Riker to bridge—"

That was all O'Brien heard for a few moments. Then the lights went off in the vicinity of the holodecks, and with them the faint hum of the ventilation system.

"O'Brien?" It was Riker again.

"Aye, sir?"

"We've cut power to Deck Eleven. Can you hear anything from inside the holodeck?"

O'Brien listened. His stomach tightened.

"Nothing, Commander."

A muffled curse. "Try to pry the doors open, Chief. There'll be a security team there in a minute or two."

O'Brien tugged at one of the doors, knowing full well that he wouldn't be able to budge it by himself—even with the power shut down. Of course, that didn't stop him from giving it his best shot.

By the time the security team showed up, he'd actually created an opening the size of a hand's-breadth. A familiar face loomed before him as other hands gripped the interlocking segments of the doors.

"Fern," he said, acknowledging her.

Resnick smiled grimly. "Any idea what happened?"

He shook his head. "Just that Lieutenant Worf's in there, and Captain Morgen as well. And they're in some kind of trouble."

He and Resnick strained along with the rest of the security team, but they weren't making much progress. It seemed that the doors had moved about all they were going to.

"Everybody step back," said Burke, the team leader. Waiting a moment while O'Brien and the others complied, he plucked his phaser off his belt, selected a setting, and trained it on one of the doors. Then he activated the thing.

The blue beam knifed out, vaporizing the duranium door in a matter of seconds. As the air filled with steam and the smell of something burning, Burke made his way through the twisted metal remains.

Resnick was right on his tail. And O'Brien was right on hers.

With the power off, the holodeck had reverted to a yellow-on-black grid. There were two figures inside. Both bloody, but both still standing—if barely.

Swaying, panting heavily, Worf waved away Resnick's offer of help. "See to Captain Morgen," he ordered, his voice little more than a rasp.

A couple of security officers approached the Daa'Vit. "No," said Morgen. "Let me be." And promptly fell to his knees.

Burke pressed his insignia. "Sickbay—we need a trauma team in holodeck one. We've got two casualties—one Klingon and one Daa'Vit. *Hurry.*"

Seven

"But I feel fine," Worf protested.

"I'm happy for you," responded Crusher, using her tricorder to check the dermaplast patch on the Klingon's back. It was adhering perfectly—a good job, if she said so herself.

"There's really no need for this, Doctor."

She glanced over her shoulder at Morgen. "Another sector heard from."

The Daa'Vit shook his head disapprovingly. "What is it about medical officers?"

"They are excessively cautious," Worf observed.

"To be sure," agreed the Daa'Vit. "No offense, Doctor, but sickbay is the one thing I will *not* miss about Starfleet."

Crusher chuckled. "Listen to you two. One would think you'd been here for days. It's been only a couple of hours." Finished with her examination of Worf's dressings, she moved over to Morgen's biobed.

"A couple of hours too many," complained the Daa'Vit as the doctor positioned her tricorder near his thigh. The gouge there had been deep, but it was healing nicely, with no sign of infection. "You can see we need no further attention."

"I can see," she countered, "that you know nothing about medicine. Or else you choose to ignore what you do know." She moved the tricorder up to Morgen's side, where he'd been badly slashed. "Just because you *feel* fine doesn't mean you *are* fine. Those healing agents and painkillers and antibiotics take their toll. The healing agents in particular—they soak up nutrients like a sponge, leaving just enough for the body's other functions. A little too much physical activity and you'll be flat on your backs, wishing you had enough strength to scratch your nose."

Worf made a derisive sound. "You underestimate the Klingon constitution, Doctor." He considered Morgen. "And perhaps the Daa'Vit constitution as well."

Morgen frowned as Crusher inspected his chest wounds. "Your colleague speaks the truth. Daa'Vit—and Klingons—are tougher than you may realize."

Satisfied with Morgen's progress, the doctor switched off her instrument and closed it up. "I underestimate nothing," she said. "Worf should know that, considering I've been treating him for years now. True, I've never had to medicate him for wounds like *these*—but I think I know a *few* things about Klingon biology." She replaced the tricorder in the pocket of her lab coat. "Now, if you were to say I've never treated a *Daa'Vit,* you'd be quite right. But I've studied up quite a bit on the subject."

"Reading and doing are two different things," Morgen reminded her.

"I agree," Crusher assured him. "That's why I went to the trouble of speaking recently with a Dr. Carter Greyhorse. You know him? Apparently, he's had some experience treating a Daa'Vit. Naturally, neither of us anticipated any problems, considering the nature of our mission to Daa'V. But he humored me all the same."

Morgen's eyes narrowed. He turned to Worf. "It's a conspiracy."

The Klingon grunted in assent. "No doubt."

Crusher noted with interest the relationship that had developed between the two. Of course, she wouldn't dare point it out to them. That would be the quickest way to destroy it.

Hell of a way to get closer, she thought. If the experience had lasted much longer, it would have killed them.

"In any case," she said, "I've got to go. The captain has called a meeting—you can imagine what it's about."

Worf slid off his biobed. "I should be there."

"No way," the doctor told him. "You'll stay right here. That's an order."

"But I am chief of security. And this is a security matter."

"I don't care if you're the"—she glanced at Morgen—"the hereditary ruler of Daa'V. No one leaves this sickbay until I tell them to. Got it?"

Neither Worf nor Morgen answered—at least, not audibly. But when Crusher left sickbay, she left alone.

Picard was the first to enter the lounge. It was quiet—almost unnaturally so. Outside, seen through the observation ports, the stars bore silent witness to his carefully controlled anxiety. He crossed the room.

Taking his place at the head of the conference table, gazing at its polished surface, the captain had an overwhelming sense of déjà vu. He could almost feel the years peeling away, the dimensions of the room shrinking . . . faces swimming up at him. Those of Ben Zoma, Simenon, Greyhorse, Idun, Pug and—of course—Jack Crusher . . .

"Is Ensign Morgen all right, Doctor?"

"Fine," said Greyhorse. "He was just a little shaken up."

"And Lieutenant Asmund?" asked Jack.

Picard could feel Idun tense at the mention of her sister—but she gave no other sign of her concern.

"Likewise, Captain. She'll live to stand trial for the attempt on Morgen's life."

"Good. I am glad to hear that she will survive."

He had to be careful what he said. After all, it was Gerda who'd committed the crime—not her twin.

"I've got two men assigned to her night and day," reported Joseph. He glanced at Greyhorse. "The doctor's not pleased about it, but I told him those were your orders."

The captain nodded. "Indeed."

"What about the Klingons?" asked Simenon.

"The Victorious *and the* Berlin *are only hours away," responded Ben Zoma. "They'll be escorting the good ship* Tagh'rat *to the borders of the Empire, where it will become an imperial matter. But the word from the emperor is that the splinter group will be dealt with harshly. After all, he wants this treaty as much as we do."*

"What a damned sorry mess," said Greyhorse.

"Could have been worse," said Jack. "She could have succeeded."

"True," said the Gnalish.

Suddenly, Joseph stood. "Sir," he said, addressing Picard, "I want to take full responsibility for what happened. If there are any repercussions—"

"We will all assume responsibility," interrupted the captain.

The security chief seemed mute for a moment. He hung his head, and when he spoke again, it was in a softer tone. "It's just that I don't know how this could have happened . . ."

". . . could have happened," said a voice outside the lounge.

Drawing himself up to his full height, Picard saw Riker entering alongside Data. The android's brow was wrinkled ever so slightly.

"It *does* seem highly unlikely," remarked Data.

"What does?" asked the captain.

Both Riker and the android regarded him.

"That what happened in the holodeck could have been an accident," said the first officer.

Data nodded as he pulled out the middle seat on the side of the table facing the stars. "That is correct, sir. It is possible that Lieutenant Worf inadvertently misprogrammed the holodeck, calling for a Level Three scenario to automatically follow Level Two. However, he could *not* have inadvertently instructed it to ignore his command to abort." Seating himself, he went on without pause. "The holodeck computer's mortality failsafe is designed to resist such instructions, to make them difficult for the user to implement—in order to avoid just this sort of occurrence."

Riker sat too—at his usual place, on Picard's left. "Of course, there could have been a malfunction—but you know how rare those are. We check the holodecks on a regular basis. Certainly, we would have caught on to a flaw that profound."

Halfway through Data's observation, Dr. Crusher, Counselor Troi, and Commander La Forge filed into the room. Geordi had something in his hand.

"And even a simple malfunction," said the android, "would not account for Chief O'Brien's inability to end the program from without. That would have depended on a different circuit entirely."

"In other words," expanded the first officer, *"both* circuits would have had to go haywire at once. A pretty big coincidence."

"Yes," confirmed Data. "The only practical explanation is that—"

"Someone tampered with the holodeck circuitry," said La Forge, tossing his burden on the center of the table. It slid a foot or so on the smooth surface before finally coming to a halt. "And that's exactly what happened." As he, Troi, and Crusher took their seats, he pointed to the bundle of wires and small black boxes. "There's the evidence. We found it behind one of the lead panels."

Picard picked up the bundle and turned it over in his hands. "Looks fairly complicated," he concluded.

"It *is*," said his chief engineer. "Ingenious, in fact. And made from parts one might find around the ship."

"Naturally," said Riker. "A device like that would have been detected in the transport process."

"It appears," said Troi, "that someone among us is out to get Morgen. Or Worf. Or both of them."

The captain felt a muscle in his jaw beginning to twitch. He did his best to control it.

Riker frowned. "Someone was after Morgen once before. On the *Stargazer.*"

Beverly turned to the captain. "But that was twenty years ago. And she was apprehended before she could carry out her mission—wasn't she?"

Picard nodded. "Gerda Asmund was found guilty of attempted murder and remanded to the rehabilitation colony on Anjelica Seven. She spent eleven years of her life there before the authorities judged her fit to rejoin society." He sighed. "Shortly thereafter, she died on a freighter en route to Alpha Palemon. The ship was passing through a meteor swarm when its shields suddenly failed. Gerda was working in the hold; it was punctured, and she was lost with seven others."

"Her body?" asked Riker.

"Never found," said the captain.

"Then she could still be alive," Geordi concluded.

"Not likely," said Picard. "There were no containment suits missing. No shuttle craft unaccounted for."

"Still . . ." Geordi insisted.

Crusher leaned forward. "Captain . . . how much did Idun and Gerda resemble each other?"

It was a chilling thought.

"They were identical," said Picard. "I could barely tell them apart, except for the fact that Idun sat at the helm and Gerda at navigation." He shook his head. "But what you're suggesting seems a bit farfetched." He regarded Troi. "Counselor . . . have you sensed anything to make you suspect Idun is not who she seems?"

Troi shook her head. "No, not really. Just the sort of ambiguities one might expect from a human raised by Klingons." She paused. "Though I must admit, I have had little experience with Idun's sort of mind. There is a discipline there that keeps me from reading her emotions very well."

"What about the transporter?" asked Geordi. "Wouldn't it have a record of her bio-profile? One we could match with her records?"

"Inconclusive," ruled Crusher. "If Gerda and Idun have the same bio-profile—which has been known to happen with identical twins—then we would have no way of knowing if Gerda beamed aboard in her sister's place."

"They *did* have the same profile," Picard noted reluctantly. "I remember that."

Riker regarded him. "And Idun was at Starbase 81 long enough for Gerda to make the switch." He looked thoughtful, then frowned. "But I have to agree with the captain. We're looking a bit far afield—especially when Idun *herself* has a motive."

"You mean revenge?" asked Troi. "For what happened to her sister?"

"Make that *two* motives," the first officer amended. "I was thinking more along the lines of her completing Gerda's mission."

"Completing . . ." Picard began. "To what purpose, Number One?"

"The same purpose as before," said Riker. "To create a rift between the Federation and the Daa'Vit. To eliminate any need for the Klingons to share a conference table with their old enemies. And with Morgen inheriting the crown of Daa'V, they could hardly have picked a better time to kill him. Not only would the Daa'Vit break ties with us, they'd be thrown into a state of internal disarray."

The captain shook his head. "Idun Asmund has served Starfleet with distinction for more than two decades. She has never given anyone any reason to doubt her loyalties." He straightened in his chair. "When Gerda made her attempt on Morgen's life, I decided that it would be the gravest of injustices to punish Idun for her sister's crime—and I have not changed my mind in that regard. If there is evidence to incriminate her, fine. But let us not judge her on her choice of sibling alone."

"All right, then," said Riker. "What about the others?"

Those at the table exchanged glances. It was not an easy thing to hold up one's fellow officers as murder suspects—particularly when the *Stargazer* survivors had become so well liked. And Picard sympathized; he was no more eager to hear such accusations than his officers were to voice them.

But someone had committed an act of violence on his ship. He could not allow that to happen again.

"Commander Riker asked a question," said the captain. "I want answers." He turned to Troi first. "Counselor?"

The Betazoid sighed. "Mr. Joseph is not a happy man, sir. He is bitter—disillusioned."

"Over his failure to advance his career?" said Picard.

Troi nodded. "Apparently."

"Do you think," asked the captain, "that his unhappiness would manifest itself this way?"

"It is difficult to say. I do not think Joseph resents Morgen in particular. If he has focused his resentment on anyone, it is Commander Cadwallader."

"Then again," said Riker, "Morgen was below him once in the chain of command—just as Cadwallader was."

"And when one is irrational," offered Crusher, "one may lash out at *anyone.*"

Troi shook her head. "Joseph is *not* irrational—at least, not as far as I can tell. But he *is* angry. At times, extremely angry."

Riker indicated the mess of wires and black boxes. "Does he have the knowhow to make something like this?"

"He is not an engineer," said Picard, "if that's what you mean. But security work does involve a knowledge of ship's systems."

"Greyhorse has some technical knowledge," the doctor offered. She shrugged. Obviously, she did not believe Greyhorse was a viable murder suspect. The captain couldn't exactly blame her.

"What about Simenon?" asked Data, who had remained silent almost from the time he sat down. *No surprise,* thought Picard. Matters of motivation were not exactly the android's specialty.

"He would certainly have the expertise," said Troi. "But does he have a motive?"

"The Gnalish and the Daa'Vit have never been best of friends," Beverly remarked. "I remember Jack expressing some misgivings about Morgen and Simenon serving together."

The captain looked at her. It was the first time she'd brought up Jack's name since the *Stargazer* contingent came aboard.

"True," he said. "On the other hand, there was never any violence between the two peoples—thanks to Federation intervention. Nor did those misgivings ever become material. In fact, Morgen and Simenon always had a healthy respect for each other."

"What about the Daa'Vit angle?" suggested Riker. He looked at Picard. "We know that Morgen has opposition at home. Would his political enemies go so far as to hire an assassin?"

The captain mulled it over. "I suppose it is possible," he conceded. "And the Daa'Vit are sufficiently spread out among the Federation for any one of our guests to have had contact with them."

Riker looked to the intercom grid in the ceiling. "Computer—has anyone in Captain Morgen's escort been to Daa'V?"

The computer responded instantly in a pleasant female voice. "Captain Ben Zoma, Commander Cadwallader, and Chief Joseph visited Daa'V one year ago on the *Lexington.*"

"Their purpose?" asked the first officer.

"To deliver medicines requested by the Daa'Vit government."

Picard nodded. Pug on Daa'V, he thought. How could he help but read into the situation? Bitterness often made a man vulnerable. And if the proper incentive was offered into the bargain . . .

No. The captain would not prejudge Joseph any more than he would Idun. Pug had served him well on the *Stargazer;* he deserved better.

And yet, he could not allow his feelings to get in the way of his duty. Picard cleared his throat.

"I must say," he told the others, "it is extremely difficult for me to believe that one of my former officers is capable of murder. I would have trusted any one of them with my life—exactly as I would trust one of *you.*" He considered the device on the table. "But one cannot ignore the facts. We have a dangerous individual aboard—and we must find that individual. *Quickly*—before he or she can strike again."

"I'll organize the security effort," said Riker. "We'll have each of them watched around the clock."

"Good, Number One. But be discreet. Security personnel are not to discuss the matter in public—not even among themselves." He turned to Geordi and then to Crusher. "That goes for engineering and medical personnel as well. I do not wish to put the assassin on guard."

Assassin. The word seemed so out of place here on the *Enterprise.*

"Counselor Troi," he said, addressing the empath in her turn. "Keep an eye on our visitors. Let me know if you sense any duplicity in them."

Troi nodded. "Aye, sir."

"In some cases, Counselor, you may have to seek them out. We may not have the time to carry on a passive investigation."

She nodded again.

Picard turned to the ship's doctor. "I trust Worf will be up and about soon?"

"I want to keep him—and Morgen as well—for observation overnight. Then they're all yours. But I wouldn't ask Worf to take on anything physically strenuous—not for a couple of days anyway."

That was fine with the captain. What he needed now was the Klingon's *mind*—his training in protecting the ship and its people from calculated harm.

"That will have to do," he said. "When you release him, send him directly to me."

Crusher promised that she would do that.

Morgen shook his head, stalking from one end of the captain's ready room to the other. Dr. Crusher had done a good job; Picard would never have noticed his friend's limp if he hadn't been looking for it. "It is out of the question."

Sitting behind his desk, the human frowned. "It is an eminently reasonable request."

"Not from my point of view."

"I am not asking you to lock yourself in your quarters—only to make yourself scarce."

The Daa'Vit eyed him. "And I categorically refuse."

"Damn it, Morgen. Someone has made an attempt on your *life.*"

"So you'd have me hide from them? Be fearful of them?" He sneered scornfully. "That is not the Daa'Vit way, my friend. I would have thought you'd know that by now."

Picard took a deep breath, let it out. He hadn't expected this to be easy, had he?

"Of course," said Morgen, "you could order me confined to quarters. That is certainly your prerogative." He stopped to face Picard, as if challenging him. "But then, you would be jailing the next ruler of the Daa'Vit worlds."

The captain decided against picking up the gauntlet. He wanted matters to proceed calmly—in an orderly fashion. And arousing Morgen's ire was the wrong way to do that.

Fortunately, a more subtle tack occurred to him.

"I would never think of it," he told the Daa'Vit. "Not even if you were still an ensign, and your crown was twenty years away."

That gave Morgen pause. "That's right," he said finally. "You didn't confine me to quarters then either." He tilted his head. "But then, the killer had already been caught—hadn't she?"

"We didn't know there weren't *other* killers aboard." Picard got up from behind his desk and came forward to sit on the edge of it. "Not for certain, we didn't. What's more, there was the matter of a Klingon escape ship to be reckoned with." He shrugged. "But at the time I was concerned with more than your well-being. I was concerned with your *education.* It occurred to me that if you were to become a Starfleet officer, you had to be treated like one."

Morgen nodded. "I'm grateful."

"You are quite welcome," said the captain. "And my trust was rewarded. Starfleet got itself a fine officer." He looked at the Daa'Vit. "A fine captain." A pause. "That is, before you became a dignitary."

"I beg your pardon?" said the Daa'Vit, his eyes narrowing.

Picard smiled. "Come, Morgen. Admit it. You are, for all intents and purposes, already the ruler of your people. You have left behind your status as a Starfleet officer—in your own mind, if not officially." He held out his hands. "You don't believe me? Recall, if you will, the threat you made a moment ago."

The Daa'Vit regarded him for what seemed a long time. "No," he said finally, his lip curling. "I was speaking in anger. Gods, the very thought of being a *dignitary*—it makes my skin crawl." He looked away from Picard and grimaced.

"Why?" asked the human. "Because dignitaries are notorious for ignoring what we captains know are best for them? Because they insist on endangering their lives for no good reason?" He nodded. "Yes, you are right. Those are things of which you could *never* be accused."

Morgen's head came up and his eyes locked again with Picard's. At that moment he looked like a prototypical son of Daa'V—one whose edges had never been softened by the Federation. Then, slowly, a begrudging smile spread across his face. "You are a master, sir. I salute you." He shook his head appreciatively. "In all that time I spent captaining the *Excalibur,* I never developed that knack you have for making a point."

"Just as well," said Picard. "Then you would have been *completely* insufferable—not unlike Ben Zoma." A beat. "You'll cooperate?"

The Daa'Vit's nostrils flared. "Up to a point," he agreed. "I'll make myself . . . how did you put it? *Scarce?*"

"That is indeed how I put it."

"But if trouble presents itself, don't expect me to run. I am still quite capable of handling myself, you know."

The captain had no doubt of it. "Fair enough," he said.

Eight

Troi waited in the corridor outside the doors of Commander Asmund's apartment. Inside, she knew, her presence was being announced by a beeping sound. Nor could Asmund fail to hear the signal; it was audible in every part of her quarters, and the computer had confirmed that she was home.

Of course, the commander could ignore the beeping—indicating that she didn't want to be disturbed. Or she could simply say so via ship's intercom.

The empath was beginning to suspect the first possibility when the intercom suddenly barked out a single word: "Enter."

She gathered herself as the doors opened, revealing one of the apartments set aside for guests. The decor was moderate and subdued—designed more to avoid offense than to delight, since the ship's visitors had such a broad spectrum of tastes and preferences.

In special instances, of course, the apartments were completely redecorated— usually to impress a foreign leader or ambassador with the Federation's respect for other ways of life. The captain's guests, however, had no need of such special treatment. They were all used to Starfleet facilities of one sort or another.

Troi came in and looked around. No sign of Asmund.

"Commander Asmund?" she called politely.

"Be right with you," came the answer from somewhere deeper in the apartment.

The empath nodded, mostly to herself, and took a seat on a small blue couch. Above it was a painting—a replica of Glosterer's famous study: "The Molecular Structure of Certain Amino Acids." She took a moment to appreciate the subtleties of tone and color.

And tried not to reflect on her ambivalence about her mission here.

On one hand, she was doing exactly what she'd aimed for when she set out to be a ship's counselor. She was trying to help an individual who was having problems adjusting to her environment.

And Asmund was certainly having problems. One had only to witness her departure from dinner the night before to know that.

But she was also attempting to pin down a danger to the ship and its occupants. And while this was a part of her job as well, she was more used to gauging murderous intent in outsiders than in fellow officers.

Coming here under the guise of counselor was, in some ways, a subterfuge. A deception, if only by half.

That didn't sit well with her. Her nature was to be sincere, honest. What's more, her effectiveness as a counselor was based squarely on those qualities. If she were to obtain someone's trust, she had to first be confident she was trust*worthy*.

Yet the threat had been so immediate, the evidence so solid that there was a murderer on board, that Troi hadn't protested when the captain asked her to probe their guests' emotions. Nor would she back down now.

"Counselor Troi," said Asmund, bringing her out of her reverie. The woman was standing in the doorway that led back to her sleeping quarters. She was wearing a tight-fitting black jump suit of Starfleet issue; her hair, still wet from the shower, was combed straight back.

The empath started to her feet, and Asmund motioned for her not to bother.

"Can I get you anything?" asked the blond woman.

Troi shook her head. "No. Thank you."

Asmund went over to the apartment's food processing unit. "I hope you don't mind," she said, "if I have something myself."

"Not at all," said the ship's counselor.

With practiced skill Asmund punched in a series of instructions. A moment later a glass of thick dark liquid appeared on a tray, along with a couple of cloth napkins.

At first Troi thought it was a Klingon drink. Then, as Asmund came over and sat on a graceful highbacked chair, the empath got a whiff of it.

"Prune juice," she said.

The blond woman nodded, tucking back a lock of wet hair that had fallen onto her forehead. "You should try it sometime." Taking a sip, she set down the tray and then the glass on the polished black table that separated them.

"Perhaps I will," the counselor agreed, smiling pleasantly.

As they regarded each other, Troi got the same impressions she'd gotten before. Conflicts, uncertainties. The strain of maintaining a façade of humanity when her natural tendency was to be Klingon.

A mirror-image of Worf, she noted, and not for the first time. One was trying to reconcile his Klingon heritage with his human upbringing; the other was trying to balance her Klingon upbringing with her human heritage.

There was a strange symmetry there. An almost poetic juxtaposition of opposites—what the Betazoid musicians of two centuries earlier would have called *aieannen baiannen.* Literally, *wind and water.*

But Troi had not come here to make esthetic observations. Probing more deeply, she searched for the emotional residue that would normally accompany duplicity in a human—the shades of feeling that would tip her off to Asmund's guilt.

"Tell me, Counselor," said the blond woman. "Why are you here?"

The empath looked her in the eye. "It is obvious that you are having some trouble coping. I was wondering—"

"If there was anything you could do to help?"

Troi maintained her composure despite the interruption. "Something like that. I know how difficult it can be to finally close a wound—and then to have it opened again by people and circumstances."

"Do you, Counselor?" Her voice was steady, giving away nothing. "With all due respect, I doubt it."

"Contrary to appearances," Troi responded, "I have had my share of heartaches. My share of loss. Of pain."

For a fleeting moment, she thought of Ian, and her heart sank. Then she recovered.

Asmund must have noticed her discomfort, because her attitude changed rather abruptly.

"I did not mean to make this a competition," she said. "I apologize." She shrugged. "I have had this conversation twice now—once with my present captain and once with Captain Picard. Both times I managed to convince myself that they were right; both times I made an effort to meet the others halfway. Both times I was unsuccessful." She shook her head. "Then I realized that the problem was not theirs, but mine."

"What do you mean?" asked Troi, though she had a fairly good idea.

"They may have forgiven me my association with Gerda—but I haven't."

Asmund straightened in her seat. "How much do you know about Klingon tradition, Counselor?"

"A little," said the empath. "Mostly from my association with Lieutenant Worf."

The other woman stared into her glass. "The ancient Klingons had a law that if a person was not available to be tried for his crimes, his siblings might be held accountable instead." Her voice hardened. "Gerda was my sister. In human terms, I had an obligation to watch out for her. In Klingon terms, it was more than an obligation. It was a *'Iw mir*—a blood-bond."

Troi leaned forward. "Are you saying that you're in some way guilty of your sister's crime? As if *you* had committed it instead of *her?*"

"I know," said Asmund. "The Federation doesn't see it that way. Neither does the human part of me. Over the years, I think, my human self managed to submerge the guilt—the implications of the *'Iw mir.*" She frowned. "I believe, however, that my reunion with my former comrades has awakened my Klingon sense of responsibility."

"And that is why you cannot mingle with them? Because they remind you of the blood-bond?"

"That is my theory. Even if no one else will punish me for Gerda's crime, I will punish myself." She raised her glass and sipped. "What do you think, Counselor? From a professional standpoint, I mean?"

It sounded plausible. Troi was forced to say so.

"As I thought." Asmund put her glass down again and smiled grimly. "So you see, Counselor, I don't need to talk with anyone. I'm quite capable of diagnosing my own problems."

The empath tried to frame her words carefully. "Diagnosis is only the first step, Commander. Now that you know there is something wrong, don't you want to do something about it?"

Asmund stared at her. "From a Klingon point of view, Counselor, it is my responsibility to bear this guilt."

It was a difficult situation. Troi had to concede that.

"Would it hurt," she asked, "if we talked again?"

Asmund thought about it. "No," she said finally. "I suppose it wouldn't hurt."

"Good," said the counselor. "Then let's do that. As often as you like." She returned the other woman's piercing gaze. "And if I do not hear from you, I will take it upon myself to call."

Asmund nodded. "Fair enough."

Troi rose. "I am glad we had this talk." She smiled.

The other woman tried to do the same as she got to her feet—but in all fairness, she wasn't very good at it. Nor did she offer any further expression of emotion—gratitude or anything else—as the empath departed.

Once out in the corridor, Troi took a deep breath and frowned. Again, she had come up hard against Asmund's wall of self-discipline—a discipline born of hiding herself *from* herself. Of course, she had gotten some insight into the blond woman by virtue of their conversation—but nothing she could offer to the captain as an indication of Asmund's guilt or lack of it.

As for easing the woman's pain . . . perhaps she had made some headway there. But not as much as she might have hoped.

All in all, an unsatisfying conclusion.

*   *   *

Riker bit his lip as the doors opened to reveal Cadwallader's quarters. *Come on,* he told himself. *The sooner you get this over with, the better.*

She was sitting by the computer terminal built into the bulkhead, wearing her mustard-and-black uniform. "Hi," she said.

"Hi." He was glad she hadn't changed yet for dinner—particularly when he saw the very feminine green shift folded neatly over the back of a chair.

Cadwallader turned and followed his gaze. "Not very neat," she apologized, "am I? I just can't help it. Leaving clothes all over is my vice."

"Tricia . . ." he began, but she was already up out of her seat and across the room. Picking up the dress, she held it before her. Riker could see that it was translucent in places—all the *right* places.

"You like it?" she asked. "I know it's bad form to show a date your dress before you've got it on, but—" She shrugged. "What can I say? Mum never trained me quite right."

He had known this wouldn't be easy. But he hadn't expected her to be so damned excited—so *vulnerable.*

"Tricia . . ."

She replaced the dress on the chair. "This is appropriate, isn't it? I mean, I've never had dinner in a holodeck. How does one dress for a meteor storm? Or a hot, steaming jungle—"

"Tricia!"

She stopped short, surprised by the tone of his voice. "Excuse me. Did I say something wrong?"

Riker cursed himself inwardly. He hadn't meant it to be like this. "No. It's not your fault. It's just that—" Here came the hard part. "Maybe this isn't such a good idea."

He might as well have told her he was a Romulan in disguise. "I beg your pardon?" she said.

"You know," he told her, "with both of us being officers . . ." It sounded lame and he knew it. But what else could he say?

Certainly not the truth—that she was a suspect in an attempted murder investigation, and that it prevented him from getting emotionally involved with her. If he listened to his heart instead of his head, if he kept on going the way he was going . . . it would be too easy to let something slip, something that would help the assassin achieve success the next time.

Not that he believed *Cadwallader* was the assassin. Far from it. But if Riker let out some detail of the investigation, and she unknowingly passed it on to the guilty party . . .

"Will," she said, "there are lots of officers who have . . . relationships with one another. It's not as if we're even serving on the same ship." She looked at him in a way that made his heart sink. "Or is there some other reason? Perhaps the bit of difference in our ages?"

He steeled himself, shook his head. "No other reason. I like you, Tricia. I like you a lot. But I just don't feel comfortable with . . . with what's happening between us."

She smiled ruefully. "That's too bad," she told him. "I thought—well, never mind what I thought." There was just the slightest trace of huskiness in her voice. "I guess I'll see you around, then, eh? Maybe in the gym or something."

Riker nodded. "I wouldn't be surprised." And before he could falter—before he could change his mind about the line he'd drawn between his feelings and his duty—he turned and left the suite.

Even after he was outside in the corridor, the doors to Cadwallader's quarters closed behind him, he could see her expression. The disbelief. The disappointment. The embarrassment.

He felt like something one would scrape from the bottom of one's boots.

It was strange. The more time passed without any other incidents, the more it seemed that the sabotage of the holodeck had never taken place.

As Picard looked around the bridge, everything seemed so placid—so orderly. It was difficult to contemplate the possibility of violence in such a setting. Even the viewscreen, with its familiar image of stars stretched into taut lines of light, conspired to create an illusion of stability.

Of course, Picard knew that this was a pitfall he would have to avoid. As much as he wanted to believe otherwise, he knew that someone had attempted to kill Morgen—and perhaps Lieutenant Worf as well.

He could feel the Klingon's presence at the tactical station—like an anchor in a sea of uncertainty. They hadn't pursued the possibility that Worf might have been the primary target and not Morgen. But then, given the presence of the *Stargazer* survivors, and the fact that the Daa'Vit's life had been threatened once before . . .

Playing devil's advocate for a moment, Picard asked himself if any of his former officers might have a reason for wanting Worf dead. As far as he knew, none of them had ever met him before they'd boarded the *Enterprise.* And the only one who had a reason to hate Klingons was Morgen—the very individual who had shared the security chief's peril in the holodeck.

It seemed far more likely that the Daa'Vit was the intended victim. But just to be sure, the captain resolved to discuss the alternative with Commander Riker. And with Worf himself, naturally, at a—

The captain's thoughts came to an abrupt halt as he felt the ship surge violently beneath him. On the viewscreen there was an accompanying shift—as the dashes of starlight shortened up considerably.

"Mr. Data," he said, "I gave no order to accelerate."

The android had stationed himself at the conn station for the day to give Solis more practice at ops. His fingers were fluttering over the controls at a quicker than usual pace.

"Nor did I initiate any change in speed," said Data. He swiveled in his seat to face Picard. "Nonetheless, sir, we *have* accelerated. We are proceeding at warp nine point nine five."

The captain shook his head, incredulous. The *Enterprise*'s engines weren't supposed to be *capable* of propelling it that fast—at least, not for more than a few seconds.

"Are you certain?" he asked Data.

The android turned back to his console and checked. "Diagnostics confirm it, sir. Unless the entire computer system has malfunctioned, we are traveling at a rate equal to five thousand ninety-four times the speed of light."

Picard felt a slight queasiness in his stomach as he rose and approached the conn station. Normally, he didn't check up on his bridge personnel—particularly Data. But there was nothing *normal* about this.

Sure enough, the monitor showed that they were clipping along at 9.95. The queasiness grew worse. Could this have anything to do with the attempt on Morgen's life?

"How is this possible?" he asked the android.

"I do not know, sir."

One thing was certain—the ship could not be allowed to continue at this speed. Who knew what it would do to the warp engines? The hull integrity? "Slow to warp six again," he instructed Solis. *"Immediately."*

The dark-haired lieutenant looked up at him. "Captain . . . I know this sounds crazy, but the engines are *already* working at warp six. Or at least, what *should* be warp six."

Picard glanced at the viewscreen, as if it could tell him something his officers couldn't. But it yielded nothing of value.

"Mr. La Forge," he called.

"La Forge here," came the response.

"This is the captain. I'm up on the bridge." Picard licked his lips. "Commander, I want you to check on the warp drive—tell me how fast we should be going."

"*Should* be?" asked Geordi.

"There seems to be some question as to our speed," explained the captain.

"Sir, I just *checked* the warp drive. I felt a surge and I wanted to make sure everything was all right."

"And?" Picard prodded.

"Everything seems to be in order. As for how fast we're going . . . let's see." The captain could picture Geordi checking his instruments. "That would be warp six."

Picard felt his teeth grinding. "Commander, what would you say if I told you we were traveling at warp nine point nine five?"

The intercom system was silent for a moment. "I'd say that's impossible," answered the engineering chief.

"And yet," the captain told him, "our external sensors indicate that we are doing just that. Nor is there any evidence of sensor failure."

This time, Geordi took even longer to react. "You mean we're exceeding top speed—and our engines *aren't?*"

Picard managed to keep his voice free of the frustration he was feeling. "That is how it appears."

"I'll be right there," Geordi told him.

The captain grunted. "Thank you, Mister La Forge." He turned back to Data. "For the time being, Commander, I think it would be wise to drop out of warp altogether."

"Aye, sir," replied the android. With practiced ease, he went through the necessary routine on his board. However, even after Data was finished, Picard could feel the vibration of warp speed in the hull—could see the streaks of light darting by on the viewscreen.

"What is going *on?*" he asked.

"I cannot say," the android responded. "The warp drive has been disengaged. Yet our sensors indicate that we are still proceeding at warp nine point nine five."

The captain felt a muscle in his jaw start to twitch. With an effort, he controlled it. "Then we cannot slow down," he concluded.

It was not a question, but Data answered it anyway. "That is correct, sir."

Picard resolved not to panic—not even on the inside. Geordi would be here in a matter of moments, he told himself. His chief engineer would shed some light on this.

He had damned well better.

Nine

With both warp and impulse engines at rest, it was ominously quiet in engineering. As Geordi entered ahead of Data, two faces turned simultaneously in his direction—those of Phigus Simenon and Wesley Crusher.

"Thanks for being so prompt," he told them.

"What's the matter?" asked Wes.

"Must be something serious," the Gnalish said. "You were up on the bridge for almost an hour."

Geordi nodded. "It's serious all right. That's why I wanted the best help I could get."

He headed for the master situation monitor and pulled up a schematic of the sector through which they were passing. The *Enterprise* showed up as a red blip in the middle of the diagram.

They all came closer to take a look.

"You'll note," Geordi pointed out, "that we're moving pretty quickly—especially in light of the fact that our engines have been turned off."

Data spoke up. "Warp nine point nine five, to be precise."

Both Wesley and the Gnalish looked at him.

"You're kidding," said the ensign.

"I am not capable of humor," replied the android. "As you know."

"I assume you've checked for quirks in the sensor systems," remarked Simenon. "After all, we know only what they tell us."

"Checked and rechecked," the chief engineer replied. "They're working just fine."

"So we're sailing along at warp nine point nine five, and without even lifting a finger." Wesley shook his head, disbelieving.

"Curious," agreed the Gnalish.

"Apparently," Geordi told them, "we've gotten caught in some sort of subspace phenomenon. A *slipstream,* for lack of a more precise description. And it's carrying us ahead against our will." He paused, looking at the others. "I don't have to tell you what this means."

"We'll be at Daa'V in a matter of hours," said Simenon. "And out into uncharted space in a few days."

"That's exactly right," the chief engineer said. "And from what I understand, there could be problems if Morgen's late for the coronation ceremony—*big* problems. After all, not everyone on Daa'V is thrilled to see him succeed to the throne, and they'd love an excuse for denying it to him. Which is why we left ourselves plenty of time to get him there."

"Or so you thought," added the Gnalish.

"Or so we thought," Geordi echoed. "And even at warp factor nine point two— the maximum speed the *Enterprise* can sustain for any extended period of time— we're going to be able to return to Federation space only one-fourth as fast as we're leaving it. In other words, every day out is going to mean *four* days back. So if we're going to solve this problem, we'd better do it soon—before we find ourselves in the middle of a major interplanetary incident."

"Or worse," said Simenon. "We don't know very much about subspace phenomena, gentlemen—but the ones we've observed seem to be quite variable. That means we may continue this way for a while—but it is more likely we will suddenly be released. Or carried along even *faster.*" He looked at Geordi in particular, his serpentine eyes slitted. "And then, of course, there is a fourth possibility."

The chief engineer nodded. "The nature of the anomaly could change altogether. We could suddenly find ourselves in a subspace whirlpool—or something even *more* violent."

"The moral being to get the hell off this roller coaster," the Gnalish amplified. "Preferably, *before* it has a chance to do us in."

Wesley straightened. "You can count on me," he told Geordi.

La Forge smiled. "I know I can, Ensign."

Data had already pledged his best efforts. The chief engineer turned to Simenon. "And you, sir?"

The Gnalish's mouth quirked, "What do *you* think?"

For a brief moment, Geordi flashed back on a question the captain had asked of him up on the bridge, when nobody else was listening: *"Commander . . . is it possible that this was accomplished by an act of sabotage? That we were somehow maneuvered into this slipstream you speak of?"*

At the time, Geordi had said it was *not* possible. And he still believed that. No one—not even the best mind in the Federation—had a good enough grasp of subspace phenomena to use one in setting a trap.

But whoever the assassin was, that individual couldn't have been too upset about running into the slipstream. It was a distraction—a complication that could only work to his or her advantage.

And if the murderer was Simenon—a possibility the chief engineer had to consider, even if he found it unlikely—he would have every reason not to see their work proceed smoothly.

"I think," Geordi said at last, "that I'm glad to have you on my team."

The Gnalish smiled. "Naturally."

As the doors parted, Riker entered the apartment.

Morgen was standing in the center of the foreroom, looking a little too much like a caged beast for the first officer's taste. "I trust," said the Daa'Vit, "that you're not here just to check up on me. I could hardly have complied better with the captain's wishes—much to the detriment of my disposition."

"No," Riker assured him, "I'm not here to check up on you."

"What then?"

"We've got a problem. And since it may affect your arrival on Daa'V, Captain Picard felt you should know about it."

At the mention of his homeworld, Morgen's attention turned up a notch. "I'm listening," he said.

"The *Enterprise* has run into a subspace phenomenon," Riker explained. "Something we've never encountered before."

"Has it thrown us off course?" the Daa'Vit asked.

The first officer shook his head. "No. Our course is unchanged. But the phenomenon has got us traveling at warp factor nine point nine five."

Morgen's forehead ridged over. "What?"

Riker nodded. "I know how it sounds, sir. But it's the truth."

The Daa'Vit gestured to one of the chairs. "Sit, Commander. Please."

The human conformed to the request. Morgen sat across from him on a rather queer-looking couch—a stone-and-moss affair which had come from ship's stores.

"Now," the Daa'Vit told him, "say that again."

Riker spread his hands. He went over the whole business, leaving nothing out. After all, it was Morgen's right to know—not only as the next ruler of his people, but as a captain in Starfleet. And his initial surprise notwithstanding, the Daa'Vit seemed to take it in stride.

"You know," he told Riker, "we had our share of close calls on the *Excalibur.* Maybe more than our share. Somehow, we always seemed to get out of them." He smiled as he remembered, the surliness brought on by his confinement forgotten. "After a while, you develop a belief that there's no problem you can't solve—no trap from which you can't devise an escape." He looked meaningfully at his guest. "Do you know what I mean?"

The first officer nodded. "Yes, sir. I do."

"Some might call that kind of confidence a trap in and of itself. And I suppose it could be. But more often, I think it's an asset. Because if you really believe you're going to upset the odds, you generally will." Morgen ran his palm over a clump of moss on the couch, studied it. "I really *believe* we're going to get out of this, Riker." He raised his head, fixing the human with his yellow eyes. "How about *you?"*

"And that," said Troi, "is our predicament as I understand it."

The rec cabin was empty but for the six of them—Troi herself, Ben Zoma, Cadwallader, Joseph, Greyhorse, and Asmund. The ship's counselor looked from face to face. "Questions?"

"I take it Simenon is already involved in solving the problem," said Greyhorse, his voice implying criticism of the idea—which was usually the case when he was talking about the Gnalish.

"That is correct," Troi told him. "He is working closely with Geordi La Forge."

The doctor added, "Much to Commander La Forge's delight, no doubt."

That drew a murmur of laughter; even the empath had to chuckle. Only Asmund, who sat in the back of the room apart from the others, seemed less than entertained by the remark.

"And Morgen?" asked Cadwallader.

"Commander Riker is discussing this with him separately. After all, there are political ramifications to his late arrival which will have to be dealt with."

"Is there anything the rest of us can do?" asked Asmund.

Troi shook her head, noting how the woman's professionalism had come to the fore as soon as she'd heard about the emergency. Otherwise, she would probably have resisted meeting with the others.

"Not at the present time," said the counselor. "But if the situation changes, you will, of course, be notified."

"Have you tried to contact any of our other ships?" asked Joseph. "The *Lexington,* for instance?"

The empath nodded. "We have sent out communications beacons. However, as long as we progress at this speed, no other ship can catch up to us—much less help us."

Ben Zoma, who was sitting next to Joseph, clapped his security chief on the shoulder. "Well," he said, "we all wanted to know what was out there. Maybe now we're about to find out." He looked at Troi, his dark eyes full of good cheer. "Don't worry, Counselor. We served on the *Stargazer*—we're used to blazing new territory."

Troi was grateful for his help in keeping his comrades' spirits up. And for Greyhorse's as well—though that had not necessarily been the doctor's purpose.

"If that's all," she said, "I should be getting back up to the bridge."

No one objected. But as she made her way to the exit, she found Ben Zoma walking beside her.

She had a feeling it was no accident, but they were in the corridor—out of earshot of the others—before he confirmed it. "Counselor," he said, looking straight ahead, "there's a problem—isn't there? I mean *beyond* this slipstream phenomenon."

"A problem?" she echoed.

He turned to her, as serious as she'd ever seen him. "I've been at this too long not to know when something's wrong. First of all, there's an excess of security officers around—even if they're trying their best not to be obvious about it. Second, Morgen's spent an awful lot of time in his quarters lately. And third, the holodecks are suddenly off limits. Now, I don't know what the others think, not having discussed this with them. But I'd be surprised if they weren't a little suspicious as well."

Troi looked him in the eye. "If you have a question," she suggested, "you should take it up with the captain." She smiled, hating the need to be evasive. "Even ship's counselors aren't privy to *everything,* you know."

Ben Zoma didn't quite buy her act; she could tell. But for now, he let the subject drop. "Very well, then," he said, a glimmer of humor creeping back into his voice. Or was it irony? "I'll let you go now. I'm sure you've got other duties to attend to."

"Thank you," she answered, and headed for the turbolift.

Picard glanced around the conference table at Geordi's four-member crisis team. "I'm afraid I don't understand," he said. "How will reversing engines allow us to escape this thing?"

"It won't," said Geordi. "But it might slow us down—buy some time."

The captain nodded. "And time is a factor here, isn't it?" He considered the strategy from all angles. "What about the stress it would place on the ship? Will the hull stand up under such circumstances?"

"There's no way of knowing for sure," said Simenon. "But my guess is that the stress will be within manageable limits."

"Plus, we can administer reverse thrust gradually," Wesley advised. "That way, if we see there's going to be a problem, we can back off."

Picard drummed his fingers on the table. "It's risky."

Data leaned forward slightly. "Captain, our present position is characterized by risk as well."

Picard looked at the android. "I suppose that is true, Commander." He turned to Geordi again, his decision made. "Very well, Mr. La Forge. We will give it a try."

Rising, he tugged down hard on his tunic and led the way out of the observation lounge. As he took his seat in the command center, he saw Data proceed to ops and Wesley to conn, replacing the personnel who had been posted there. At the same time, Geordi took up his position at the engineering station.

Since the seats on either side of the captain's were unoccupied, Simenon took one of them—where Riker usually sat. "You don't mind, do you?" he asked Picard. "After all, I have to sit somewhere."

The captain almost smiled. "I thought you *hated* to be on the bridge."

"It wasn't such a novelty back then," explained the Gnalish, already intent on the viewscreen.

"Really," said Picard. It felt good to have Simenon beside him again—just like old times. Nor could the suspicion that had fallen on the Gnalish quite dampen the captain's confidence in him.

Putting such thoughts aside for the moment, Picard raised his head and spoke. "This is the captain speaking. Secure all decks. In a few seconds we will be attempting a maneuver which may toss us about a bit—but not to worry. The ship is well under control."

It sounded good. Now they would see how much *truth* there was to it.

Picard nodded to Wesley, who had turned around in his chair to wait for the captain's signal. Facing forward, the ensign made the necessary preparations.

"Warp factor one," said the captain. "Reverse thrust."

"Warp factor one," Wesley confirmed. "Reverse thrust."

"Engage," said Picard.

A shudder went through the ship, but only for a second. Then it stopped.

"No problems with hull integrity or ship's systems," reported Geordi. "But we haven't slowed down one iota."

The captain frowned. "Warp factor two, Mr. Crusher. Engage."

Wesley executed the order. Again, there was a brief vibration.

"Still nothing," Geordi said. "No cause for alarm, no change in speed."

Picard noticed that Simenon was staring at him. He turned to face his former chief engineer, and the Gnalish looked down at his hand on the armrest. Four of his scaly gray fingers were extended; his thumb was folded back. When he looked up again at the captain, his meaning was clear.

"Warp Factor Four," commanded Picard.

"Warp Factor Four," said Wesley, complying.

This time the ship's trembling was more pronounced, and it lasted longer. But when it was over, the streaks of starlight on the viewscreen were longer and a little less frantic.

"Progress," announced Geordi triumphantly. "We're down to warp nine point nine one."

"Which means we've cut our speed by a third," said Simenon. He looked at the captain. "Sorry. It's the professor in me."

"Quite all right," said Picard. If they had been alone, he would have clapped the Gnalish on the back—as he'd had occasion to do so many times on the *Stargazer*. "How is the ship holding up?" he asked.

"Considerable stress on hull integrity," Geordi told him. "But we can handle it."

"Should we try Warp Factor Five?" asked Wesley.

The captain glanced at Simenon's hand. There were still only four fingers extended.

"I wouldn't recommend it," called La Forge. "I think we're on the edge now. And we've slowed down considerably—why take the risk?"

"Then we will remain at Warp Four," Picard decided. "And Mr. Crusher—do not anticipate."

The back of the ensign's neck turned red. "Acknowledged, sir."

"All right," said Geordi. "We've bought ourselves that time we wanted. Let's do something with it. Data, Crusher, Professor Simenon—you're with me."

The Gnalish gave the captain one last look as he swept past—a look that said his contribution was all in a day's work. Then he was on his way to the turbolift along with Wesley and the android, his tail switching back and forth over the carpeted deck.

Geordi was leaning on a bulkhead, his arms locked across his chest. He looked at Simenon, Data, and Wesley in turn.

Not the most upbeat bunch, he remarked to himself. But then, he wasn't feeling too upbeat himself just then. Of them all, only Data was still holding his head erect—and that was only because he wasn't human enough to know when he was licked.

"We've been at this for hours, and we've got nothing to show for it," Geordi said. "I'm opening the floor to any idea, no matter how wild. Hell, it doesn't even have to be an idea—just a half-baked notion."

The others looked at him. Simenon grunted.

"I mean it," Geordi said. *"Anything."*

Wesley straightened a little. "Okay. What if we separated the saucer section from the battle bridge?"

Simenon shook his head. "It wouldn't help. If we were moving strictly under engine power and you disconnected the saucer, it would drop out of warp. But since the warp field is being imposed on us externally, the saucer would continue to be dragged along with the battle bridge."

The android nodded. "That would be the most likely result."

"I agree," said Geordi. "All right—forget separation. How about the shuttles?"

"Same thing," responded the Gnalish. "They'd be stuck here just as we are."

"They might proceed more slowly," offered Data, "because of their lesser mass. Remember, we are not in normal space; Newtonian principles may not hold here."

"And what if they *did* proceed more slowly?" asked Simenon. "It would only be a stop-gap maneuver."

"Besides," said Wes, "none of them can travel faster than warp one—so whatever advantage we enjoyed on the way out we'd lose in spades on the way back."

Geordi nodded. "Even assuming there were enough of them to evacuate the ship—which there aren't, even including the lifeboat pods. Next."

"We launch a probe," said the Gnalish. "And then we blast it with photon torpedoes. Our shields should protect us from any damage, but the backlash—" Abruptly, he waved the idea away. "No. If we wanted to go backward more forcefully, all we'd have to do is go to warp five."

"That's right," said Geordi. "And we've already scotched that idea because of the safety factor."

Data's brow creased. "It may be that we are approaching the problem the wrong way."

"What do you mean?" asked Wes.

The android looked at him. "We seem to be focusing on finding a way to slow down. Perhaps it would help us more to *speed up.*"

That *was* a fresh slant. "Go on," said Geordi.

"The slipstream is carrying us forward at warp nine point nine five. If we can exceed that speed, we might be able to outrun the phenomenon's frontal horizon—assuming it has one—and thereby free ourselves."

It was almost childlike in its conception. And yet, in a common-sense kind of way, it seemed as if it could work.

Of course, there was a rather large *practical* problem.

"You're talking about the ship traveling in excess of warp nine point nine five," Geordi pointed out. "We've never done that before."

"We've never *tried,*" said Wes.

"And if Mr. Data is right about there being a frontal horizon," added Simenon, "it might take only a fraction of a second to pierce it."

"Or it could take millennia," the chief engineer reminded him.

"Yes," the Gnalish conceded. "Or that. It depends on the magnitude of the phenomenon. And where we are in relation to its boundaries."

Geordi mulled it over. "I usually like to give the captain more than one option."

Silence from Data and Wesley. Simenon rolled his fiery red eyeballs at the notion. After all, it had taken so long to come up with *this* plan . . .

"But in this case," said La Forge, "I think I'll make an exception."

Standing in the corridor outside Morgen's door, Crusher was starting to become a little concerned. After all, she'd been there for more than a minute, waiting to give the Daa'Vit his routine follow-up exam, and there had been no response to her presence. Of course, Morgen could have been taking a nap—but it seemed unlikely with all that was going on.

Finally, she tapped her communicator. "Computer—where is Captain Morgen?"

The reply was nearly instantaneous. "Captain Morgen is in the forward lounge on deck seventeen."

"Thank you," the doctor said out loud. As she headed for the turbolift, she thumped herself on the head.

Dumb, Beverly. You should have checked out Morgen's whereabouts before you came all this way.

Nor could she just call him via the intercom system. If someone were with the Daa'Vit, they'd wonder why the ship's doctor wanted to see him. No, she would have to seek him out in person—and drag him back to his apartment only if he were alone.

The turbolift doors opened at Crusher's approach. She stepped inside.

"Deck seventeen," she instructed. "Forward lounge."

The lift's movement was imperceptible except for a subtle hum. And since she hadn't been more than a couple of decks away, she arrived in a matter of seconds.

As she exited, she made a left and followed the curve of the corridor. The lounge appeared on her right, its doors open—not uncommon, if there was nothing going on inside that would disturb others on the ship.

Voices. One was Morgen's—subdued yet resonant. The other was female, human. Not Troi's, or she would have recognized it. Nor Asmund's, unless things had changed drastically since dinner the other night.

Cadwallader's, she decided. And as she entered the lounge, she saw that she'd guessed correctly. Ben Zoma's Number Two was sitting across a small table from the Daa'Vit, engaging him in a game of *sharash'di.*

At Crusher's arrival, they both looked up. Cadwallader smiled. "Greetings, Doctor. Fancy meeting you here."

Beverly smiled back. "I saw the doors open and I couldn't resist peeking inside." She indicated the game board. *"Sharash'di,* eh?"

Morgen nodded. "Commander Cadwallader thought it was high time I left that stuffy apartment you've given me—and spent some time in this stuffy lounge."

The doctor wondered about that. Had Cadwallader lured the Daa'Vit in here for something other than a simple diversion?

Certainly, the woman didn't look like the type to go around assassinating people. But the captain hadn't omitted anyone when he'd ordered his former officers watched—and he knew them better than she did.

Maybe I should stick around, she told herself. For a while anyway, just in case—

Abruptly, they heard Picard's voice addressing them over the intercom. All three of them looked up.

"As you know by now," said the captain, "we are caught in a subspace phenomenon. We will be attempting to escape that phenomenon in a few moments. Once again, I must ask that all decks be secured."

Well, Crusher mused, so much for whether I should stay or go. Picard's announcement had taken that decision out of her hands.

Cadwallader gestured to a chair. "Have a seat, Doctor. After I thrash Captain Morgen, you can have a whack."

Picard sat back in his command chair. In front of him, Wesley and Data had once more taken up their positions at the forward stations. And as before, Geordi was off to the side at the engineering console.

But with Riker and Troi on the bridge, Simenon was content to take the proverbial backseat. He now stood next to Worf at tactical, no doubt scrutinizing the efficiency with which the Klingon did his job.

"Mr. Crusher," said the captain, "reverse engines."

Wesley carried out the order. Abruptly, the ship seemed to shoot forward again. The light streaks on the viewscreen resumed their earlier velocity.

"Engines reversed, sir," said the ensign. "We are now proceeding forward at warp four—or at least that's our engine speed." He glanced at another monitor. "Our actual speed is warp nine point nine five—just as it was before."

Picard nodded. "Thank you, Mr. Crusher. Go to warp nine point six."

"Aye, sir." Wesley touched the necessary controls.

It had absolutely no effect on their velocity. The captain knew that even before Data announced it.

"Warp nine point nine," Picard instructed.

Still no change—other than the fact that their warp drive was laboring as hard as it ever had before. At this speed, the engines would hold out for only a few minutes—then they'd simply turn themselves off.

And as they accelerated beyond warp nine point nine, their ability to maintain speed would no doubt diminish accordingly—perhaps to no more than a matter of seconds. Nonetheless, the captain was inclined to approach his goal by degrees. He refused to play Russian roulette with in excess of a thousand lives.

"Nine point nine three, Mr. Crusher."

"Nine point nine three, sir."

Geordi spoke up: "Estimate one minute and forty-five seconds until engine auto-shutdown."

Picard could feel the thrum of the engines through the deck. "Nine point nine five," he said.

"Nine point nine five, sir."

The vibration in the deck grew worse, joined by a high-pitched whine. Picard set his teeth against it.

They were moving as quickly as the slipstream now. Keeping pace with it, as remarkable as that seemed. He thought he could feel the g-force pressing him back into his seat. But of course, that was just his mind playing tricks on him—wasn't it? Or had the inertial dampers reached their limit?

"Estimate auto-shutdown in nine seconds," Geordi said over the whine. "It's now or never, sir!"

With an effort, the captain leaned forward. *Come on, Enterprise!*

"Nine point nine six, Mr. Crusher."

"Nine point nine six!" Wesley repeated, unable to keep the excitement out of his voice. Nor did Picard blame him—no Federation vessel had ever traveled even *this* fast under its own power.

The ensign made the necessary adjustments—and holding his breath, or so it appeared to Picard, pressed the "enter" key.

Suddenly, the bridge was caught in the grip of chaos. The viewscreen seemed to burst with blinding light, while the whine became the worst kind of spine-shivering squeal. Worst of all, the captain felt himself thrust back as if by a giant hand, crushed into his command chair.

Then, as abruptly as it began, it was over. No whine, no vibration, no intrusion of g-forces. The viewscreen was blank, the ship's visual sensors having apparently overloaded. Picard took a deep breath, let it out.

He looked around. "Is everyone all right?"

Everyone was, though some of the bridge officers seemed to have lost their footing in that last violent moment. Geordi was one of them.

"Mr. Crusher," said Picard, rising and approaching the Conn station. En route, he gave his tunic a short, effective tug. "What is our situation?"

When Wesley turned around, he looked disappointed. "The warp engines are down, sir. And we're still moving at warp nine point nine five."

A bitter thing to swallow. But the captain accepted it with equanimity. "I see" was all he said.

"Life-support nodes have switched to impulse power," Data reported. "However, lighting and ventilation systems are experiencing widespread failures, though none that suggests imminent danger to the crew."

Picard nodded. "Thank you, Mr. Data." It occurred to him to pose another question. Turning to Geordi, he asked: "Did we achieve warp nine point nine six, Commander?"

La Forge shook his head. "I'm not sure, sir. We had some instrument malfunctions."

Picard accepted that too. "See what data you can collect," he advised. "Perhaps we can learn something from this."

"Aye, sir," said the chief engineer. "Just as soon as I get the engines up and running again."

The captain turned back to the viewscreen. Despite its emptiness, he could see imagined stars streaming by all too quickly.

Picard sighed. They had given it their best shot—and failed.

In the lounge on Deck Seventeen, the only illumination was supplied by the starlight that came through the observation port—and that wasn't much at all. However, Crusher's eyes were adjusting to the darkness. She could now discern her companions from the shadowy silhouettes of the furniture.

"Whatever our captain did," said Cadwallader, "it destroyed more than a few circuits. Even the emergency lighting's not working."

"Other parts of the ship may be in better shape," Morgen offered. "We should try to reach them."

"Seems like a good idea," said the doctor.

"The doorway is over *there,*" the Daa'Vit announced. Beverly felt him take her by the arm and usher her toward the exit.

"Careful of that chair." That came from Cadwallader, apparently guided by Morgen as well.

"I see it," said the Daa'Vit. "Thanks."

And a moment later they emerged into the corridor. Windowless, it was even blacker than the lounge. Crusher pointed to the left—a pretty useless gesture, she realized. If *she* couldn't see her hand, how could her companions?

"Turn to the left," she told them. "There's a turbolift a few meters from here. On the right—just past the curve."

"It's a good thing you're with us," said Cadwallader, "or we'd have a devil of a time trying to—"

Suddenly, the darkness ahead of them exploded in a burst of fiery red light. Instinctively, the doctor brought her arm up to protect her eyes—but before she could do even that much, she was wrenched off her feet by a pair of hands and sent flying backward.

A second blast followed the first; this time there was no doubt. *Someone was firing a phaser at them.* And judging from the odor of burning duranium in the air, that someone was out for blood.

Morgen cried out, then Cadwallader. Through the prism of her hot, burning tears, Crusher tried to see who it was that had attacked them, and where he was aiming his weapon.

But it was no use. There was too much happening and it was happening too quickly; all she could do was press herself against the bulkhead and call for help, and hope that the intercom was working better than the lighting system.

A third blast—a shriek and a curse, and the muffled thump of a body hitting the deck. Putting aside her fear, the doctor crawled in the direction of the sound, bracing herself for what she might find.

After all, the beam had pierced the bulkhead. There was no limit to the havoc it could have worked on a human body—or a Daa'Vit, for that matter.

But if she got there in time, she might be able to help. To stabilize the victim's condition until he or she could be transported to sickbay.

Never mind the fact that she might be a victim *herself* by then. She was a doctor, damn it!

Zzt—

She dropped flat against the deck as another ruby bolt sliced across the corridor—not more than a foot above her head. By its light, she saw the shape of the fallen figure before her.

Cadwallader.

Crusher couldn't tell how badly the woman was hurt, but the way she just lay there wasn't encouraging. As the darkness closed down again, the doctor snaked forward—far enough to close her fingers around Cadwallader's shoulder.

Suddenly, the corridor echoed with distant voices. Faraway lights cast grotesque shadows, and Crusher had an all-too-vague impression of the killer as he—or she—disappeared around the curve.

Morgen—visible also now—took off in pursuit, as the Starfleet captain in him gave way to the Daa'Vit hunter. She called after him, to remind him that the killer was still armed and had the advantage over him. He seemed not to hear.

Turning her attention back to her patient, the doctor noted gratefully that Cadwallader was still breathing. Her face was a mask of pain and the entire right side of her tunic was already crimson, but there was still hope for her.

She tapped her communicator. "This is Dr. Crusher. I need a trauma team on Deck Seventeen—*now.*"

Stripping off her lab coat, she tucked it under Cadwallader and up around her shoulder. Then she pressed down hard, in an attempt to staunch the flow of blood. The phaser emission had stabbed right through the woman, and the hole in her back was worse than the entry wound—but with any luck the weapon had been set on narrow aperture. Cadwallader moaned, her eyelids fluttering.

Come on, Crusher exhorted inwardly, as the security team bounded past her after Morgen and the assassin. *Come on, before she bleeds to death . . .*

Ten

As the captain strode into the specially blocked off critical care area, Crusher and Morgen were there waiting for him. Cadwallader, he noted with some relief, was well enough to turn her head a bit in recognition of his approach.

The doctor looked worn out herself, but she managed a smile. The message was clear: in time, Cadwallader would be all right.

Picard nodded gratefully to her. Then he looked down at his former communications officer. She was pale—terribly pale—but her eyes were as warm and vibrant as ever. Her hand lay on top of the thermal blanket; he took it, squeezed it. Cadwallader squeezed back, surprising him.

"She's tougher than she looks," Morgen observed.

The captain grunted his assent, replacing the woman's hand on the blanket, then looked up at the Daa'Vit. "What happened?" he asked, the cold, flat calmness of his voice belying the anger that raged inside him.

"We were assaulted in a corridor during the power outage," Morgen explained. "A single assailant with a phaser. Adjusted to setting six, if the holes in the bulkhead are any indication."

"Setting six?" repeated Picard. "But—"

"I know," said the Daa'Vit. "Our killer must have disabled the communications module in the phaser so it couldn't talk with the ship's computer."

"The phaser didn't know it was on the ship," Beverly expanded. "So it didn't restrict itself to setting five."

"Then you recovered the weapon?"

"Unfortunately, no," the doctor said. "At least, not yet. Worf is looking for it now; I'm just speculating."

The captain frowned. "And you couldn't tell who it was? Not at all?"

Morgen shook his head. "It was too dark, and we were blinded by the phaserlight. After the security team scared him—or her—off, I tried to follow. But as I said, it was dark. And our assailant knew how to go quietly."

Picard gazed at Cadwallader again. "You say Mr. Worf is investigating?"

Crusher nodded. "He mentioned something about blocking off the area—so he could keep what happened from becoming common knowledge."

"I see," the captain said. "In that case, I'll be on Deck Seventeen if you need me." He looked down at Cadwallader again, managing a smile. "You do everything the doctor tells you," he advised. "I want you up and about in time for the ceremony on Daa'V."

Cadwallader's eyes smiled back at him.

When the call for Picard came up from sickbay, a chill played along Riker's spine. And when Dr. Crusher subtly declined to discuss the matter in public, the first officer's fears were pretty much confirmed.

There had been another attempt on Morgen's life. And as before, someone had gotten hurt. But who? Had the assassin been injured in the course of being apprehended? Or was there another victim—maybe even a fatality?

Of course, Deanna was as much in the dark as he was. She wasn't a mindreader—not as a full-blooded Betazoid would have been. She could only gauge emotions—and neither the captain's nor Crusher's were telling her anything instructive.

On the other hand, someone had to look after the ship. So he and Deanna remained on the bridge, striving to remain calm—trying not to exchange too many worried glances.

In the past, when they were in trouble, Riker had been able to take solace in the celestial beauty captured on the viewscreen. But now, with the starpaths stretched as taut as tightropes—reminders of the slipstream that was propelling them toward who-knew-what—even that option was closed to him. He almost wished that Geordi's engineering team hadn't gotten the damned thing working again.

It seemed like years before they heard from Picard. And though his voice was well under control, the nature of his request only aggravated their misgivings: "Commander Riker. Counselor Troi. Avail yourselves of my ready room, please. I would like to have a word with you."

Getting up from the captain's chair, the first officer escorted the empath to the captain's private office. Since Picard wasn't actually inside, there was no need to wait until their presence was acknowledged. Instead, they walked right in.

Riker looked up at the intercom grid. "We're in your ready room, sir. What's happening down there?"

"Nothing good, Will. There's been another attack, as you probably guessed. A *phaser* attack. Cadwallader's been hurt."

Riker felt his throat constrict. "How badly, sir?"

"She'll recover completely, Dr. Crusher tells me—though it'll be a few days before she's ready to leave sickbay. And a couple more than that before her tissues have fully regenerated." A pause. "She was hit with a phaser beam at setting-six intensity."

The first officer gritted his teeth. At setting six, a phaser beam could punch a hole in duranium. Cadwallader was lucky she was even alive.

"Where and when was she attacked?" Deanna Troi asked.

"Deck Seventeen," Picard answered. "She was with Morgen and Dr. Crusher, in one of the lounges, when we tried to outrun the slipstream. The killer took advantage of the power blackout to try again. Morgen and Dr. Crusher escaped without injury, but Cadwallader was not so fortunate."

Riker bit back his anger. "Did they get a look at the assassin?"

The captain's sigh was audible. "They did not. However, Mr. Worf is engaged in an analysis of the scene now. Perhaps he will turn up some clues as to the killer's identity. In fact, that is where I am headed once our discussion is over."

"Is there anything we can do?" the first officer asked.

"Not right now, Number One—you are needed on the bridge. I just thought you should know what happened."

"Thank you, sir," Riker said.

Picard didn't reply. Apparently, he had already started out for Deck Seventeen. In the silence, the first officer turned to the ship's counselor.

"Rotten news," she commented.

He nodded. Right about then he should have said something clever and optimistic—"silver linings" kind of stuff. That would have been characteristic of him.

But somehow, he didn't feel like it. All he could think about was Cadwallader, and how she might have died without ever knowing why he'd canceled their dinner. It was sort of maudlin—but hell, it was the way he *felt.*

He desperately wanted to see her. To sit down at her bedside and explain. But he couldn't. The captain had left specific instructions that he was to remain on the bridge.

"Will?"

Abruptly, he remembered that Deanna was standing in front of him. He'd been staring right past her.

"Sorry," he said. "I've got a lot on my mind."

She smiled—half sadly, he thought. "You care for her, don't you?"

He started to ask to whom she was referring—and then stopped himself. Denying something to Deanna was like denying it to himself.

"Yes," he told her. "I guess I do."

There was a time when he would have felt funny admitting that to her—a time when their own relationship was too fresh in their minds for them to talk about other lovers. But things had changed between them—for the better, as far as he was concerned.

"Now I understand," she said.

"Understand what?"

"The feelings I have been sensing in you lately. The conflicts. As long as Cadwallader was a suspect, you had to submerge your feelings for the sake of the investigation."

He said, "I had to break a date with her. It was one of the hardest things I've ever done—believe it or not."

"I believe it," she told him.

Riker looked at the empath. "Deanna, be careful out there, all right? If this could happen to Cadwallader . . ."

She put a hand on his shoulder—a gesture of reassurance. "I am a big girl," she told him, grinning. "But thanks all the same."

And gently but firmly she steered him toward the door.

Worf turned as the turbolift doors opened, cursing inwardly. He had programmed the lift to bypass this floor until their investigation was over.

Then he saw the captain come out into the corridor, and he realized that his order had been overridden by one of the few individuals on the ship capable of doing so. Nor did he have any problem with that—the bypass would be back in place as soon as the doors closed behind Picard.

He squared his shoulders as the captain approached, making his way through the crowd of security personnel carefully analyzing the assault from all angles. "Sir," said Worf.

Picard gazed with distaste at the phaser burns on the bulkheads—samples of which were being taken by Burke and Resnick. Then he turned his attention to the Klingon. "At ease, Lieutenant." He took a deep breath, let it out through his nostrils. "Anything to report—beyond the obvious, that is?"

The security chief extracted the phaser from his belt and handed it over. Picard's eyes narrowed as he accepted it.

"The weapon used in the assault," Worf explained, though it was all but unnecessary. "As we suspected, its communications module has been disabled." He paused. "We found it in a refuse bin about twenty meters forward of here. Apparently, the assassin did not want to take a chance that it would turn up in a room search—but was in too much of a hurry to decompose it."

The captain examined the phaser for a moment. Slowly, his eyes widened. "Lieutenant—this phaser—"

Worf nodded. "It is one of ours. Stolen from the security section."

Picard regarded him. "How could that have happened?"

The Klingon looked past him, trying to contain his shame. "Loyosha—the officer on duty—was found unconscious shortly after the attack. He was drugged—something in his food, I believe. It appears he was eating his dinner when he passed out. Of course, it is only a theory. We have secured the remainder of the food so it can be tested."

The captain frowned and returned the phaser. Worf replaced it on his belt. "Where did Loyosha's meal come from? The food service unit outside Security?"

"That is the most likely possibility," the Klingon confirmed. "We have secured the unit as well."

Picard nodded. "Good." He started to walk along the corridor, away from the main focus of activity, in the direction from which the attack had come. He would, of course, have been able to tell that from the phaser scars on the bulkheads. Worf walked along with him, silent at first.

Finally, the security chief swallowed. "Sir?"

"Yes, Worf." The captain wasn't looking at him. He was looking back and forth from one end of the corridor to the other, apparently trying to satisfy himself as to some aspect of the attack.

"Sir," said the Klingon, "if the food service unit was tampered with, it is my fault. I insist on taking full responsibility for the incident."

The captain turned to him. He had a strange look in his eyes—as if Worf's comment had struck some kind of chord.

"Lieutenant," the older man said finally, "we are dealing with someone who has an extraordinary grasp of this ship's systems. Considering the unit's proximity to Security, I am certain the assassin did not reprogram it in person. And if he—" He paused. "Or *she* reprogrammed it from afar, I am certain even Mr. La Forge would be hard pressed to say *how*."

Worf scowled. "Nonetheless—"

Picard dismissed the idea with a wave of his hand. "Nonetheless *nothing*. You have more important things to do than waste time on self-recrimination. Do I make myself clear?"

The Klingon straightened, feeling appropriately chastised. "Aye, sir," he said.

"Now take me through this assault as you've reconstructed it. And don't leave out any details."

Worf nodded. "As you wish."

The critical-care area was off limits to all nonmedical personnel, with the exception of Picard, Riker, and Worf. Those were the orders Crusher had left when she'd gone to her office, in order to more closely analyze the vital-sign readings she'd taken from Cadwallader.

Simple. In retrospect, *too* simple.

She'd forgotten that Carter Greyhorse was a medical officer, and that none of her doctors and nurses—who knew only half Cadwallader's story themselves—would have a reason to keep the high-ranking visitor out.

So when Crusher returned to critical care, satisfied that the patient was safe from any serious complications, there was her former colleague—hovering massively over Cadwallader's unconscious form, one huge hand brushing a stray lock of hair off her forehead. Before she could say anything—after all, what *could* she say?—Greyhorse had sensed her presence and turned around.

She had never seen him display much emotion. But she saw it now. His eyes blazed beneath lowered brows.

"Damn it," he said. "Why didn't you *tell* me about this, Beverly?"

Crusher shrugged. "It happened just a few minutes ago. And we don't normally bring in visitors to help with patient care."

He struck the biobed—hard. "When it comes to Cadwallader, I am *not* just a visitor. I've put a lot of effort into this woman over the years. When she's hurt, I want to know about it."

"I'll take that under advisement," Crusher told him, stiffening under his barrage. Then she remembered the circumstances, and she forced herself to take a gentler approach. "I know how you feel, Carter. She's your friend—"

"She's *more* than my friend," Greyhorse said. He glanced back at Cadwallader. "At Maxia, we had taken some direct hits. Sickbay was a mess—fires all over. And debris—I was pinned under some of it. It was nearly impossible for me to get out—or for anyone else to get in." A pause. *"She* refused to leave—at least until she knew if I was alive or dead. Cadwallader and Picard and a few others stayed behind while the shuttles were taking off. Finally, she found me—cut me free of the wreckage just before sickbay became a bloody inferno. And with some help hauled me onto the last shuttle. By then I'd lost consciousness—too much smoke inhalation." He turned back to Crusher. "If not for Cadwallader, I would have died a pretty grisly death."

"I didn't know," said Crusher.

Greyhorse cleared his throat, a little embarrassed. "Now you do." He tilted his head to indicate the patient. *"Phaser* burns? Where in God's name did she get *those?"*

Crusher cursed inwardly. Too late, she looked up at the monitor above the bed, which had a full display of Cadwallader's tissue damage. Any doctor worth his salt could tell the molecular disruption patterns had been caused by a phaser beam.

There was no point in lying. Greyhorse was good; he would see through any explanation she could make up.

"Come on back into my office," she told him. "It's a long story."

Geordi shook his head. "This is crazy. Absolutely crazy. As if the slipstream wasn't trouble *enough!"*

Picard's intercom voice was ominous: "Keep an eye out in your section, Commander. If this killer of ours is as enterprising as he seems, and as adept at engineering . . ."

"I get the picture, Captain."

"Good. Picard out."

Geordi regarded Data, who was sitting on the other side of the chief engineer's desk. He took a deep breath, let it out. "It's getting scary," he told the android.

Data looked apologetic. "Intellectually," he said, "I recognize the concept. However, as I am myself incapable of fear, I cannot share the feeling."

Geordi grunted. "No need to be sorry about that. Right now it's important we keep our heads. No matter *who's* getting shot at—or sabotaged in the holodecks."

He regarded Wesley and Simenon through the transparent wall of his office. They looked as tired as he felt—particularly the Gnalish. With his snappy sense of humor and his alien appearance, it was easy to forget that he was verging on elderly. But a few days' worth of theoretical headbanging had made him start to look his age.

One thing he knew, at least, was that Simenon hadn't been responsible for the phaser attack. The Gnalish had been with him during the power dip and every moment thereafter.

Unless he had an accomplice . . .

"Should we not join the others?" Data prompted. "They will be wondering what is keeping us."

"I was just thinking," Geordi told him. If there was *more* than one person involved in the murder attempts . . . a *conspiracy . . .*

Simenon could have arranged the holodeck incident—and left the phaser attack to someone else. Maybe the Gnalish was able to get a signal to his co-conspirator that a blackout was in the offing, and that it would be a good time to take another shot at Morgen. Maybe—

"Nah," he said out loud. Why look for a complicated solution when it was most likely a solo operation? It was hard enough to believe *one* person was nutty enough to want to kill Morgen—much less *two*.

"Nah?" echoed the android.

Geordi smiled. "Just discarding a theory, Data. Nothing to be concerned about." He got up. "Come on. Maybe we can finish those subspace field calculations before I conk out completely."

Data looked at him in that puzzled sort of way. He was doing that less and less these days—but the engineering chief must have hit on a colloquialism with which the android wasn't yet familiar.

"Conk out," La Forge repeated. "As in stop due to lack of sleep."

As understanding registered on his face, Data rose too and followed Geordi out of his office.

Picard had never been more grateful for his ready room. Right now he needed time. Time to think. Time to absorb the sights of Cadwallader stretched out on a biobed and the corridors of deck seventeen blackened with phaser fire.

Time to put aside Worf's insistence on claiming responsibility—which had sounded so much like Pug's comments twenty years before, after another, equally horrible occurrence. . . .

In a little while he would return to his command chair. He would exude confidence. He would inspire others.

But not just now. For a moment at least he would lean back and close his eyes and try to obtain some perspective on the whole bloody mess.

Obviously, Cadwallader was no longer a suspect. The captain had read enough Dixon Hill stories to know that a murderer might injure himself to avoid suspicion—but Cad had been hurt too badly for him to believe that. And besides, the phaser had been in someone else's hands; both Beverly and Morgen had sworn to it.

Picard chewed the inside of his cheek. He couldn't help but feel that he was overlooking something. That there was a clue huddling in some dark corner of his brain, waiting only for him to shed some light on it.

I should know who is doing this, he told himself. *I was their captain, for godsakes. I should have some insight into them.*

Indeed, how could he ask Worf or Will to find the killer when *he* couldn't? Who knew Idun and Pug and the others better than Jean-Luc Picard?

The answer welled up unbidden. *Jack.* Jack Crusher knew them better than their captain—better even than their own mothers, in some cases.

Yes. Jack would have known who was trying to kill Morgen. People had trusted him with secrets they entrusted to no one else. After all, how could anyone with that earnest, well-scrubbed farmboy face be capable of betrayal?

And in an uncomfortable way, the captain had been jealous of that quality in his friend—hadn't he? Picard shook his head. He hadn't thought of that for a long time—his envy of Jack Crusher.

It had never gotten in the way of their friendship, certainly. Nor had Jack ever known about it. But there was something in the young Jean-Luc Picard—the one who had taken command of the *Stargazer* with somewhat less assurance than he'd let on—that yearned to be loved the way Jack Crusher was loved. Not just respected or admired, but *loved*.

In time, of course, he had gotten over that. And it was precisely then that he realized he *was* loved—though in a slightly different way. People seemed to have an affection for Jack the first time they met him. In the captain's case, love was something earned over the course of days and months and years.

And who was to say which kind of love was better? Certainly not Jean-Luc Picard, for whom affairs of the heart were still more dark and terrifying in some respects than the farthest reaches of the unknown.

The captain gazed at the empty chair opposite him. *Ah, Jack . . .*

For a moment Picard imagined his friend sitting on the other side of the ready room desk, his long body folded up into the most businesslike posture he could manage.

"A problem, Jean-Luc?"

The captain nodded. *"A big one,"* he confirmed.

"Anything I can help with?"

Picard sighed. *"There is a killer on board, Jack. One of our friends—and he or she is after Morgen."*

Jack's features took on a more serious aspect. *"Trying to accomplish what Gerda couldn't."*

"Exactly. And I haven't a clue as to which of them it is."

His friend nodded grimly. *"When you have problems, you don't fool around."*

"There's an answer, Jack. I know there is. I just wish I knew where to find it."

Jack appeared to want to say something—as if he had the answer to the riddle. As if he knew who the killer was. But in the end, he couldn't get it out. All he could do was shrug.

"It's all right," Picard said.

"I'm sorry," Jack whispered at last.

"No." The captain regarded his friend, missing him more than ever. *"Really. It's all right."*

Suddenly, the chair was empty again, though Picard wished mightily it were otherwise.

Eleven

Riker had wanted to come before this, but he couldn't exactly leave the bridge in the middle of his shift to pursue personal matters. As he entered sickbay, he caught sight of Dr. Crusher.

She was just emerging from behind the critical-care barrier—the one that separated Cadwallader's biobed from the rest of the facility. Noting his presence, Crusher regarded him. "Something I can do for you, Commander?"

"Yes," Riker said, "there is." He indicated the barrier. "I was hoping to visit with our guest."

The doctor frowned slightly. "She's sleeping now. She really shouldn't be disturbed."

His first impulse was to protest—but he subdued it, knowing it wouldn't do him any good. Beverly Crusher could be pretty stubborn when it came to protecting her patients' interests.

Besides, if Cadwallader needed her sleep, who was he to deprive her of it? His explanation of what had happened the other night could wait.

"If you need to know anything about what happened," Crusher told him, "you can ask me."

It took him a second or two to figure out what she was talking about. He shook his head. "No. Nothing like that. I just wanted to see how she was."

Crusher looked at him for a moment—and she seemed to understand. "Oh," she said. "In that case, why don't you come back a little later?"

He nodded. "I'll do that." A second thought. "Would it be okay if I just peeked in on her?"

The doctor thought about it. "I suppose that I can allow that," she decided finally. There was a twinkle in her eye as she said it.

The first officer smiled. "Thank you." And under Crusher's scrutiny, he advanced to the barrier.

Sticking his head around the side of it, he peered inside. As the doctor had informed him, Cadwallader was asleep. But her face was turned in his direction.

Riker sighed. To tell the truth, he had expected worse. But it was still something of a shock to see her lying there wan and weak-looking, when she had been spinning around a horizontal bar not so long ago.

"Commander . . . ?"

He turned and saw Crusher standing behind him. "I know, Doctor. I know." Reluctantly, he retreated from the barrier.

"Perhaps," she suggested, "I could let her know you were asking for her."

"I'd appreciate that," he told her.

As they walked back toward the center of sickbay, Crusher looked up at the first officer. "There's no need for worry," she said. "Actually, our patient is doing quite well."

He nodded. "That's good to hear, Doctor."

But he would continue to worry—and not just about Cadwallader.

There were the rest of the *Stargazer* survivors to consider as well. . . .

Data sat in engineering, going over computation after computation in his positronic brain. He had been engaged in this activity ever since Geordi had sent everyone on the crisis team to bed.

"No sense in killing ourselves," the chief engineer had said. "We'll be able to think a little straighter in the morning."

Simenon had agreed. Wesley too, though reluctantly.

But Data needed no sleep. So when Geordi and the others left for their quarters, he remained. And hours later he was still there.

Unfortunately, he hadn't gotten very far. There were too many variables in his equations, too many unknowns. If only he had a better understanding of subspace dynamics . . .

"Pardon me."

The android turned at the sound and saw Dr. Greyhorse standing behind him. The man shrugged his large shoulders.

"I guess everybody's called it quits for the evening."

"On the contrary," Data responded, swiveling around in his seat. *"I* am still here. Therefore, not *everybody* has called it quits."

Greyhorse's eyes crinkled slightly at the corners. "Right you are, Commander. Your logic is impeccable." He looked around. "But everyone *else* has called it quits—yes?"

"That is true," Data replied.

The doctor pulled up a chair and sat down heavily. "Too bad. I was hoping to lend a hand."

"In what way?" the android asked, curious now.

Greyhorse shrugged again. "You know. With this damned slipstream problem we've run into. I come from a long line of engineers, and I've had some training in the field myself. I just thought that I might be of service."

"I see," Data said. "I apologize. I did not know of your engineering background."

"It's all right. No one does, really."

"Are you familiar with the problem?" the android asked.

"Not exactly." Greyhorse chuckled dryly. "Or to be more blunt about it, hardly at all. I just know that we're caught up in a subspace phenomenon that's affecting our velocity."

Data nodded. "Allow me to give you a more detailed picture."

And for the next half hour, that's just what he did. For the doctor's part, he listened intently, interrupting only once or twice when he needed something explained in greater detail. Toward the end of the briefing, he didn't interrupt at all—a fact which Data took as a token of Greyhorse's increasing understanding. As it turned out, he was right.

As soon as Data was finished, the man began to rattle off suggestions. Good ones too. But they had all been suggested—and rejected—already. And of course, Data was forced to say so. After a while Greyhorse's enthusiasm began to wind down; he began to run dry of ideas.

"Lord," he said, "I guess I was right to go into medicine after all. I wouldn't have made a very good engineer."

"On the contrary," the android told him, "your suggestions were quite good. The fact that they were made already is a tribute to your ability, not a condemnation of it." He saw Greyhorse's expression take on new life. "Remember, Doctor, three of the finest engineering minds in the Federation could not do any better."

The man looked at him. "Three? Who are you excluding, Data—not yourself, I trust?"

"I do not consider myself highly skilled in the area of engineering," the android explained. "A good engineer, as I have been told time and again, is one part knowledge and two parts intuition. I certainly qualify in terms of knowledge, but intuition is one of my weak points."

Greyhorse shook his head. "You know, Data, there's intuition and there's intuition. My relatives would fit your great-engineer model to a T. They're intuitive as hell—when it comes to machines, at least. But put them in a room with other humans and they have as much intuition as the furniture. Same with me, I'm afraid. I never wanted to be like them, but . . . well, you know the saying. The apple doesn't fall far from the tree. I'm a whiz when it comes to dealing with people's bodies.

But when it comes to dealing with their minds—dealing with them as people—I'm a zero. A *robot.*" He smiled. "You, on the other hand, appear to be a machine. You *believe* yourself to be a machine. But trust me on this, Data. You're more human—more intuitive in many respects—than the entire Greyhorse clan put together."

The android found that hard to believe. He said so.

"You haven't met the Greyhorse clan," the doctor pointed out.

"No," Data agreed. "But I have met *you.* And you do not seem to be lacking in positive human qualities."

The doctor peered at him from beneath the ridge of his brow. "Appearances can be deceiving, Commander. Deep down I am a very uncaring person. You need an example?"

The android didn't quite know what to say.

"I'll give you one anyway," Greyhorse offered. He leaned closer. "I know about the attack on Tricia Cadwallader. I walked into sickbay and saw her lying there, and your Dr. Crusher told me the whole story."

Data was surprised, given the captain's orders to keep the assassination attempts secret. However, he didn't interrupt. He merely filed the information away for future consideration.

"I know," the doctor continued, "and yet I cannot really say I feel for Commander Cadwallader. Oh, I am concerned on a professional level—I have as much pride in my work as the next surgeon, and I hate to see it marred or mucked up. But as far as my feelings for Cadwallader the individual—the person with whom I worked closely for years and years—I find I have none. The fact of her injuries leaves me cold as clay."

Data cocked his head as he so often did when comprehension eluded him. "But what about your efforts regarding the slipstream?" he asked. "Did you not say you came to help?"

Greyhorse waved the suggestion away with his large, meaty hand. "Self-preservation, my friend. Nothing more, nothing less. If the ship is lost or destroyed, so am I. And I prefer to survive—to return to Starfleet Medical, where I can go on with my charade: the humane and dedicated healer."

He got up. Data watched him, trying to make sense of what the doctor had said.

"Sorry I couldn't be of more help, Commander. If anything comes to me, I'll let you know." He paused. "Oh, and . . . I'd appreciate it if you didn't mention my visit to Professor Simenon. He'd only mock me. You know, for overstepping my professional bounds."

"I understand," the android assured him.

"You see?" Greyhorse said. "You really *are* more human."

Then he left.

The captain was still sitting in his ready room, still thinking, when the sound of chimes interrupted his reverie. Someone out on the bridge wanted to see him. Picard looked to the room's only entrance, wondered briefly who might be out there. Then, reluctantly, he straightened in preparation for *whoever* it was.

"Come," said the captain.

The doors opened.

It was Ben Zoma. And he did not look very happy.

"Have a seat," said Picard.

His former first officer sat down on the opposite side of the captain's desk. It was a familiar position for both of them; they'd conversed this way on the *Stargazer* hundreds of times.

But this is not the Stargazer, the captain had to remind himself. And Ben Zoma was no longer his exec. What had his life been like for the past decade? Could he have changed enough to become a killer?

"Jean-Luc," began the olive-skinned man, no longer his usual jovial self. "I want some answers. And I want them now."

Picard met his gaze. "What sort of answers, Gilaad?"

Ben Zoma leaned back in his chair. "Where is Cadwallader? And don't tell me you don't know. She doesn't answer my intercom calls. And when I went to her quarters, there was no answer there either."

The captain decided to be truthful—if only up to a point.

"She is in sickbay," he said. He watched for his friend's reaction, hoping to discern something that would give away Ben Zoma's guilt. And at the same time, hoping even more fiercely *not* to.

"Sickbay," echoed the other man, suddenly concerned. And as far as Picard could tell, the concern was quite genuine. "Is she all right? What happened?"

Here came the lie. It didn't exactly emerge trippingly from his lips.

"During the engine shutdown, emergency life support short-circuited on Deck Seventeen, causing an explosion in the ventilator shaft. An air vent blew out; Cadwallader was in the wrong place at the wrong time."

It *could* have happened that way. In fact, Geordi swore he'd actually *seen* an accident just like it—years ago, back on the *Hood.*

Ben Zoma nodded, taking it in. "And Cadwallader?"

"She's fine," said Picard. "Some minor surgery, that's all. She could probably be up and about tomorrow, though Dr. Crusher will no doubt want to keep an eye on her a little longer."

Ben Zoma nodded again. The skin between his brows crinkled.

"You know," he said, "when you serve under a man for almost twenty years, you come to know him pretty well. You know when he's tired, or frustrated, or saddened. Even a man like *you,* Jean-Luc—one who hides his feelings well." He leaned forward, not so much angry as hurt. "And you know when he's lying through his teeth. You, my friend, are lying through your teeth."

"Indeed."

"That's right. As I told your Counselor Troi, there's something happening on the *Enterprise*—something you're not telling us about. The beefed-up security, the holodecks being out of order . . . and Morgen's sudden inclination toward solitude. And now Cadwallader." He shook his head. "You can't tell me that you're not hiding something."

The situation dictated that Picard carry on the charade—that he continue to suspect Ben Zoma along with the others. But his instincts told him otherwise. And a starship captain, he had learned early on in his career, had to ultimately follow his instincts.

He took a deep breath. "You are quite correct," he told his friend. "I am lying. In fact, Cadwallader was wounded by a phaser blast. And Morgen has become a hermit at my request—after he nearly lost his life in a sabotaged holodeck."

Ben Zoma was silent for a second. Then he said: "Details. Please."

Picard sketched out the situation for him. By the time he was done, the man's eyes had narrowed to slits.

"So you see," the captain said, "someone is trying to kill Morgen. And more than likely, the assassin is one of *us.*"

Ben Zoma frowned. "I wish I could disagree with you." A pause. "Do you think it was Idun?"

"Personally," said Picard, "no. It's too obvious—especially after the way she has alienated herself from the group. Though I am sure the assassin would like us to *believe* Idun is guilty."

"Obvious or not, she's the only one with a clear motive," Ben Zoma pointed out. "Revenge for her sister's death."

"Commander Riker came up with another one—the completion of Gerda's mission."

Muscles rippled beneath the other man's graying temples. "I hadn't thought of that—but he's right."

Picard shook his head. "No. I still think Idun is innocent."

"A hunch?" asked Ben Zoma.

"If you like."

"You can't operate on hunches, Jean-Luc. Not in a matter like this one."

The captain smiled grimly. "It was a hunch, Gilaad, that led me to trust *you.*"

Ben Zoma smiled back. "Good point," he said.

Picard recalled something else from the meeting in the observation lounge. "Tell me about your mission to Daa'V. You were with Pug and Cadwallader, delivering medicines, as I understand it?"

The dark man looked surprised at the seeming non sequitur. "Yes. Decacyclene. The Daa'Vit were hit hard by Marionis syndrome, a virus that originated on Marionis Six—" He stopped as he saw what Picard was getting at. "You want to know if we came in contact with anyone opposed to Morgen's return. And if they could have influenced one of us."

"Exactly."

Ben Zoma shrugged, his eyes glazing over as he gave the proposition some thought. "There were those who asked after Morgen—but no one who actually came out for or against him. Not in my presence, anyway. And as far as influencing the others . . ." He shook his head. "I couldn't vouch for all the medical personnel—you'd have to ask my chief medical officer about that. But Cadwallader and Pug hardly left my side while we were down there. I doubt anyone could have tampered with them in any way."

The captain looked at him. "In Pug's case, it might not take much tampering at all." He chose his words carefully. "Gilaad . . . you see him on a daily basis. Has his resentment gone so far that it would make him want to kill?"

Ben Zoma answered without even thinking. "He's resentful, all right. And in some ways—small ways—it has affected his performance. Certainly, his drinking doesn't help in that regard either. You've seen how he puts away the synthehol."

Picard nodded.

"But I would bet my life that Pug has nothing to do with these murder attempts. Down deep, he's a gentle man. He always *was* a gentle man."

The captain sighed. "All true. But *someone* has designs on Morgen's life. And if it's not you or Cad or Pug . . ."

"I know," Ben Zoma said. "It's hard to imagine Simenon or Greyhorse practicing violence. And if Idun is innocent, as you say, that doesn't leave a huge number of suspects, does it?"

Picard looked at him. "No. It doesn't."

Ben Zoma spread his hands. "I wish I could be of more help, Jean-Luc. I really do."

For a fleeting moment he resembled Picard's vision of Jack Crusher. The captain blinked.

"That's all right," the captain assured him—just as he had assured Jack. "Eventually, I suppose, we will find the person we're looking for. I just hope Morgen survives until then." He squared his shoulders. "In the meantime, Gilaad, not a word of this to anyone. Not even Morgen or Cadwallader."

"You've got my word," said Ben Zoma. He stood. "And thank you."

Picard was genuinely confused. "For what?"

"For having enough trust in me to confide all this."

The captain nodded. "Just do me one favor."

"What's that?" asked Ben Zoma.

"Don't turn out to be the murderer."

His friend nodded. "It's a deal," he said.

Just then Beverly Crusher's voice came over the intercom. "Captain Picard?"

"Here, Doctor. One moment, please." He looked at Ben Zoma meaningfully.

"You want me to leave?" asked the other man.

"I do."

"But I already know what's going on. And it might be news about Cad."

"If it is," the captain assured him, "I'll let you know."

Ben Zoma frowned. "All right," he said finally. "It's your ship. I suppose you can conduct your investigations any way you like."

Reluctantly, the former first officer of the *Stargazer* got up and left. The ready room doors closed silently behind him.

Looking up, Picard addressed the intercom grid. "Sorry, Doctor. I had some company."

"I understand. In fact, I had some myself a few moments ago."

"Really."

"Yes. Greyhorse." She took a deep breath—so deep it was audible over the intercom system. "Captain, I told him what was going on. He barged into sickbay and saw Cadwallader and—and it was pretty obvious what had happened to her. At that point it made more sense for him to know than to have him asking a lot of questions all over the ship."

Picard cursed inwardly. If he'd been aware of this, he'd never have—

"Sir?"

"Doctor . . . our friend Greyhorse is not the *only* one who knows. I just let Ben Zoma in on the details myself."

For a second or two, Crusher was silent. "Well," she said, "it seems our secret is no longer as secret as we would like."

"That much is certain. I think it's time we had another meeting. I'll see you in the conference lounge in ten minutes."

"Aye, sir."

The captain stood. He could feel matters getting out of hand.

It was time to rein them in.

Twelve

Picard looked around the table—at Riker, Troi, Worf, and Crusher. "And so," he said, "I take full responsibility for my decision to confide in Captain Ben Zoma—just as Dr. Crusher takes responsibility for confiding in Carter Greyhorse. But I do not want anyone else let in on this—not under any circumstances."

"It's going to get harder and harder to keep it under wraps," Riker pointed out. "If Ben Zoma noticed, others will too."

Troi nodded. "Ben Zoma said as much."

"Nonetheless," the captain insisted, "we will do everything we can to maintain security. Any questions?"

There were none.

"Very well, then. Let us turn to our investigation. Counselor Troi?"

"Unfortunately," the empath said, "I have nothing of substance to report. A couple of our visitors—specifically Asmund and Joseph—have problems. But none I could point to as a prerequisite for murder."

Picard turned to Worf. "Lieutenant—your findings."

Worf scowled. "We analyzed the meal eaten by Loyosha just prior to his losing consciousness. As we suspected, it was laced with a narcotic that induces sleep. The source of the meal was the food service unit near security—which was programmed to include this narcotic in three of Loyosha's favorite dishes." He looked at Picard. "The unit showed no signs of tampering, sir. So it must have been reprogrammed from another location—just as you suggested."

"Reprogrammed from another location?" Riker whistled softly. "Our assassin's grasp of technology gets more impressive all the time."

Picard grunted. "What about the rest of your inquiry?" he asked Worf.

The Klingon's scowl deepened. "I personally traced the whereabouts of each visitor at the time of the blackout. Morgen and Cadwallader, as we know, were with Dr. Crusher. Professor Simenon was in engineering with Commanders Data and La Forge. Captain Ben Zoma, Dr. Greyhorse, Commander Asmund, and Chief Joseph were in their quarters. At least, that is the information recorded by the computer, based on the locations of the suspects' communicators."

"But," Riker reminded them, "it's a simple matter to remove one's communicator. Then one need not worry about being located—either at the moment of the crime or later on."

The captain nodded. "But thank you, Lieutenant. It was worth a try." He regarded the others. "Suggestions?"

No one seemed to have any.

"Are we beaten that easily?" he asked. "Perhaps we should just concede defeat now and get it over with."

That seemed to shake them up a bit.

Picard stood. "I do not care what it takes," he insisted. "I want this would-be assassin found. Before he becomes an assassin in *fact.*"

He scanned the faces at the table. For a moment he could have sworn Jack Crusher's was among them. Then he looked again, and Jack was gone.

Steadying himself, the captain said: "This meeting is adjourned."

The holodeck doors opened on a majestic scarlet forest shot through with long shafts of golden sunlight. Wesley took a step inside, applying his weight to the seemingly mosslike substance that covered the open spaces between the trees. It was springy underfoot—so springy, in fact, that it was difficult to keep his balance. But after a few more steps, he found the way to negotiate it was to bounce along instead of trying to resist it.

The Gnalish wasn't immediately visible, but there seemed to be a path full of the springy stuff that cut the forest in two. Half walking and half bouncing, Wesley followed it, shading his eyes when the sunbeams got in them.

It was still along the path, windless and empty of animal life. No doubt, his presence had sent all the earthbound creatures scurrying into the bushes.

But it hadn't done anything to hamper the activity above him. Small flying things darted from branch to branch, looking carefree and idyllic. They weren't a whole lot different from the birds Wesley remembered from his childhood on Earth—though no Terran bird ever made those deep-throated sounds, or shed so many feathers as it flew.

Smiling, the ensign watched the flight of one feather as it descended directly in front of him. It glistened in the sun, dark purple around its stem and green at its fringes. Intrigued, Wesley knelt to pick it up—and drew his hand back quickly as he felt the prick of something sharp. Examining his finger, he saw a bead of blood at the tip.

"If we were really on Gnala," said a voice, "you would have about twenty seconds to make peace with your gods."

Wesley jumped at the sound. He'd been so intent on the feather, he'd forgotten that he wasn't alone in the holodeck. Turning, he saw the Gnalish sitting with his back against a tree trunk, his scarlet robes exactly the same color as the foliage.

"I didn't mean to scare you," Simenon said, getting to his feet. "It just occurred to me that you might find a little background information interesting. Including what's poisonous and what's not."

The ensign looked at the feather in a fresh light. "It's so pretty. It's hard to believe it's harmful."

"Appearances can be deceiving." The Gnalish smoothed out his robe. "There's an antidote, of course—but you would have to have taken it in advance. Once you've been pricked, it's too late." He shaded his eyes and pointed to the flying things among the branches overhead. "That's how they secure their sustenance. They wait until an animal brushes against a feather and is incapacitated by the poison. Then they descend and pick it apart. Quick workers too. Usually, they can clean a carcass before the poison shuts down the victim's brain."

It wasn't a pretty image. Wesley shuddered involuntarily, imagining a path full of tiny four-legged skeletons.

"Of course," Simenon went on, "the poison doesn't affect the *columnu*—the flyers. They have a natural immunity to it."

Wesley let go of the feather. He watched it waft to the mossy ground. "I'm glad," he said, "that you decided to leave a few details out of your program."

The Gnalish grunted. "So am I. Back on Gnala, I used to have to wear thick boots to go for a walk in the woods." He picked up the hem of his robe. "Here, I can go au naturel."

Wesley looked at Simenon's feet. For the first time, he realized that the Gnalish was barefoot.

"So, young man, have you followed me in here for a reason? Or just to chat?"

Wesley smiled, a little embarrassed. "Geordi—I mean Commander La Forge—wanted me to make sure you were all right. You didn't show up in engineering this morning."

"If I was all right?" Now it was Simenon's turn to smile. "He could have found that out over the intercom. Commander La Forge just wonders what I'm doing in this holodeck when we have a problem to solve."

The ensign nodded. "I guess that's another way of putting it."

"And to solve a problem," the Gnalish went on, "we must stand around the master situations monitor, looking ominously at one another."

Wesley winced. "I don't think that's *exactly—*"

Simenon dismissed the notion with a wave of his hand. "It's all right. You need not defend your Commander La Forge. At his age, I would probably have approached it the same way." He regarded the ensign. "However, I am older and wiser now. And I know that the best way to approach a problem, sometimes, is to forget about it entirely." He indicated the scarlet forest with a sweeping gesture. "To play a little hooky, as your Earth expression goes."

He began to walk down the path. Wesley just watched him, not knowing exactly what to do. Should he continue to badger the Gnalish? Or consider his mission completed and return to engineering?

Suddenly, Simenon turned around. "Well?" he asked. "Are you coming or not?"

The ensign hesitated for a moment. "Me?" he repeated lamely.

The professor snorted. "I don't see anyone else standing there."

What the hell, thought Wesley. It wouldn't hurt to take a break—just a short one. He started after Simenon.

"That's better," said the Gnalish.

"Where are we going?" asked Wes.

"Down to the lake. Where else?"

It wasn't very far. A couple of twists in the path, and they were there, the water reflecting the splendor of the trees that towered all around it.

Simenon stopped in the vicinity of a small pile of stones—one which he had gathered some time before, apparently, or else simply programmed into the scene. Abruptly, without a word to his companion, he knelt, his ruby eyes darting around until they fixed on something a meter or so away. Using his tail to sweep the ground, he brought his find closer to him—and when it was close enough, picked it up with his fingers.

Another stone. The Gnalish examined it. But after a second or two, he tossed it away. Watching the whole strange scenario, Wesley couldn't help but chuckle. It seemed so funny for an Academy professor to be squatting barefoot and scavenging for rocks.

"What are you laughing at?" asked Simenon, abruptly indignant. "It takes time to select the right specimens." Holding yet another one up at eye level, he turned it around, inspecting it from various angles.

"The right specimens?" the ensign echoed. "Right for *what?*"

The Gnalish put the stone down in the pile and began to scrutinize another.

"For skimming, of course."

Wesley looked at him. "What's *skimming?*"

That got the Gnalish's attention; he looked up. "You mean you don't know?"

The ensign shrugged. "Should I?"

Simenon looked at him as if he'd just eaten one of the rocks. *"Should* you? Of course you should. Weren't there any lakes where you grew up?"

Wesley thought about it. "I . . . I guess so. But that was when I was really young. I've spent a lot of time on starships since my mom joined Starfleet."

The Gnalish looked a little sad—or was that the ensign's imagination? "You mean," he said, "you've never skimmed a rock? That's absurd! Every youngster skims rocks." He shook his serpentine head. "Well, we'll have to rectify that gap in your education right now."

He picked up one of the rocks he'd put in the pile—a small round one with one flat side. Aligning one of its edges with the inside of his scaly forefinger, Simenon took a couple of steps down to the edge of the lake, stopping only when the water was lapping gently at his bare feet. Then he leaned his upper body at a funny, almost awkward kind of angle—and sent the rock flying with a flick of his wrist.

The rock sailed over the water, hopping high into the air three times before it finally sank some twenty meters away. The Gnalish turned back to Wesley, looking quite satisfied with himself.

"That," he instructed, "is how one skims a rock." He returned to the pile, bent, and picked up a replacement. Then, straightening again, he offered it to Wesley. "Care to try it?"

The ensign took the rock and tried to fit it into the curl of his forefinger as Simenon had done. The edge cut painfully into his skin.

"No," said the Gnalish. "You're holding it too tight. Let it rest on the side of your middle finger." And manipulating Wesley's hand, he showed him what he meant.

The ensign nodded. That felt better. Trying to lean as Simenon had, he looked at the Gnalish. "Now I just throw it?"

Simenon shook his head. "You don't *just* throw it. There's a knack to it." He pantomimed the procedure with his own empty hand. "You see? The bottom of the rock must be held parallel to the surface of the lake. And when you release it, you put a backspin on it—so that it remains stable when it hits the water."

Wesley went through the motion a couple of times until he felt he'd gotten the hang of it. Then he turned toward the lake, drew the stone back, and flipped it out over the water.

It turned sideways as it flew, made a loud *plunk* when it hit the lake, and sank like a—well, like a stone. The ensign frowned.

Simenon sighed. "I can see we've got some work ahead of us."

Riker had expected to see Beverly Crusher presiding over sickbay. It was only after he walked in and saw Dr. Selar standing there giving orders that he realized Crusher had gone off duty. A few minutes ago, he calculated—the same time his own shift had ended.

Usually, he was on top of little things like that. But right now he was a little preoccupied.

He waited patiently for Selar to finish her other business. When she finally saw him standing there, she didn't seem the least bit surprised. "Commander," she said, inclining her head slightly by way of a greeting. "I was told you might be coming by."

That caught him a little off his guard. "Really?"

"Yes. Dr. Crusher mentioned it."

"Oh," he said. "Right." Boy, he really *was* preoccupied, wasn't he?

The Vulcan indicated the barrier behind which Cadwallader's biobed was situated. "You wish to see our patient?"

He nodded. "If it's not a bad time."

"Actually," Selar told him, "it is not a bad time at all." And without further ado, she led him back to the critical-care area, where they stopped as she leaned around the barrier. "Commander?"

"Mmm?"

"A visitor for you."

A rustling of the bedcovers. "By all means," the patient said, "let him in."

Riker smiled. Cadwallader's voice was stronger than he had expected it would be.

But Selar didn't allow him to go right away. "Please be brief," she advised. "Her progress is exemplary, but she looks better than she feels. We must help her conserve her strength."

"Don't worry," he said. "I won't wear her out."

The Vulcan gave him a wary look before departing to attend to her duties. Riker watched her go.

Then he came around the barrier and found Cadwallader looking up at him. She was propped on a pillow, her arms entwined across her chest.

She wasn't as pale as when he saw her last. But he remembered what Selar had said about that appearance being deceiving.

"You look rather comfortable," he told her.

She shrugged. "I suppose—considering I took a phaser beam not so long ago. Isn't modern medicine wonderful?"

He looked into her eyes. They had that old sparkle.

"Listen," he said, "I promised Dr. Selar that I'd stay only a min—"

Cadwallader frowned. "Bugger Dr. Selar," she told him. "I'm in much better shape than she thinks. Stay as long as you like."

His eyes narrowed in mock-reproach. "I think Dr. Selar deserves a little more respect."

Cadwallader grunted. "Dr. Selar deserves a good pinch." She considered him. "And for that matter, so do you."

He gave her his best apologetic look. "I know. I'm sorry."

"That was a lousy thing you did, Will Riker."

He nodded. "Just try to see it from my point of view. At the time, you were a murder suspect."

She looked at him questioningly. "You didn't really think that, did you?"

Riker shook his head. "No. But I couldn't take the chance that I was wrong. And even if you weren't the murderer, I couldn't just come out and tell you about the investigation. You might've given it away without realizing it—a nervous look at the wrong time, a slip of the tongue . . ." He let his voice trail off. He shrugged.

Suddenly, Cadwallader grinned. "You look pretty foolish when you're trying to apologize—you know that?"

He feigned injury. "Thanks a lot."

"Especially," she added, "when there's no need. I've had a little time here to think, you know. And it didn't take me long to understand why you did what you did." She put out her hand; he took it. "So don't get all maudlin on me. You're forgiven, as far as that goes."

Riker squeezed her hand. "I'm grateful."

"Besides," she said, "you'll have plenty of opportunity to make it up to me. That is, after we catch the murderer and give this subspace phenomenon the slip. And dodge whatever other perils pop up in the meantime."

He chuckled. "You sound pretty confident."

"I am," Cadwallader replied. "But then, I've looked death in the eye and lived to tell of it."

Riker rolled his eyes. She laughed softly—just as he intended.

"You know," he told her, "you're pretty remarkable, Tricia Cadwallader."

"Yes," she said. "I know."

Someone cleared her throat behind him. Even before the first officer turned around, he knew it was Selar standing there. She looked at him, one eyebrow arched meaningfully, not needing to say a word to make her message clear.

He turned back to Cadwallader. "Time to go. I'll see you soon," he said.

She nodded. "Soon," she echoed—showing just the least bit of doubt, and thereby giving the lie to all her brave talk.

It was with that unsettling impression lingering in his mind that he headed for the exit.

Beverly Crusher flopped down on her bed, bone tired. Not so much from tending to Cadwallader, though seeing to the woman's care had kept her in sickbay for quite a long time. After all, that was her job; she was prepared for it.

What had *really* worn her out was the *wondering*. The suspicion. And the knowledge that no place on the ship was really safe.

If the assassin could make the holodeck a deathtrap, why not sickbay? Or engineering? Or the bridge?

The killer had known the blackout was coming. Had been able to find Morgen at just the right time, under just the right circumstances. The attempt's failure might have come down to the only unlooked-for element—the doctor's presence. By being there, Crusher had given the murderer three targets instead of two. And that might have meant the difference between a timely rescue and a bloodbath.

If she hadn't thought to go looking for the Daa'Vit, or if she hadn't arrived before the blackout . . . the assassin might have succeeded. And Daa'V might have found itself without a monarch.

She couldn't avoid the thought: *it still might.* They had no more idea who the murderer was now than they'd had after the first incident.

He could even get me *here,* she mused. *Even here in my own quarters.* At any moment she might turn around and see those phaser beams stabbing at her again. Or maybe something else—something equally deadly.

No. The murderer is after Morgen, she assured herself. That's what all the evidence suggests. Alone, you're safe.

Before she knew it, she'd taken out the box of tapes. And a moment later she was rummaging through Jack's recorded messages again. Seeking security in the sound of his voice? Maybe. And why not? She had never felt so safe with anyone as she had with her husband.

She selected a tape at random—just as she had before. And as before, as she read the stardate, she recalled her circumstances at the time.

It was the hardest part of her stay in San Francisco. Still plugging through med school. Still pre-Wes, though many of her friends at the time were either pregnant or raising young children. And still waiting for that first shore leave, missing Jack terribly.

Maybe not the most riotous time in the life of Beverly Crusher. But that didn't mean Jack's tape would be gloomy as well. It always seemed his most upbeat messages came when she needed them the most—as if he'd had a sixth sense about her that transcended the thousands of light-years separating them.

What the hell. Without giving it another thought, she popped the tape into the player.

"Hi, Bev. I hope things are as exciting for you as they are for me."

Crusher closed her eyes and smiled. *Just what the doctor ordered.*

"We've just gotten back from Coryb, the fourth planet in the Gamma Shaltair system, where we were surveying the Coryb'thu civilization as a precursor to formal first contact. Up until now, the only surveys I'd been on were the flora-and-fauna kind—never anything that involved a living, breathing civilization. You can't imagine what it was like walking through their cities, brushing against them, exchanging smiles with them—and none of them ever suspecting that you weren't one of them. Kind of eerie and exhilarating at the same time. And whenever it got more eerie than exhilarating, there was Ben Zoma or Pug or Idun nearby to haul me back to reality.

"The funniest part was having to wear these prosthetics that Greyhorse designed for us. The Coryb'thu are basically humanoid, but the middle part of their faces extend forward into kind of a snout. The prosthetics created the same effect. And they weren't even all that uncomfortable. The only problem is they take a while to remove, which is why I'm still wearing mine as I speak. We cut a deck of cards to determine the order in which we'd have our faces restored to us—and I picked the two of diamonds. Oh, well. You know what they say—lucky in love, unlucky in prosthesis removal. And speaking of love—either that relationship of Greyhorse's ended as soon as it began, or I really *was* seeing things. I'll keep you posted on that."

Greyhorse's relationship? Beverly shook her head. There could hardly have been two subjects farther apart in her mind than romance and the former medical officer of the *Stargazer.* She wondered who the lucky girl might have been—assuming, of course, that it hadn't just been Jack's imagination getting the best of him. She'd have to ask Carter about it.

"Got to go now. As you know, we get only so much time in these subspace packets. Love you. Miss you like crazy. And study hard, damn it—someday, I want to be able to turn around and see you standing there next to me."

End of tape. Crusher sighed. Hearing Jack's voice had had the desired effect. She felt better—much better.

Almost safe, in fact.

* * *

"There," said Simenon. "That's more like it."

Wesley frowned, visualizing the flight of his last toss before it sank beneath the surface of the lake. Two hops—not bad, but not great. The Gnalish had gotten as many as four without even trying.

"Don't stop to think about it," Simenon advised. "Thinking has nothing to do with it. After all, you're only throwing rocks—your ancestors did that with brains a good deal less developed than yours."

The ensign chuckled and picked up another stone. Positioning it the way the Gnalish had taught him—the procedure having become second nature by now—he pulled back and let it fly.

One hop, two.

Three.

And it wasn't done yet. With one last burst of energy, the stone leapt in a high fluid arc—the rock-skimming equivalent of a grace note.

Four. The ensign turned to Simenon. "Well?" he asked.

The Gnalish puckered up his face and grunted approvingly. "Much better," he said, studying Wesley intently. Something changed in his eyes, softened.

Wesley hesitated, then decided to say what was on his mind. It didn't look like he'd get a better opportunity. "Professor? You said you'd tell me more about my father—about how he died."

Simenon nodded, cleared his throat. "I did, didn't I? Very well, then." The Gnalish switched his scaly, gray tail back and forth over the forest floor, as if gathering himself. Then he began. "You're familiar, I assume, with the problem we encountered?"

"The Nensi phenomenon," Wes told him. "A ball of matter and energy thought to have its origin in a special category of supernova. Very rare, but very destructive—and almost impossible to distinguish from a rogue comet except at close range."

"Exactly. Of course, back then we had no idea as to its origin—and neither did Nensi—considering it was the first time anyone had ever encountered the bloody thing. In any case, it all but stripped the *Stargazer* of her ability to defend herself. Shields went down. Sensors went down. Weapons went down. And we started to record an overload in the starboard warp field generator. Shutting down the warp drive stabilized the situation, but there was still a lot of energy cycling through the nacelle. We were afraid that the generator would just blow up—and whether it would take the rest of the ship with it was anybody's guess. Remember, we had no shields with which to protect ourselves.

"Unfortunately, we couldn't just separate into two parts as the *Enterprise* can. But we had to disassociate ourselves from the starboard nacelle, and as quickly as possible. We batted the problem around until we were ready to chew one another's heads off. Any moment, we knew, we might be obliterated in midsentence. Finally, your father came up with a solution. Someone had to get outside the ship and sever the nacelle from the rest of the *Stargazer.*"

Wesley had gone over this part in his head a thousand times. Going outside, cutting away the nacelle with phaser rifles, had been the only way. The *Stargazer* wasn't set up to fire on itself, even if ship's phasers had been working at the time. And to approach the project through the power transfer tunnels was unthinkable— they were too full of energy seepage from the warp field generators.

"Naturally," Simenon said, "your father volunteered—it was his plan. Others came forward also—Ben Zoma, Morgen, Asmund, Vigo. Even Greyhorse. The captain didn't like the risk involved. Hated it, to tell the truth. But in the end, he chose a team of two: your father and Pug Joseph. Both of them had had experience in hull repairs. Both of them knew how to negotiate the ship's skin. And since the transporters had been damaged along with nearly everything else, that was pretty important—to be able to get to the nacelles and back again.

"They set out from the airlock nearest their destination—a tiny one, used only in drydock to check the torpedo-launch mechanism. For us, it served a different purpose. The worst part was our inability to track your father and Pug on our sensors. We could talk to them through their helmet communicators, but that was about it. And once they got going, there wasn't a great deal of conversation—as little as possible, in fact. Just a remark now and then to let us know everything was all right."

The Gnalish snorted. "Anyway, they reached the nacelle assembly pretty quickly. But it took forever to cut through it. The *Stargazer*'s transfer tunnels weren't as wide as what you've got here on the *Enterprise*—but they weren't pipe cleaners either. And as you know, phaser rifles can't sustain a beam indefinitely. They've got to be given time to cool down. So while we waited on the bridge, strung tight as Vulcan harpstrings, your father and Pug hacked away until their limbs were trembling with the strain.

"The tricky part was when they got into the transfer tunnel. With all the energy in there already, the phaser beam could have stirred it up even more—or had no effect at all. Most likely, we knew, it was going to be something in between—which is why Pug and your father had been cautioned to approach that juncture carefully.

"For a long time after they began that stage of the work, we heard nothing from them. The captain was as worried as the rest of us. He was about to call for a progress report, when your father's voice was heard over the intercom: 'We're in,' he said. 'And no problems to speak of. Just a lot of fireworks.' We thought the worst was all behind us.

"A couple of moments later, their communicators went dead. Nothing to worry about, necessarily. In fact, I'd predicted it would happen, what with all that energy running out of the assembly. But it was an ominous thing, that silence. Someone began to pace—I forget who. Ben Zoma, maybe.

"It went on like that for quite a while. The waiting, the pacing. The faces that looked like they'd been stretched too tight. Finally, there was no denying it—they'd been out there too long. Something had happened—something bad. Picard said as much. He said that someone had to go out and bring them back.

"As before, there were volunteers. But the captain wouldn't listen. He was determined to keep the body count down, he said; he was already thinking in those terms. Ben Zoma argued with him, but to no avail. Pulling on a suit, he went after your father and Pug.

"The explosion came sometime later. I don't remember exactly when. It felt as if we'd been pummeled by a giant fist. And when it was finished, we all stood there, afraid to move—because moving was a step toward facing the reality of what had happened.

"The worst possible event hadn't occurred—we hadn't been destroyed, the ship was still intact. The instruments showed us why. It wasn't the generator that had blown; it was just a pocket of accumulated energy. And the nacelle was floating free, which was what we'd wanted all along.

"But three of our friends were still out there. At last, Ben Zoma got up from his seat and headed for the turbolift. I followed. So did Greyhorse, though he was barking orders to his trauma team the whole time. The others had to stay at their posts.

"We got to the airlock about the same time as Greyhorse's people. There were also a couple of security guards, handpicked by Pug beforehand. They started to put on containment suits—but before they could get out of the lock, they saw Picard coming in. And he had Pug with him—alive.

"The captain had found him drifting alongside the hull, unconscious. There was no way he could have brought both Pug and your father in at once—he had to make a choice, and Pug was closer. As it was, he barely managed to get them around the curve of the ship before the explosion. If he'd gone after your father instead, all three of them would have died."

He looked at Wesley. "The captain went back for your father, of course, but we all knew it was too late to help him. Afterward, Pug explained that the energy build-up had been too much for them, that they blacked out—first your father, then Pug himself."

He grunted. "With the nacelle assembly ripped away, we were able to stagger away on impulse. So in the end, your father and Pug accomplished everything they set out to do. The only problem was one of them didn't live to see it."

Wesley found he had an ache in the back of his throat. He tried to swallow it away, found that he couldn't.

The Gnalish's eyes narrowed. "Are you all right, Ensign?"

Wes nodded. "Yes," he said finally, his voice huskier than he would have liked. "I'm fine. Really." He bent for another rock, trying to take his mind off his feelings. "Let me see if I can repeat that last performance."

After a moment, he heard Simenon grunt. "Of course." A pause. "The trick is to be consistent. There, that's a good one—the one to your—"

Abruptly, a voice came out of nowhere.

"Wesley?"

The ensign looked up at the holodeck's intercom grid, hidden in the illusion of scarlet treetops. *Oh, no.* How long had he been here? It seemed like only a few minutes, but Geordi's tone suggested it had been much longer.

Wesley steeled himself. "Yes, Commander?"

"What the devil is going on up there? When I sent you after Professor Simenon, I didn't expect the *two* of you to disappear."

The Gnalish snorted derisively and shook his head. Wesley tried to ignore him. "Sorry, sir. I guess I, um . . . just lost track of time."

"Lost track of—damn it, Wes! Did you forget what kind of mess we're all in? Maybe Professor Simenon has the option of fiddling while Rome burns—but you don't, not as long as you're wearing that uniform. Understood?"

The ensign grimaced. Out of the corner of his eye he saw Simenon pick up another rock. "Aye, Commander."

"Then get down here on the double. You can tell me in person what you found so enthralling that you—"

Geordi was interrupted by a high-pitched yelp that made Wesley whirl in alarm. His first thought was that the Gnalish had fallen into the water and was drowning. Of course, that was unlikely given his reptilian anatomy—but that didn't come to mind until moments later.

In any case, Simenon wasn't in any trouble, aquatic or otherwise. He was just standing there with a strange expression on his face. A wide-eyed, open-mouthed sort of expression.

"Wes? Is everything all right?" Geordi asked.

The ensign looked at Simenon. "I think so," he replied. He tilted his head to get the Gnalish's attention. "It is all right—isn't it, Professor?"

Suddenly, Simenon's features broadened into a smile. "You're damned *right* it's all right," he said. He looked up. "Mr. La Forge—make some tea. We'll be there in a minute."

Wesley regarded him. "Make some tea?" he echoed.

"I *like* tea," said the Gnalish. "Who do you think introduced your captain to Earl Grey?" He hurried past the ensign on his way to the holodeck exit.

Wesley fell in after him. "But—that *sound* you made—"

Simenon dismissed it. "I always make that sound," he shot back over his shoulder, "when I'm about to save the ship."

As Riker entered the turbolift, leaving sickbay behind, he knew that the place where Cadwallader had been attacked would yield no physical evidence of what had taken place there. The curving stretch of corridor had already been restored, the phaser-scarred sections of bulkhead replaced, and the bloodstains leeched from the floor covering.

But he still wanted to see it again for himself. He had the feeling that if he stood there long enough, if he gave sufficient thought to the details imparted by Morgen and Dr. Crusher, he would find an angle that Worf's security teams had overlooked.

At worst, he would feel as if he were making a contribution. The idea that there was a killer aboard had certainly concerned him before—but Cadwallader's close call brought the problem closer to home. Now it was *personal*.

"Deck Seventeen," he said. Though he couldn't feel it, the turbolift started to move. A moment or two later the doors opened. He stepped out.

And saw Ben Zoma kneeling in the middle of the corridor, eyes narrowed, intent on something in the distance.

The captain of the *Lexington* looked up as Riker exited the lift. He seemed surprised—but just a little. And he made no effort at all to cover up his interest in the place.

For a second or two they just stared at each other. Then Ben Zoma cracked a smile. "Fancy meeting you here, Commander."

The first officer refrained from smiling back. "Mind if I ask what you're doing, sir?"

The older man stood, winced, and massaged the back of his neck. "Damn," he said. "There's that tightness again. The old body's not what it used to be—though I'll deny it if you tell anyone I said that."

"You haven't answered my question," Riker reminded him.

"True," Ben Zoma said. "That was rude of me. On the other hand, I think you know why I'm here. I imagine it's the same reason *you're* here—to go over the scene of the crime. To see if there might not be something the others overlooked."

Riker nodded. "How long have you been here?" he asked.

"Just a few minutes."

"And?"

Ben Zoma shook his head. "No brilliant insights—unfortunately." He gazed past Riker. "The killer came from that direction—more than likely was already waiting for Cad and the others when they came groping for the lift in the dark." His nostrils flared. "I wish he were here now. And I wish I had a phaser too."

Riker regarded him. "Not exactly the kind of talk Starfleet encourages in its captains."

"No," agreed Ben Zoma, "it's not." He turned back to the first officer. "But then, there's no one around to hear it but the two of us." He cocked his head. "And if it were Dr. Crusher who'd gotten hurt, or Counselor Troi, wouldn't you feel the same way?"

Riker hesitated.

"Come now—be honest."

The first officer decided to be as honest as the dark man had been. "Maybe. But wanting and doing are two different things."

"No argument there," Ben Zoma told him. "Many's the time I wanted to take someone's head off—and didn't."

"I'm glad to hear it," Riker remarked.

"Well," said the *Lexington*'s captain, "I should be going. Cadwallader could probably use some company. Though I'm sure Dr. Crusher will be as suspicious of my intentions as you are—*still.*"

The younger man shrugged. "The fact that the captain chose to trust you is a mark in your favor. But it doesn't *necessarily* mean you're not the killer."

"Absolutely right," Ben Zoma said, the corners of his eyes crinkling. "Now I know why Picard described you the way he did."

While Riker tried to decipher that last remark, the captain's friend walked past him into the empty turbolift. Just before the doors closed, he heard Ben Zoma utter a single word: "Sickbay."

Once inside the lift, Ben Zoma shook his head appreciatively. Some officer, that Riker. Jean-Luc's instincts had been right five years earlier, when he'd offered the man the first officer's position on the *Enterprise.*

He still recalled vividly their conversation on Starbase 52, where the *Lexington* had put in for repairs. Ben Zoma had been pleasantly surprised to find his former captain there, awaiting transportation to his new assignment, and Picard had insisted on standing him to a few drinks.

"I tell you, Gilaad, I never thought I would find an exec like you again. But I think lightning has managed to strike twice."

"Who is he?"

"His name is Riker. Will Riker. He's with DeSoto on the Hood.*"*

"Yes. I think I've heard of him. His father's a civilian strategist, isn't he? Specializing in the frontier regions?"

"That's correct. He's one of the top men in his field. And for my money, his son is even better." Picard leaned forward. *"You know DeSoto—he never says a good word about anyone unless he absolutely has to. And he sings young Riker's praises like a nightingale. Of course, DeSoto is not happy about the man leaving—he hates like hell to lose such a fine first officer. But he says Riker has earned the right to choose his own destiny."*

"Very impressive, Jean-Luc." Ben Zoma shook his head. *"A* Galaxy-*class vessel and a first-rate exec. What lucky star were you born under?"*

"You know, my friend, I ask that question of myself sometimes."

It was a moment before Ben Zoma realized that the turbolift had come to a stop. And another moment before he could wipe the nostalgic grin off his face, so whoever entered wouldn't think he was some sort of imbecile.

Then he saw who was standing there, and he smiled anyway.

"A pleasant surprise," he said. "I meant to come see you."

"Oh?" said the newcomer as the lift doors closed again.

"Yes. I thought we should—"

Suddenly, there was a flash of something metallic. Too late, Ben Zoma realized what it was. Before he could prevent it, the knife had slipped between his ribs and out again.

Lord, he thought, *I've found the killer. But not the way I had in mind.*

As a second strike headed for his face, he ducked—and the blade hit the turbolift wall instead. Carried forward by the momentum of the attack, his adversary fell against him and they grappled. Ben Zoma somehow found the hand that held the knife and managed to keep it at bay.

But he didn't have much time and he knew it. Already, his side was a fiery, gut-wrenching agony as his nerves woke to the damage inflicted on them. Nor did he dare look down to see how much blood he had lost—no doubt, it was considerable. Putting all his ebbing strength into a single uppercut, he managed to stagger the knife's owner backward. And at the same time to bellow at the intercom grid for security.

Unfortunately, his adversary recovered sooner than Ben Zoma had expected. This time he couldn't avoid the knife altogether—and it cut deep into his shoulder. Gritting his teeth against the pain, he slumped against the wall of the lift and kicked desperately at his attacker's knee.

By then, however, he was too cold and numb to know if his blow did any damage. The last thing he saw was the knife descending yet again. The last thing he felt was it plunging into his chest.

Worf estimated that four minutes had gone by. Four minutes from the time he heard the request for help until he reached the turbolift on Deck Thirty-three. It would have been faster for him to override the last occupant command and bring the damned thing up to the bridge—but for some reason the lift doors wouldn't shut.

Half a corridor away, he'd seen why. There was an arm stretched out across the threshold—to prevent just the sort of quick attention the Klingon had had in mind. Cursing out loud, he'd noted the blood on the bare hand.

And now, as he knelt beside the body, he cursed again. It was Ben Zoma.

The man had been stabbed a half-dozen times—at least twice in the chest. Nor could Worf ignore the fact, even in his eagerness to do his job and preserve Ben Zoma's life, that he had seen this kind of wound before.

Very *definitely,* he had seen it before.

Removing his honor sash and stripping off the top of his uniform, Worf wrapped Ben Zoma tightly in the fabric of the shirt. It would help to keep the man warm—an important measure, since he'd already gone into shock. Also, it might slow down the loss of blood—which had already been excessive, judging by the pool of gore on the floor of the turbolift.

Placing his forefinger against Ben Zoma's neck, the Klingon felt for a pulse. There was movement there—terribly weak, but discernible nonetheless.

"My God!" said a voice.

Worf looked back over his shoulder and saw the two women in civilian garb, grimacing at the sight of Ben Zoma. He couldn't recall their names, but he knew they were in one of the science sections. A moment later two other civilians approached from the other direction, immediately as stricken by horror as the first two.

"What's happened?" cried a man.

"Keep back," the Klingon growled. "The situation is under control."

It was only another moment before Dr. Crusher arrived with a medical team in tow. Making their way through the swelling throng of onlookers, they lifted Ben Zoma onto a gurney and moved him into the turbolift.

"Sickbay," Crusher said. At the same time, she was taking readings with her tricorder. "Give him twenty cc's of cordrizene. That ought to keep him going until we can stabilize his condition." Her voice betrayed none of the emotion she must have been feeling.

But when she looked up at Worf, her anger was hard not to miss. "How long," she asked in a subdued tone, "is this going to go on?"

"It is finished," he rumbled.

Her brows came together. "What do you mean? Did you get a look at the killer?"

He shook his head. "No. But I *know* who it is."

Thirteen

As Riker followed Picard out of the turbolift, the younger man had to hustle to catch up. He had never seen the captain so intense—so driven.

It had to be hard on him, the first officer thought. He could only imagine how hard.

If it were anyone else, he would have suggested that they stay on the sidelines, commanding officer or not. In cases like this one, personal involvement usually led to trouble.

But Picard wasn't just anyone. Riker had never once seen him lose his composure, not in the four years and more that he'd served under the man. He could only trust that the captain would not make this instance the exception.

Down the corridor, the trio of armed security personnel was doing exactly what they'd been told—remaining silent and well back from the door monitor, so that they wouldn't alert anyone inside to their presence. They'd been instructed not to make any move on their own unless the killer tried to leave.

As Riker and Picard approached from one direction, Worf approached from the other. Momentarily, the first officer wondered why the Klingon was naked from the waist up—and then he remembered Worf's account of his discovery of Ben Zoma. He swallowed as he recalled the bloody details.

Quickly, wasting no time, the captain pointed to Worf and to Burke, who'd been in charge up until now. Then he indicated either side of the door, showing them where he wanted them to position themselves.

Even as he drew out his phaser, the Klingon looked none too happy about the idea. "Captain," he whispered, "you cannot go in first—"

But Picard cut him short with a simple raising of his hand. "I can," he whispered back, "and I will." He turned to the door, gathering himself. "This is my responsibility. I should have discharged it some time ago."

It was a clear admission that he'd been wrong about the assassin's identity—and that Riker had been right. But the first officer derived no satisfaction from the fact. There were no winners in this situation, only losers. And, unfortunately, Ben Zoma had been the biggest loser of all.

While the captain and Worf were engaged in their exchange, Burke had been working to override the door's programming with a security-level code. Finished now, he nodded to Picard.

"Ready, sir," he breathed, taking out his phaser. Holding it close to him, he pointed it at the ceiling.

Without hesitation, the captain walked forward, confident that there would be no beeping inside the apartment to serve as a warning of his approach. Stripped of any programming instructions to the contrary, the doors opened to admit him.

As luck would have it, the apartment's occupant was sitting at a table in the center of the reception room. She barely turned her head as Picard entered with Riker close behind.

Idun Asmund looked from one to the other of them, remarkably calm—though she had to know that they were on to her. Captains and first officers didn't just march into their guests' quarters unannounced. "To what do I owe the honor?" she asked, half smiling.

"You are charged," Picard responded, his voice flat and mechanical, "with the attempted murder of your fellow officers. On three separate occasions—including one just moments ago, when you savagely attacked Gilaad Ben Zoma with a *Klingon ceremonial knife.*"

The woman's brow creased. "What are you talking about? I haven't touched my knives since I came aboard. If this is a joke—"

"It's no joke," said Riker.

Asmund stood. She darted a glance out into the corridor, where she must have caught sight of Worf and his security team—because the crease in her brow deepened. She turned back to the captain. "Sir, if Ben Zoma's been hurt, I had nothing to do with it. You must believe that."

Picard's nostrils flared. "I wish I could, Idun. I truly do. But both Worf and Dr. Crusher agree—only a Klingon ceremonial knife could have inflicted wounds such as Ben Zoma sustained. *You* carried such weapons onto the *Enterprise.* And outside of Worf, you are the only one here practiced in their use." A pause. "What's more, you have no alibi—other than the computer record of your having been in your quarters at the time. But the computer only records the presence of your *communicator.*" He scowled—a sincere expression of his pain and regret. "I have no choice but to place you under arrest."

She shook her head. "You're making a mistake, Captain. If you'll tell me what's going on, I can—"

"You'll be notified of the charges in detail," said Picard, "once you're in the brig." He looked to Riker. "See to it, Number One. And don't forget to check her for poisons."

The first officer nodded. "Aye, sir." Worf had told him how Klingons imprisoned by their enemies often chose suicide as an honorable alternative to captivity.

"Thank you," Picard said.

It might not have been plain to anyone else, but Riker knew how this was tearing the captain up inside. Asmund had been part of his crew—just as he and Troi and Worf were now. No, more than his crew—his *family*.

It wasn't easy to confront the fact that a member of one's family was a murderer. Not under *any* circumstances.

As Picard turned to leave, Asmund appealed to him. "Captain—this is insane. I would never do anything to hurt Ben Zoma or anyone else. If anyone knows that, it's you."

Picard headed for the doorway, appearing not to hear her. And after he was gone, Worf filled the opening, glancing meaningfully at Riker. The first officer nodded.

He turned to Asmund. She stared back at him, hard. As if she were fighting to keep her grip on emotions so powerful they might rip her apart.

Momentarily, Riker's heart went out to her. It was a terrible thing to see one who had been Klingon-bred fighting to maintain her dignity.

Then he remembered what had been done to Ben Zoma. And to Cadwallader. And his sympathy for the woman melted away.

"If you please," he told her, indicating the exit.

With a visible effort, Asmund collected herself. Then, without another word, she gave herself up to the security officers waiting outside in the corridor.

"Let me get this straight," the engineering chief said. "You think we can *skim* the *Enterprise* out of the slipstream?"

"In a word," Simenon answered, "yes."

They were gathered again around the master situations monitor in engineering—Geordi, the Gnalish, Data, and Wesley. And the ensign was finding it increasingly difficult to keep quiet.

It was Simenon's theory, Simenon's plan. So it only made sense for Simenon to explain it. But Wes was so sure it was going to work that he could feel himself bubbling inside with excitement.

"You see," said the professor, "I was teaching Wesley how to skim stones. You know—flat rocks?"

Data looked puzzled. "I am not familiar with the activity."

"That's all right," said Wesley. "You don't really have to be."

The android took the ensign's word for it. "Very well," he said. "Please proceed, Professor."

"Anyway," Simenon went on, "in all my years on Gnala and elsewhere, I've skimmed hundreds—maybe even thousands—of stones. But I never gave much of a thought to the principles of physics that govern it. After all, they are so basic, so simple, as to be taken for granted. The stone's surface and the water's surface collide; the resulting exchange of energy between the two objects impels the stone upward as well as forward. In short, it *skips*. Its momentum has been diminished some, thanks to things like friction and gravity and the energy absorbed by the water in the collision—but not by much, as long as two conditions are satisfied: the angle of collision must be fairly oblique and the stone must be relatively flat."

As the Gnalish paused for effect, Geordi leaned forward over the monitor to look at him. "Professor, this is all very enlightening. But what's it got to do with—"

Simenon stopped him with a raising of his scaly hand. "All in good time, Commander. All in good time." He frowned. "Where was I?"

"Fairly oblique and relatively flat," Wesley reminded him.

"Oh, yes." He punched up a schematic of the *Enterprise* on the monitor screen. "Let's say this ship is such a stone. It has left our hand, and is hurtling along parallel to and just above the slipstream."

"Excuse me," said Data, "but we are *in* the slipstream—not on it."

Simenon snorted. "Commander, you would never make it as an engineer—or a Gnalish, for that matter. There are very few precise analogies in this life—particularly when we're talking about something as esoteric as a warpspace phenomenon."

Geordi nodded, placing a reassuring hand on Data's shoulder. "It's all right, Professor. We'll bear with you."

"My gratitude," the Gnalish muttered, "is boundless. In any case, the *Enterprise* is hurtling along, basically parallel to the surface—perhaps skipping every now and then without knowing it, because so little energy is lost in each collision. However, the collisions are what serve to keep us on the right path. Now, if we could somehow change the angle at which we strike the surface, we might go shooting off in a different direction entirely. If we approach it edge-down, for instance, we might go *under* the surface—which would put us in a completely different medium. A slower medium—just as regular space is a slower medium than subspace. Still with me?"

"Still with you," Geordi replied. "Of course—"

"Of course," the Gnalish interrupted, "we *can't* change our position. The slipstream won't let us—because we're dealing with not one surface, but many. In fact, they're all about us, surrounding us—bouncing us back on course with every little collision, channeling us forward. A good assumption?"

"It would appear so," Data replied.

"Fine. That leaves us only one other option—to change the shape of the rock. Or, rather, in this case, the *Enterprise.*"

The android looked more puzzled than ever. "Professor, are you suggesting we separate the saucer from the battle section—as was suggested earlier?"

Simenon shook his head. "Not at all. Because it's not really the ship that presents a surface to the slipstream."

Geordi snapped his fingers. "That's right. It's the *shields!*"

"Exactly." The Gnalish punched some additional information into the situation monitor, and the schematic began to move. "All we need to do is change the shape of our force shields—"

Finally, Wesley couldn't stand it any longer. "And in effect," he continued, "we'll be changing the shape of the rock. Instead of a streamlined object designed for maximum efficiency in flight, the slipstream will be confronted with an angled surface front and back."

"Which," Simenon resumed, seemingly without breaking stride, "should skim us out of the slipstream. No muss, no fuss. All we have to do is present opposition to the flow—at precisely the right angle. One that's obtuse enough to substantially change the force vector situation, but not so obtuse as to place intolerable stresses on the *Enterprise.*" He looked around, with particular attention to Geordi. "So? What do you think?"

The engineering chief frowned as he considered the idea. "It might work," he said, "and it might not. Even if the theory is sound, we're going to have to find the correct angle at which to pitch the shields—or we could be so much subspace debris."

"Isn't that what computer models are for?" Wesley asked.

For a moment Geordi thought about it some more. Then his frown dissipated. "All right," he decided, starting to input instructions to the situation monitor. "Let's see what we can come up with."

Picard frowned as he stood in Beverly Crusher's office, staring at the opaque barrier that separated critical care from the rest of the medical facility. The doctor sat across her desk from him, holding a cup of coffee in both hands. She looked terrible—worn out.

"Jean-Luc?"

He turned to face her.

"Are you all right?" she asked.

He nodded. "I am fine." Then: "What are his chances?"

Crusher took a deep breath, let it out. "Hard to say. We've transfused him, stabilized him—done everything we could. But . . ." She shook her head. "He suffered massive trauma. Lost a lot of blood." She looked down at her coffee. "He was in excellent health when it happened—that's a mark in his favor. But I can't tell you what the outcome will be."

He had never felt so helpless—so frustrated. *He is one of my oldest friends. And all I can do is wait. And hope.*

But not here. He had other business to attend to.

"Excuse me," he told Beverly.

"Of course," she said, managing a smile. "Don't worry. I'll hold down the fort."

As the captain left her and made his way through sickbay, he could see Riker waiting for him at the entrance—just as he had requested. The first officer straightened as he noted Picard's approach.

His eyes searched the captain's face as he wheeled out into the corridor. A moment later Riker used his long strides to fall into step beside him. "Not good," he concluded without even having to ask.

"Not good," Picard confirmed. Then, since there was nothing more that could really be said on that subject, he turned to another. "It appears we were mistaken, Number One—about Morgen being the only target, I mean. Gilaad Ben Zoma was alone when he was attacked. And in retrospect, one must wonder if Cadwallader's shooting was as unintentional as we first believed."

As the turbolift came up on their right, they turned and headed in. The doors opened as soon as the mechanism's sensor recorded their presence and closed after they were inside.

"Bridge," Picard instructed. Silently and without even a hint of motion, the lift began to carry them upward.

"Revenge," the younger man concluded, as if he had come to the end of an internalized dialogue. He turned to the captain. Judging by Riker's expression, the word had left a bad taste in his mouth. "Revenge on everyone who had anything to do with her sister's apprehension—and imprisonment." He paused thoughtfully. "But talk about a warped sense of justice. Gerda did what she did of her own volition; no one on the *Stargazer* twisted her arm. And once you knew about it . . . what else could you do but try to stop her?"

Picard frowned. "There was no other choice. You and I know that. But to Commander Asmund . . . who can say? It is not easy to accept the death of a loved one, much less a twin. Tragedy can do strange things to people's judgment—make them see villains where there are none."

Riker shook his head. "And not just tragedy."

The captain looked at him.

"Sometimes," the first officer explained, "the desire to protect will do that too. Look at us." He smiled ruefully. "I was seeing assassins everywhere I turned."

Just then the doors opened and the bridge was revealed to them. Though the command seat was empty, all seemed to be in order, so they proceeded to the observation lounge.

Once again a set of doors opened for them. They walked in and saw that everyone who was supposed to be there *was* there. With one exception.

The captain turned to Counselor Troi, who had chosen to wait for them by the door. "Simenon?" he asked.

"He's in engineering—a can't-wait kind of meeting, apparently. Geordi says that they may be on to something." She paused. "Under the circumstances, I thought I would speak to the professor later—on my own."

Picard nodded. "I agree, Counselor. You were correct to let them be." He turned then to those positioned about the conference table. Morgen, standing by an observation port and frowning, his arms crossed over his chest. Pug, sitting at the table already, drumming fingers and looking more than a little leery. Greyhorse, waiting stoically with his hands locked behind his back.

"Ah," the doctor said. "At last. Now, perhaps, we can find out what's going on."

"Indeed," the captain assured him. "Please—all of you—sit down."

They sat. Picard and Riker were the last to push their chairs in.

The captain gazed at the expectant faces of his former officers. And at Pug Joseph's in particular.

"Before I go any further, Pug, I must tell you that the others here have an advantage over you—at least *some* knowledge of what has transpired. It was not by my choice that this became the case; it was dictated by circumstances."

Joseph shifted in his seat. He seemed more curious than resentful.

"Nonetheless," Picard went on, "I regret that it was not possible to let you in on the secret as well. I trust that you will understand—as a security officer and as a friend."

He turned to the others. "I have bad news. Gilaad Ben Zoma was assaulted just a little while ago in a turbolift on deck seventeen. He is in sickbay now—in critical condition."

Morgen cursed elaborately.

"My God," Greyhorse whispered. *"How* critical?"

The captain regarded him. "Dr. Crusher says there's no way of knowing at this point."

Pug just sat and stared. He seemed lost, unable to connect with what he was hearing.

"On the other hand," Picard added, "we have found the assassin. She is in the brig, under guard."

To Morgen and Greyhorse it was fairly obvious to whom he was referring. Besides Cadwallader, Asmund was the only female in the Daa'Vit's escort.

To Pug, however, it was not quite so obvious. The captain spelled it out: "Idun is the one who tried to kill Ben Zoma, Pug. Just as she tried to kill Morgen and Cadwallader earlier."

The security officer leaned back heavily in his chair. Finally, he uttered his first word since Picard had entered the room: "Why?" He looked around for help from his *Stargazer* shipmates. "What the hell would she want to do that for?"

Picard told him—about the attacks, the suspicions, everything. By the time he was finished, Joseph's complexion had darkened to an angry red.

"But now it is over," the captain announced. "It hurts me that Commander Asmund could have come to this. And it hurts me even more that Captain Ben Zoma is in such straits. But at least it is over."

Greyhorse sat up a little straighter. "Captain, if there's anything I can do . . ."

Picard shook his head. "Nothing at the moment. But I will relay your offer to Dr. Crusher."

The Daa'Vit trained his feral yellow eyes on the captain's.

I know, Picard responded silently. *We need to talk.*

O'Brien scanned Ten-Forward from his vantage point near one of the observation ports. The place was buzzing like crazy.

"News spreads fast around here," Eisenberg noted.

The transporter chief nodded, regarding the young man across the table from him. He'd met Eisenberg only a couple of weeks before, when the medical technician expressed an interest in joining O'Brien's notorious poker enclave. Of course, O'Brien had had to explain about the length of the waiting list, which was longer than ten *Enterprise*s put together.

But at the same time, he'd taken a liking to the fellow. In fact, in some ways, Eisenberg reminded O'Brien of himself at the outset of his first starship assignment. Eager but unseasoned, and a little daunted by the danger—which was considerable at the moment, the transporter chief had to admit.

That's why O'Brien had made it his personal mission to lighten the younger man's load. To help him forget his worries, if only for a little while. And Ten-Forward had seemed like the best place to do it—until the crowd began to pour in, all a-flutter with accounts of Ben Zoma's discovery and Asmund's subsequent arrest.

"Fast?" O'Brien gave out with a short, sharp laugh. "That's an understatement if I ever heard one." He used his glass to indicate the entirety of the lounge. "On a good day, you can start a rumor on the bridge at 0800 hours—and it'll reach the last table in Ten-Forward before you have a chance to close your mouth."

Eisenberg looked at him a little skeptically. "Really?"

The transporter chief shrugged. "Well, maybe I'm exaggerating just a bit. I don't get up to the bridge that often, y'know. But I think you get the idea."

The med tech took a drink, then put his glass down. "I guess everyone's just relieved. Can't say I blame them, either." He shook his head. "Can you imagine? A murderer on board—shooting phasers, plunging knives into people . . ."

"Tampering with holodecks," O'Brien added, thinking it sounded a little more benign—as long as one left out the details.

"That too. It gives me the willies just thinking about it. And for the murderer to turn out to be one of the captain's guests . . . damn. I thought they served with him a while back. I thought they were his *friends.*"

"They are," the transporter chief explained. "A bad apple doesn't make a bad bunch."

Eisenberg didn't seem to have heard him. "You know what they say. With friends like those, who needs the Romulans?" He sighed. "You should have seen that poor Ben Zoma fellow. I've never seen so much blood." The younger man's gaze grew distant.

O'Brien eyed him mock-seriously. "Y'know, Davey, you're starting to depress me. And that's not easy."

The med tech leaned back in his chair, genuinely repentant. "Sorry."

"Why don't you take a peek at the bright side? The woman's been caught. She's in the brig, where she can't hurt anybody else."

"I suppose so," Eisenberg told him. For a brief moment he seemed content. Then he started to think again. "But that's not our only problem, is it?" He glanced out the port, where the stars continued to streak by at an ungodly speed. "What about *that?* I heard that this phenomenon can suddenly change shape—become something else. And tear us apart like old-fashioned tissue paper."

O'Brien could see he had his work cut out for him. "You *could* look at it that way—doom and gloom and all that stuff. Or you could tell yourself that Commander La Forge and his helpers will get us out of this—like they always do. And in the meantime, we have ringside seats for the greatest show in the galaxy."

O'Brien swung his chair around to face the observation port and the flat lines of light beyond it. Raising his glass in a toast, he said: "To warp nine point nine five. May she always be so beautiful."

Then, without looking to see Eisenberg's reaction too quickly, he took a sip of his synthehol and savored it. "Ah," he commented with a bravado he didn't quite feel. "What life's all about."

Finally, he gave his companion a sidelong glance. The younger man was staring at him.

"Join me?" O'Brien asked.

Gradually, Eisenberg lifted his glass. And smiled—if only faintly. "When you put it that way," he said, "how can I refuse?"

After everyone else left, it was just the two of them. Morgen paced the length of the observation lounge, looking for all the world like a caged beast. And the captain watched, leaning back against the edge of the conference table, his arms folded over his chest.

"Damn her," the Daa'Vit growled. "No—damn *me.* How could I have brought her aboard? *How?"*

"There was no way of predicting this," Picard told him.

"You're wrong," Morgen insisted. "I knew I was inviting trouble—in my heart, I knew. But I wanted to show her that I could put the past behind me. I wanted to be forgiving. Benevolent. All the things my years in Starfleet taught me to be." He shook his head. "And look where my benevolence has gotten me. Your security officer is endangered. Cadwallader gets a hole burned through her. And Ben Zoma— brave, goodhearted Ben Zoma—"

Suddenly, Morgen seemed to erupt—to go mad. He growled hideously at the top of his lungs and pounded his fists on the table. Picard's instinct was to retreat from the spectacle, but he stood his ground—reminding himself that the tortured creature before him was his friend. That he had nothing to fear from him.

Still, it was not easy. He had never seen such an explosion of Daa'Vit fury before—and he had no wish to see it ever again.

In the end, Morgen's fit lasted just a few seconds. But even when it was finished, his chest still heaved. "I am sorry you had to see that," he said.

"It is all right," the captain told him. "We are friends. Old friends."

"No," the Daa'Vit insisted in a deep slow voice. "It was . . . inappropriate." He massaged the fingers of his left hand. "But even so, I was right. I should have listened to my head, not my heart. I should have known better."

Picard could see no good coming of further self-recrimination. He decided to change the subject. "Will it hurt your ability to ascend to the throne?" he asked.

The Daa'Vit looked at him. "What?"

"Being without Ben Zoma and Asmund. Will it hurt you politically?"

If Morgen saw what the captain was doing, he didn't object. He thought for a moment, then shook his head. "It shouldn't. True, it will make people wonder when I show up with a smaller escort than that which was announced. But there will still be four of you—yourself, Pug, Cad, and Greyhorse. And four is the minimum required by law." He cleared his throat, which must have been scoured raw by his outburst. "Blazes—anyone who hasn't got four friends in the whole universe isn't *fit* to rule."

The Daa'Vit began to pace again. But he seemed under control, contemplative. Almost calculating, in contrast to the fit of unbridled emotion Picard had just witnessed. Preferring this Morgen to the other—at least for now—the captain didn't interrupt.

"Of course," the Daa'Vit said after a little while, "the size of my escort is one thing—and the circumstances in which it was diminished is another. If the true story gets out on Daa'V, it could be embarrassing. *Most* embarrassing."

The captain shrugged. "Then no one on Daa'V need *know* the circumstances."

Morgen nodded. "Good." His eyes narrowed. "Now all we have to do is get there. What about this idea that Simenon's had?"

Picard shook his head. "I don't know anything about it—except that Commander La Forge seemed to think it was promising."

"Perhaps we should find out, then." A hint of irony had crept back into his voice. Of amusement, almost.

The captain saw it as a good sign. "Perhaps we should," he agreed.

Fourteen

As Worf negotiated the corridor that led to the brig, he asked himself exactly why he'd come.

Initially, he had decided it made sense for the chief of security to check up on a prisoner like Asmund—one who had proved both so brutal and so resourceful. But by the time he was descending in the turbolift, he had been honest enough to admit—if only to himself—that there was more to it than that.

He was curious about this female—and had been since the beginning. After all, she had been raised on the Klingon homeworld. She had been exposed early on to the customs and traditions *he* had missed—that is, until he sought them out as a teenager.

But he was also repelled by her. She was an anomaly—neither human nor Klingon, but a strange admixture of the two. Just as Worf himself was—and that was what made him so uncomfortable.

Up until now, his repulsion had dominated his curiosity. He hadn't exactly avoided her—he was too busy avoiding Morgen—but he had managed to keep busy enough with his duties to prevent any chance meetings.

Then there had been the incident in the holodeck, and he had had a more compelling reason for shunning the woman. As long as she was a suspect in the murder attempts, he could not afford to have his vision clouded with emotion. What if he came to respect her? To like or even admire her? It could only have been an encumbrance in the discharge of his duty.

And of course, once he realized it was she who had made the attempts on Morgen and the others, personal contact had been out of the question. She had become an adversary, and a deadly one.

But now, with Asmund sequestered in the brig, his curiosity had come to the forefront.

Why? Because she had committed a violent crime—more than one, in fact. And because of the possibility that her Klingon upbringing, in some way—twisted or otherwise—had had something to do with it.

Hadn't there been a fear deep inside him, since the day he arrived at the Academy, that the Klingon in him would rise up at the wrong time—with grisly results? That a superior would confront him in the heat of an armed conflict and pay the price? Or that a crewmate would simply surprise him in the gym—and regret it for days afterward?

Gradually, on a purely rational level, he'd discovered that his fear was unfounded. He'd learned that he was sufficiently in control to subdue his instincts, dysfunctional as they sometimes were in the context of accepted Starfleet behavior.

That had driven his anxiety into a dark corner of his psyche. But it hadn't kept it from gnawing at him.

Now he could see the product of his fear—given flesh and substance. Given reality. What was the expression? *There but for fortune* . . .

It was the *real* reason he was coming to see Asmund. Because he had to determine for himself if her immersion in Klingon ways had had any bearing on the murders she'd attempted. He had to know to what extent Asmund herself was responsible—and to what extent it was the fire in her blood.

One final turn of the corridor and the brig came into view. In accordance with Worf's orders, there were two gold-shirted security officers—Burke and Nevins—standing guard outside. *Despite* the fact that the facility's force field had been activated.

After all, Asmund had already proven her ingenuity in using shipboard technologies to her advantage. She might have had the foresight to tamper with the brig—just as she tampered with the holodeck and the food service system. It was a long shot, given the highly secure nature of the detention area—but why take chances?

The security officers straightened at his approach. He acknowledged them with a nod. "At ease," he said. Then, turning to Burke, who was the senior of the two, he asked: "Problems?"

"None, Lieutenant. Commander Asmund hasn't said a word for hours." He paused. "Any luck with the other knife, sir?"

Inside the detention cell, Asmund was sitting by herself, watching the conversation on the other side of the transparent energy barrier. She was looking at the Klingon in particular. Worf met her gaze for a moment, then turned back to Burke.

"No," he told the man. "No luck. At least, not yet."

"I guess it would be easier if it were made of *shrogh,* or some other distinctly Klingon material."

"Yes," Worf agreed. "That would have made our search a good deal easier."

But by the end of the sentence, he was no longer looking at Burke. Once again he was regarding the prisoner—who had stood up and was approaching the threshold of her cell.

"Careful, Commander," Burke warned her—not out of compassion, but because it was his duty. "That barrier has a kick to it."

"I know," said Asmund, addressing the human. "I am familiar with starship security facilities, thank you." She turned her gaze on Worf. "Lieutenant, I would like to have a word with you." Her eyes were hooded, her chin held high. All in all, a very Klingonlike posture.

"I am listening," he responded.

She shook her head. "Alone."

It came out sounding more like a demand than a request. If he hadn't been so curious about her to begin with, he wouldn't have given it a second thought.

But the idea of gaining insight into her motives was an alluring one. Too alluring for him to pass up.

"Sir," Burke said as if he could read his superior's thoughts, "the commander isn't your typical prisoner. I wouldn't advise it."

Asmund's mouth twisted up at the corners. Worf read the scorn in the gesture, calculated to sting his Klingon pride.

"Are you so frightened of me," the blond woman asked, "that you dare not face me even across an energy barrier? Is that what it's come to—Lieutenant?"

He knew what she was up to. He knew that she was taunting him for a reason. But try as he might, he couldn't believe she was in a position to harm him. Even if she somehow managed to remove the barrier, she was unarmed—and he had his phaser.

"Leave us," Worf told his security people, never taking his eyes from Asmund's.

"But Lieutenant—" began Burke.

"Leave us," repeated the security chief—this time a little more forcefully.

Burke and Nevins had no choice but to comply. With obvious reluctance, they withdrew down the corridor until they disappeared around the bend.

"All right," Worf told the prisoner. "We are alone."

Asmund nodded. "Thank you." Her gaze seemed to soften a bit. "You didn't have to do this."

It caught him off guard. Up until then, her attitude had been haughty—dancing on the edge of arrogance. Suddenly, there was a touch of weakness in her. A sense of vulnerability no true Klingon would have permitted himself. Was it an attempt to lull his suspicions? If so, he resolved, it wouldn't work.

"Agreed," he told her. "I did not have to do it. Now, what is it you wished to speak about?"

She took a half-step toward him. It brought her dangerously close to the energy field. "You were the one who identified the knife wounds," she said. "It could only have been you. Correct?"

"Correct."

"And it was your duty to report what you found."

"Correct again."

Asmund nodded. "Then you believe I am guilty."

Something shifted uncomfortably in Worf's gut—as if he'd eaten too many serpent worms. "That is for others to judge."

"Of course it is. But what do *you* believe?"

He shrugged. "I must believe the evidence."

"But there *is* no evidence," she insisted, her voice rising an octave. With a visible effort she took hold of herself again. "Or, rather, what there is is circumstantial."

"I leave the shades of legality to the advocate general's office," he told her. "My job is to see that the ship and her crew are safe."

"Then do your job. But look beyond the evidence—if you want to call it that. Follow your instincts." A pause. "What do they tell you? That a Klingon would have tampered with a holodeck? Or opened fire on three unarmed and unsuspecting victims? Or tarnished a ceremonial knife with an enemy's blood?" She struck her chest suddenly and viciously. "*I* am a Klingon, Lieutenant. I would not have dishonored my family with such behavior—even if I *were* inclined to kill someone." The woman's eyes blazed with a cold fire. "My sister tried to kill Morgen—a fact it seems I will never live down. But she wasn't a coward. She didn't do it with sabotage or attacks in the dark; your files will confirm that. Misguided as she was, Gerda's attempt on Morgen's life was in keeping with the Klingon tradition of assassination. I say it again: she did *not* act like a coward."

The thing in Worf's gut began to writhe. He had to admit it—Asmund's words had the ring of truth to them.

"You know I'm telling the truth, Lieutenant. And you know also the importance of one's name—one's honor."

The Klingon flinched inwardly. Did she know of his discommendation? Apparently she did. But then, it was hardly a secret in the Empire. And if Asmund maintained any contact at all with the family that raised her . . .

"Yes," he said with as much dignity as possible. "I know of that."

"I must clear my name, Worf." She had dropped the Starfleet title and was using his given name; the significance of that choice was not lost on him. Asmund was calling upon him as a Klingon might call on another Klingon—as a warrior might call on another warrior. "I must find the assassin and bring him to justice. And I can't do that while I'm sitting in the brig."

The security chief's eyes narrowed. "What would you have me do? *Free* you?"

She regarded him. "Talk to Captain Picard. Make him see—he'll listen to you." Her hands became fists. "I'm not your killer, Worf. I am *not* the one you're after."

He looked at her—looked deep into those strange, blue-shadow eyes—and found he believed her.

"Please," the blond woman said—not like a warrior this time, but like a human. "There is no one else on this ship who might understand. You are my only hope."

Worf took a breath, let it out. "I will consider what you've said. Beyond that, I make no promises."

"Tell him I can help in the investigation." She came closer, her face only inches from his now. "Tell him I can be of use to you." Asmund reached out to him. "I *can* be of use, you kn—"

She must have reached out just a little bit too far—because there was a savage burst of light and the woman was flung back into her cell.

Worf resisted the impulse to go in and help her. The energy barrier worked in both directions; he would have suffered the same fate.

So he could only watch as Asmund shook off the effects of the force field and pulled herself to her feet. Watch—and gain a measure of respect for her stamina. Humans weren't supposed to be able to get up so quickly after being jolted like that.

She looked at him. "That was stupid."

He agreed. He said so. Then he added: *"Maj doch SID ghos nagh."*

It was a Klingon saying—in essence, "Good things come to those who wait."

Asmund must have wondered exactly what he meant. But she nodded. *"Tuv nagh."* I will be patient.

A moment later Worf called for Burke and headed back to the turbolift. There were no computer stations in the corridors of deck thirty-eight—for security reasons—and he wanted to learn more about Gerda Asmund's approach to the murder of Ensign Morgen.

"Come in," Morgen told him.

The doors to the Daa'Vit's apartment opened and the Klingon walked in. Their eyes met and locked, their instincts taking over for just a moment before they remembered who they were and the experience they had shared.

"Sorry to bother you," Worf said.

"Don't be," Morgen assured him. He indicated a seat. "Please."

The security chief acknowledged the kindness with a slight inclination of his head. He sat.

"What can I do for you?" the Daa'Vit asked.

Worf frowned. "I need to know about that first attempt on your life. The one that Gerda Asmund staged twenty years ago."

Morgen looked at him. "Any particular reason?"

"Yes," the Klingon told him. "But for now I would prefer it remain my own."

The Daa'Vit considered the response. "All right," he said finally. "I will respect that. But couldn't you have found what you seek in the ship's computer?"

"No. I tried that, and all I could get was a reference to the crime. No details."

"What sort of details were you looking for?"

"Everything," Worf said. "As much as you can remember."

Morgen considered it. "Let me see, then." He leaned back on his couch—a strange rock-and-moss affair. "I was an ensign at the time. One of my duties was to periodically check the shuttle bay operation consoles—in essence, to run the self-diagnostic sequences. It was something the regular shuttle deck personnel could have done easily enough, but Captain Picard insisted I learn everything there was to know about a Federation starship. In retrospect, not a bad idea." His bright yellow eyes lost their focus as he reentered the past. "That particular day, a crewman named McDonnell was in charge of the shuttle deck. A slow-moving, slow-talking sort of fellow, but one you could always rely on. When I arrived, he was nowhere to be seen. The deck was empty."

"There was only *one* crewman on duty?" Worf asked.

"That is correct. The *Stargazer* was a deep-space explorer, remember. *Constellation*-class. We didn't carry the same kind of crew that the *Enterprise* does. We didn't need to."

The Klingon nodded. "Of course. Please proceed."

"I called for McDonnell, but there was no answer. What I should have done at that point was alert Pug Joseph. But I was young and cocky—and besides, I didn't expect that there was really anything very wrong. So I took a look around.

"Finally, I found McDonnell. He was stretched out behind one of the shuttles, either dead or unconscious. Later, I found out he had only been knocked out. But at the time I wasn't sure, so I rushed to his side. And as I bent down to see him, Gerda leapt down on me from her perch on top of the shuttle.

"She must have hit me pretty hard. The next thing I knew, there was the taste of blood in my mouth. My vision was blurred and my ears were ringing too loudly for me to think. I didn't know it was Gerda attacking me. I wasn't even certain I'd been attacked. I just knew that something bad had happened, and that I should try to keep it from happening again.

"As I tried to get my bearings, I caught a glimpse of something swinging toward me—something long and heavy-looking. Just in time, I rolled away; it missed me. There was another blow, which I also managed to elude. Gradually, I came to realize that my life was in jeopardy—and that it was Gerda who was jeopardizing it, though I couldn't understand why.

"By the time Gerda came at me again, I had made a further connection with reality: I recognized the weapon she held in her hands. It was a *rikajsha* stalk. What the Federation science manuals refer to as Klingon ironroot."

The reference prodded Worf's curiosity. *"Rikajsha?"* he repeated. Ironroot grew only on the Klingon homeworld. "Where did she get it?"

"From the ship's botanical garden," Morgen explained. "Gerda brought it aboard when she signed on with the *Stargazer.* Apparently, she was planning my assassination even then—arranging to have a weapon at hand that need not arouse anyone's suspicion. After all, it was only a long, skinny garden plant—even if it was capable of breaking someone's skull when placed in the right hands."

"Actually," Worf told him, "Klingon legend is full of references to the *rikajsha* being used as a weapon. I assure you," he said, "I would allow no such plants in the botanical gardens of the *Enterprise."*

Morgen nodded. "I know. I checked." A pause. "At any rate, I couldn't avoid Gerda's attacks forever. That first blow had been a telling one, and it put me at a severe disadvantage. Before she was done, she'd broken one of my arms in two places and cracked a couple of ribs. But I was able to reel and stagger around long enough to avoid being killed before help could arrive. And arrive it did—compliments of dumb luck.

"It seems a crewman named Stroman, a geologist with a bent toward charcoal sketching, had been doing studies of some of the specimens in the botanical garden. Noticing that the *rikajsha* was missing—had been violently uprooted, in fact—this crewman notified Pug Joseph on the bridge. Picard and Ben Zoma overheard and wondered about it, and they contacted Gerda. Seeing it was she who had brought the plant there in the first place, they thought she might know something about it.

"Unfortunately—for Gerda, not for me—their call went unanswered. Gerda had left her communicator in her sleeping quarters so as not to be traced to the shuttle deck. She had no idea that anyone was trying to reach her—nor, I suspect, would she have cared very much at that particular moment.

"Concerned, Picard queried the computer about her whereabouts. It told him that she was in her room—even though she was supposed to be on her way to engineering, to help calibrate a new navigation system.

"Even more concerned now, the captain had Pug Joseph dispatch a security team to Gerda's quarters. At the same time, Ben Zoma ordered Cadwallader to conduct an internal sensor search for Gerda—just to confirm that she was truly in her room. We'd had instances of people forgetting their communicators, and he didn't want the security team wasting time on a wild chase of—what is the expression?" He looked to Worf for help.

"Goose," the Klingon offered. "A wild goose chase."

"Right. Thank you. After a little while—internal sensor searches being the slow things they are—Cadwallader determined that Gerda was not in her quarters at all. She was on the shuttle deck—where neither McDonnell nor myself were responding to Cad's intercom calls. Moments later the captain, Ben Zoma, and Pug burst in and rescued me—just as Gerda's blows were starting to connect again."

Morgen smiled humorlessly. "You see what I mean? Dumb luck. Except for anticipating Stroman's desire to sketch the *rikajsha,* Gerda did everything right. She picked a time and a place when I would be relatively isolated from other crewpeople. McDonnell was the only one who would be around—and he was someone she could easily deal with. What's more, there was little chance of anyone finding my body before she made good her escape." He stopped himself. "Do you know about that? The escape, I mean?"

The security chief shook his head. "Not very much. As I said, the computer was far from helpful."

"It was masterful—in theory, anyway. The *Tagh'rat*—the Klingon splinter group's ship—was awaiting Gerda's signal. When she finished with me, she needed only to contact her allies and open a hole in the shields—using the shuttle deck's instrumentation. By the time the hole was recognized and closed by bridge personnel, the *Tagh'rat* would have gotten close enough to snare Gerda in its transporter beam and take off."

Worf had to agree. It was a good plan. If Gerda had been successful in her assassination attempt, it would probably have worked.

"I wish," the Daa'Vit said, "that I could have made Stroman part of my escort. I didn't have that option, though. He died at Maxia Zeta."

"Too bad," the Klingon remarked.

"Yes. It is."

Worf let a moment go by before he resumed his questioning. "Tell me . . . did Gerda try to take her life after she was apprehended?"

Morgen looked at him. "I believe she did."

The security chief nodded once. "Thank you. You have been most helpful."

Fifteen

Picard sat in Geordi's office and scrutinized the readouts on Geordi's desk monitor. "Insufficient data," he read.

"That's right," said the chief engineer. "We can't construct a really dependable model for the professor's theory—we simply don't know enough about subspace physics." He sat back in his chair. "Of course, we've been able to come up with some *relatively* dependable models. But to do that, we had to make some rather large assumptions." Touching a space on his keypad, he brought up one of the models to which he was referring. "This is an example. If all our assumptions are correct, we ought to be home free at twenty-six degrees. But if we're off a bit here or there, we could need as much as *thirty*-six degrees."

The captain looked at him. "However, you still think the basic theory is sound." Geordi nodded.

"And the warp engines are capable of bearing that kind of burden again?" He nodded again.

Picard gauged his officer's confidence level. It was about as high as he'd ever seen it—despite the trouble with computer modeling.

"All right, then," he told La Forge. "Let's give it a chance."

Geordi leaned forward again. "You've got it, sir. I'll just need a few minutes down here to finalize things."

The captain stood. "Take as much time as you need. I will be up on the bridge." He paused, gazing in the direction of the master situations monitor, where Simenon, Data, and Wesley were fiddling with yet another set of variables. "Commander . . . how did the professor take the news?"

Geordi shrugged. "Right in stride. But then, that's more or less what I expected of him. He's not one to let his feelings show—is he?"

Picard shook his head. "No. He's not." Another pause. "I just wondered."

As the captain and the chief engineer exited La Forge's office, the crisis team looked up. They waited for a sign.

Geordi gave it to them. Thumbs-up.

"It's about time," the Gnalish commented. Wesley probably thought the same thing, but he kept his sentiments to himself—and wisely so. He had a lot of dues to pay before he could get away with Simenon's brand of antics. Only Data seemed to take the go-ahead in stride.

Without a comment, Picard left engineering and headed for the nearest turbolift. Stepping inside, he said: "Bridge."

In the silence that followed, he had a moment to ponder his decision. To wonder if he was doing the right thing.

He was still wondering when he emerged from the lift—only to be confronted by his Klingon security chief. Judging by the expression on Worf's face, there was a matter of more than routine concern on his mind. And with all that had occurred on the *Enterprise* lately, Picard was not eager to anticipate what it might be.

"You wish to see me," Picard said. It wasn't a question.

The Klingon nodded his massive head. "Aye, sir." He indicated the ready room with his eyes. "In private, if you don't mind."

"Of course," the captain responded, and led the way inside. As the doors closed behind them, he took a seat behind his desk. Worf sat down as well. "All right," Picard said, leaning back. "I take it this is a security matter."

The Klingon hesitated. "Yes," he replied at last. "But perhaps not in the way you mean."

The captain found his curiosity piqued, but he decided to let Worf proceed at his own pace. "I am listening," he said simply.

His chief of security frowned as he searched for the right words. "Sir," he began at last, "I don't believe Commander Asmund is the killer."

The statement caught Picard off guard. *"Not* the killer," he echoed, giving himself time to recover. He leaned forward. "Lieutenant, you yourself presented the evidence that damned her. Are you now saying that you were *wrong?"*

"Not about the knife wounds," Worf explained. "They were made by a ceremonial blade—I would stake my life on the fact." He licked his lips. "But I no longer believe that Commander Asmund was the one who wielded the knife."

Picard regarded him. "And what has occurred to change your mind?"

Worf's brow lowered—a sign of sincerity, of earnestness, Picard had learned over the years. "Captain, I had occasion to speak with Commander Asmund. She claimed that she was innocent—no surprise under the circumstances. But in the process of defending herself, she made some points that rang true. About honor— *Klingon* honor."

Picard was interested enough to hear more. "Go on," he said.

"In essence, Commander Asmund told me that the murderer's approaches weren't worthy of a Klingon—which she considers herself to be. In this, I had to agree. None of the attempts fit in with the Klingon tradition of assassination."

"But we know that some of your people take that tradition less seriously than others," the captain pointed out. He had firsthand knowledge of that fact, having been the intended victim of a *dis*honorable attempt back on the Klingon homeworld.

"True," Worf conceded. "That is why Commander Asmund referred me to the details of her sister's crime. You recall those details?"

"I do." Picard saw the scene again, just as it had been presented to him when he and Ben Zoma rushed onto the shuttle deck: Gerda swinging the deadly ironroot. Morgen lurching to avoid the blow, and only barely succeeding. And McDonnell lying prone in the foreground. "They are not easy to forget."

"You recall, then, that Gerda Asmund did not kill the one called McDonnell— though it would have been well within her power, and even advisable. A loose end is a loose end, yet Gerda chose to avoid unnecessary death."

The captain nodded. "That is correct."

"What is more, Gerda used a simple weapon—as prescribed by Klingon tradition. Usually a knife is the weapon of choice, but certainly an ironroot is not out of the question."

"The point being that she probably could have gotten her hands on a phaser— but chose not to."

"Exactly." Worf paused to let the significance of that sink in. Then he went on. "Note also that the assassination attempt was carried out by a single individual—one on one. And finally, that the first blow was not a killing one—giving the intended victim an opportunity to view the face of his killer, so he would know whom to curse in the afterlife." His voice grew weightier. "Finally, there is the matter of the poison."

The captain couldn't help but wince at the memory. No one had expected

Gerda to have a *ku'thei* nodule under her armpit—not even Idun, who had shaken off her shock long enough to warn them about a suicide attempt. Fortunately, Greyhorse had gotten to Gerda in time.

"Again," Worf finished, "all in accordance with Klingon custom. All honorable."

Indeed. And the crimes committed on the *Enterprise* had been anything *but* honorable—just as Idun had pointed out. Picard measured one set of facts against the other. "What you are saying, then," he told Worf, "is that since Gerda Asmund acted according to your code, Idun—as her identical twin—would have done the same. And because the murder attempts were conducted dishonorably, by Klingon standards, they could not have been the work of Idun. Eh?"

Worf scowled. "Is it not a logical conclusion?"

"Perhaps," the captain conceded. "And if less were at stake here, I might be inclined to accept it. But we are dealing with life and death; we cannot take the chance that our logic is flawed." He leaned back again. "It is no secret that I have been one of Idun Asmund's staunchest supporters. Even when some of your fellow officers were ready to condemn her, I refused to believe them—to judge her on the basis of her sister's actions. But now . . ." Picard shook his head. "I cannot release her. I cannot risk another murder. You may log your observations for the judge advocate general's office, Lieutenant—but the matter is really out of my hands. I am sorry."

The Klingon lifted his chin. "I understand," he said. Though his disappointment must have been keen after all the trouble he had gone to—after what he had deemed the truth was proven to have no practical value—he still held his duty above all. And his sense of duty dictated that he accept the captain's decision. "Nonetheless, I have increased security to the point at which it stood before Commander Asmund's arrest."

"Naturally," Picard agreed.

Having received the captain's blessing, the Klingon rose.

On the other side of his desk, Picard got up as well. But one matter was still unresolved. "A question, Worf."

The Klingon, who had just started to turn away from him, looked back. "Captain?"

"Where did you get all this information? It is not available in the ship's computer files. I know—it was by my order that the details were left out."

Of course, they were still on file at Starfleet Headquarters. But he had not wanted the material to be available to curiosity seekers—especially since it might have hampered Idun in her career.

"I spoke with Captain Morgen," the Klingon answered.

Picard swallowed his surprise. What had happened to that fabled hostility between Klingons and Daa'Vit?

"I see," he said. "Carry on, Lieutenant."

Worf inclined his head slightly. "Aye, sir."

A moment later the chief of security had departed, leaving Picard with even more to ponder than when he arrived on the bridge.

Good God, he mused. *Is it possible that a murderer is still loose on my ship?*

Guinan stood behind the bar, looked around, and smiled.

Ten-Forward was quiet again. Not *really* quiet, of course; there were murmured conversations and the tinkling of glasses and the sound of chairs clattering against tables. But it was placid in comparison to the rush of the last several hours.

Commander Asmund's arrest had raised quite a stir. And understandably so.

Asmund wasn't some hostile life-form who'd invaded the *Enterprise* with her phasers blazing; she was a Starfleet officer who had walked beside them, even sat down to dinner with them—all the while plotting to commit murder in their midst.

For once, even Guinan had been caught off guard. Usually, there was very little that occurred on the ship that got past her. But neither she nor Troi nor anyone else had managed to catch on to the killer—not until Worf identified her by her handiwork. It was disconcerting, to say the least.

As the doors opened, Guinan glanced in their direction. It was a reflex by now, part of the routine of running Ten-Forward. She felt more comfortable knowing who was coming in and who was leaving. And people liked the idea that she took note of them; it made them feel special.

Then she saw who had just entered her domain. *Well,* she mused, *maybe "special" isn't quite the right word in this case. "Hunted" or "persecuted," but definitely not "special."*

It was Pug Joseph. And he'd been drinking again. She could see it in the dark, puffy rings under his eyes and in the waxy pallor of his skin.

For a moment, Pug didn't seem to notice her—maybe because there were a couple of waiters obscuring his view. She watched him scan the area out by the observation ports, eyes narrowed. Looking for his nemesis, she thought: *me.* Failing to find her, he smiled and took a couple of steps toward the nearest concentration of tables.

Apparently, Pug had gotten tired of drinking in his room. And despite his earlier failures, he still thought he had a shot at taking his binge to Ten-Forward.

Then the waiters moved away, and Guinan was revealed to him. As their eyes met and locked, his expression changed—became tense, almost hateful.

Stifling his fury, he turned and walked out of the lounge.

Beverly lay stretched out on her bed, staring at the ceiling, trying to face the prospect that Ben Zoma was beyond her help. It wasn't easy. She had done her best, brought to bear all the medical technology at her disposal—and he still had less than a fifty-fifty chance.

That irked her. It wasn't as if she had never lost a patient—every doctor in Starfleet had to deal with occasional failure. But Ben Zoma had been her husband's friend, his comrade. He had joked with him, shared sorrows and triumphs with him. In a way, she felt that losing Gilaad Ben Zoma would be letting Jack down. And she desperately didn't want to do that.

Jack. The thought of him made her turn to the box of tapes resting on her commode. She wanted—needed—to hear his voice.

Opening the box again, Beverly peered inside. She longed to hear something upbeat, optimistic, like the last one—but after a moment she realized that she didn't remember the content of any individual tape very well. In fact, they were pretty much a blur to her.

It took her a few minutes, but she eventually found a tape that seemed to fit the bill. In fact, she realized with a little pang of delight, it was one of the first subspace messages Jack had ever sent her. She even remembered the messenger who had brought it—a stocky young woman who took her duties quite seriously. She used to check and double-check Beverly's signature against her records before releasing a tape, no matter how many she brought—at least until they replaced her with someone less memorable.

And it was summer, wasn't it? Beverly remembered that too, because she couldn't understand how it could be summer and be so cold. Of course, she'd never lived in San Francisco before. She'd never even lived on *Earth* before.

But Starfleet's medical college was in San Francisco, and it was the best in the Federation. And when she'd actually gotten *accepted* there, she could hardly justify staying on Arvada Three, as much as she loved the colony.

So, shortly after her marriage to Jack, they'd moved to a second-floor apartment in the shadow of Starfleet headquarters—which seemed a little oppressive at first. Later, however, she came to appreciate it; it had made her feel closer to her husband and his work. And it enabled her to get subspace messages that much more quickly.

Shaking her head, she inserted the tape into the player. It took a second or two before Jack's message came up.

"Hi, sweetheart. Life on the *Stargazer* is . . . how can I put it? Eventful. For the last couple of weeks we've been charting a couple of gas giants on a collision course in the Beta Expledar system. The theory was that if two of these gas giants come together with enough force, the resulting body will be heavy enough for its own gravity to instigate fusion—in other words, for the thing to become a star in its own right.

"Well, it's no longer a theory. I wish you could have seen it. You can't imagine the outpouring of light . . . the sheer magnitude of the spectacle . . . I know I'm not very good with words, but I think you get the idea. It was magnificent.

"On a more mundane note, I've made friends with my first Pandrilite—a fellow named Vigo, who's in charge of the weapons around here. Don't worry—he hasn't had any chance to use them yet, and he probably never will. In any case, he's trying to teach some of us this game called *sharash'di*. I've never heard of it, but it looks interesting, and Vigo says I've got quite an aptitude for it. I think he means for a *human*—but I just might surprise him one day.

"Fortunately, we've got a good group on the *Stargazer*. When you're working in close quarters, that's pretty important. You've been hearing about Jean-Luc for a long time, of course, but my respect for him grows each day. There can't be a man alive better suited to head up a deep-space exploration. Ben Zoma's another born leader—though he's got a much more low-key approach. Sometimes I think he'd rather hear a good joke than eat. And then there's—"

Jack's voice was drowned out by that of Jean-Luc Picard, coming over the *Enterprise*'s intercom system: "This is the captain. Once more we will be attempting to free ourselves from the subspace anomaly. The maneuver may take some time and involve a fair amount of turbulence; please take all necessary precautions."

Reluctantly, Beverly switched off the tape mechanism and got to her feet. She would resume, she promised herself, once this "maneuver" was over.

Off duty or not, she wasn't about to let sickbay get bounced around without being there to pick up the pieces.

As Worf approached the brig, the two security officers faced him and straightened. He set them at ease with a nod and came to stand before the force barrier.

Asmund had been sitting on her bunk. She looked up—and saw immediately that he had nothing in the way of good news for her.

"I am sorry," he said. "I spoke with the captain on your behalf—"

The woman finished the sentence for him: "But he won't take the chance."

He eyed her. "That is correct."

She nodded. "I suppose I'm not surprised. As one who was raised a Klingon, I hate the idea of sitting here, caged, while the one who arranged it runs loose." Her eyes blazed with dark fire. "The very idea," she began, her voice trembling, "the very idea consumes me."

It took her a few moments to achieve control again. "But as a Starfleet officer," she said, "I can't blame the captain. I would probably have made the same decision myself."

"If you are innocent, it will come out in a court-martial." He did not expect that to be of much comfort to her now—but what else could he say?

Asmund grunted. *"Tuv nagh?* Wait for weeks, months, while someone else decides my fate? And I remain an object of scorn and loathing? I am not *that* patient, Lieutenant. But then, that is not your concern. You have done all you could; I am grateful."

Turning away from him then, she went back to her bunk and sat down. He stood there for a moment, watching her. Wondering what he would do, how he would feel, if he were in her place.

Then he turned and, with a brief acknowledgment of the officers on guard, made his way back to the bridge.

Sixteen

Standing at his engineering console, Geordi scanned the bridge. Every one of his fellow officers was in his or her place—not to mention Morgen and Simenon, who had gotten the captain's permission to witness the maneuver from a position near the aft stations.

Getting up from his command chair, Picard turned to look at the chief engineer. "You may proceed, Commander."

"Aye, sir," Geordi answered. Focusing his attention on his monitor, where the shields were depicted as a series of blue lines surrounding the ship, he took a last look at such items as environmental resistance, energy consumption, and field integrity. Satisfied, he tapped in the first set of alterations. Immediately, the blue-line configuration began to writhe and change.

"Forward shields flattening," Data reported. "Forming a surface perpendicular to the axis of our passage."

For Geordi, the information was redundant. His monitor showed him the effect in some detail.

"Obverse stress increasing," Wesley announced.

The ship quivered momentarily—just as it had when they'd tried reversing engines. It was a good sign, La Forge told himself.

Unable to keep the excitement out of his voice, Wesley said: "We're slowing down, Captain. Warp nine point nine four five . . . warp nine point nine four zero." He leaned back. "Stabilizing at nine point nine four zero."

"Hull integrity?" Picard snapped.

"Stresses are well within acceptable limits," Worf replied from tactical.

A *very* good sign, Geordi noted.

Simenon had been right—shield structure had an effect on their progress through the slipstream. But would it have enough of an effect to dump them out of it?

There was only one way to find out. A second time, his fingers skipped nimbly over the console.

"Rear shields flattening," Data informed them.

A shiver ran through the deck, through the bulkheads. It was more strident, more noticeable than the one before it.

"Obverse stress *de*creasing," Wesley declared. "Accelerating . . ." He shook his head. "Back up to warp nine point nine five now."

Worf raised his gaze from his monitor board. "Stress has intensified considerably, sir. It is as if we were being sandwiched between two forces."

Picard looked over his shoulder at his security chief. "Any danger, Lieutenant?"

"No *immediate* danger," the Klingon advised him.

In his seat at the captain's side, Riker consulted the readouts built into his armrest and frowned. "So far, so good."

Yes, Geordi mused. *So far, so good.* But the easy part was over. From here on in, the going would get a lot rougher.

With careful precision, he instructed the computer to tilt both shield surfaces—forward and rear. Not a lot—just ten degrees.

This time, the deck didn't just shudder—it jerked. So badly, in fact, that La Forge had to grab on to the edges of his console to keep from falling.

Through it all, Data's voice was as calm and matter-of-fact as ever. "Shield surfaces pitched ten degrees," he said.

Picard let go of his chair, which he'd used to steady himself. Straightening to his full height, he looked around. "Mister Worf?"

The Klingon's answer was a second or two in coming. "Minimal damage, sir." Another pause. "No serious injuries."

The captain nodded. "Good." He turned to Wesley. "Velocity? Bearing?"

"No change," the ensign told him.

Picard cast a glance in Geordi's direction. The chief engineer looked back, and a wordless communication passed between them.

Continue?

Continue.

Adjusting the blue lines on his monitor another ten degrees, La Forge input the change. And hung on.

It didn't help. The ship bucked so badly that he found himself on the floor anyway. And it didn't stop bucking—not completely—though the echoes weren't nearly as vicious as the original jolt.

"Shield surfaces—" Data began.

But Worf's cry drowned him out. "Structural damage to Decks Twenty-two and Twenty-three. Evacuating affected areas and sealing off!"

Could have been worse, Geordi mused, lifting himself up off the carpet. Twenty-two and twenty-three were engineering decks which were less than crucial at the moment. And since they were sparsely populated, it would only take a few moments to clear them.

"Same speed and heading, sir!" Wesley called out.

More importantly, Geordi noted, the shields were maintaining their shape, despite the forces imposed on them. The drain on the engines was tremendous, but they were doing their job—and doing it well.

Behind Worf, Morgen was helping Simenon to his feet. The Gnalish had hit his head on something; he was bleeding. But he refused to leave the bridge.

La Forge didn't blame him. Under the circumstances, he wouldn't have left either.

As he got another grip on his console, Geordi exchanged looks with the captain again. Picard looked a little rumpled; he must have fallen as well. But he seemed no less resolute than before.

"Decks Twenty-two and Twenty-three evacuated," Worf growled.

The captain nodded. Geordi nodded back.

Turning to his monitor, the chief engineer manipulated the shields. *Ten degrees more. That's thirty altogether—pretty much an average of what the models said it would take.* On the screen, it looked like a lot. But would it be enough to free them?

Or just enough to tear them apart?

He called out: "Hang on, folks." Then, bracing himself, he pressed "enter."

Idun Asmund hadn't said a word to the two security officers outside her cell since they started their shift an hour or so ago. Nor had she spoken to any of the guards on the shifts before that.

A cool customer. That's how one of them had put it, thinking she hadn't heard. Well, she'd heard all right. And though she hadn't corrected the woman, she was anything but *cool*.

She was hot. She was *seething*. Just as any Klingon would have seethed, penned in like an animal.

Of course, this time it was more than her breeding that made her crave freedom so intensely. She had a *job* to do—a job that couldn't wait. And she couldn't do it from the brig. It ate at her, that while she sat, helpless, blood-justice went unsatisfied.

But she had long ago learned to contain her Klingon-bred tendencies to vent emotion. So well, in fact, that those on the *Stargazer* and elsewhere had seen her as some sort of iron maiden—highly disciplined, highly controlled. *A cool customer indeed.* She savored the bitter irony of it.

When the captain's announcement came over the intercom, the goldshirts exchanged brief remarks. But she remained silent—even though she had an idea of the risks they had to be incurring. The last set of maneuvers had blacked out parts of the ship—and they hadn't accomplished a thing. She didn't know much about warpspace engineering, but she knew this—any serious attempt to escape the slipstream would place an even greater strain on the *Enterprise*. A strain that would put them all in jeopardy.

If her guards hadn't fully appreciated that fact, the first jolt gave them an inkling of what was to come. She noted the look of alarm that crossed both their faces.

"Huh," one of them muttered—a big man whose hair was as pale as hers. His first name was John—she'd overheard that. "The captain wasn't kidding."

His companion was smaller, dark and bearded; name unknown. "That's all right," he said. "Let's just hope it does the trick."

The second shock was worse. The blond man was thrown to the floor. The dark one managed to keep his feet by clutching at the bulkhead behind him.

And even then, it wasn't over. There were aftershocks that made the ship tremble unnervingly.

"Damn." John picked himself up, despite the continuing disturbances. "What's going *on* up there?"

The other man just shook his head. He was looking at the light that indicated the barrier was still in effect.

Though Asmund couldn't see it from her bunk, or indeed from anywhere in her cell, she gathered that the light was still on. Otherwise, her guards would have reacted to the fact. But the dark one was still scrutinizing it.

"What's the matter?" asked the blond man, noting the direction in which his colleague was staring.

"I thought I saw the light flicker."

John considered it himself. "It's not flickering now," he said.

"No. It's not." He shrugged. "My imagination, maybe." He turned to his companion. "I guess that was it. My imagination."

That's when the third jolt came. Actually, it was more of an upheaval.

The floor of her cell came crashing up at her, and the world went black.

Lifting himself off the deck, Geordi straightened his VISOR. In the grinding, shifting moment of chaos that followed his implementation of the last shield-shape alteration, it had fallen askew. *Along with half my vertebrae,* the engineering chief remarked inwardly, noting the pain that was only now emerging in his lower back. And both his knees. And his left wrist.

He winced as the VISOR clicked softly into place. *Must have hit my head too,* he decided. *Damn. What a mess.*

Then, as his unique variety of vision was restored to him, he realized just why he was so sore. He was no longer at the engineering console—he was no longer anywhere *near* the engineering console. Their effort to escape the slipstream had flung him clear over to the food dispenser—a good thirty feet!

As he looked around he saw that other members of the bridge contingent had been similarly strewn about. The captain, Riker, and Troi, for instance, had all been pitched forward and to the right, so that they were now dusting themselves off near the emergency turbolift. Worf was in front of the command area instead of in back of it, and Wesley had been plastered against the forward viewscreen—which had gone blank somewhere along the line.

Neither Morgen nor Simenon was immediately visible—not until they poked their heads up from behind the tactical station. The Gnalish muttered a curse.

Only Data had somehow managed to remain in his seat—though now that Geordi looked more closely, he could see that it had been at the expense of his control board. The thing was flipped up and mangled at one end—no doubt, where the android had gripped it to anchor himself.

This kind of stuff wasn't supposed to happen on a ship like the *Enterprise,* Geordi noted. Not with all the damping and stabilizing features built into her. But then, no spacegoing vessel was designed to do what they had done.

"Is everyone all right?" Picard asked.

There were some groans, but no seriously negative replies. The captain nodded. "Good. Now let's see where we stand."

By then La Forge was already making his way back to the aft stations. He was pleasantly surprised to see that his monitor had fared better than the viewscreen: it still showed the blue-lined diagram that he'd been using to set up each maneuver. Unfortunately, most of the blue lines were gone.

"Damage?" Picard demanded, having resumed his place in the command center.

By then Worf too had returned to his original position. "Reports coming in from all decks, sir. Damage to ship and systems is considerable." He looked up. "Nothing, however, that cannot be corrected by repair teams."

"Warp drive is disabled again," Geordi chimed in. "But we pretty much expected that. What shields we've got left are running on impulse power."

"Injuries?" the captain asked.

The Klingon consulted his board again. "Widespread. But so far, none appears to be life-threatening."

Picard's forehead wrinkled. "I would say we were lucky, under the circumstances." He turned to Wesley. "The question is *how* lucky. Mister Crusher?"

The ensign hunched over his monitor and frowned. He shook his head. "I wish I could tell you, sir. But astrogation is down." He swiveled in his chair to face the captain. "I don't know if the maneuver worked or not."

Picard grunted, unable to quite conceal his disappointment. "I see."

"There's a way to find out, though," Geordi reminded them. "All we have to do is find an observation port."

"Good idea," Simenon said. And without waiting for anyone else to agree, he headed for the observation lounge.

A half-dozen others moved to follow him—Morgen, Picard, Riker and Troi. And finally, Geordi himself.

The lounge doors parted, revealing the cabin and its conference table. And beyond it, a generous helping of starlit space.

La Forge smiled. Past those who had entered before him, he could see that the stars were standing still—no longer streaks of light, but mere points.

They were out of the slipstream, back in normal space. And though it wasn't clear yet exactly *where* in normal space, it felt pretty good to be there.

Simenon was standing in the front of the group. As Geordi watched, he turned his serpentine head and looked back at him. And winked. As if to say *we did it!*

Though nobody saw it—not even Simenon—La Forge winked back.

When Asmund regained her senses there was a nauseating, dull ache in the vicinity of one of her temples. She touched the area gingerly, winced at the pain even that light contact provoked, and inspected her fingertips. Blood—and not a little of it.

But her guards had come through even worse. The bearded man was out cold, one of his legs twisted in such a way that it had to have been broken. And the one called John, while conscious, was gripping his side and grimacing in anguish. For the moment, he seemed to have forgotten about his phaser; it was lying on the deck a couple of feet from where he lay propped against the bulkhead.

She saw all this in darkness, aided only by the strobe of a naked, fizzling circuit—though she couldn't at first pinpoint its location. Then it dawned on her. It was the one just to the side of her cell—the one that controlled the energy field.

Rising from the floor, she approached the place where the barrier should have been. Carefully, ever so carefully, she reached out.

And watched her hand pass over the threshold, unscathed. No flash of light, no energy charge to make her regret her trespass. No barrier.

No barrier.

Then she looked down and saw that John was watching her. That he had realized the barrier was down as well.

Without a word, he launched himself in the direction of his phaser. Ignoring the pounding in her head, Asmund dived for the weapon too. Unfortunately for her, he got to it first, managed to raise it and fire.

Twisting in mid-air, Asmund somehow eluded the narrow beam of red light. And before the blond man could take aim again, she grabbed hold of his wrist with both hands.

Knowing what she knew about pressure points, it wasn't difficult to make him scream out and drop the phaser. But all her faculties focused on the task, she never saw the blow from his free hand. It hit her in the back of the neck, stunning her, intensifying the spike of pain in her temple.

Still, she found the strength to lash out backhanded—to hit her adversary across the face hard enough to knock him out. As he slumped beside her, she laid claim to the weapon and got to her feet.

The other guard was still unconscious, his breathing shallow but regular. She passed up the temptation to look for his phaser as well, deciding a second one would be of only marginal value—and she had no time to waste. At any moment, they might realize she was free and send a security team after her.

Phaser in hand, she took off down the corridor.

Like everyone else on the bridge, Wesley was still shaking his head over the success of Professor Simenon's idea. The ensign grinned as he watched the Gnalish regale Picard with the third retelling of his stone-skimming exploits in the holodeck. With Riker and Troi having departed to oversee repair and relocation efforts, and Morgen gone along with them, the captain and Simenon had the command center all to themselves.

Suddenly, the professor pointed to Wesley, and the others turned his way as well. The ensign felt himself blush as Picard smiled appreciatively and nodded; he could just imagine what Simenon was telling him. *Wonderful boy you've got there. Couldn't have done it without him. So how is it he never skimmed stones before? Who's responsible for his education anyway?*

Swiveling away before his blush became permanent, Wesley returned his attention to his board. Much to his surprise, the astrogation function had been returned to it; that section of the display was outlined again in green light.

Touching the appropriate keys, he called up their position. Instantly, the coordinates appeared on the screen.

He froze as he realized the significance of what he saw. No, he told himself. *Please* say this isn't right. With an effort, he forced his fingers to run the system through a diagnostic check.

There was nothing wrong with it. It was functioning perfectly. Swallowing, Wesley turned again toward the captain.

And drew Picard's attention. Abruptly, the captain stopped smiling—and came striding down to the conn station.

"What is it, Mister Crusher? You look positively green."

Then Picard looked past him and saw the coordinates. As Wesley watched, the muscles in the man's jaw rippled.

"Commander La Forge," the captain called, hardly raising his voice. His eyes remained fixed on the astrogation readout.

"Aye, sir?" Geordi came down the ramp from the aft stations. "Something wrong?"

Picard nodded. "Apparently."

"What is it?" Simenon asked, rising from his seat in the command center.

"Come see for yourself, Phigus."

By that time, Geordi had arrived and was beginning to appreciate the situation. He whistled soft and low.

Wesley knew that *someone* had to come out and say it. But he waited dutifully for the Gnalish to arrive and curse beneath his breath before he fit words to the problem.

"We're in Romulan space," he announced—a bit more loudly than he'd intended. It attracted some stares from around the bridge.

"Indeed," Picard said. Then, a little more softly: "The question is, what are we going to do about it?"

As if sensing that the question was directed toward him, Geordi looked up. "Captain, the engines are in bad shape. And even if we *had* warp speed, I don't think I'd want to risk using it."

Picard's eyes narrowed. "Because we might get ourselves stuck in the slipstream all over again?"

"That's right, sir." La Forge bit his lip. "To be safe, we've got to put some distance between ourselves and the phenomenon. And even at full impulse, that's going to take some time. Hours, anyway."

"At least," Simenon chimed in.

Picard frowned at La Forge. "We don't *have* time, Commander. There could be a Romulan ship on our tail at any moment." His frown deepened. "How quickly do you think you can give me warp one?"

La Forge shrugged. "I don't know. A day, a few hours—it's hard to say, sir."

"Three hours," Picard told him. It wasn't a request and it wasn't an order. It was just a statement of what they needed.

Geordi sighed. "You'd better excuse me," he said, and headed for the forward turbolift. Without waiting to be asked, Simenon fell in right behind him.

Picard turned to Wesley. "How far are we from the Neutral Zone at full impulse?"

Wesley quickly performed the necessary calculations. "Sixteen hours, thirty-two minutes," he said, though the captain had moved close enough to the Conn to see the computations on-screen himself.

Picard nodded. "Lay in a course, Mister Crusher. When the use of our warp drive is restored to us, we'll be that much closer to salvation."

Sixteen hours, Wesley thought. *There's no way we can go unnoticed for that long.*

Behind him, he heard Lieutenant Worf grunt—as if in agreement with the ensign's unarticulated analysis. Then the Klingon spoke.

"We have another problem, sir," he said evenly.

Picard turned away from the newly restored viewscreen to face his security chief. "Yes, Lieutenant?"

Worf's expression was grim. "Commander Asmund has escaped."

Seventeen

Picard's eyes narrowed as he absorbed the information. "I see," he said, his voice level and controlled. "And her guards?"

"Injured, but not badly." The Klingon added: "The brig's security systems were damaged in the escape from the slipstream."

"Is she armed?"

"She has a phaser, sir."

He nodded. "And potential victims all over the ship." The captain frowned. "Go after her, Worf. *Find* her." His tone was decisive, authoritative—but his eyes were full of regret. "And give her no quarter. Commander Asmund is a most resourceful individual."

Worf nodded, already starting to move toward the turbolift. "On my way, sir."

"Lieutenant . . ."

The Klingon stopped.

Picard opened his mouth to say something—but thought better of it. He shook his head. "Nothing. Just keep me posted."

"Aye, sir," said the security chief. But he knew what the captain had been about to say—something about not allowing personal feelings and beliefs to keep one from doing one's duty. It would have been an unnecessary instruction; he was glad that Picard had kept it to himself.

As the captain turned back to the viewscreen, Worf entered the turbolift. "Computer," he asked, "what is the location of Commander Idun Asmund?"

The response was quick and concise. "Commander Asmund is in a lift compartment in the vicinity of Deck Eight, primary hull."

Worf straightened as if he'd been slapped in the face. The battle bridge was located on deck eight of the *secondary* hull. It would be a simple maneuver for Asmund to move from one hull to the next—and if she could rig the holodeck and the food processor, she could probably gain access to the battle bridge as well.

And she could control the entire ship from there.

She was clever. She had fooled him once, with her protestations of innocence. She would not fool him again.

"Deck Eight," he said, his teeth clenching as he prepared himself for the inevitable confrontation.

Had Morgen been more familiar with the layout of a *Galaxy*-class vessel, he might have had some prior idea of which cabin he was entering. As it was, he was almost as surprised to see the roomful of young children as they were to see him.

There were about a dozen of them, peering up at him with eyes fresh from crying. A couple still had trails of tears on their faces.

A woman who was kneeling among them—their teacher, apparently—looked up at Morgen. "Hello," she said, unable to conceal the trepidation in her voice.

It wasn't the first time he'd evoked that kind of reaction since he'd set foot on the *Enterprise.* Nor was it difficult to understand, given the imposing Daa'Vit physique and the fact that so few of his people were seen on Federation starships.

A moment later, noticing the pips on the Daa'Vit's collar, the woman said, "Oh. You must be one of Captain Picard's guests."

"Yes," he told her. "I'm Captain Morgen. Is everyone all right in here?"

She nodded. "We're fine." She scanned the faces of the children. "A little frightened, but fine."

Just as she said that, a little girl began sobbing. And before the woman could comfort the child, a little boy followed suit.

Smiling, Morgen lowered himself onto his haunches. "Come on, now," he said, glancing from the girl to the boy and back again. "If you cry, it's going to make *me* start crying too. And when I start crying, I can't stop."

Then, before he lost their attention, the Daa'Vit opened his tear ducts and let the clear serum inside them flow copiously down his cheeks.

As he'd intended, it got the children's attention. So fascinated were they by the sight of his tears, they forgot their own problems. A couple of them even started giggling.

Morgen mugged an expression of sadness, and they giggled some more. More mugging, more giggling. Before they knew it, they were laughing out loud.

The woman shot him a look of gratitude. He nodded a little and went on with his act—one that had become a favorite of the children on his own ship over the years.

One little boy even came over and put his arm around the Daa'Vit. "It's all right," he said. "There's nothing to be scared of."

Morgen turned to him, still releasing great globby tears. "Are you sure?" he asked.

"Uh huh," the child assured him. "Captain Picard will take care of us. That's what my mom always says."

As if on cue, the Daa'Vit's communicator beeped. Tapping it out of reflex, he opened the communications channel on his end. "Morgen here."

"This is Picard," the captain told him. "We've got a problem—or more accurately, *another* problem. Are you alone?"

"One second, please." Standing, the Daa'Vit winked at the children. Then he retreated to the other side of the cabin. "All right. You can go on now."

The captain didn't waste any time. "Asmund has escaped her cell. She's at large and she's got a phaser."

Morgen digested the information. "Acknowledged."

"I want you to return to your quarters."

The Daa'Vit made a sound of disgust. "I've spent enough time in my quarters," he complained. "More than enough time. Your people need my help."

"My people," Picard said, "will survive better without you." The level of authority in his voice went up a notch. "You are a *target,* Morgen. And as such, you are a danger to everyone around you."

The Daa'Vit looked back at the children.

"Report to your quarters, my friend. Or I will have a security team escort you there."

The Daa'Vit forced himself to be objective—to see the wisdom in his former captain's words. "As you wish," he answered finally. "Morgen out."

He lingered only another second or two—just long enough to consider the little ones and the woman in their midst. None of them had any idea what kind of dangers they faced—both from within and without. And that was probably just as well.

"Do you have to go?" a little girl asked.

He nodded. "I'm afraid so. But thanks. I feel a lot better now that you've cheered me all up."

Then, before he could entertain any rebellious second thoughts, he took his leave of them.

The Klingon in Worf urged him to face Commander Asmund alone—but the security chief in him recognized he had a greater chance of success if he called in backups. In the end, the security chief won out.

As he reached Deck Eight, however, none of his backups had arrived. And the situation didn't allow for delay. Drawing his phaser, Worf pressed his back against the bulkhead, and quickly but silently made his way along its curving surface.

At any moment, he knew, he might come face to face with the fugitive—though given the head start she had, it was far more likely she'd already gotten into the battle bridge. And that was the reason for his haste.

When he slid within view of the bridge doors, he noticed that they were closed. Nor did they show any signs of having been forced.

A neat job indeed. He'd hardly completed the thought when reinforcements arrived in the forms of Nevins and Loyosha.

"Is she in there, sir?" asked Nevins.

Worf was about to answer in the affirmative when he realized he was only going on a supposition. Turning his face upward, he queried the computer as he had earlier: "Computer—what is Commander Asmund's location?"

Again, the answer was immediate. "Commander Asmund is in a turbolift on Deck Eighteen."

Worf looked at his security officers. They looked back.

"Deck Eighteen?" Loyosha echoed.

What was she doing? Trying to forestall the inevitable?

Worf didn't believe it. Asmund was too smart to believe she would elude them for long this way.

Putting himself in her place, the Klingon conceded he might throw a single curve at his pursuers—and the battle bridge would have served him well in that regard.

But Deck Eighteen? What was on Deck Eighteen except living quarters and—

He cursed. If he could locate Asmund, then Asmund could locate *Morgen*. Why didn't he think of that before?

"Computer," he barked, "where is Captain Morgen?"

"Captain Morgen," the computer replied, "is in the educational facility on Deck Eighteen."

Worf hurtled down the corridor, with Loyosha and Nevins in close pursuit.

"Commander?"

La Forge looked up from his workstation, where he'd been working feverishly to get the warp drive back online. On the other side of engineering, the Gnalish was standing at an identical workstation, complementing his efforts.

"Progress?" Geordi asked hopefully.

Simenon shook his lizardlike head, never taking his eyes off his monitors. "Not enough. I've still got a long way to go."

Turning back to his own instruments, La Forge smiled. He was getting to know Simenon pretty well—he could tell when the professor had something on his mind. "Then what?" he asked.

A pause. "Tell me about the Romulans."

La Forge was a little surprised by the request. Then he remembered that the *Stargazer*'s famous twenty-year voyage had taken place during the Romulans' decades-long period of withdrawal. Very likely, he realized with a bit of a jolt, Simenon had never even seen a Romulan—except in tapes, and even those were bound to have been pretty old.

Nor was it hard to figure out what had prompted the Gnalish's curiosity. When you were sneaking through enemy territory, it was only natural to want to know a little about the enemy.

"Tell you about them," the chief engineer echoed. "Where would you like me to start?"

"Start anywhere," Simenon instructed.

La Forge smiled again. "All right. For one thing, their technology has come a long way since their alliance with the Klingons. Their ships are bigger, faster, and deadlier."

"All very comforting," the Gnalish commented.

"And of course," La Forge continued, "no one schemes better than the Romulans. No one's more merciless." He thought about the *Enterprise*'s various encounters with its Vulcanoid adversaries over the last few years. And of his personal experiences. "On the other hand," he went on, "they're people, with their own concepts of honor and loyalty, of right and wrong."

Simenon grunted. "Ah-hah. A ray of hope. Does that mean they refrain from shooting first and asking questions never? Is there a chance they'll believe our tale of woe and let us go?"

La Forge shrugged. "Depends on the exact circumstances."

"In other words, no."

"In other words, it's pretty unlikely."

The Gnalish sighed. "Sorry I asked."

Worf couldn't understand it. As he made his way down from Deck Eight in a parallel turbolift, his adversary didn't move out into the corridor. In fact, she didn't move at all.

She just maintained her position in the lift. And the lift maintained its position on Deck Eighteen.

But why? Had she been hurt in the course of Geordi's maneuver, or maybe in an ensuing melee with her guards—hurt so badly that she'd had only enough strength to go this far, and no farther?

Or was she up to something else entirely? Something he had failed to figure out?

The doors of Worf's lift opened and he swung out, breaking into a run. Nevins and Loyosha pelted along behind him.

All of them had their phasers at the ready—just in case.

"Computer," the Klingon barked one more time. "Location of Commander Asmund."

"Commander Asmund is in a turbolift on Deck Eighteen," the computer confirmed.

Worf's mind raced as fast as the rest of him. He had a vision of her standing there in the lift, doors open, a grim smile on her face—and then, when she heard him coming, closing the doors and watching the look on his face as she escaped him.

Was that it? Was she trying to humiliate him, knowing he would lead the search for her?

For what reason? Sheer spite?

Or was she truly mad now—not only homicidal, but out of touch with reality in other ways as well?

This time, when the Klingon arrived to confront the fugitive, he had plenty of company. Not only Nevins and Loyosha, but an additional trio of security officers approaching from the other end of the corridor.

Contrary to Worf's premonition, the lift doors were closed. He took in his people with a glance.

"Phasers on stun. Be prepared for anything."

Then, careful to keep his eyes on the doors, he touched the lift security override pad on the bulkhead.

Not that he expected the action to accomplish anything. With the technical expertise Asmund had demonstrated, Worf fully expected that she'd jammed the door-opening mechanism, which would force him to find an engineer capable of bypassing or otherwise nullifying her handiwork.

Much to his surprise, however, the override worked. The doors opened.

The security officers tensed, training their weapons on the interior of the compartment. As it turned out, it wasn't necessary.

There was no one inside.

Muttering a curse, Worf took a step forward—and noticed something on the floor of the lift. Grunting, he went in and picked it up.

A communicator. He turned it over in his hand.

Asmund had led him on a merry chase. And he had been too concerned with more complicated explanations for her behavior to consider the simplest one of all.

What was the expression humans used? About failing to see the forest for the trees?

The fugitive had asked the computer for Morgen's whereabouts and then programmed the lift for that destination—with a stop on Deck Four, just to prolong the chase. And while her communicator was buying her time, she was using it to serve her purposes.

He should have known she'd try something like this, the security chief told himself. He should have *known*.

He scowled. Asmund could be anywhere on the *Enterprise* now. Absolutely anywhere. He had no choice but to have his people comb the ship for her, inch by inch.

And Morgen . . . he had to contact the Daa'Vit, alert him to—

"Lieutenant Worf?"

The Klingon turned at the sound of his name. He was a little startled to see Morgen standing there, casting a curious eye over the proceedings.

"Is something wrong?" the Daa'Vit asked innocently.

Worf's scowl deepened. "That," he growled, "is one way of putting it."

The bleeding from her temple had stopped, but Asmund's head hurt mercilessly. Taking a deep breath, she leaned back against the cargo container and tried to put her thoughts in order.

By now, she thought, they would have found the communicator in the turbolift. And begun the search in earnest.

But it was too late. Avoiding the use of the lifts completely, she'd found an entrance to the cargo bays on Deck Thirty-eight and slipped inside.

Fortunately, the bay's manifest had told her it had the kind of cargo she needed. And the *Enterprise* crew had been every bit as efficient as it was reputed to be; the dolacite containers she sought were all in their proper locations.

Used extensively these days to line the insides of warp nacelles, dolacite was the only substance routinely carried on Federation starships that could foil internal sensor systems. By hiding among containers full of the stuff, Asmund had effectively rendered herself invisible to the ship's internal security systems.

She glanced at the phaser in her lap. Picking it up, she felt its reassuring heft.

Under other circumstances, it might have been a liability to her. After all, every phaser was hooked in with the ship's computer—to prevent the use of power levels at which a random blast could punch through a hull wall. And with that kind of hookup, it wasn't all that difficult to scan the *Enterprise* for phaser locations—there were only a few dozen of them on board.

It was certainly a lot easier than trying to find a single human bio-profile among a mostly-human population of more than a thousand individuals.

But the dolacite protected her from that kind of detection as well. Which was a good thing. She needed the phaser.

You've bought yourself some time, she mused. You'd better put it to good use.

If only her head didn't hurt so much.

All in all, Beverly decided, they'd been pretty fortunate. Not only had Simenon's strategy gotten them out of the slipstream, but they had avoided any truly serious injuries. The worst was a compound fracture of the leg, suffered by a man named Starros—one of the security officers who had been watching Idun Asmund. Nor had sickbay sustained any damage; there wasn't even a tricorder out of place.

Of course, Asmund had escaped in the course of the beating the ship had taken. And according to Worf, she was armed with a phaser and dangerous as hell.

But so what? They were also in Romulan space, in peril of being blasted to atoms or—if Fate was kind—merely becoming prisoners of the Empire.

Somewhere along the line, the doctor had decided it wasn't worth getting scared. And so, when the last of those injured in the attempt to break free of the slipstream had been treated, she'd decided to return to her cabin, and enjoy some much-needed rest.

As soon as she stepped out of the lift, Beverly noted the beefed-up security presence in the vicinity of her door. She asked what it was about.

"Lieutenant Worf's orders," one of the officers on duty replied.

"I see. Then you've got squads like these by the captain's quarters as well? And Commander Riker's?"

"In every occupied residential corridor, Doctor."

Crusher nodded. "Good," she said. "I wouldn't want to be singled out for special treatment or anything."

The security officer looked at her. "I beg your pardon?"

"Don't mind me," the doctor told her. "I'm just asserting my right to be in as much jeopardy as everyone else."

And while the officer tried to decipher her last statement, Crusher walked by her and entered her apartment. It felt good not to be afraid anymore.

As she stepped inside, she saw a tiny red light shining at her from her bedroom.

It was on the tape player—a reminder that the thing was on "pause." And a reminder as well that she'd made a promise to herself about listening to the end of the tape.

She let the light draw her on. Hell—if she was going to be space dust before long, she was at least going to hear the end of Jack's story first.

Without even ordering the lights to activate, she sat down on her bed and touched the display marked "play." Immediately, the tape picked up where it had left off.

"—there's Greyhorse and Pug Joseph and Simenon, who you've heard about also, and—hell, I'd better stop before I read off the whole roster. As I said, though, they're a good bunch."

Crusher sat back against her cushions. Maybe *that* was what had given her this spurt of resolve—the cumulative effect of hearing Jack's voice these last few days. Exposure to the courage that had spurred him to life—and ultimately death—among the stars. It was as good an explanation as any.

"And while we're on the subject of Greyhorse," Jack went on, "it seems there's more to him than meets the eye. He comes off pretty quiet, pretty studious. But the other day, I think I caught him in a compromising position . . . with Gerda Asmund, of all people. You see, Vigo and I were—"

Crusher's finger darted out and stopped the tape. In the dark of her bedroom, she could hear the thumping of her heart against her ribs—the sudden urgency of her breathing. Touching the mechanism's control display again, she rewound for a few seconds. Then she played it back again.

"—more to him than meets the eye. He comes off pretty quiet, pretty studious. But the other day, I think I caught him in a compromising position . . . with Gerda Asmund, of all people. You see, Vigo and I were repairing to the lounge for a game of *sharash'di.* We didn't know there was anyone in there. And as we came in, we saw Greyhorse and Gerda sort of—well, sort of moving apart, as if they'd just been embracing one another. Anyway, I didn't want to embarrass them, so I just ignored it, and so did Vigo. We went straight to the—"

The doctor shut off the machine. She had heard enough. *Oh my god,* she thought. *Oh my god.*

Heart hammering in her chest, she punched her communicator.

In the dim light he'd come to prefer, Carter Greyhorse sat in his quarters and considered the Klingon ceremonial knife. It was sheathed almost to the hilt in a black crust of dried blood—Ben Zoma's blood.

But not enough of it, apparently; the captain of the *Lexington* was still alive. The murderer cursed softly. He knew now that he should have inflicted a few more wounds before he fled. But if he'd stayed a little longer to do that, some crewman might have stumbled onto the scene.

And he couldn't afford to be found out. Not then—and not now. There was still so very much to do.

Turning the knife in his hand, he admired its cruel, cold lines, its sturdiness. It was a good tool; it had been made well. As well as the knives that Gerda had owned—but then, that was no surprise, considering Gerda and Idun had gotten them from the same source.

Idun . . . it was strange to see her again, after all these years. She was even more beautiful than he remembered—just as Gerda would have been, if she'd lived. It made him ache to think about that. *If she'd lived . . .*

Straightening, he put the thought from his mind. There was no time for senti-mentality. He had to think—to prepare.

What was that line from Robert Frost? *"Miles to go before I sleep . . ."* He smiled grimly. Rising, he crossed the room and slipped the blood-blackened blade beneath his mattress—pushing it in just enough so that it couldn't be seen.

Eventually, he knew, someone would suspect him and search his room. And the knife would be found. But by then, it would be too late for those who had wronged Gerda Asmund.

And he would no longer care what they did to him.

Picard was sitting in his ready room, reviewing all his options, when Beverly reached him.

"It's Greyhorse," she said without preamble. "Greyhorse is the killer."

Picard started. A chill climbed the rungs of his spine. "How do you know?" he asked.

Crusher's voice was trembling. "One of Jack's tapes. He and Vigo saw Greyhorse and Gerda embracing."

The captain thought about it. Gerda . . . and Greyhorse? "He never told me."

But then, he wouldn't have. That was why people had trusted Jack Crusher. He would sooner have died than given away a confidence.

"If Gerda and Greyhorse were involved—" the doctor began.

"Hold, Doctor." Picard didn't wait for the rest. "Lieutenant Worf," he called out.

"Worf here," came the reply.

"I want Doctor Greyhorse arrested and confined to his quarters. This as-signment takes priority over all others—including the hunt for Commander Asmund."

Picard could imagine the confusion on the Klingon's face. But to his credit, Worf's hesitation lasted only a moment.

"Aye, sir. Worf out."

Picard was silent a moment.

"I thought I knew him, Jean-Luc," Crusher said. "I worked with him for a year at Starfleet Medical."

She sounded as if she were on the verge of tears.

"I thought I knew him, too," he said. "I thought I knew them all."

When the doors opened on the cargo deck where Asmund was hidden, the first thing she did was check the power charge on her phaser. Not that it was at all nec-essary—she already knew how many shots it had left. But her instincts compelled her to make sure.

The second thing she did was move forward into a crouch. Her legs hurt in a number of places—small injuries she must have suffered when she was thrown about the brig. But she had to endure all that now—just as she had managed to en-dure the pain in her temple for the last hour or so.

It was disappointing that they had thought to look for her here so soon. She hadn't had nearly enough time to consider what had gone before—to come up with even a halfway reasonable theory as to who the murderer might be.

Of course, it wasn't *necessarily* a security officer who'd just entered. It could have been a crewman coming down for supplies, or to make sure the environmental controls were working. After all, there were certain containers that carried temperature-sensitive cargo.

But Asmund had to be ready for the worst. She had to assume that Worf or someone else had outguessed her.

As the doors whispered shut again, she heard voices. *Two of them. Or more.* Leaning forward a little more, she strove to hear what they were saying.

But they had stopped. Definitely security, then. A couple of cargo handlers wouldn't have had any reason to become so quiet. She held the phaser a little tighter.

Then the silence was broken by the beep of a communicator. One of the security officers muttered something beneath his breath.

"Bednarik here," she heard someone say.

"Our orders have changed," said the voice on the intercom. Asmund recognized it immediately as Worf's.

"Changed, sir?" Bednarik was still trying to speak softly, though it must have been obvious to him that he'd lost the element of surprise.

"That is correct," the Klingon confirmed. "We are no longer searching for Commander Asmund. Our new objective is Doctor Carter Greyhorse."

Greyhorse. Asmund felt her teeth grind together.

"The big fella," Bednarik said.

"Precisely," came Worf's reply. "You are to report to Deck Twenty-four. Greyhorse has shown himself to be a consummate technician—he may decide to strike at the environmental support equipment."

"Aye, sir." A beep signaled the end of the conversation.

Bednarik's companion spoke up for the first time since they entered the cargo deck: "What about Asmund?"

There was a pause. "We forget about her," Bednarik said, "for now. But if we happen to run across her, I'll tell you what—I'm going to shoot first and ask questions later."

Asmund nodded. She wouldn't have expected anything else.

Then the cargo deck doors opened and closed again, and she was alone. She relaxed—though not completely.

Worf and his security people had given her what she'd been looking for—the identity of the murderer. If she just sat tight, they would eventually find Greyhorse and stop him. But the Klingon in her couldn't accept that as a solution.

The man had soiled her honor—tried to kill her comrades. It was *her* job to deal with him—no one else's.

She would get to him first. She promised herself that.

Carter Greyhorse was on his way to sickbay. He had some unfinished business there.

Once before, he'd visited sickbay to complete a job he'd started. But just when he thought he was alone with Cadwallader, just when he was about to slip the *ku'thei* pill between her lips, Beverly Crusher had come in and ruined everything.

This time, Crusher would not interrupt. The computer had already assured him that she was in her quarters. And with the murderer caught—or so everyone thought—it would be simple enough to smile his way into critical care. And pay Ben Zoma back.

As he would pay them *all* back. Each and every one—for taking from him the only person who'd ever made him *feel* anything.

Turning the corner, he entered the medical facility. It was crowded with those who had been injured in Simenon's maneuver. None very badly, he saw—which was just as well. He hated to see innocent people get hurt; he was, after all, a doctor.

A few steps in, a nurse turned and looked up at him. She smiled. "Doctor Greyhorse," she said, recognizing him.

He smiled back in a perfunctory sort of way and kept going. She had no idea; his expression, as reserved as ever, hadn't given her a clue.

Critical care was just ahead and to the right. The barrier obscuring the area was still up, though it was meaningless now. The murder attempts were common knowledge. There was nothing left for Picard to hide.

As Greyhorse approached the barrier, he resolved to be patient. His lack of success in finishing off Cadwallader would not make him hurry. This was a slow game, this killing—slower than he had anticipated. But he would ultimately be the winner. All he had to do was keep going and not make any mistakes.

Then he saw that there was no one attending to Ben Zoma at the moment. My luck is changing, he thought. I will not need to be patient after all.

For a moment, he studied the readings on the monitor above the bed. Interesting. Ben Zoma was putting up quite a fight. It was a good thing he'd had the opportunity to come by—and change that.

Glancing around quickly to make sure they were still alone, he reached for the *ku'thei* pill. Fortunately, it left no traces. Nor was it a substance the transporter's bio-filter was programmed to red-flag. But then, he'd selected it on that basis. Working in the upper echelon of Starfleet Medical gave one some knowledge of bio-screening systems.

Sitting down in the chair at Ben Zoma's bedside, he leaned over the patient. To an intruder, it would appear as if he were examining him. Ben Zoma's face was pale and waxy-looking; the only color in it was where the skin had been irritated by the tubes in his nostrils and his mouth.

Gilaad Ben Zoma, this is for Gerda Asmund. For the—

Suddenly, Greyhorse heard sounds of alarm outside the barrier. The *ku'thei* pill was poised just above Ben Zoma's parched lips. He had to do something—he couldn't allow himself to be found like this. Gripped by panic, he thrust the pill into the man's mouth as far as it would go.

That's when Dr. Selar came dashing around the barrier. One look at him was all she needed. Without breaking stride, she gripped him by the shoulder and spun him away from Ben Zoma.

She knows, he realized. The knowledge jolted him. But how? How can she? And who *else* knows?

Shortly, they all would. No matter if he killed her now as she tried to get the pill out of Ben Zoma's throat. If she lived, she would spread the word—assuming it was not spreading already. And if she died, there would be witnesses to the fact that he had done it.

Better to escape while he still could. To follow the steps he'd outlined for himself if he should ever be found out.

Bolting through the space between the barrier and the bulkhead, Greyhorse flung himself through the gathering crowd. Someone tried to grab him by the wrist; twisting down savagely, he snapped the man's grip and left him screaming.

Then he was hurtling toward the exit, his mind locking down like a machine.

Which, in the end, was what he was born to be. Not a man, but a machine. No more human, in all the ways that mattered, than the android Data. *A machine.*

In the corridor, people stopped to look at him. But that was all. Obviously, no one had warned them about him. They hadn't heard yet.

Taking advantage of the fact, he headed for the turbolift. A female crewman was in his way; he hurled her aside. Once he got to the lift, he knew, it would be impossible to stop him. His objective was only two decks away—a matter of moments.

As he passed a joining of the corridors, however, he saw something out of the corner of his eye. A flash of red and black. There was an impact, though he was too deep into his battle-state by now to feel it, and he was shoved sideways into the bulkhead on his right.

Recovering, he caught sight of his attacker's face—recognized the blue eyes, narrowed in determination. And of course, the beard.

Riker was quick. He got in a solid blow to the side of Greyhorse's head—a blow that jarred the big man but did not stop him. Before the first officer could follow up on his attack, Greyhorse retaliated.

First, he snapped Riker's head back with a well-placed *kave'ragh*—just as Gerda had taught him. Then, while the smaller man was still stunned, he lifted him off his feet by the front of his tunic and flung him hard into the bulkhead.

Before Riker slipped to the deck, Greyhorse was lunging for the turbolift again. A fraction of a second later, the doors opened and he was inside.

"Transporter room five," he said, breathing just a little harder than normal. Removing his communicator, he flung it on the floor. Then the doors closed and, though he couldn't feel it, the lift started to move.

"Captain? This is Doctor Selar."

On the bridge now, Picard glanced at Data before replying. "Yes, Doctor. What the devil is going on there?"

"Apparently, you were right to warn us about Doctor Greyhorse. He was putting something in Captain Ben Zoma's mouth when I interrupted him. A pill—poison, I would guess. Fortunately, I was able to retrieve it."

Picard swore softly. It had been close.

"Where is Greyhorse now?" asked the captain. "Were you able to detain him?"

A slight pause. "No, sir. My priority was the safety of the patient."

Picard nodded. "Of course. Thank you, Doctor."

"We must stop him, sir," Data said. He looked at the captain. "With what he knows about ship's systems—"

Before he could finish, Picard was calling Worf over the intercom.

"Aye, sir?" the Klingon replied.

"Mister Worf, we have located Doctor Greyhorse. He fled sickbay just a few moments ago."

The Klingon grunted. "I'll dispatch a team to the area—and limit the turbolifts to security use only."

"Very good," the captain said. He almost warned Worf about Greyhorse using his communicator to lay down a false trail—but he was sure the security chief was well aware of that tactic by now.

He stood and turned to Worf's replacement at tactical.

"Get Commander Riker up here right away. And—"

"Captain?"

Picard responded without turning. "What is it, Commander?"

Data seemed to hesitate for just the smallest fraction of a second. "Sir, we have made contact with the Romulans."

Picard turned and faced the main viewscreen—and his mouth went dry. Before him was a Romulan warbird—immense, powerful. And he knew without asking that all its disruptors were trained on the *Enterprise*.

Eighteen

Picard stared at the image of the Romulan warbird. "Open hailing frequencies," he instructed.

A moment later the screen filled with a typically Romulan visage—finely chiseled, with hooded eyes and long, pointed ears. The man was seething with confidence—and why not? By now his scanners would have picked up the *Enterprise*'s lack of warp drive activity—not to mention its inadequate shielding. He had the Federation ship at a disadvantage and he knew it.

The only thing he couldn't have divined was the set of circumstances that placed the *Enterprise* in Romulan territory. But then, he might not have cared. The fact was they were *there*.

The human decided to take the initiative. "I am Jean-Luc Picard, captain of the Federation vessel *Enterprise*. Whom do I have the honor of addressing?"

His mouth curling into a faint smile, the Romulan responded. "My name is Tav. I command the *Reshaa'ra*." The smile faded. "You are in Romulan space. You will surrender your ship immediately."

No give in this one, Picard observed. No inclination toward satisfying his curiosity; he's going to go strictly by the book.

The captain frowned. He didn't have many tools at his disposal—just the truth, really. "We are not here by choice, Commander Tav. We were brought here by a subspace phenomenon which we only recently escaped."

The Romulan's eyes narrowed ever so slightly. "How intriguing," he commented. "Our engineers will no doubt be fascinated when they have the opportunity to debrief you. In the meantime, I repeat: you will surrender your vessel. The alternative is destruc—"

Picard never heard the end of Tav's threat.

Normally, Data's duties at ops would have kept him from seeing what happened to the captain. However, the android had been halfway turned around in his chair, awaiting instructions, when Picard was enveloped in the scintillating pillar of light associated with molecular transport.

A fraction of a second later the captain was gone. It was as if he'd never been there in the first place.

There were curses and murmurs of apprehension from the other officers on the bridge. Data found that they were all looking in his direction, including Dr. Crusher.

Of course, he told himself. I am the ranking officer. They want to know what to do.

Using his control panel, the android cut into their link with the Romulan vessel. On the *Reshaa'ra,* it would appear to be a technical failure. With that done, Data turned and addressed the bridge contingent.

"Please remain calm," he said. "We must not let the Romulans know that anything has happened to our captain; it would only place us at a greater tactical disadvantage."

They understood. A moment later there was no trace of the confusion that had resulted from Picard's disappearance. Satisfied, Data restored the video portion of the link; after all, he didn't want the Romulans to think they'd been cut off on purpose.

Lastly, looking straight ahead at the Romulan called Tav, the android availed himself of the intercom system: "Commander Riker, please respond . . ."

It had been a long time since someone had handed Riker as bad a beating as Greyhorse had. As the first officer slowly got to his feet, he found he hurt in a dozen places. Could've been worse, he thought. He'd had no idea the doctor was so strong—though his size should have been a clue.

"Commander? Are you all right?"

He turned and saw Pug Joseph making his way through a gathering crowd. The man's face was lined with concern.

"Fine," the first officer replied, dusting himself off. He looked about, saw that the woman Greyhorse had flung aside was recovering too. A couple of crewpeople were helping her up. "You didn't by any chance see what happened to Dr. Greyhorse, did you?"

Joseph's brows came together. "Greyhorse? *He* did this to you?"

Riker nodded. "I'm a little stunned myself—no pun intended."

"I don't get it. What's the matter with him?"

The first officer met the other man's gaze. "Greyhorse is the murderer, Mr. Joseph."

Pug just stared at him.

By that time Worf was approaching from one end of the corridor, trailed by a couple of security people. The Klingon navigated briskly through the clot of on-lookers, his expression one of urgency.

"He was here," Riker said. "Unarmed, as far as I could tell."

Worf took in the scene at a glance, finally turning back to the first officer. "The turbolift?" he asked.

Riker was about to plead ignorance when someone in the crowd spoke up: "Yes. He went into the lift."

"No doubt," Worf said, "before we restricted access to them." He had begun to bark out a security clearance code to open the lift doors, when another voice cut in—over the intercom.

"Commander Riker—please respond." It was Data. And though Riker knew it was an impossibility, the android sounded . . . agitated.

He tapped his communicator. "Riker here."

"We have encountered a problem," Data informed him.

"What *sort* of problem? Not the Romulans?"

"Aye, sir—the Romulans."

The first officer cursed inwardly.

"But that is not all, Commander. The captain has disappeared."

Worf looked at Riker. "Disappeared?" he echoed.

"That is correct," the android said. "Shortly after he established communications with the Romulan commander, he vanished—in what seemed to be a transporter effect."

The first officer's mouth went dry. "Speculation, Data."

"We cannot rule out the possibility that the Romulans have captured him," the android explained. "But with our shields up, even at partial strength, it seems highly unlikely."

True. The Romulans didn't have the technology to transport through shields. Hell—neither did the Federation.

Then, what—?

Like sequenced grippers in a perfect docking maneuver, everything seemed to fall into place. Riker's conclusion hit him even harder than Greyhorse had.

"All hands!" the first officer called suddenly—thereby opening the entire intercom system to his message. "Remove your communicators immediately! I repeat—remove your communicators!"

It took those around him a couple of seconds to follow his line of reasoning—but follow they did.

"Greyhorse," Worf spat out, complying with Riker's order.

"He's gotten hold of a transporter," Joseph expanded, complying also.

"That's right," Riker said, taking off his communicator and tossing it onto the deck with everyone else's. Before his eyes, one of the badges—it was hard to know whose—shimmered with an unholy radiance and vanished. The sight sent a shiver through him.

Not a moment too soon, he reflected. If they'd waited any longer, one of them would have been Greyhorse's prisoner. Or worse—transporter soup.

"Data," he called, opening up a channel through the intercom grid. "I'm coming up to the bridge. Just stay where you are—don't do or say anything." He turned to Worf. "Find out what transporter room Greyhorse has occupied. Cut off his power, jam his annular confinement beam—whatever. Just stop him before he starts transporting away pieces of the hull."

The Klingon looked at him. "What about the captain?"

Riker frowned. What he was about to say went directly against his grain as first officer. "If he's still alive, try to keep him that way. But as long as Greyhorse has an operative transporter in his possession, Captain Picard is not the priority."

Worf looked as if he'd swallowed something rancid. But he obeyed, turning and leading his officers back through the crowd. Riker needed the nearby turbolift; the Klingon would find another one.

"I'm coming along," Joseph insisted, falling in behind the security team. He sounded determined.

Nor did Worf protest. Apparently, he was willing to accept all the experienced help he could get.

Riker turned to the lift and freed it with his own clearance code. As the doors opened, he got inside. "Bridge," he commanded.

And tried to figure out what in blazes he was going to say to the Romulans.

One moment, Picard was on the bridge; the next, he was somewhere else. And before he could determine exactly *where,* he felt something hard smash into his chin. Staggering under the impact, he was hit a second time, even harder. And a third. Finally, he fell, his legs refusing to hold him up any longer. As he lay there fighting off the lurching blackness that was threatening to engulf him, he felt the floor start to slide by.

His head felt like a block of stone, but he managed to lift it—to look around. He saw that he was in the transporter room, being dragged by someone—someone massive, who had a handful of the captain's tunic in his fist. After a second or two, he realized that it was Carter Greyhorse.

They were headed for the transporter controls. Why? Picard had no idea. His brain was too sluggish—he couldn't seem to pull his thoughts together. But instinctively, he knew that he had to stop the big man from reaching his destination.

Grabbing Greyhorse's wrist and swinging around at the waist, he fought off a black wave of vertigo and wrapped his legs around the man's ankle. Then he twisted his hips as hard as he could.

Caught unawares, the doctor reeled wildly. When Picard twisted a second time, he toppled altogether.

With an effort, the captain rolled away, already anticipating retaliation. But the big man was much faster than he seemed. Before he could scramble to his feet, Greyhorse whirled and kicked him in the ribs.

The pain was excruciating. Somehow, Picard weathered it and kept his legs underneath him. But it only made him an easier target. Putting all his weight behind the blow, Greyhorse leapt and kicked again. It was like being hit with a phaser set on heavy stun.

The captain skidded backward across the deck, the breath knocked out of him. As he wheezed and struggled to fill his lungs, Greyhorse advanced on him purposefully. A second time, Picard rolled in the opposite direction—it was all he could manage. Lights exploded behind his eyes; his pulse thundered in his temples. But he hung on to consciousness, greedily gulping each painful breath.

"You're as much a fighter as you ever were," the doctor said. He sounded as if he were speaking to him from a great distance. "But it won't help. Your crimes have finally caught up with you."

And with uncanny ease he lifted Picard's limp form and flung him across the room. The captain felt himself hit the deck, tumble, and finally come up hard against the base of the console. When it was all over, the taste of blood was strong in his mouth. He spat it out, lifted his head.

The transporter platform was being activated again. Dimly, through the layers of wool in his brain, he realized what Greyhorse might have been up to—and curling his fingers over the lip of the control console, digging his heels into the carpet, he slowly dragged himself to his feet.

Too slow, he told himself. *Too slow.* With each passing second, Greyhorse was destroying another life.

But as Picard inched up high enough to see his adversary, he knew that he hadn't been too late after all. Something had gone wrong for Greyhorse.

He could see it in the man's eyes—trained on him now instead of on the controls. They were fierce and dark, full of unbridled fury. His lower lip trembled savagely.

"Damn you!" Greyhorse rasped. He pounded on the transporter console with his huge right fist; it shuddered beneath the blow. "They're on to me! They've taken off their communicators."

A wave of relief swept over the captain. Someone had seen Greyhorse's strategy in time.

The big man reached over the console and took hold of the front of Picard's tunic. *"You.* You delayed me, or I would've killed them all by now—scrambled them in transit." His lip curled. "I wanted you to watch, Captain. I wanted you to see your friends die—that was the worst thing I could've hoped to do to you." His face was just inches from Picard's. It was a shaman's mask of pure, writhing hatred. "I never should have cut it so close. I should have scrambled you too, and been done with it. I just didn't think you'd fight so hard."

Trembling with rage, Greyhorse let go of the captain with one hand and started resetting the transporter controls. Picard grasped the man's wrist with both hands, but he couldn't seem to break that monstrous grip.

"Maybe I can't scramble *them,"* the doctor muttered. He looked up, his eyes suddenly alight. "But I can still scramble *you."* He turned his attention back to the board. "And don't expect anyone to stop me from outside; I made sure they couldn't interfere once I got started."

Picard believed it. He knew what kind of technical expertise Greyhorse had demonstrated in his other attempts at violence.

"Carter," he gasped, still fighting to get air into his lungs. He needed time—to get his strength back. To make the room stop spinning. "Carter—*why?"*

The big man sneered at him. "Why? You have the gall to ask that—after you stripped Gerda of her honor? Of her life?"

The captain shook his head. "No," he got out. "I only stopped her . . . from killing Morgen . . ."

"Lies!" the doctor cried. With one hand he pulled Picard halfway up over the transporter console. His other hand curled into a claw and hovered just over Picard's face. "You dishonored her! You deprived her of her right to suicide! And then you dishonored *me*—by making me the instrument by which you saved her!" Spittle clung to the corner of his mouth. "Do you know how she looked at me afterward? How she *hated* me? For that alone you deserved the worst torture I could devise. But her hatred wasn't the worst of it—the worst was what happened in that rehab colony." His large brow rippled painfully with the memory. "Klingons aren't humans. They're not *meant* to be put in cages like beasts—day after day, month after month. It deprives them of everything that makes them Klingon . . ." He swallowed hard. "It *changes* them."

Picard knew it would be no use arguing that rehab colonies weren't cages. Greyhorse was mad—truly mad. He felt another surge of vertigo wash over him and fought to keep himself from succumbing.

"I saw her after she came out," the big man went on. His upper lip curled back. "She wasn't the same. She wasn't Gerda. I wanted to hold her, to help her after all she'd been through—but she told me to just go away, to just get the hell away from her." A sob came up from deep in his massive chest. "She said I was no good for her. That she'd paid for what she'd done, and she didn't want to be reminded of it."

Another sob, worse than the first. He shook with it. "I thought that she'd change her mind—get over it—and we'd be together again. And then . . ." His eyes went blank. "And then she died, and there was nothing left for me to think about—except what I would do to the ones who hurt her."

Past Greyhorse, Picard saw something happening to the transporter room doors. They were glowing in a couple of places—with a distinct pinkish radiance. Phasers, he realized. Of course. Security was trying to burn its way in.

But he couldn't let Greyhorse know—not until it was too late. Quickly, he looked away.

How long would it take for Worf to cut his way in? At one of the higher settings, only a few seconds. But there was less control that way. He might burn through and hit someone inside—someone like the captain—so he'd be using a lower setting.

And how long then? A minute? Maybe two? Could he stall Greyhorse that long?

As if in response to Picard's silent question, the doctor punched in the balance of the transporter's instructions and came around the console—jerking his captive along with him. They were headed back to the platform. And Picard could see that one of the disks was live—hungry for an object to transport.

The captain took a second to gather his strength and tried the same maneuver that had worked before. But this time he was too slow, or else Greyhorse was ready for him. Before he could get a good grip on his tormentor's wrist, the doctor stopped and swung him forward with all his strength. Unable to stop himself, Picard tumbled end over end, finally coming to rest against the base of the transporter grid.

When he looked up, he saw Greyhorse advancing on him. But behind the doctor, the phaser glow was getting darker.

"Carter," Picard gasped. "Don't do this. I hated what happened to Gerda too—but there was no other way."

The big man stopped, towering over him. He grunted scornfully. "That's it," he said. "Go ahead. Beg." He got down on his haunches, came closer than he should have. "I *want* to hear you beg."

The captain knew he wouldn't have another chance. Planting his heel against the side of the platform to get his whole body into it, he launched a blow at the center of the doctor's jaw. It landed more solidly than he might have hoped, jarring him all the way to his shoulder. There was a sound as of cracking ice and Greyhorse fell backward.

Pressing his advantage, Picard staggered to his feet and made for the door, where the hot spots were getting angrier than ever. I can make it, he told himself. I can—

Then he felt something grab his ankle, and his feet went out from under him. He hit the deck and Greyhorse whipped him around again toward the transporter platform. Clawing at the carpet, the captain managed to stop himself short of the live disk.

But the doctor had other ideas. Again, he drove a booted foot into Picard's ribs, robbing him of what sense had been restored to him. Then, picking the captain up like a rag doll, he took a step backward, preparing to hurl him to his death.

He was stopped short by a sound like all the banshees of hell as the doors to the room burst open. Greyhorse whirled to see what had happened and the captain groped for the big man's shoulder, trying to anchor himself against being flung into the transparent beam. But with what seemed like no effort at all, Greyhorse lifted him even higher.

The room was filling with a flood of security officers, led by Worf. To Picard's surprise, Pug Joseph was right beside him. They pointed their phasers, but stopped short of using them on Greyhorse once they saw the situation. Numbed, battered, the captain could only watch.

"Go ahead," cried the doctor. "Shoot me. And before I fall, I'll see to it that Picard's atoms are scattered through the void."

Worf stuck out a hand to hold his people back. "Put him down," he said, "and we will talk."

Greyhorse laughed. "What is there to talk about? A rehab colony—maybe the same one where Gerda lost her soul?" He shook his head. "I don't think so."

"Carter," Pug interjected, taking a step forward. "What are you doing? He was your captain, for godsakes. He was your friend."

The doctor's mouth twisted. "My *friend?* Then why did he kill the only person I've ever loved—the only one who ever made me feel *human?*" He glared at Joseph. "Why did *you?*"

The security chief shook his head. "I didn't kill Gerda, Carter."

"Didn't you?" the doctor asked. "You stood by like all the others and watched as they took her away. You—"

Picard wasn't quite certain what happened next. But somehow, it seemed that Greyhorse was hit from behind. The deck rushed up and hit the captain hard, and a moment later Pug was kneeling at his side.

Twisting his head, Picard tried to see what was going on. What he saw was Greyhorse, crouching like a beast at bay—held there by a figure in black and gold wielding a phaser. It took the captain a moment to realize that the figure was Idun Asmund.

She glowered at the doctor. "You forgot to lock out the other disks," she said. "You remembered everything else—but you forgot that."

"Traitor," he spat out. "How can you side with them? They killed your sister!"

Asmund's eyes narrowed. She raised the phaser just slightly.

Picard saw that it was set for "kill." The woman took a couple of steps toward Greyhorse.

"Idun," the captain said, "stop and think." With his arm slung over Pug's shoulder, he got to his feet. "You don't really want to do this."

Worf was just a few feet behind Greyhorse. He had his phaser in his hand as well. Set on stun, it was pointed at Asmund's breast—but he seemed unwilling to press the trigger. "It's over," he told her. "Your name has been cleansed."

"No thanks to him," she replied, taking another step toward the doctor. She was almost close enough now to reach out and touch him. "He would have stripped me of the only thing left to me—my honor. Knowing how hard I'd worked to disassociate myself from Gerda's crime, knowing what it meant to me to be trusted and respected again . . . he would have obliterated that without a second thought."

"Yes," Greyhorse agreed. "That and more. For Gerda. Someone had to *remember* her—*avenge* her."

The muscles in Asmund's jaw worked. Her eyes narrowed a notch.

"Commander," Worf entreated, "you *have* your honor. It is *intact.* Don't blacken it now. Don't finish the job he started."

For a long moment she stared at her former comrade. Then, suddenly, she replaced the safety on her phaser and tossed it to the Klingon. Worf caught it in midair.

Greyhorse grinned derisively. "Your sister had more courage. *She* would have killed me."

Asmund appraised him, her dark blue eyes as hard as stone. "No," she decided. "Gerda was too honorable to kill a madman."

Without another word, she walked over to Picard and took his other arm. "Let's go," she said, "Captain."

Picard looked at her and squeezed the hand that held his. "Yes," he responded. "By all means. We have some Romulans to deal with."

And as Worf and his security people surrounded Carter Greyhorse, the captain let his two former officers escort him out of the room.

"You are not Captain Picard," the Romulan commander observed.

Riker stood before the command center, where Beverly Crusher sat on the edge of her seat and sized up his adversary. He still had no idea of how he was going to get them out of this one.

Clearing his throat, he said: "I am Commander William T. Riker, first officer. The captain has been called away to deal with an emergency."

That elicited a certain degree of interest from the Romulan. "An emergency," he repeated. He made a derisive sound—loud enough to be heard over the communications link. "Something more pressing than a Romulan warbird with its talons around your throat?" He shook his head. "You take me too lightly, Commander. Perhaps I need to remind you where the *true* emergency lies."

Looking back at one of his officers, the Romulan barked an order. As the officer complied, his fingers dancing over his console, Riker had a feeling about the kind of reminder the commander had in mind.

And there was no way they could escape it. Not at impulse speed.

A moment later the bridge of the *Enterprise* shuddered. The first officer's teeth ground together; he hated being so helpless.

"Shields at eighteen percent," Data reported. He turned to face Riker. "One more such assault will result in extensive damage to the ship."

Riker nodded, still staring at the screen—and the Romulan. He cursed softly. Come on, Will—*think!* Do something—before it's too damned late!

The Romulan raised an eyebrow. "Now," he said, "will you surrender—or must I incapacitate you first?"

The first officer's mind raced, but to no avail. He was drawing a blank at the worst possible time.

Ironic, wasn't it? They couldn't move fast enough to even give these Romulans a run for their money, when not too long ago they were breaking every speed record in the—

Blazes! That was it!

Frowning at his adversary, he said: "I can't hear you, Commander. Your transmission is jumbled."

Of course, that wasn't the case at all—Riker could both see and hear the Romulan much better than he cared to. But he needed a minute to work on his idea.

The commander's head tilted ever so slightly. He was trying to decide whether to believe the human or not—particularly in light of the apparent glitch that had occurred earlier.

Riker didn't have the luxury of waiting to see the outcome. Turning toward tactical as if he wanted to know what had happened to communications, the first officer subtly drew a forefinger across his throat—a signal that Picard had used in the past. It meant *cut transmission.*

Recognizing the gesture, the tactical officer complied. Nodding to Riker, he said: "Done, sir."

"Good," the first officer told him. He glanced at the viewscreen, where the Romulan was consulting with another of his officers. He looked skeptical—but at least he wasn't firing on them. Not yet.

Lifting his eyes to the intercom grid, Riker called on Geordi La Forge.

"Aye, sir," came the chief engineer's response.

"We've got trouble," Riker advised. "Romulans. I need warp one—and I need it now."

For a moment Geordi hesitated. The first officer's heart sank. If they couldn't rouse the warp engines even *that* much, his plan was useless.

"All right," La Forge said finally. "We can give it a shot. But I've got to warn you—we're probably not far enough from the slipstream yet. Even if we can get the warp drive to respond, it's probably only going to get us stuck in subspace again."

Riker smiled. "I'm counting on it." He turned to Wesley. "Heading one four five mark nine oh, Mr. Crusher. Warp one—on my order."

"Warp one," the ensign confirmed, locking in the new information.

Riker looked at the viewscreen. The Romulan commander was glaring at him, considering his options. He still appeared confident; he wouldn't act hastily. Not unless something changed.

Something like the powering up of the *Enterprise*'s warp engines.

"Got 'em going," said Geordi over the intercom. "But we'd better move quickly—I don't know how long they'll last."

A split second later, the Romulan received the news. His brow furrowed as he saw the possibility of his prey slipping through his net. He whirled to address his weapons officer—

And the viewscreen reverted to an exterior view of the Romulan vessel. The enemy had made the communications blackout mutual.

"Engage," shouted Riker, bringing his hand down for emphasis.

Wesley carried out the order.

The first officer steeled himself against the jolt of the Romulans' barrage. A second ticked off. Another . . .

No impact. That could mean only one thing . . .

"Proceeding at warp one," Wesley announced. He made no effort to disguise the mixture of relief and uncertainty in his voice. "At least, that's what the engines are—"

Before he could finish, there was an abrupt surge in speed. They could hardly help but notice it. And the starstreaks on the viewscreen began darting by with frenetic intensity.

"Commander—the Romulans are giving pursuit," the man at tactical reported.

Riker nodded. Now, if there was any justice at all in the universe . . .

"What's their speed?" he asked.

The Tactical officer was prompt. "Nine point nine five, sir. The same as ours."

"Commander?" It was Geordi.

"It worked," Riker told him. "We're back in the slipstream. And so are they."

"Which is just the way you wanted it."

Geordi had caught on. And judging from the look on Dr. Crusher's face—a mixture of admiration and relief—Geordi wasn't the only one.

"That was the plan," the first officer agreed.

Of course, he'd taken a big chance. They were still sitting ducks if the warbirds decided to fire. But by now the Romulans were no doubt discovering they had more important matters to worry about.

"How's the warp drive?" he asked Geordi.

A pause. "Better than I figured it would be."

"Have we got enough juice to try your shield maneuver again?"

Another pause. "Not yet. Can you give me an hour?"

Riker said just what the captain would have said. "Take a *half*."

Geordi said he'd see what he could do.

The first officer returned his attention to the forward viewscreen. After all, his work wasn't over.

"Raise the Romulan commander," he told the Tactical officer.

Seconds later, his adversary's face filled the screen again. But this time that air of confidence had been replaced with suspicion.

"What have you done?" the Romulan asked angrily.

"I have lured you into a trap," Riker explained. "The same one that forced us into Romulan space. Of course, we've since discovered a way out of it—which we'll be employing shortly."

The commander's eyes narrowed. "Do not taunt me, human. I still have my weapons trained on you. And your shields are at low power."

"True," the first officer conceded. "But we're your only hope of escape. If you destroy us, you'll never see your homes again." He smiled affably. "Sometime prior to our departure from subspace, we'll give you the data you need to follow us."

The Romulan looked incredulous. "What kind of fool do you take me for? If you truly know a way out, why would you share it with us?"

"Because we have no reason to do otherwise. It will take you some time to decipher the information—and by the time you do, we'll be safely out of Romulan territory."

The commander mulled the matter over. "There is a way to insure that you do not leave us here. We could take hostages."

Riker shook his head. "I'm afraid not. Any attempt to board us will force us to try to escape prematurely. If we succeed or fail, you will be left here alone—without the information you need. And if we fail—we will be destroyed," he lied. "Again, leaving you here alone, with no inkling of how to extricate yourself."

The commander's mouth became a hard, taut line. How much did he know about the Federation? About human attention to such things as honor? About a poker-faced bluff?

At last, he uttered a curse—one the computer had trouble translating—and relented. "We will allow you to prepare whatever maneuver you have in mind. At the slightest hint of treachery, however, I will not hesitate to destroy you."

That was fine with Riker. He had no intention of being treacherous. Or, for that matter, even giving the *appearance* of treachery.

In the next moment, the Romulan's image blinked out again, to be replaced by the streaking stars of the slipstream. The first officer took a sobering look at them, then remembered that the Romulans were only half his problem.

"Lieutenant Worf," he called. "What's going on down there?"

The Klingon's answer wasn't long in coming. "Dr. Greyhorse has been taken into custody."

Riker swallowed. "And the captain?"

The words were hardly out of his mouth when the turbolift doors opened and Picard emerged. His face was swollen and bruised, his uniform was torn in a number of places, and there was a decided limp in his gait. But he was alive, damn it— he was alive!

A moment later, Asmund and Joseph stepped out of the lift as well. The blond woman had the look of one who'd just been exonerated.

"The captain is on his way up to the bridge now," replied the security chief.

"Actually," the first officer responded, "he's just arrived. Thank you, Mr. Worf."

Out of reflex, Crusher had started out of her seat—but Picard waved her away. "It's all right," he said dryly. "I'm much better than I look."

Riker smiled. As Picard made his way to the command center, he said: "It's good to see you, sir."

The captain nodded stiffly. "Good to see *you*, Commander." He glanced at the viewscreen and saw the telltale effects of the slipstream. *"Mon Dieu,"* he muttered. And turning again to his next in command, he asked the question with his eyes.

"It was the only way to escape the Romulans, Captain."

"We left them behind?" Picard asked.

Riker straightened. "Not exactly, sir. They entered the slipstream behind us."

And then the strangest thing happened. Slowly, gradually, a grin spread over the captain's battered visage. He regarded his first officer.

"Clever move, Number One."

Riker smiled again, "I try, sir."

Nineteen

Picard leaned back in his ready room chair, trying to ignore the damage Greyhorse had inflicted on him. Unfortunately, as his mind cleared, he was becoming that much more aware of the pain.

His former shipmates—Idun and Pug—apparently intended to wait with him until Dr. Selar arrived. Beverly Crusher had wanted to stay as well, but Picard had assured her again that his injuries were not all that serious, and that she was needed more down in sickbay. After all, should past prove to be prologue, she would have her hands full with slipstream-exit victims.

That is, he told himself, if an exit is even possible. The fact that we did it once is no assurance we can do it again.

No—he stopped himself. There was no point in entertaining morbid thoughts. The finish line was in sight; all they needed was a little luck and they'd win this race.

"You know," Pug said, "there are a couple of things you still haven't told us." He was standing by the captain's desk, addressing Idun, who was halfway across the room gazing into the captain's aquarium.

The blond woman looked back over her shoulder. "What's that?"

"How you knew where Greyhorse would be holed up. And how you managed to show up when you did."

Picard nodded, reminded that Idun hadn't finished the story she'd begun in the turbolift. "Yes," he said, his curiosity aroused, "how *did* you accomplish all that?"

She shrugged, turning to face them. "It really wasn't all that difficult. I was tipped off by Commander Riker's warning over the intercom—the one that instructed everyone to remove their communicators. I asked myself why that might be necessary—came up with the fact that the communicators are used to establish beaming coordinates—and realized that someone with dangerous intentions must have gotten hold of a transporter."

Pug grunted. "Good thinking."

"Indeed," the captain said. "But to beam yourself into the room which Dr. Greyhorse had taken over—" Suddenly he stopped, realizing the implications.

"That's right," Idun told him. "I had to find another transporter room and stun the operator on duty. Likewise, the security officer who came to provide reinforce-ments—no doubt following Mr. Worf's orders." There was a tinge of regret in her voice. "In any case, they should have regained consciousness by now."

Picard frowned. That wasn't exactly the kind of thing he liked to hear about—even if it *had* been a prelude to saving his life.

Pug, on the other hand, shook his head in appreciation. "Beautiful. And once you had a transporter, you could use it to trace other transporter activity in the ship. So when you found something going on in room one, you just set the con-trols, stepped on the platform, and beamed over."

"Yes," Idun said. "Fortunately, Greyhorse planned to use the entire platform in working his revenge on us, so all the stations were operational. Which was a good thing, because I couldn't have beamed over with any assurance of success other-wise. Having never been on a *Galaxy*-class ship before, I would only have been guessing at the coordinates." She cast a glance at the captain. "Of course, Greyhorse might have realized the stations were open and locked them down—if he hadn't been distracted." A faint smile took shape on her lips. "I'm willing to wager you provided *more* than a small distraction."

Picard harumphed. "Not *much* more, I'm afraid."

"Don't sell yourself short, Captain," Pug told him. "I never thought of Greyhorse as a fighter, but anybody that big . . ." He left the conclusion hanging in the air.

"And if he was . . . *involved* with Gerda," Idun added, "he knew how to use his size to good advantage. Klingons are taught that at an early age."

For a moment, her dark blue eyes seemed to lose their focus; she folded her arms over her chest. Was she thinking about her sister and the relationship Gerda had kept secret—even from *her?*

"Be that as it may," Picard said, cutting into the silence, "I—"

His sentiment was interrupted by a beeping at the room's single entrance.

"Come," he instructed, expecting Selar. But as the doors parted, it was Worf who entered instead.

"Sir," the Klingon said. He acknowledged Pug and Idun with a couple of brief nods.

"You've attended to Dr. Greyhorse?" the captain surmised. His discomfort was getting worse—harder to put aside.

"I have," Worf replied. "As a precaution against his escaping from the brig the way Commander Asmund did"—he shot Idun a sidewise look as he said this—"I've stationed additional personnel at the site. They have grappling devices to secure them against turbulence. Also, the brig's restrictive barrier has been repaired and placed on battery power, so it should not be affected by any damage to ship's systems."

"Excellent," Picard told him. "What about the possibility of suicide?"

"I have scanned the doctor's person. He will have no opportunities to take his own life."

"And my knife?" asked Idun.

Worf turned to her. "It was discovered in his quarters. It will be necessary to hold it as evidence."

Idun frowned, but she seemed to accept the necessity.

Turning back to the captain, the Klingon said: "Our search of Dr. Greyhorse's quarters also revealed a small supply of *ku'thei* pills. It was one of these that he used in his attempt to finish Captain Ben Zoma."

"I see," Picard responded. However, his attention was starting to wane as the pain mounted—particularly in his side, where Greyhorse must have fractured a rib or two when he kicked him. Where in blazes was Selar?

Coincidentally, his door chose that moment to beep again.

"Come."

This time it was the Vulcan. And she had her medical tricorder with her, slung by its strap over one shoulder. Also, what Picard recognized as a small case full of commonly used drugs.

Snatching a chair as she came in, she pulled it with her as she approached him. "I assume," Selar said in a very businesslike tone, "that the captain would prefer to be examined in private."

Picard started to protest to the contrary, but his guests were already on their way out.

"Commander Asmund," he called, stopping her in her tracks. She regarded him. "Aye, sir?"

"There is something I would like to say to you." He looked to Selar. "If you would give us a moment, Doctor—"

"No." Idun shook her head. Her posture was as stiff as ever—but there was an uncharacteristic vulnerability in her eyes. "There's no need, sir. I *know.*"

And before he could insist, she was out the door and on her way.

Picard sighed. He was glad he had been wrong about Idun Asmund. Very glad. He only hoped that she would finally get what was coming to her—the friendship and admiration of her *Stargazer* colleagues.

It was long overdue.

Before he had completed the thought, Selar was running her tricorder over him and making those discouraging sounds that doctors seemed so good at. Sighing, he submitted to the scrutiny.

It was Eisenberg's turn to monitor Ben Zoma when the captain's warning came over the intercom. They would be trying that maneuver again—the one that had gotten them out of the slipstream once before. And it would probably shake them up as much as it had the last time.

That was all right. Sickbay had fared pretty well once; there was no reason to believe it wouldn't do so again.

As he checked Ben Zoma's readouts for the umpteenth time, he thought about what O'Brien had told him in Ten-Forward—about "ringside seats" and "the greatest show in the galaxy." For a little while there, the transporter chief had made it seem so exciting, so heady. But if the stars were a little more tame next time he visited Ten-Forward, Eisenberg wouldn't be too upset.

And neither, he expected, would O'Brien—despite his brave talk and his toasts to "warp nine point nine five."

Completing his review of the readouts, the med tech started around the divider that separated Ben Zoma from their other patient—Cadwallader, no longer a critical-care case. But before he could reach the woman's bedside, he caught a glimpse of a couple of cranberry-colored uniforms coming his way.

Instinctively, he turned to see what had occasioned a visit from the captain and his first officer—especially when the maneuver was to take place in a matter of minutes. Then he realized that it wasn't Picard and Riker at all. It was Captain Morgen and Commander Asmund. And right behind them, Lieutenant Joseph, and the Gnalish—Professor Simenon.

As Morgen led his companions past the curiosity-ridden med tech, he saw Cadwallader get up on her elbows and smile.

"To what do I owe the pleasure?" she asked.

"Our fear," remarked the professor. "We heard that it was safer here than any-where else on the ship."

Cadwallader chuckled dryly. "You know," she said, "I think I believe you."

"Don't," Morgen told her. He laid his great bony hand on her bed. "I just thought it was time you received a visit from your friends." He regarded Asmund. *"All* of them."

The blond woman nodded, returning the Daa'Vit's gaze. "That's right. Or at least, that's the reason he gave *me*. And when the ruler of the Daa'Vit Unity sum-mons you, you don't dare disobey."

Morgen laughed and turned to the patient again. "For the record, it was actually more of a *request.*"

Cadwallader's smile got a little broader. "That's all right. Frankly, I don't give a damn why you're here. I'm just glad that you are."

"Guttle's Maw," the professor spat out. "What's next? Hugs and kisses all around?"

"What's going on here?" Morgen followed the voice to its source, and saw Dr. Crusher standing at the threshold of her office.

"I thought Commander Cadwallader might want some familiar faces about her—particularly now." The Daa'Vit smiled charmingly. "Won't you join us?"

Crusher seemed surprised—pleasantly so. "I'd be delighted."

Joseph turned to Morgen. "If it's all the same to you," he asked, "I'd like to be with Captain Ben Zoma." He glanced at Cadwallader. "You understand, Cad?"

"Of course," she told him.

"Wait," Asmund said. She looked at the doctor, indicating with a jerk of her thumb the divider that hid Ben Zoma from view. "Can we remove it?"

Crusher thought about it for a moment. "I don't see why not," she said at last.

Simenon snorted. "This is getting more sickly sweet all the time."

"Hush, you," Cadwallader told him as Crusher got two burly nurses to move the divider aside.

When Ben Zoma was revealed, they all stared at him for a moment. Then Joseph went to stand by his bed, and Asmund as well.

Morgen nodded approvingly. Old comrades banding together against the tide of events—no matter where that tide might take them. He was mightily glad he could call these people his friends.

Then he realized that it was almost time for the maneuver to begin, and the Daa'Vit held on to a convenient projection from Cadwallader's biobed.

* * *

This time things were a little different. On the downside, they didn't have full warp speed capability. On the upside, they knew what to expect.

Hunched over his engineering console, Geordi ran a couple of last-minute checks. Satisfied that all was in readiness, he turned to the command center.

"Ready to go," he told the captain, who'd been standing in front of his chair and looking back at the chief engineer, waiting patiently for just those words.

Picard looked just slightly the worse for wear—a big improvement over his condition a little more than half an hour before. Or so Geordi had been told, and by no less dependable a source than the first officer himself. Of course, Dr. Selar's ministrations had helped the captain regain some of his form—and a change into a new uniform hadn't hurt either.

"Thank you, Commander," said Picard. With perfect aplomb he sat down in his chair. "You may commence."

Without further ado, Geordi turned back to his monitor, where the blue-line representation was once again in effect. Rather than approach the desired configuration by stages, as he had before, he went right to the final product: two flat surfaces, one fore and one aft, each pitched at an angle of thirty degrees to the ship's long axis.

After all, they had no time to fool around. Geordi was confident that their current warp capability would be enough to hold the shields in place for the duration of the maneuver—but maybe not much longer than that.

For just a second before he input the change, he paused to consider the possibility that they had pushed their luck a bit too far—that this time the maneuver wouldn't work, or that they'd be torn apart in the process. Geordi looked around at the familiar figures on the bridge—defined in electromagnetic patterns that only he and his VISOR could decipher. Even in that tiny tick of time, he was able to consider them one by one: Picard. Riker. Troi. Worf. Data. Wesley.

The chief engineer smiled. If the maneuver failed this time, if they had miscalculated, it had at least been one hell of an adventure.

Steeling himself, he gave the computer its marching orders.

Idun Asmund studied the face of Gilaad Ben Zoma. It was gaunt and bloodless, so different from the handsome, smiling countenance that had been the man's trademark. It was painful for her to look at him—but being a true Klingon, she forced herself to do it anyway.

After all, he was dying. Not quickly, not without a fight, but he was dying nonetheless. And there might not be too many more opportunities to see him while there was still breath left in him.

Asmund looked at Pug. He knew also that Ben Zoma wasn't long for this world. She could see it in his eyes. It occurred to her that Pug might even feel responsible for what had happened. After all, he was a security chief—one of a breed that would sooner die themselves than see something happen to their commanding officers.

She sympathized, feeling responsible as well. Hadn't it been her knife that had stabbed Ben Zoma? And wasn't it her lapse of vigilance that had allowed Greyhorse to obtain it?

Asmund recalled the first time she'd ever seen anyone die. Though she and Gerda had been too young to understand at the time, her family was embroiled in a feud with another clan. There had been threats, then violence. And finally, in the middle of the night, two men had brought her father's older brother into the house.

She remembered her mother closing the door against the billowing mists. She saw her father again as he helped lay his sibling on a table—as he tore aside Lenoch's cloak and inspected his wounds. And she felt anew the mixed sense of fear and fascination—the guilt that had taken hold of her as she and Gerda peeked into the room all unnoticed by the adults.

Like Ben Zoma, Lenoch had been stabbed over and over again. Even in the dimly lit foreroom of her father's house, even against the dark hues of Lenoch's clothing, she had been able to see the blood—a lot of it and in many places. Her father had cursed at the sight.

The rest was a blur. She had a vague impression of being discovered by her mother—of being sent back to bed. Not that she and Gerda had been able to sleep. They'd lain awake all night gazing at each other, wide blue eyes a-glitter with moonlight, listening to the guttural exchanges in the rooms below them. Listening and wondering—until the night was shattered by the sound of a half dozen voices bellowing all at once. Like the cry of the *taami*-wolves that roamed the hills back on Alpha Zion, but with a tinge of something distinctly Klingon. And by that howling, they knew that Lenoch was dead.

But there was more—wasn't there? Before she and her sister had been shooed upstairs, hadn't she seen something else? Something that Gerda had remarked about once they were alone in their bedroom?

She frowned. It bothered her that she couldn't remember. *Gerda* would have remembered—but Gerda wasn't around to be asked. Idun forced herself to concentrate.

What was it? What had they seen?

Suddenly, the deck beneath her feet shuddered and shifted, forcing her to hold on to Ben Zoma's biobed in order to maintain her balance. It lasted only a couple of seconds, however. Idun looked around.

Certainly, the lack of a more violent tremor was encouraging. But no one was saying anything. At least, not until they received official word.

Then it came: "Attention, all decks. This is Captain Picard. We have returned to normal space with minimal damage to the warp drive and other systems."

There were murmurs of approval, sighs of relief. One doctor slapped another on the back.

"Please note," the captain's voice resumed, "that the crisis is not yet over. Our emergence from the slipstream phenomenon has deposited us once again in Romulan space. However, we are much closer to the Neutral Zone this time." A pause. "We will maintain yellow alert status until we leave Romulan territory—which, if all goes well, should be a matter of just a few hours. I thank you all for your cooperation."

Of course, Asmund thought, there was still the possibility of an encounter with another Romulan ship. But at least it wouldn't be the *Reshaa'ra*. It would take Commander Tav some time to unravel Picard's encrypted directions for emerging from the slipstream. And in the meantime, the Romulans would get a taste of—

Idun could feel the blood rushing to her face. A *taste* . . .

That was *it*—the thing she couldn't remember. Before their mother had chased them upstairs, she and Gerda had seen their father *taste* Lenoch's wounds!

But why? Why would he do that?

Unless . . . he suspected them of being *poisoned.*

It was a dishonorable thing to do in the course of an assassination. But then, whoever attacked Lenoch might have been a dishonorable individual.

Suddenly, a connection snapped into place. She looked down at poor, haggard Ben Zoma and wondered: what kind of person was *Greyhorse?*

"Dr. Crusher," she snapped—before she'd even completed her chain of reasoning. Crusher rushed over. "What's wrong?" she asked.

"Poison," Idun said. "I think Ben Zoma's been poisoned."

The doctor shook her head. "No. Greyhorse never got that pill into him. Besides, I administered the antidote for *ku'thei*—just in case."

"I'm not talking about a pill," Idun insisted. "I'm talking about the *knife* Ben Zoma was attacked with."

Crusher's brow creased. "You think there was poison on the blade?"

Idun nodded. "Not enough, perhaps, to do the job as quickly as Greyhorse desired. But in the long run, enough to kill him."

Crusher glanced at her patient—and recognized the possibility that Asmund was right. "I don't suppose you know *which* poison?"

Idun shook her head. *Ku'thei* was widely used, but hardly the only option. Klingons used a number of untraceable toxins.

Nor could the doctor administer the antidote for each and every one—not all at once, or their interaction would prove as fatal as the poison itself. And Ben Zoma didn't have that much time.

Both she and Crusher knew all this. But how could they narrow it down?

"Idun," the doctor said, "Greyhorse never treated a Klingon in his life. Much of his knowledge of Klingon medicine must have come from Gerda."

So the question became: What poison would *Gerda* have used? Given what they'd seen the night of Lenoch's death, there could be only one answer: the poison their father had tasted. But what was it?

Idun bit her lip. She tried to picture her father again, dabbing his fingers in their uncle's wound. Lifting the fingers to his mouth. He'd said a word—hadn't he? A single word.

"Choc'pa," she told Crusher. "Try the antidote for *choc'pa.*"

Twenty

The stars outside were back to normal once again.

Guinan was surveying the newly restored Ten-Forward lounge, such as it was, when the doors to the place opened and revealed Pug Joseph. As he had the last time she saw him, he hesitated just inside the entrance.

This time, however, he wasn't drunk. She noticed that right away. But he looked off-balance, confused, as if he'd been staring at the sun for too long.

When he saw her standing behind the bar, he didn't get angry. He didn't turn tail, either. He walked right up to the bar and confronted her.

"Nice to see you again," she told him.

"Sure it is." For a while, he just stood there looking at her. Looking through her, she thought. Then he spoke up: "Listen, you were right. I've got a problem."

Guinan was genuinely surprised. She hadn't expected him to come around so quickly.

He smiled, though there was no humor in it. "You didn't expect me to say that, did you?"

She had to be honest. "Frankly, no, I didn't. What made you change your mind?"

He wet his lips. "A lot of things," Joseph said. "My captain was attacked—nearly fatally. And a good friend—make that two good friends—were seriously injured. All by a man I thought I knew." He breathed in once, out once. "I didn't know anything! I didn't know where my captain—my responsibility—was, or where he was going. I couldn't see the hurt that Greyhorse was carrying inside him, the hurt that twisted and changed him. I was too busy getting soused for anything else."

Guinan nodded. So that was it. Well, it wasn't the kind of therapy she'd have wished for, but it seemed to have done the trick. Admitting that a problem existed was half the battle.

But now that he had made the admission, there was no need for him to torture himself. "This isn't the *Lexington,*" she reminded him as gently as possible. "You're not in charge of security on this ship."

"Doesn't matter," replied Joseph. "At the least, Ben Zoma was my captain. My responsibility." He looked down at the bar. "The last thing I wanted was to be the cause of someone else's death."

His emphasis on "else's" sent a chill up her spine. "You mean this happened before?" she asked softly.

"That's right. A long time ago." He raised his head until their eyes met. His were like black holes. "That's what I carry around inside of me. That's the reason I drink the way I do. Because I killed somebody, somebody who depended on me." A pause, as he wrestled silently with his demons. "You don't know what that's like. No one does—except ol' Pug." His face twisted. "So what do I do? What does anyone do when he has that hanging around his neck?"

Guinan's heart went out to him. She'd been right about this one, about his self-hatred. But like Troi, she'd thought it rooted in disappointment—with his career, with the way his life had turned out. She hadn't had any idea how heavy his burden really was.

"You could start," she said, "by talking about it."

Joseph shook his head. "It's not a real nice story." His expression suggested that he meant it.

"No problem," she insisted. "I hear all kinds."

That was all he really needed—those few words of invitation. Slowly, painfully, he began to tell her what had happened.

Normally, she would have heard him out—listening ever so carefully, speaking only if he needed a push to keep going—until he had purged himself of whatever was plaguing him.

But this time was different. It was wrong.

"Stop," she said.

Joseph looked at her, a little shocked.

"I'm not the one who should be hearing this."

The man's eyes opened wide. He knew exactly what she meant.

"No," he told her. "I can't."

Guinan smiled her most serene smile—the one she used only when absolutely necessary. "You can," she assured him. "What's more, you have to. It's the only way."

Beverly wasn't expecting any visitors, so she was more than a little surprised when she saw Pug Joseph in sickbay, heading in the direction of her office.

As he filled her doorway, the *Lexington*'s stocky security chief appeared uncomfortable. Fidgety. Or at least that's how it seemed to the doctor.

"Pug." She smiled. "Hi. Care for some coffee?"

He shook his head. "No. Thanks."

"How about a seat, then?"

He nodded, pulled the chair out from the other side of the doctor's desk, and sat. For an awkward moment or two he just looked at the floor. When he raised his eyes, they looked . . . what? Haunted?

"How's the captain?" he asked.

"Fine. He'll be out of bed in no time."

Joseph bobbed his head. "Good." He glanced fiercely at something on the wall, and then at something else on her desk. But not at her—not exactly.

The doctor was acutely aware of sounds that she hardly ever heard otherwise . . . the murmur of physicians and nurses as they discussed some minor-injury case . . . the hum of an overhead light fixture that hadn't worked right since Simenon squeezed them out of the slipstream . . . the sharp clatter of a tricorder as it dropped onto a tabletop.

And still Joseph looked around, not quite facing her and not quite facing away—anger and hurt passing over his face in waves.

Beverly leaned forward. "Pug—is something wrong?"

He looked directly at her now, and his mouth became a taut, hard line. "Yes. Something's wrong," he got out. He swallowed. "It's been wrong for a long time."

She returned his gaze, not having the least idea what he was talking about. "I don't understand."

"No," he said. "I guess you wouldn't." He sighed deeply. "You've heard the story about how Jack was killed, right? About the problem with the nacelle, and how we had to go out there and sever it? How the energy buildup overcame us, and Jack died in the explosion?"

Crusher nodded. "Of course."

"Well, it didn't exactly happen the way you heard."

The doctor felt the blood drain from her face. "What do you mean?"

Joseph thrust his chin out. "I mean, Jack didn't have to die." He paused. "It was because of me that he got killed. Because of *me.*"

Crusher felt as if someone had hit her in the stomach. Clutching the armrests of her chair for support, she stared at Joseph. Watched him hang his head, watched his shoulders rise once and sag.

"It was hard work cutting through the nacelle assembly," he told her. His voice was distant. "We were drenched with sweat despite the cooling systems in our suits. And as hard as we worked, it didn't seem we were making much progress. Being out there, being so focused on what you're doing, you lose track of time. You feel like you've been hanging out over the edge forever, your whole life.

"And all the time, the energy is cycling through the warp field generator. Building and building, getting ready to explode. And you don't know when—you just don't know. Any moment could be the one." He shook his head. "It gets to the point where you believe you can feel the explosion—the heat, blistering your skin. And the impact—like someone's taking a hammer to all your bones at once. And the shrapnel—the tiny pieces of hull ripping through you like razors.

"We thought about that. I did. Jack did too—you could tell by the expression on his face, by the feverish look in his eyes. He was just as scared as I was. But he didn't panic. He just kept at it, slicing away with his phaser rifle. Talking with the captain every now and then, putting on a show of confidence despite the emptiness he felt in his gut.

"Getting into the transfer tunnel was the worst part. The *worst.* We could imagine all the energy jumping around inside. Lightning in a bottle. And yet we were pouring on all that phaser fire—like lighting a giant fuse. It was crazy. We knew that, I was *telling* myself that, but we kept firing at the tunnel as if we were too stupid to accept it.

"Suddenly, we were in. We were in and we hadn't blown up. Jack told the bridge and everyone was happy. I was happy too. I was giggling like a madman." A muffled groan. "I think I lost it then. I used up all my nerve getting into the transfer tunnel. After that I had nothing left—nothing. I fired away, I did what I was supposed to, but it wasn't me that was doing it. It was somebody else's arms holding the rifle, somebody else's eyes staring into that mess of tangled metal and circuitry and hellfire. And after a while, that someone didn't have the brass to stick around."

He raised his head, looked at her. If Crusher had thought his eyes were tortured before, she knew now that that had been nothing—compared to *this.*

"At one point Jack was grabbing my arm. He tried saying something to me, but our communicators were dead—silenced by all the energy running wild around us. And even if they'd been working, I don't think I would have heard him. I was too rattled by then. Too intent on just getting out of there, getting back inside the ship. Getting *safe.* I let go of my rifle and started back for the hatch. And I screamed—I think—for him to do the same thing.

"He didn't. He stayed out there, cutting at the assembly—trying to do it by himself. More than halfway to the hatch, I looked back and saw him." Joseph's brows came together into a twisted knot. "I'll never forget it. There he was, blasting away like he couldn't stop." Pug's eyes went wide. "And the energy leak from the nacelle was getting worse. It looked like something alive, something fierce—like the bloody Angel of Death or something. But he'd done some damage. It looked as if he was close to severing the nacelle entirely. Maybe with a little help from me, he would have.

"Suddenly, without warning, the energy leak began accelerating—growing like crazy. It was obvious that something was going to blow. But Jack didn't budge. He kept firing his rifle, even though you couldn't even see the phaser beam anymore for all the radiation pounding at him. He must have known how near he was to accomplishing his mission. And while he was trying to blast away the last of the assembly, I started moving again toward the hatch—even more out-of-my-head frantic than before. As fast as I was going, I should have gotten tangled up in my grapples. Somehow, I didn't."

Joseph bent his head again, ran his fingers through his closely cropped hair. "Then I saw the captain coming from the other direction, and I realized what I'd done. And I knew what the others would say about me—how I chickened out, how

I lost my nerve. I couldn't stand the thought of that, I couldn't. So I just went limp, just pretended I was unconscious. It was all I could think of.

"I didn't expect him to drag me back. I thought he'd go after Jack—after his friend. But I was closer, I was a sure thing. A part of me wanted to tell him I didn't need his help, that he should have gone after the other guy to talk some sense into him. But then he would have known I was a coward, and he would have told everyone else. So I stayed quiet.

"When the energy pocket exploded, we were sheltered from the impact. All I saw of the blast was the radiation from it, and then the nacelle, or what was left of it, spiraling off into space. And I knew Jack was gone. The captain knew it, too; I could see him—"

Joseph's voice broke and he had to stop. "Howling," he whispered, shaking his head from side to side. And then a little stronger, as he drew on some inner reserve of strength: "Howling on the inside of his damned face plate, as if it was him that was dying, and not Jack. But just for a second or two. Then he pulled himself together and got me to safety."

A muttered curse. "That's when I told everyone the story—about how we'd blacked out from all that energy coming out of the transfer tunnel. About how we'd done our best, but it was just too much for us." Now the sobs came, wracking him, shaking the man like a rag doll. "And they believed me," he rasped angrily. "God help me, how they believed me."

Crusher sat there in her chair, not sure what to feel. Should I be angry, she wondered? Bitter? Should I pity him—or should I pity *me?*

Slowly, she got up and came around her desk. Pug wouldn't—or couldn't—look up at her. He was too ashamed—and not only of the tears that had to be in his eyes. He covered his face with his square, powerful hands.

How long ago was Jack killed in that accident? It seemed like forever. And Joseph had been carrying this secret—this burden—all that time. Until now he probably thought he'd be carrying it to his grave.

Tentatively, she reached out—and placed her hand on his shoulder. It was like a rock, clenched against the pain. She could feel it.

"It's all right," she said mechanically. And then she realized—it *was* all right, wasn't it? Whatever crime this man had committed, if one could call it a crime, was a long time ago. And he had been her husband's friend; Jack wouldn't have wanted to see him this way, no matter what. She said the words again, with more conviction this time: "It's all right, Pug. *I forgive you.*"

Joseph looked up at her, his eyes red-ringed and swollen. Taking her hand off his shoulder, he held it against his cheek. And shamelessly cried some more.

It wasn't really Cadwallader's fault that she was running a few minutes behind schedule. After all, they hadn't let her see Ben Zoma until just a little while ago, and she hadn't wanted to leave sickbay before welcoming her captain back to the world of the living. Hell, she'd have done that much even if he'd been only her commanding officer—and not her friend as well.

Nonetheless, she hated like the devil to be late. Especially when it came to something as mysterious as the dinner experience Will Riker had created for her. Despite her protests, he'd told her nothing at all of what was in store—advising her only to wear "that dress" he'd seen the evening of their *last* scheduled appointment.

Finally, a little out of breath, she turned the corner and came in sight of their rendezvous point—the entrance to holodeck one. But Riker was nowhere to be seen.

Oh, come on, she remarked silently, slowing down as she approached the place. I'm not *that* late. And even if I were, he owes me one after the way he—

Abruptly, the doors to the holodeck opened and Riker stepped outside. He was wearing a fitted black suit, the kind worn on Earth for formal occasions. The first officer smiled and extended his hand to her.

She looked past him into the holodeck. What she saw looked like a patch of lush green fir forest, with shards of deep azure sky showing between the needled branches.

"Don't just stand there," Riker said. "Come on in."

She turned to him. "Are you, um, sure I'm *dressed* for it?"

He nodded reassuringly. "You couldn't be dressed more perfectly."

Laying her hand in his, Cadwallader let him draw her into the holodeck. As the doors closed behind her, she got a better idea of her surroundings.

They were perched on a steep mountainside—or more specifically, on a wooded ledge jutting *out* from a steep mountainside. She could see other mountains all around them—a chain stretching in every visible direction to the horizon. And above them was a perfect dome of blue heaven, uninterrupted by even a single wisp of cloud. It looked like the kind of place that should have been quite cold, but the sun was hot and strong, and the trees protected them from the winds.

"You approve?" Riker asked.

She nodded. "Where are we?"

"Alaska," he told her. "Not far from where I grew up." He tapped his foot on the moss-covered ground. "I got a chance to see this place only once—just before I left for the Academy."

"Helipod?" she guessed.

"Nope. I *climbed* up. Took three whole days and a lot of bruised body parts, but I made it."

Cadwallader looked down into the valley below. She whistled.

"And it was just as beautiful as I thought it would be," he went on. "Only one problem. There was nobody to share it with."

She chuckled, amused. "I think I get the picture. But wasn't this supposed to be a *dinner* date?"

Riker snapped his fingers. Suddenly, a gas-fired stove materialized in front of them. There were a couple of pans on the cooking grill. The aroma that came to Cadwallader was spicy and faintly fishy.

"Smells good," she said. "What is it?"

"Trout remoulade," he replied. "An old family recipe."

He snapped his fingers a second time, and a red-and-white checkered tablecloth materialized not far from the stove. It sported a basket of bread and a couple of glasses of wine.

This time, Cadwallader actually laughed. "You think of everything, don't you?"

Riker shrugged. "When I'm inspired."

She turned to him. "And when it gets dark?" she asked. "What do we do to keep warm?"

"I don't think that will be a problem," he told her.

"Really? And why is that?"

He was completely deadpan as he said it: "You'll have to wait until *after* dinner to find *that* out."

Today, there were only two of them at Ben Zoma's bedside—Troi and Commander Asmund. Of course, the empath had a professional reason for remaining there. It was disconcerting to regain consciousness and find that so much had changed while one was unaware. Often, a ship's counselor could smooth the transition.

But not all Troi's reasons for visiting were of the professional variety. She also *liked* Ben Zoma. Hell—it was difficult not to.

And to be honest, she felt a little guilty for having had to deceive him when he confronted her that time in the corridor. She was glad the time had come when she could drop the pretense and be honest with him.

Just as she was glad she didn't have to lie to Idun Asmund anymore. Or to probe her emotions for evidence of murderous intent.

"How long until we reach Daa'V?" Ben Zoma asked softly. With the poison completely neutralized, he was considerably stronger than he had been the day before. He'd even gotten most of his color back.

"Another four days," Troi told him. "And that's at warp nine."

Full warp capability was a luxury she'd never take for granted again. Not after crawling into and halfway through the Romulan Neutral Zone at warp one.

He thought for a moment, then seemed surprised. "We'll be on time."

"That's right," she said. "Even with all that's happened, we'll be on time. Thanks to Geordi and his engineering staff—and a little help from your friend Simenon."

Ben Zoma smiled. But a moment later the smile faded.

"It's too bad. About Greyhorse, I mean."

She nodded. "We all feel bad. Perhaps with some rehabilitation . . ." She shrugged. "One can only hope."

He turned to Asmund. She returned his gaze attentively.

"Funny," he said, "isn't it—that the one we were most eager to pin the problem on . . . should be so instrumental in the solution. And in saving my life to boot."

Idun grunted. "Remember Beta Gritorius Four?"

After a second or two it came to him. "So I do. Then we're even?"

The blond woman shook her head. "Not at all. It's just *your* turn again to save *my* life."

Ben Zoma laughed—which turned out to be a bad move, as it drew the attention of Dr. Selar. The Vulcan was suddenly standing at the foot of the biobed.

"I think we should be going," Troi said, rising.

Asmund stood too. "If we must. But I'll be back," she told Ben Zoma.

The captain of the *Lexington* pointed at her with mock-solemnity. "I'm depending on it, Commander."

Troi grinned—and not just at Ben Zoma's antics. She saw the look on Idun Asmund's face, and she knew that she was happy. For the first time in years the woman felt as if she *belonged.*

One didn't always have to be an empath to know what was going on in people's hearts. And to rejoice with them.

Worf looked at the entrance to his quarters, where the alarm was beeping insistently. "Enter," he said.

As the doors opened, Morgen's angular frame filled the gap. "I hope I am not interrupting anything," he remarked, his yellow eyes glinting.

Worf made a point of not paying excessive attention to the long, leather-wrapped object tucked under one of the Daa'Vit's arms—though when this voyage began, he would have been more than a little leery of it. "No," he replied evenly. "Not at all. Come in."

Morgen walked directly to the chair he sat in last time. Momentarily, the Klingon considered placing himself on the other side of the room, as he had before. Then he thought again and took a seat much closer to Morgen's—separated from it by only the width of a low, s'naiah-wood table.

Their eyes met and locked. Klingon and Daa'Vit—though no longer *just* Klingon and Daa'Vit. With a hint of ceremony, Morgen laid the leather-wrapped object on the table.

"Open it," he instructed. His inflection rendered it more of a request than a command.

Worf picked it up and unwrapped the thing. Before he was entirely finished, he saw the curved, razor-sharp blade. It gleamed even in the subdued light. The Klingon regarded his visitor.

"Go ahead," Morgen said.

Carefully, Worf unwrapped it the rest of the way. He noted the grim elegance of the weapon, its surprising lightness, the intricately woven leather of its pommel. He nodded appreciatively.

"I only regret," the Daa'Vit told him, "that it could not be a real *ka'yun*. But I was quite pleased with the job your ship's computer did in fabricating this one. You'll find it handles slightly better than the one *you* gave *me* when we participated in your 'calisthenics' program."

The Klingon looked at him and suppressed a frown. It was only reasonable to expect that a Daa'Vit would make a superior *ka'yun;* they were trained to do so from the age of three.

"The hardest part was convincing your captain to authorize a bypass of the computer's security restrictions. As you know, it will not create a weapon without the prior approval of either the captain or the security chief." Morgen smiled. "And I could hardly have asked *you*—not if I wanted it to be a surprise."

Worf rewrapped the *ka'yun* and set it down again. He didn't know what to say. It was the first time in the history of the universe that a Daa'Vit had ever offered a Klingon such a gift. "I am honored," he managed to say at last.

"Of course you are," Morgen quipped. "But you understand—it's only a temporary thing."

The Klingon's forehead ridged over. "Temporary?" he echoed, not understanding at all.

"That's right," the Daa'Vit informed him. "When my coronation is over, I'll beam you back with a real one."

Worf shook his head. Now he *really* didn't understand.

Morgen leaned closer. "Unfortunately, I have a couple of vacancies in my escort. Dr. Crusher has graciously agreed to fill one of them. I am asking you to fill the other."

The security chief looked at him. "A Klingon . . . on Daa'V . . . ?"

Morgen waved aside the objection. "I'm not saying it will be easy, Lieutenant. Not for you—and not for me. But I'm willing if you are."

Worf sat back in his chair. "You will be denounced as a traitor. Your throne will be forfeit."

"Does that mean you're turning me down?" the Daa'Vit asked.

The Klingon attempted a grin. "No," he said. "Once again, I am honored."

"And perhaps a little crazy," Morgen suggested.

Worf nodded. "That as well."

As the holodeck doors opened, Wesley recognized the scene. It was just as he remembered it—a scarlet forest set ablaze wherever a sunbeam pierced it. The flying things were there too, hurrying from one overhead branch to another, making their deep-throated cries and dropping their beautiful, deadly feathers.

As the ensign entered, he remembered also to adjust for the strange springiness of the turf—and to look for the path that cut through the woods.

Simenon was just where Wes had expected to find him. This time, however, he was dressed in regulation Starfleet attire—not the casual robe he'd been wearing when they last visited this program.

As Wesley approached, the Gnalish was picking up a stone from the pile. "Greetings," he said without turning around. Then, pausing—as if savoring the moment for as long as he could—he pulled back and let fly.

The stone sailed effortlessly over the bright, placid water. It skipped once, twice, and then three more times in quick succession. Brushing his hands against each other, Simenon turned to his young companion.

"It's like piloting a shuttle," he said. "Once you've got it, you never lose it."

The ensign smiled. "I guess you're right."

The professor trained his ruby eyes on him. "Come to polish your technique?"

Wesley shook his head. "To wish you luck."

Simenon snorted. "What sort of luck will I need on Daa'V? One diplomatic mission is much like another." His tail switched back and forth; his expression eased just a bit. "But thanks for the thought."

"You know," said Wesley, "I'm hoping to get to the Academy one day. As soon as possible, in fact."

The Gnalish tilted his head as he regarded the human. "And?"

Wesley shrugged. "I don't know. I guess I'm looking forward to seeing you there."

"I see." He bent and picked up another rock, appraised it. "I should tell you— I'm not the most popular fellow in the place. Cadets see me and run the other way."

"Then they're not very bright," the ensign told him. "I've already attended one of your classes." He glanced at the pile of flat rocks at Simenon's feet. "I wouldn't mind at all taking another."

The professor snorted again—more softly this time. "That's what you say *now.* Just wait until exam time."

Wesley laughed. And after a moment Simenon joined him.

Beverly Crusher smoothed out her dark blue and black dress uniform and considered herself in the mirror. She looked fine. But then, her appearance wasn't the source of her dissatisfaction.

Her door mechanism beeped. The captain, no doubt. Right on time, as always.

"Come in," she said, and left her bedroom to meet him in the apartment's reception area.

Picard was idly taking in the furnishings when she emerged. He smiled at the sight of her.

"Very becoming," he said. "Very becoming indeed. It has been some time since you've worn your dress uniform, Doctor."

She smiled back. "Thank you. And yes, it has."

He held his hands out, palms up. "All ready?"

Crusher nodded. "I guess so."

The captain regarded her. "Is something wrong, Beverly?"

She sighed. "I just wish I'd had more time to prepare for this. Ever since Morgen asked me to be part of his escort, I've been studying Daa'Vit culture. But there's still a great deal I don't know."

"And you are afraid you will do something to embarrass Captain Morgen—or even jeopardize his ascension to the throne."

"Exactly," Crusher said.

Picard shook his head. "No need to worry. Unlike you, I have had time to veritably immerse myself in Daa'Vit custom. And I can tell you there are no hidden traps to catch you by surprise."

She looked at him. "You're sure?"

"I'm sure. Do you feel better now?"

"As a matter of fact," she told him, "I do." Taking a quick survey of her quarters, Crusher turned and headed for the door. The captain followed her out.

Once in the corridor, they headed for the nearest turbolift. There was a spring in Picard's step that the doctor hadn't noticed for days. She approved—and not just in her capacity as chief medical officer. It was good to see the man feeling so chipper after all that had come before.

Maybe his good spirits were contagious, she mused—because by the time they reached the lift, she felt pretty chipper herself.

"You know," she said, surprising herself a little, "I was actually dreading seeing the people from the *Stargazer*."

The captain shot her a glance. "Oh?"

"It's true. I didn't even want to come out of my quarters."

He grunted. A moment later, the lift arrived and the doors opened. They stepped inside.

Once they were in the privacy of the conveyance, Picard cleared his throat. "To be perfectly candid," he said, "I was a little apprehensive myself."

Crusher saw him in a new light. "*You* were apprehensive? For godsakes, why?"

He turned to look at her. "I thought our visitors would bring back memories. Matters I hadn't quite laid to rest."

And suddenly, she understood. She'd been so wrapped up with her own ghosts, she'd forgotten the captain had some of his own.

"What about now?" she asked.

"Now," he said thoughtfully, "I am glad I had a chance to see my old friends again. *All* of them—living and dead."

She took his arm and squeezed it affectionately. "I know the feeling, Jean-Luc. I know it quite well."

That was how they emerged from the lift—with her arm tucked into the crook of his. And it was still there when they entered the transporter room, where they found the others already waiting for them.

Epilogue

Guinan gazed out of Ten-Forward's observation port at the huge, blue disc of Daa'V. Picard and the others had arrived there minutes earlier, having beamed down to the planet's surface for Morgen's coronation ceremony.

Guinan couldn't help feeling bad about Greyhorse. She had met him years earlier, on the same occasion when she met Ben Zoma, Joseph, Simenon, and the Asmund sisters.

Had she listened to the doctor a little more closely then—really *listened*—she might have picked up his obsession with Gerda Asmund, and stopped him from becoming someone driven to murder his friends.

For that matter, Guinan reflected, she might have kept Gerda from committing the crime that landed her in a penal facility. And if Gerda hadn't committed that crime, Greyhorse wouldn't have had a reason to kill.

"*If,*" she whispered, and heaved a sigh.

But at the moment Guinan's path crossed the *Stargazer*'s, she had been laboring under problems of her own, and her level of awareness wasn't anywhere near what it might have been. She just wasn't doing much listening in those days.

Except to Picard, of course.

She chuckled. After all, *that* Picard wasn't the veteran who commanded the *Enterprise*-D so deftly now, plying his course with the kind of grace and wisdom other captains could only dream of. Not by a long shot.

The Picard whom Guinan knew back then was still new at the game of commanding a starship. He was raw, untested, making the best decisions he could.

And they weren't always the right decisions. Even in those days, he would probably have conceded that.

But then, Fate had thrust Picard into the limelight well before his time. It was a wonder, Guinan supposed, that her friend had survived the ordeal at all. . . .

PART TWO

United Federation of Planets Starship
U.S.S. Stargazer NCC-2893
2333

One

Jean-Luc Picard regarded his opponent through the fine steel mesh of his fencing mask.

Daithan Ruhalter was tall, barrel-chested, and powerfully built . . . and for all of that, quick as a cat. Like Picard, he was clad entirely in white—the accepted garb for fencers for the last several hundred years.

At first, Ruhalter just stood there on the metallic strip in a half-crouch, only his head moving as he took stock of Picard's posture. Then he edged forward with a skip step, lunged full length and extended his point in the direction of his adversary's chest.

It wasn't his best move—Picard knew that from experience. It was just an opening salvo, Ruhalter's effort to feel his opponent out—and Picard, who had been trained by some of the best fencing masters in twenty-fourth-century Europe, didn't overreact. He merely retreated a couple of steps and flicked his opponent's point aside.

Undaunted, Ruhalter advanced and lunged again—though this time, he took a lower line. Picard had no more trouble with this attack than the first. In fact, he launched a counterattack just to keep his adversary honest.

Ruhalter chuckled in his mask, his voice deep and resonant. "Let's begin in earnest now, eh?"

"If you say so," Picard rejoined.

Suddenly, the other man's point was everywhere—high, low, sliding in from the left, zagging in from the right. Picard wove an intricate web of protective steel around himself, defending against each incursion as soon as he recognized it.

Ruhalter used his fencing blade the way he commanded his crew. He was aggressive, improvisational, inclined to go with his instincts first and last. Also, he was a devout believer in the philosophy that the best defense is a good offense.

It was an approach that had garnered the man his share of prestigious medals and left more than one hostile species cursing his name. Years earlier, before the landmark Treaty of Algeron, Ruhalter had even gotten the best of the crafty Romulans.

However, Picard was no pushover either. Though his style was to rely on skill, discipline, and a carefully considered game plan, he was so surgically precise that few opponents could prevail against him.

Ruhalter continued to advance against the younger man, relentless in his onslaught. His sword darted like a living thing, a steel predator hungry for a taste of its prey.

Picard had no chance to go on the offensive, no opportunity to drive his opponent back in the other direction. It was all he could do to keep Ruhalter's point away from himself—but he did that admirably well.

And he knew his adversary couldn't keep up his intensity forever. Eventually, Ruhalter would have to falter. If I bide my time, Picard told himself, I'll find the opening I need.

Then, suddenly, there it was . . . *the opening.*

In an attempt to lunge in under Picard's guard, Ruhalter had failed to extend his lead leg quite far enough. As a result, he had dropped his upper body. Off-balance, he was eminently vulnerable.

Picard moved his opponent's point out of the way, encountering little resistance. With practiced efficiency, he leaned forward into a forceful but economical counterthrust.

Too late, he saw his error. Ruhalter hadn't made a mistake after all. His overextension had been an act, a ruse designed to draw Picard into a subtle trap . . . and it had worked.

Thwarting the younger man's attack with the polished dome of his guard, Ruhalter came at Picard with a roundhouse right. Before Picard could retreat and erect a new defense, Ruhalter's point was pushing against the ribs beneath his left arm.

"Alas!" the older man barked, making no effort to mask his exuberance.

The best fencing masters in Europe would have been ashamed of him, Picard thought. On the other hand, it was devilishly difficult to deal with someone who was so unpredictable.

"Your point," Picard conceded drily.

Careful not to forget his manners, he swung his blade up to his mask in a gesture of respect. Then he settled back into an en garde position. Ruhalter, who was smiling behind his mask, did the same.

"You know," he remarked good-naturedly, "you look a little sluggish this morning, Jean-Luc."

"Only in comparison to my opponent," Picard told him. *Though that will change,* he added, resolving to win the next point.

He succeeded in that objective. However, Ruhalter came back and won the next two in succession. In the end, Picard's determination notwithstanding, he lost the match 5-3.

Ruhalter removed his mask, revealing his rugged features and thick, gray hair. "Thanks for the workout," he said.

Picard removed his mask as well. "Thank *you,* sir," he responded, ever the good sport.

"You know," Ruhalter told him in a paternal way, "you need to trust your instincts more, Commander. A man who ignores his instincts is defeated before he starts."

Tucking his mask under his sword arm, Picard managed a smile. "I'll try to keep that in mind, sir."

He would, too. After all, Ruhalter was more than his captain. He was also the twenty-eight-year-old Picard's mentor—a man the second officer greatly admired, despite the differences in their personalities.

"Perhaps you would care for a rematch," Picard suggested.

Before the captain could answer, a voice echoed throughout the gym: "Leach to Captain Ruhalter."

The captain looked up at the ceiling, as if he could see the intercom grid inside it. "Yes, Mr. Leach?"

Stephen Leach was Ruhalter's first officer. He had been left in charge of the ship's bridge while the captain and his second officer took their exercise in the gymnasium.

"You have an eyes only message from Admiral Mehdi at Starfleet Command, sir," Leach reported. As usual, he projected an air of cool efficiency.

Ruhalter looked at Picard. "Eyes only, eh? I guess I'll have to ask for a rain check on that rematch."

Picard nodded. "I understand, sir."

The captain glanced at the ceiling again. "I'll take it in my quarters, Mr. Leach. Ruhalter out." Replacing his mask and sword on a wall rack, he nodded in Picard's direction and left the gym.

As the younger man watched his captain depart, he wondered what the message from Starfleet Command might be about. After all, it was rare for headquarters to send an eyes only missive to *any* vessel, much less a deep-space exploration ship like the *Stargazer*.

The second officer ran his fingers through his sweat-soaked, auburn hair. Few eyes only messages remained that way for long, he mused. He hoped this one wouldn't be an exception.

Idun Asmund was running a diagnostic routine at her helm console when the turbolift doors opened and her twin came out onto the bridge.

Gerda Asmund was Idun's mirror image—tall, blond, and eminently well proportioned. Men invariably found the two of them attractive, though the reverse wasn't true nearly often enough for Idun's taste.

One of the drawbacks of having been raised among Klingons, she reflected. Unless a man smoldered with a warrior's passions, she wasn't likely to give him a second look.

Negotiating a path around the captain's chair, which was occupied at the moment by the tall, rail-thin Commander Leach, Gerda relieved Lieutenant Kochman at the navigation console. Then, as she sat down and surveyed her control settings, Gerda shot her sister a look.

Idun had no trouble divining the intent behind it. Clearly, Gerda was bored. For that matter, so was Idun.

They had joined the *Stargazer*'s crew with adventure in mind. After all, the *Stargazer* was a deep-space exploration vessel, its mandate to push out the boundaries of known space. However, in more than seven months of service, they had seen nothing but routine planetary surveys and the occasional space anomaly— hardly the kind of excitement they had hoped for. Gerda had even broached the subject of transferring to another ship.

Idun was a bit more optimistic than her sister. And less than fifteen minutes ago, she had been given reason to believe her patience might finally be rewarded.

"Commander Leach?" came a voice over the ship's intercom system. It was the captain, Idun realized.

The first officer looked up, his dark eyes alert in their oversized orbits. "Yes, sir?"

"Set a course for Starbase two-oh-nine," the captain said. "And don't spare the horses."

Idun saw Leach frown. He was a man who liked to deal in hard facts, not colorful colloquialisms.

"Warp eight?" the first officer ventured.

"Warp eight," the captain confirmed. "Ruhalter out."

Leach turned to Gerda. "You heard Captain Ruhalter, Lieutenant. That survey of Beta Aurelia will have to wait."

"Aye, sir," said Gerda, bringing up the appropriate cartography on her monitor and charting a course. A few moments later, she sent the results to her sister's console.

A comment went with it: *Warp eight. Sounds serious.*

Idun sent a return communication: *Preceded by an eyes only message not fifteen minutes ago.*

Surprised, Gerda looked up from her monitor and glanced at her sister. For the first time in months, a smile spread across her face.

Gilaad Ben Zoma, the *Stargazer*'s chief of security, heard a beep and looked up. "Come in," he said.

A moment later, the doors to his small, economically furnished office slid apart, revealing a compact, baby-faced young man with short, sandy hair in a uniform that seemed a tad too big for him. He looked uncomfortable as he stepped into the room.

But then, Ben Zoma mused, Lieutenant Peter "Pug" Joseph probably had an idea as to why he had been summoned. The security chief smiled to put the man at ease and gestured to a chair on the other side of his desk.

"Have a seat, Mr. Joseph."

"Yes, sir," said the younger man. He sat down, but he didn't look any more comfortable than before.

Ben Zoma leaned forward. "As you may have guessed, I called you here to talk about what happened last night."

Joseph looked contrite. "Yes, sir."

"You know," said the security chief, "it's good to be alert, especially when we're dealing with something as tricky as the inlet manifold. But sometimes, it's possible to be a little *too* alert."

"Sir," Joseph replied, "I thought there was a real danger—"

Ben Zoma held his hand up, silencing the man. "I know exactly what you thought, Lieutenant. And I must say, I admire the quickness with which you responded. But for heaven's sake, you've got to be a little more certain before you sound a shipwide alarm."

"But, sir," Joseph argued respectfully, "if there *had* been a problem with the inlet manifold—"

"Then it would have been picked up by our engineers," the security chief assured him. He reached for his computer monitor and swiveled it around so the other man could see its screen. "Just as they would have picked up that field coil overload you were certain you saw a couple of days ago . . . and that apparent injector malfunction over which you shut down the warp drive."

The other man sighed and slumped back into his chair.

"Then," Ben Zoma went on as gently as he could, "there was the time you called an intruder alert without verifying your sensor data. And the time before that, when you thought an unidentified ship was approaching and it turned out to be a neutrino shadow."

Joseph hung his head.

The security chief was sympathetic. Not too many years earlier, he himself had been a fresh-faced, junior-grade officer.

"I don't bring up these incidents to make you feel bad," Ben Zoma explained. "I just want you to see that you're overreacting a bit. Granted, a threat to life and limb occasionally rears its head on a starship . . . but it can't be lurking *everywhere*."

Joseph nodded. "I see what you mean, sir."

"Good," said the security chief. "Then we've accomplished something."

The younger man looked up, his eyes hard and determined. "I'll do better," he vowed. "I promise you that."

"I'm sure you will," said Ben Zoma.

But in reality, he wasn't sure at all.

Chief Medical Officer Carter Greyhorse hadn't intended to walk into the ship's gym. Distracted as he was, he had believed he was entering the neighboring biology lab, where he meant to review the work of a Betazoid biochemist who claimed to have synthesized the neurotransmitter psilosynine.

The doctor had expected to be greeted by the sleek, dark forms of a computer workstation, an industrial replicator and an electromagnetic containment field generator, all of them packed into a small, gray-walled enclosure. Instead, he found himself gazing at a tall, blond woman in a formfitting black garment pursuing some exotic and rigorous form of exercise.

The woman's cheeks, he couldn't help noticing, were flushed a striking shade of red. Her full lips had pulled back from her teeth, endowing her with a strangely wolflike appearance, and her ice-blue eyes burned with an almost feral intensity.

And the way she moved . . . it took Greyhorse's breath away. She punched and kicked and spun her way through one complex maneuver after another, her skin glistening with perspiration, her long, lean muscles rippling in savage harmony.

Harsh, guttural sounds escaped her throat, occasionally devolving into a simple gasp or grunt. But they didn't signal any pause in her routine. Despite whatever fatigue she might have felt, she went on.

In the presence of such passion, such vigor, Greyhorse felt oddly like an intruder. He experienced an impulse to go back the way he had come, to retreat to his safe and familiar world of scientific certainties.

But he didn't go. He couldn't.

He was mesmerized.

The woman, on the other hand, didn't even seem aware of the physician's presence in the room. Or if she *was* aware of it, it didn't appear to faze her. She pursued her regimen with uninhibited energy and determination, pushing her finely tuned body to levels of speed and precision that few other humans could even contemplate.

Then she did what Carter Greyhorse would have thought impossible. She turned it up a notch.

As the doctor watched, spellbound, the woman attacked the air around her as if it were rife with invisible enemies. She whirled, struck, gyrated, and struck again, faster and faster, until it seemed her heart would have to burst under the burden.

Then, suddenly, she stopped . . . and in a spasm of triumph and ecstasy, tossed her head back and howled at the top of her lungs. The sound she made was more animal than human, Greyhorse thought, more the product of the woman's blood than her brain.

Finally, her chest still heaving, sweat streaming down both sides of her face, she fell silent. Only then did she turn and take notice of the doctor standing by the door. Their eyes met and he could see the raw emotion still roiling inside hers.

He felt he should say something, but speech escaped him. All he could do was stare back at her like an idiot.

The woman drew a long, ragged breath. Then she went to the wall, pulled a towel off the rack there, and stalked past him. A moment later, Greyhorse heard the hiss of the sliding doors as they opened for her. Another hiss told him they had closed again.

Looking back over his shoulder, he saw that the woman was gone. A wave of disappointment and relief swept over him.

The doctor was new on the ship, so he didn't know many people outside of Ruhalter and his command staff. Certainly, he didn't know the woman he had just seen . . . not even her name.

But he would make it his business to find out.

Lieutenant Vigo was sitting in the *Stargazer*'s mess hall, staring at his plate of *sturrd,* when his friend Charlie Kochman sat down next to him and lowered a tray of food onto the table.

"Now that," said Kochman, who was the ship's secondary navigator, "is what I call a replicator program."

Vigo glanced at Kochman's tray, which featured a large wooden bowl full of hard, gray mollusk shells with dark, rubbery tails emerging from them. "Steamers?" he asked.

"Steamers," his colleague confirmed with a grin. "It took a while, but the replicator finally got them right." He glanced at Vigo's plate. "You've got some more of that Pandrilite stuff, I see."

"Sturrd. It *is* the signature dish of my homeworld," Vigo noted.

Kochman held up a hand. "Don't get me wrong, buddy . . . the last thing I want to do is keep a big blue guy like you from eating what he really likes. I just figured you might want to try something else sometime."

Vigo glanced at his friend's mollusks, which he didn't find the least bit tempting. "Sometime," he echoed.

Kochman chuckled. "To each his own, I guess." And with unconcealed gusto, he used his fork to crack open one of the clams.

Vigo considered his own food again. One of the other humans on the ship had described *sturrd* as a mound of sand and ground glass smothered in maple syrup. But to a Pandrilite, it was as appetizing as any dish in the universe.

Usually, he amended. At the moment, Vigo didn't have much of an appetite.

Kochman noticed. "What's wrong?" he asked between mollusks.

Vigo shook his head. "Nothing."

His friend looked sympathetic. "It's Werber again, isn't it?"

Wincing, the Pandrilite looked around the mess hall. Fortunately, Hans Werber was nowhere to be seen. "I told you," he reminded Kochman. "There's nothing wrong. Nothing at all."

"Right," said his friend. "Just like there was nothing wrong a couple of days ago, and a couple of days before that. Admit it—Werber's on your back and he won't get off."

Vigo didn't say anything in response. He was a Pandrilite, after all, and Pandrilites were taught from an early age not to complain. They shouldered their burdens without objection or protest.

However, Kochman was right. Lieutenant Werber, the *Stargazer*'s chief weapons officer and therefore Vigo's immediate superior, was a supremely difficult man to work for.

He routinely held Vigo and the ship's other weapons officers to unrealistic standards. And when they didn't meet those standards, Werber would make them feel unworthy of serving on a starship.

Kochman shook his head sadly. "Somebody's got to stand up to the guy. Otherwise, he'll just keep on making people feel like dirt."

Perhaps my colleague is right, Vigo reflected. Perhaps the only way to improve the situation in the weapons section is for someone to let Werber know how we feel.

But the Pandrilite knew with absolute certainty that that someone wouldn't be him.

Standing at his captain's left hand, Picard watched Idun Asmund bring the *Stargazer* to a gentle stop. Then he eyed the bridge's main viewscreen and the Federation facility that was pictured there.

Starbase 209 was shaped roughly like an hourglass top, its bulky-looking extremities tapering drastically to a slender midsection. In that regard, it was no different from a dozen other starbases Picard had visited in the course of his brief career.

What's more, he had seen plenty of ships docked at those facilities. But none of them even vaguely resembled the dark, flask-shaped vessel hanging in space alongside Starbase 209—a vessel whose puny-looking warp nacelles projected from its flanks as well as its hindquarters.

Ruhalter leaned forward in his center seat. "Interesting design, isn't it?" he asked, clearly referring to the ship and not the base.

"Interesting, all right," said Leach, who was standing on the captain's right. "And if I may hazard a guess, it's the reason we're here."

The captain didn't respond to the remark. But then, he didn't seem to know much more than the rest of them.

Suddenly, Picard was struck by a feeling that he had seen the flask-shaped vessel somewhere after all . . . or something very much like it. But if not at a starbase, where would it have been? The second officer wracked his brain but couldn't come up with an answer.

"Sir," said Paxton at the communications console, "I have Captain Eliopoulos, the base's ranking officer."

Ruhalter sat back. "Put him through, Lieutenant."

A moment later, the image of a fair-haired man with a dark, neatly trimmed beard appeared on the screen. "Welcome to Starbase two-oh-nine," he said. "You must be Captain Ruhalter."

"Pleased to meet you," said Ruhalter. "Your place or mine?"

The casual tone seemed to catch Eliopoulos off guard. It took him a moment to reply, "Yours, I suppose."

"Done," said Ruhalter. He turned to Leach. "See to Captain Eliopoulos's transport, Number One. The command staff and I will be waiting for you in the ship's lounge."

The first officer darted a glance at Picard, no doubt wondering why his subordinate couldn't have taken care of Eliopoulos's arrival. Then he turned and entered the turbolift.

As the doors slid closed with a whisper, the second officer regarded the viewscreen again. The more he studied the strange vessel, the more familiar it seemed to him. He could barely wait to hear what Captain Eliopoulos had to say about it.

Two

Picard watched the ship's new chief medical officer enter the lounge with some difficulty. Carter Greyhorse was so big and broad-shouldered, he could barely fit through the door.

"Good of you to make it, Doctor," said Ruhalter, from his place at the head of the dark, oval table.

Greyhorse looked at him, then mumbled an apology. Something about some research he was conducting.

"Be thankful I'm inclined to be lenient with ship's surgeons," the captain told him. "I never forget they can relieve me of my command."

The doctor's brow furrowed beneath his crop of dark hair.

"That was a joke," Ruhalter informed him.

Greyhorse chuckled to show that he got it, but his response lacked enthusiasm. Clearly, Picard reflected as the doctor took a seat beside him, humor wasn't Greyhorse's strong suit.

In addition to Ruhalter and Picard himself, five other section heads had arrived before Greyhorse. They included Weapons Chief Werber, Chief Engineer Phigus Simenon, Communications Chief Martin Paxton, Sciences Chief Angela Cariello and Security Chief Gilaad Ben Zoma.

Simenon was a Gnalish—a compact, lizardlike being with ruby-red eyes and a long tail. Everyone else at the table was human.

The assembled officers sat in silence for more than a minute. Then, just as some of them were beginning to shift in their seats, Leach arrived with Eliopoulos in tow.

"Commander Eliopoulos," said Ruhalter, "may I present my command staff." He reeled off their names. "Naturally, they're all most eager to learn why we've made this trip."

"I'm not surprised," the bearded man responded.

Leach indicated a chair and Eliopoulos sat down. Then the first officer took a seat next to him and said, "Go ahead, sir."

Eliopoulos looked around the table. "No doubt," he said, "you noticed a strange-looking ship as you approached the base. It arrived here seven days ago. There were only two people aboard—a man named Guard Daniels and a woman named Serenity Santana."

"Humans?" asked Werber, a stocky, balding man with piercing blue eyes and a dense walrus mustache.

"From all appearances," Eliopoulos confirmed. "But from what they told us, they weren't just any humans. They were descendants of the crew of the *S.S. Valiant* . . . the ship that went through the galactic barrier nearly three hundred years ago."

The remark hung in the air for a moment as its significance sank in around the room. Picard, who was more excited by history than most, felt his pulse begin to race. *Three hundred years . . .*

It was then that he realized where he had seen the strange-looking ship before. Or rather, not the ship itself, but elements of it.

Back at the Academy, one of his professors had showed him a picture of the *S.S. Valiant*. He recalled its wide, dark body and its abundance of small, curiously placed nacelles. The vessel hanging in space alongside the starbase could easily have evolved from that primitive design.

Then something occurred to Picard—something that seemed to preclude the claim made by Eliopoulos's visitors. "Wasn't the *Valiant* destroyed by order of her captain?"

Ruhalter nodded. "That was my understanding as well."

The second officer knew the story. For that matter, everyone did. James Kirk, the last captain of the original *Starship Enterprise,* had embarked for the galactic barrier on a research mission in 2265. Just shy of his destination, he encountered an antique message buoy—a warning sent out by the captain of the *Valiant* two centuries earlier, chronicling his experiences after penetrating the barrier.

Though the details provided by the buoy were sketchy, it seemed one of the *Valiant*'s crewmen had become a threat to his colleagues . . . and to Earth as well, if he lived to return to her. To eliminate that possibility, the *Valiant*'s captain was forced to blow up his ship.

That seemed like a good reason to turn back. And as far as most people in Kirk's time knew, that was exactly what he had done.

But he hadn't turned back. He had braved the barrier despite the warning. And in doing so, he had shed some light on the fate of the *Valiant* . . . albeit at a terrible price.

The man who paid it was Kirk's navigator, Gary Mitchell, in whom exposure to the barrier had touched off a gradual but startling transformation. Mitchell became a superman, a being capable of increasingly improbable feats of mental and physical prowess . . . telepathy and telekinesis among them.

Unfortunately, Mitchell's perspective began to change as well. He came to see his crewmates as insects, hardly worthy of his notice . . . much less his compassion. In the end, Kirk was compelled to kill him.

Had he hesitated, he might have found himself in the same predicament as the captain of the *Valiant,* who had likely been confronted with a superman of his own—or so Mitchell's transformation seemed to indicate. Then Kirk too might have been forced to destroy his vessel as a last resort.

"But Daniels and Santana," Ruhalter continued, "are saying the *Valiant* wasn't destroyed after all?"

"They agree that it was destroyed," Eliopoulos replied. "However, they maintain that a portion of the *Valiant*'s crew survived her destruction . . . then found an M-Class planet and settled there."

"Hard to believe," said Simenon, his speech harsh and sibilant. "Hundreds of years ago, escape pods didn't have any real range. And M-Class planets weren't any easier to find then than they are today."

Ruhalter regarded Eliopoulos beneath bushy, gray brows. "Assuming for the moment that your guests were telling the truth, what made them decide to return to our side of the barrier?"

Eliopoulos smiled a tired smile. No doubt, he had grown weary of disseminating the information.

"They say they're here to warn the Federation about an impending threat—an immensely powerful species called the Nuyyad, which has been conquering the scattered solar systems on the other side of the barrier and sending native populations running for their lives."

Ruhalter stared at Eliopoulos for a moment. They all did. Then the captain said, "I see."

"Quite a revelation," Picard remarked.

"Stunning, actually," said Leach. He cast the second officer a sideways look. "Assuming it has some basis in fact."

"You sound skeptical," Ruhalter observed.

"I'm more than skeptical," the first officer told him. "I'm afraid—and not of the Nuyyad."

"Of what, then?" asked Picard.

"Of Daniels and Santana," said Leach. "Think about it, Commander. If these people's ancestors went through the galactic barrier more than two hundred years ago, they might eventually have developed some of the same powers Gary Mitchell displayed. And in Mitchell's case, those powers came with a need to dominate others."

The second officer smiled patiently. "But that doesn't mean—"

"I know what you're going to say," Eliopoulos interrupted. "The need to subjugate might have been a quirk of Mitchell's personality. But I have to confess, I had the same concerns as Commander Leach. I had to be careful—I had a starbase to think about."

Ruhalter cocked his head. "Wait a minute . . . didn't Mitchell's transformation have something to do with extrasensory perception?"

"It did," Eliopoulos agreed. "He was a documented ESPer and therefore more sensitive to the barrier effect. So, apparently, was the affected crewman on the *Valiant.*"

"And so was that other crewman on the *Enterprise,*" Cariello added. "The woman who became Mitchell's ally . . ."

"And later turned against him," said Eliopoulos. "That would be Dehner. And yes, she was an ESPer as well. However, the *Enterprise* had better shielding with which to filter the barrier's effects. The *Valiant* was all but naked, by today's standards."

Picard tried to imagine it. The chaos . . . the destruction . . . the blinding flash of powerful, unknown energies . . .

"For all we know," Eliopoulos told them, "even a hint of ESP might have been enough to trigger an eventual transformation—and how many humans aren't blessed at least a little in that regard?"

There was silence around the table. Werber was the one who finally took the air out of it.

"So what did you do with them?" the weapons chief asked. "Daniels and Santana, I mean?"

Eliopoulos scowled. "I did what I had to do. I had the two of them placed in detention cells, pending orders from Starfleet Command."

He paused, looking just the least bit uncomfortable with his actions. And Picard knew why. The pair was human . . . and as far as he could tell, they hadn't done anything to merit imprisonment.

"They seemed disappointed, of course," said Eliopoulos. "And more than a little displeased, I might add. But not surprised."

"Why's that?" asked Ruhalter.

Eliopoulos scowled again. "They said their colleagues had warned them that they would be taking a chance. As they were escorted to the brig, they quoted a twentieth-century Earthman . . . a fellow named Thomas. Apparently, he's the one who said, 'No good deed ever goes unpunished.' "

Picard smiled a grim smile. "It sounds like the type of remark one might make if his ancestors were Earthmen."

"Or if it served one to create that impression," Leach added cynically.

"Go on," Ruhalter instructed the bearded man.

"Naturally," said Eliopoulos, "I didn't like the idea that I might be detaining inno-cent people. But when I contacted Command, Admiral Gardner-Vincent applauded my judgment . . . and ordered me to run a battery of tests on Daniels and Santana."

"Tests?" Picard echoed.

"Brain scans, for the most part," the starbase commander elaborated. "Also, some blood workups."

"And what did you find?" asked Ruhalter.

Eliopoulos looked at him gravely. "While both Daniels and Santana looked perfectly normal—perfectly *human*—on the outside, their brains were different from those of normal *Homo sapiens*. Their cerebellums, for instance, were a good deal more developed, and the blood supply to their cerebral cortices was greater by almost twenty-two percent."

"Which suggested what?" Ruhalter wondered. "That they had been born with the mind-powers that Mitchell acquired?"

"That was the inescapable conclusion," Eliopoulos told him. "With the cooper-ation of our guests, we performed additional tests designed to gauge the extent of their telepathic and telekinetic abilities."

Picard leaned forward in his chair, eager to hear the results. Ruhalter leaned forward as well, he noticed.

"Mind you," said Eliopoulos, "Daniels and Santana could have been holding back and we would have been hard-pressed to detect it. However, what we *did* see was remarkable enough. They could tell me what I was thinking at any given mo-ment, as long as I didn't make any effort to conceal it. And they could maneuver an object weighing up to a kilogram with reasonable precision for an indefinite period of time."

Remarkable indeed, thought Picard.

"In addition," Eliopoulos went on, "Daniels and Santana underwent psycholog-ical tests. If we're to believe the results, they're a good deal more independent and desirous of privacy than the average human being. Whoever said that no man is an island never met these two."

"Did you ask them why that might be?" Picard inquired.

Eliopoulos turned to him. "We did. They told us that in a society where people can read each other's thoughts, privacy necessarily becomes an issue of paramount importance."

"I'll bet it does," said Werber.

"So you were right about them," Leach observed. "Both of them had powers like Lieutenant Commander Mitchell's."

"*Like* them, yes," Eliopoulos noted. "But we didn't find any evidence that their abilities are as devastating as Mitchell's were. For what it's worth, both Daniels and Santana claim that they demonstrated the full extent of what they could do."

Leach grunted. "And if you believe that, I've got some prime land to show you in an asteroid belt."

Werber laughed at the remark.

"This is all very interesting," Ruhalter said, his tone putting a lid on his offi-cers' banter, "but what's the *Stargazer*'s role in it?"

Eliopoulos looked at him. "Despite our suspicions about Daniels and Santana, we've yet to prove they're telling anything but the truth. As a result, Command wants a vessel to go through the barrier and investigate their story about the Nuyyad invasion force."

Leach rolled his eyes, making clear his incredulity. At the same time, Werber muttered something under his breath.

Ruhalter eyed them, the muscles in his jaw bunching. "Let's maintain an air of decorum here, shall we, gentlemen?"

"Of course, sir," the first officer responded crisply.

Werber frowned and said, "Sorry, Captain."

But to Picard's mind, neither of them looked very apologetic.

"I don't blame your officers for being wary of Santana and Daniels," said Eliopoulos. "As I said, I was wary too . . . until I received verification that the Nuyyad exist."

Leach's brow creased, just one indication of his discomfort with the announcement. "Verification? From whom?"

"I'd like to know that myself," said Ruhalter.

"From Nalogen Four," replied the starbase commander.

Picard knew the place. "There's a colony there," he said. "A *Kelvan* colony, if I'm not mistaken."

Eliopoulos nodded. "Since it was established more than a century ago by refugees, they've been accepting other Kelvans from the far side of the galactic barrier."

"And they've encountered the Nuyyad?" Cariello asked.

"One of them has," Eliopoulos told her. "One of the colony's more recent arrivals—an individual named Jomar. He told a Starfleet investigator that he had witnessed Nuyyad aggression and atrocities with his own eyes just a few years back."

"Was he told of the claims made by Daniels and Santana?" asked Ruhalter. "That the Nuyyad were gearing up to cross the barrier?"

"He was," Eliopoulos reported soberly. "And according to Jomar, those claims could well be true."

Ruhalter leaned back in his seat and regarded his officers. "All right," he declared. "I think we understand the situation. When does Command want us to leave for the barrier?"

"Immediately," said Eliopoulos. "But on the way, you're to make a stop at Nalogen Four. Apparently, Jomar is an engineer by training. He feels certain that he can adapt Starfleet tactical systems to make them more effective against the Nuyyad."

That got Werber's attention. Simenon's, too.

"What's wrong with the systems we have now?" asked Leach.

"I don't have the details," Eliopoulos told him. "You'll have to ask Jomar that question."

"I intend to," the first officer said.

"One other thing," Eliopoulos remarked. "For the sake of convenience, Jomar will assume a human appearance. However, he'll be more comfortable in his natural form and at times may wish to revert to it."

"His . . . natural form?" asked Paxton. "And what might that be?"

"Something with a hundred tentacles," Eliopoulos told him. "That's all I know, I'm afraid."

"That's enough," said Cariello.

"We'll accommodate our friend Jomar as best we can," Ruhalter declared. "Just as we would any guest on the *Stargazer.*"

Picard changed the subject. "Naturally," he said, "we'll need the coordinates of the Nuyyad positions if we're to investigate them."

Leach scowled at the notion. "Assuming, of course, that there *are* any Nuyyad positions." Clearly, he wasn't convinced yet.

"You'll have the coordinates," Eliopoulos promised them. "But Command doesn't want you searching for the Nuyyad on your own, given our lack of experience beyond the barrier. That's why they've provided you with a guide."

Simenon looked at him askance. "Meaning?"

Eliopoulos glanced at the engineer. "Meaning Jomar won't be your only guest. Either Daniels or Santana will accompany you as well."

Werber cursed beneath his breath. Simenon didn't look very happy either.

"Captain," said Leach, turning to Ruhalter, "someone didn't think this through very well. As soon as these people arrived, they were thrown into the brig . . . that's how little we trusted them. And now we're ready to give them the run of the *Stargazer?*"

"Not the run of her," Ruhalter assured his exec. .

The captain seemed a good deal less perturbed about the prospect than Leach was. At least, that was how it appeared to Picard.

"In fact," Ruhalter added flatly, "whoever comes with us will be watched day and night. Isn't that right, Mr. Ben Zoma?"

The security chief nodded. "It is, sir," he said crisply.

"Nonetheless, sir . . ." Leach began.

"Thank you for your input," the captain told him pointedly.

Then he turned to Eliopoulos again. "Tell me," he said, "did Starfleet Command determine which of your guests I'm to take along?"

The bearded man shook his head. "They left that up to us."

"In that case," Ruhalter told him, "I'd like to meet Daniels and Santana. Now, if possible. And unless you've got some objections, I'd like to bring a couple of my officers with me."

Eliopoulos shrugged. "Suit yourself, Captain."

"I usually do," said Ruhalter, quirking a smile. He turned to his second officer. "Commander Picard, Lieutenant Ben Zoma . . . you're with me." He glanced at Leach. "You've got the conn, Number One."

His first officer didn't look very happy about the decision. Clearly, he would rather have beamed over to the starbase with the captain. However, he couldn't object to Ruhalter's choice . . . not in front of Eliopoulos and the entire senior staff.

"Aye, sir," was all he said.

On that note, the captain dismissed his officers and sent them back to their respective assignments. Then he led Eliopoulos, Picard, and Ben Zoma out of the lounge.

As he followed Ruhalter down the hall, the second officer caught sight of Leach out of the corner of his eye. The first officer was standing with Simenon and Werber and scowling at him.

Ben Zoma leaned closer to him and spoke sotto voce. "Looks like you're developing quite a fan club, Commander."

Picard glanced at the security chief. Gilaad Ben Zoma was a handsome, darkly complected man with a ready smile. He was also the second officer's closest friend and colleague on the ship.

Like Picard's father, Ben Zoma's had disapproved of his joining Starfleet. From the day they met, the coincidence had given the two men a common ground, something about which to commiserate—and had created a warm rapport between them.

"Fan club indeed," the second officer responded in the same soft voice.

Up ahead, Ruhalter was too engrossed in conversation with Eliopoulos to pay much attention to what his officers were saying. Still, Picard didn't want to utter anything even vaguely insubordinate.

"That's all you have to say?" Ben Zoma wondered. "You know, if you're not careful, our pal Number One is going to stab you in your sleep."

Picard chuckled drily. "He's welcome to try."

Three

Picard stood outside a pair of gray sliding doors, alongside Ruhalter, Ben Zoma, and Eliopoulos, and watched an armed Starfleet security officer punch a code into a wall pad.

A moment later, the doors parted, revealing a fairly large, well-lit chamber. A translucent force field bisected the place, denying access to two separate cells. One was empty. The other contained two very human-looking figures—a man and a woman in dark green jumpsuits.

The man was of average build, with curly, red hair and a robust mustache. The woman was dark and petite, her thick, black tresses drawn back into a long, unruly ponytail.

Daniels, Picard thought. And Santana.

They eyed Eliopoulos and the others as they entered. There wasn't any anger in their expressions, despite their captivity. There wasn't any apparent resentment. But there *was* an almost palpable sense of impatience.

"Commander Eliopoulos," said the redhaired man. "I hope these gentlemen are from the ship you told us about."

"They are," Eliopoulos confirmed. He introduced Ruhalter, Picard, and Ben Zoma one by one.

"Pleased to meet you," the woman replied.

Up close, Serenity Santana was strikingly beautiful, with big, dark eyes and full, cherry-colored lips. So beautiful, in fact, that Picard had difficulty taking his eyes off her.

It seemed to him that her gaze lingered on him for a moment as well. But then, the second officer was quick to concede, that might well have been a product of his imagination.

"And your mission?" Daniels asked, his eyes narrowing. "To investigate what we've been telling you about the Nuyyad? That's still on, I hope."

"It is," Eliopoulos confirmed for him. "In fact, that's what we're here about. Captain Ruhalter wants to decide for himself which of you he'll take along as a guide."

Santana frowned. *"Which of us?"*

"Starfleet Command has decided it would be better for one of you to remain here," Eliopoulos explained. "For security reasons."

Picard saw Santana and Daniels exchange glances. Judging from the looks on their faces, this was yet another indignity in what they perceived as a long list of indignities.

"Fine," said the red-haired man.

Santana looked at Ruhalter. "Who are you going to take?"

The captain returned her gaze for a moment. Then, in a voice that betrayed nothing, he said, "I'll take you."

The woman seemed unprepared for such a quick decision. "Just out of curiosity," she asked, "why me?"

Ruhalter smiled an easy smile. "As my second officer will tell you, I like to go with my instincts."

Santana glanced at Picard. Again, it seemed to him that her scrutiny lasted a little longer than necessary. Then she looked at Daniels, and finally at the captain again.

"I'm ready when you are," the woman told him.

Idun Asmund had been waiting at her helm console for what seemed like forever before she heard her captain's voice flood the bridge: "We're aboard, Number One. Take us out of here."

Commander Leach, who had been sitting in Ruhalter's center seat, responded to the order. "Aye, sir." He turned to Asmund. "You heard the captain, Lieutenant. Half impulse."

"Half impulse," the helm officer confirmed.

She had laid in a course already, based on the coordinates transmitted to her minutes earlier by Commander Eliopoulos. Applying starboard thrusters, she gently brought the *Stargazer* about. Then she engaged the impulse engines and left Starbase 209 behind.

As usual, Gerda was bent over the navigation station. Idun glanced at her sister— and saw that she was typing something on her comm pad. The helm officer was able to guess the sense of the message before she saw it appear on one of her monitors.

Where now? Gerda wanted to know.

Idun smiled to herself. Where indeed? Clearly, they were headed for the other side of the galactic barrier—her sister knew that much already. But what did they expect to find there? What did they hope to accomplish? That was what Gerda was really asking.

Eventually, both Idun and her sister would be briefed by Commander Leach or Commander Picard and given the answer to Gerda's question. But for now, Idun was more than content to savor the question itself.

And judging by the expression on her sister's face, Gerda felt the same way.

Pug Joseph had taken a turbolift down to the brig just as soon as Lieutenant Ben Zoma contacted him.

After all, he'd had to make certain that everything was in running order. The last thing he wanted was to have his superiors arrive with their prisoner and find that the force field was on the blink.

Of course, the security officer reflected, as he leaned on the wall beside the field controls, Ben Zoma hadn't actually *called* the woman a prisoner. But if she was anything else, she would have been given a suite of guest quarters instead of a small, spartan cell with a guard outside.

Abruptly, Joseph heard the clatter of boot heels from around a bend in the corridor. Straightening, he listened to the sounds grow closer, louder. Finally, Lieutenant Ben Zoma turned the corner.

He wasn't alone. Fox and Sekowsky were with him, carrying phasers. And a woman was walking between them—a small, slender woman with a black ponytail and dark, exotic eyes.

"Mr. Joseph," said Ben Zoma, acknowledging him. "This is our guest, Serenity Santana. Please see that she's not any more inconvenienced than she needs to be."

"I will, sir," Joseph answered.

Santana, he repeated inwardly. The name suggested energy and exhuberance, spice and spirit. In his mind, at least, it seemed to fit her.

The woman didn't wait to be escorted into her cell. She walked in of her own volition. Then she sat down on the bench seat within and watched as Fox manipulated the force field controls.

A moment later, a not-quite-transparent barrier sprang into existence across the cell mouth. It was powerful enough to cause any human who came into contact with it to lose consciousness.

But Joseph, along with every other security officer on the ship, had been warned—Santana wasn't just any human. It was possible, if only remotely, that the electromagnetic field wouldn't hold her. Hence, the need for live, armed guards, who would monitor her every minute of the day.

And if she was as adept a telepath as they suspected, even armed guards might not be enough to keep her from escaping. So Joseph and whoever else was watching Santana would have to check in with a superior every five minutes . . . just in case.

Not so long ago, Ben Zoma had lectured him about his overzealousness. But surely, this was one case where he *couldn't* be overzealous. No amount of caution would be too great, Joseph told himself.

Even if the woman *did* look pretty harmless.

Ben Zoma put his hand on Joseph's shoulder. "You'll only be here a couple of hours. Then I'll get you some relief."

The security officer nodded. "Acknowledged."

Ben Zoma smiled at the terseness of Joseph's response. Then he left, and Fox and Sekowsky followed in his wake.

Joseph turned to Santana. For a moment, their eyes met and locked. Then, made uncomfortable by the contact, the security officer turned away.

"I don't bite," she told him.

He looked back at her, but he decided not to reply. He didn't want to be distracted by conversation.

Santana smiled a wan smile. "You know," she said in a friendly, almost playful tone, "the guards on the starbase talked to me. Are the rules that different here?"

It seemed rude not to speak to her at all. No, Joseph reflected, more than rude. Cruel, really. After all, the woman was going to be in that cell for a long time.

"If you need anything," he responded finally, "let me know."

"Ah," said Santana, her smile blossoming into something lovely. "So you *can* talk. That's good to know."

With an effort, he kept from smiling back. "Is there?" he asked. "Anything you need, I mean?"

She thought about it for a moment. "Not right now," she told him. "But if I think of anything, you'll be the first to know."

Then he *did* smile.

"We're making progress," Santana observed. "First a conversation. Then a smile. Next thing you know, I'll have you in my power."

Joseph felt his heart jump up his throat. Instinctively, his hand went to the phaser on his hip.

She took note of it. "Actually," she said, her voice a good deal more measured, "I was joking with you."

As quickly as he could, he took his hand off his weapon. "So was I," he answered, trying to salvage some of his dignity.

Santana smiled again. "Listen," she said, "I should probably let you believe you fooled me just now, but . . . well, I'm a telepath. I can tell when you're joking and when you're not. And just now . . ." She shrugged.

Joseph blushed.

"So," she said, "now that we've shared an incredibly awkward moment . . . what's your name?"

There didn't seem to be any harm in telling her. "Joseph. Peter Joseph. But everyone calls me 'Pug.' "

"Pug," Santana echoed, tilting her head to the side as if to get a better look at him. "Yes . . . I can see why."

The scrutiny made Joseph feel self-conscious. But in a way, it was also flattering. It wasn't often he had beautiful women staring at him.

"Tell me something, Pug."

"What's that?" he asked.

"I don't mean something in particular," she explained. "I mean tell me anything. Anything at all. It'll make it easier to pass the time."

The security officer tried to think of something, but he couldn't. He had never been much of a conversationalist.

"All right, then," said Santana. "I'll tell you something. I'll tell you about the place I come from."

And she did.

Picard reported to the ship's lounge as soon as he received the captain's summons. But by the time he arrived, Ruhalter and Leach were already seated around the sleek, black table.

"Have a seat, Jean-Luc," said the captain.

Picard pulled out a chair across from Leach and sat down. Then he gave Ruhalter his attention.

"I think one of us should get to know Santana better," the captain declared. "I'm not saying Eliopoulos's conclusions aren't valid, but I'd prefer to have a second opinion."

"Makes sense," Leach agreed.

Ruhalter regarded the second officer. "I noticed some . . ." He smiled. "Let's call it magnetism . . . between you and Santana."

Picard felt his cheeks heat up. "Magnetism?"

"That's what I said," came Ruhalter's reply. "I didn't get where I am by being oblivious to that kind of thing. She's attracted to you, Jean-Luc, no question about it."

Suddenly, the second officer's uniform seemed a size too tight for him. He lifted his chin. "If you say so, sir."

"I'd like you to spend some time with her," the captain told him. "Take her out of her cell, if you like. See what you can learn."

Picard didn't entirely like the idea of weaseling his way into someone's confidence. On the other hand, he knew there might be a lot at stake.

"As you wish," he responded.

"I object, sir," said Leach.

Ruhalter turned to his first officer, making no effort to conceal his surprise. "On what grounds, Commander?"

Leach didn't even glance at Picard as he spoke. "On the grounds that I've got a degree in xenopsychology and a higher rank . . . all of which makes me better qualified to do the job."

There was a rather obvious note of bitterness in the first officer's voice, but the captain seemed willing to ignore it. "You know I'm a man who listens to his gut," he told Leach. "And right now, my gut is telling me this assignment should go to Mr. Picard."

Leach seemed to wrestle with the decision. Finally, he conceded the point with a nod. "I understand," he said.

But he *didn't* understand. Picard could tell. And so could Ruhalter, the second officer imagined.

Nonetheless, the captain thanked them for their help and dismissed them, and remained in the lounge for a scheduled meeting with Simenon and Werber. Picard and Leach left the room together, the silence between them thick and full of hostility.

Finally, as they made their way toward the nearest turbolift, the first officer spoke. "I know what you're doing," he said.

Picard glanced at him. "What do you mean?"

Leach's mouth twisted with unconcealed resentment. "Don't play innocent with me, Commander. You're worming your way into the captain's good graces more and more each day, hoping to squeeze me out and land yourself a fat promotion. But I've worked too long and hard to let someone like you undermine my authority."

"Undermine your . . . ?" Picard smiled incredulously and shook his head. "I had no such thing in mind, I assure you."

"The hell you didn't." Leach's eyes had become as sharp as chips of obsidian. "Don't push me, Commander. I'm liable to push back."

Picard didn't know what to say to that. And before he could think of anything, two crewmen turned the corner ahead of them. The second officer recognized them as Pernell and Zaffino—a couple of Simenon's engineers.

"Just the men I wanted to see," said Leach.

The engineers looked surprised. "Us, sir?" asked Zaffino.

Picard doubted that Leach had any real business with Pernell and Zaffino. More likely, he was simply looking for an excuse not to share a turbolift with the second officer.

That was fine with Picard, who hadn't been looking forward to the company either. Leaving his colleague with the two engineers, he made his way down the corridor on his own.

The second officer wasn't thrilled that he had made an enemy—especially of the ship's first officer, who happened to be his immediate superior. However, he wouldn't let it stop him from discharging his duty. Turning left at the first intersection, he came to the turbolift and summoned it.

When the compartment arrived, Picard stepped inside and uttered a single word: "Brig." Then, his command filed and noted, he let the lift carry him to the vicinity of Santana's cell.

Four

Picard gazed at Serenity Santana across a table in the *Stargazer*'s mess hall. She, in turn, was gazing into her drinking glass, her raven hair liberated from its pony-tail.

The woman had been happy to leave the brig, no question about it. It couldn't have been a picnic sitting in the same small enclosure hour after hour, denied access even to the ship's library computer lest she stumble across something of some small tactical value.

The second officer glanced at the open doorway, through which he could see a watchful Pug Joseph. A necessary precaution, he conceded, but one that made having a casual conversation a bit awkward.

"You're right," Santana observed. "It *is* a little awkward."

Picard turned to her. "You read my mind," he said, hearing a mixture of surprise and delight in his voice.

"Of course," she returned.

"You know," he said candidly, "I haven't had much experience with telepathy. Few Federation species are capable of it. And none of them are capable of telekinesis."

"Unfortunately," Santana replied, "neither talent is very highly developed in our case. Captain Eliopoulos must have mentioned that."

The commander nodded. "He did. Still . . ."

The woman's dark eyes narrowed with mock suspicion. "Are you angling for a demonstration, Commander?"

He chuckled. "Can't you tell?"

Santana looked at him askance. "If you've spoken to our friend Eliopoulos, you know I'm only privy to active thoughts."

"I do know that," he admitted. "And for the sake of expediency, I'll make no bones about it . . . I *would* like to see a demonstration."

She seemed charmed by his manners. "All right. One feat of mental dexterity coming up."

Gradually, her eyes took on a harder cast. Then the skin around them began to crinkle. It was clear that she was focusing on something, concentrating as hard as she could, though the second officer didn't know what kind of task she had set for herself.

Then he heard a tinkling sound and he looked down. Santana's drink was moving, levitating off the table, the ice in it clinking merrily against the sides of the glass.

As Picard watched, the drink gradually rose to a height of perhaps twenty centimeters. Then, just as slowly, it descended, eventually coming to rest on the table again.

He looked up at Santana. "Impressive." He meant it.

She shrugged. "Eliopoulos didn't think so. He kept waiting for me to send his station spinning through space like a top."

"You have tops where you come from?" Picard asked.

"We *are* human," she reminded him. "If you saw my world, I'm sure you'd see a lot that's familiar about it."

He found himself smiling. "And a lot that's *not,* no doubt. To be honest, it's the latter that intrigues me."

"You want to know how we're different?"

"I do indeed."

Santana thought for a moment. "As Eliopoulos must have told you, we value our privacy."

"He mentioned that," Picard conceded. "But surely, that's not the only quality that sets you apart from us?"

She thought some more. "We're good gardeners, as a rule. And good musicians. Unfortunately, I'm one of the few exceptions to the rule. I couldn't carry a tune if my life depended on it."

"Anything else?"

Santana shook her head. "Nothing. Except for our mental powers, of course. But I think we've already covered that topic."

"Not completely," the second officer said. "You haven't shown me much of your telepathic abilities."

She waved away the suggestion. "They're not very impressive in comparison to my drinking glass trick."

"Nonetheless," Picard insisted.

"Persistent, aren't you?"

"So I'm told."

Santana sighed. "Have it your way, Commander. You'll have to think of something, of course. Something pleasant, I hope."

"I'd be happy to," he told her. And he did as she had asked.

Santana's brow furrowed for a second. Then she said, "Your mother was a lovely woman. And if I'm not mistaken, a wonderful cook."

Picard was intrigued. He had created an image of his mother in his mind's eye, but he hadn't pictured her preparing food.

"Why do you mention her cooking?" he wondered out loud.

"The smell of her," Santana explained. She closed her eyes. "I don't recognize it, but it's some kind of spice. Sharp, pungent . . ."

Abruptly, the second officer realized what she was talking about. "Cinnamon," he said. "She would use it in her apple tarts."

Her eyes still closed, Santana inhaled deeply, as if she were in Picard's mother's kitchen. "And you liked those tarts, didn't you? In fact, you used to think about them on your way home from somewhere."

"School," he confessed.

She opened her eyes. "Yes. School."

"Extraordinary," said Picard.

Santana shook her head. "No. What would be extraordinary is if I could read your mind like a book, finding any memory at all. They say some of our people could do that in the days when the colony was first founded. But we can't do it anymore."

Perhaps it was the look on her face, a little sad and a little dreamy, as she contemplated something she considered wondrous. Perhaps he had crossed some invisible threshold of familiarity. Perhaps many things.

Picard couldn't explain it. He just knew that he was intensely aware of how beautiful Serenity Santana was, and that that awareness was making his heart beat faster.

Then he saw her blush, and he realized that she had read his thoughts again. He felt embarrassed and ungainly, like a youngster whose crush on some girl had inadvertently been exposed.

"I'm sorry," the second officer told her.

Santana looked sympathetic. "Don't be."

"No," he said, shaking his head, "I didn't mean to—"

She held up a hand for silence. "I'm serious, Commander. There's no need to feel awkward." Unexpectedly, her expression turned coquettish. "After all, who knows how embarrassing *my* thoughts might be."

For a heartbeat, Picard was lost in the dark, sorcerous pools of Santana's eyes. Then he swallowed and pulled himself back out again.

"An . . . intriguing notion," he replied.

She seemed on the verge of saying something in response. But instead, she picked up her glass and sipped her drink. By the time she put it down again, the second officer had regained his composure.

"I hate to say it," the commander began, "but—"

"I know," Santana said, saving him the trouble. "It's time I was returning to the brig."

He nodded soberly. "Yes. After all, I have a shift starting on the bridge. But I enjoyed our conversation. Perhaps we—"

"Could have another one some time? Here in the mess hall?" The woman shrugged. "Why not?"

Picard couldn't help feeling there was more to say. However, he didn't want to make this any more personal than it had to be. When it came to Serenity Santana, he was simply doing his duty. He was following the orders his captain had laid out for him.

He didn't dare consider the possibility of falling in love with the woman.

Without another word, the second officer got up and gestured to the doorway. Santana rose as well and preceded him out into the corridor. Then she allowed Pug Joseph to accompany her back to the brig.

Picard watched them go for a moment. Heaving a sigh, he turned and headed for the bridge.

Carter Greyhorse was sitting behind his desk, studying the results of the examinations he had already conducted, when he spied Gerda Asmund through one of his office's transparent walls.

The last time the doctor had seen the woman, she had been wearing a tight-fitting exercise garment, her lips pulled back from her teeth, her skin tantalizingly moist with perspiration. Now, she was dressed in the cranberry tunic and black trousers of Starfleet, looking like anyone else in the *Stargazer*'s crew.

No, Greyhorse corrected himself quickly and emphatically . . . *not* like anyone else. Not at all. Even in her standard-issue uniform, with her spun-gold hair woven into an austere bun, Gerda Asmund was a most attractive woman.

A most *exciting* woman.

But she was there to see him as a physician, not someone with whom she might share a love interest. He forced himself to remember that. Taking a deep breath, he assumed his most professional demeanor.

Unaware of Greyhorse's inner turmoil, the blond woman came to a stop at the entrance to his office. "Lieutenant Asmund," she said in a husky but eminently feminine voice, "reporting as requested."

The doctor smiled—not an activity at which he had had a lot of practice—and gestured for his patient to take a seat on the other side of his desk. She complied without comment.

Her eyes were so blue it almost hurt to look at them. He tried his best not to notice. "Thank you for coming," he told her. "Do you have any questions about why you're here?"

She shrugged. "You need to test my extrasensory perception quotient before we penetrate the barrier. It's straightforward enough." She frowned. "Though, as you must know, I've been tested before."

Greyhorse tapped his key pad and brought up Gerda's medical file. It took no time at all to locate the results of her last ESP test, which showed she had no talent in that area whatsoever.

"Let's see," he said. "ESPer quotient . . . oh-one-one. Aperception quotient . . . two over twenty-five. As you say, you've been tested before." He looked up from his monitor. "However, things can change, and Starfleet regulations are rather specific in this regard."

The woman nodded. "Of course. Let's just do what we have to."

The doctor pretended to review other parts of her file, though he had come to know them pretty much by heart. "You're the primary navigator," he noted, "and have been since the ship left Utopia Planitia some seven months ago."

"That's correct," she said.

"Prior to that," he observed, "you served on the *da Gama,* and before that you graduated from the Academy with honors."

"Correct again," Gerda told him.

Greyhorse looked up at her. "It also says here that you were raised in a . . . Klingon household?"

"Yes," the navigator said matter-of-factly, as if such things happened all the time. "As children, my sister Idun and I were the only survivors of a Federation colony disaster. After several days had gone by, Klingons intercepted the colony's distress signal and rescued us. Apparently, we impressed them with our resourcefulness."

He grunted thoughtfully, seeing an opportunity to establish some kind of rapport with her. "It must have been quite . . ."

"Yes?" Gerda prodded.

He felt himself wither under her scrutiny. "Nothing," he said at last. "Nothing at all."

It was no use, he reflected. He wasn't good at small talk. Truthfully, he wasn't good at *any* kind of talk.

If someone gave him a disease to cure or an injury to heal, he was as sharp as any physician in the Federation. But when it came to being a person, a social creature capable of interacting with other social creatures, he fell significantly short of the mark.

Greyhorse had come to grips with his shortcomings a long time ago. He had gotten to the point where they didn't bother him. But they bothered him now, he had to admit.

And it was all because of Gerda Asmund.

"Doctor?" she said.

He realized that he had been silent for what must have seemed like a long time. "Yes," he responded clumsily. "Sorry. I was just thinking of something. Er . . . let's begin, shall we?"

Gerda nodded. "Indeed."

"I'll bring a picture up on my screen," Greyhorse explained for the fifteenth time that day. "You try to develop an impression of it in your head, using any means that occurs to you. And while you're at it, the internal sensors in this room will monitor your brainwaves."

She smiled a weary smile. "I know. As we've established, I have undergone this test before."

He smiled back as best he could. "So you said."

And he began the examination.

Picard studied the small, blue-and-green world on the *Stargazer*'s forward viewscreen from his place beside Captain Ruhalter.

"Establish a synchronous orbit," said Ruhalter.

"Aye, sir," replied Idun Asmund from the helm console.

Nalogen IV was an M-Class planet, which meant it was inhabitable by most oxygen-breathing species. Indeed, there was only one sentient form of life on the planet, and it required oxygen to survive. However, it wasn't an indigenous form of life. It had originated in a solar system one hundred thousand light-years away.

Nearly a century earlier, several ships' worth of Kelvans had set out from their home in the Andromeda Galaxy to find a new place for their people to live. One of their vessels was damaged as it penetrated the galactic barrier and its crew was forced to abandon ship.

Since Kelvan technology allowed them to change form, they took on the appearance of humans—a populous species in that part of the Milky Way galaxy—and put out a distress call. Ultimately, they hoped to commandeer a starship and use it to return to their homeworld.

However, their takeover attempt was thwarted by Captain James Kirk—the same near-legendary Starfleet officer who had dealt with the menace of Gary Mitchell a few years earlier. Once the threat to his vessel was defused, Kirk arranged for the Kelvans to settle on a world in Federation space.

That world was Nalogen IV.

"Hail the colony," said Captain Ruhalter from his captain's chair.

"Aye, sir," responded Paxton.

The comm officer's fingers flew over his communications panel. A few moments later, he looked up again.

"I've got the colony administrator," Paxton reported. "His name is Najak. But he says he'd like to restrict communications to audio only."

Ruhalter frowned as he considered the viewscreen. "Very well, Lieutenant. Tell him I'll comply with his request."

Picard had to admit that he was disappointed, if only to himself. He had hoped to get a glimpse of Kelvan civilization. Now it looked as if he wouldn't get the chance.

Abruptly, a deep and commanding voice filled the bridge. "This is Administrator Najak," it said.

Ruhalter looked up at the intercom grid. "Captain Ruhalter here. It's a pleasure to speak with you, Administrator."

"The pleasure is mine," said Najak. "And thank you for respecting my privacy, Captain. Over the years, we have come to appreciate how monstrous we seem to other Federation species. This fact has occasionally led to . . . let us call them 'misunderstandings.' "

"It's no problem at all," Ruhalter replied. "We don't want to intrude on you any more than we have to."

"Jomar will be ready in a matter of minutes," Najak advised. "If you give us the coordinates of your transporter room, our technicians will be pleased to effect his transport."

"Acknowledged," said the captain. He turned to Paxton. "Send them whatever they need, Lieutenant."

"I'll do that, sir," Paxton responded.

Ruhalter returned his attention to the Kelvan. "With luck, I'll have good news when I bring Jomar back to you."

"With luck," the administrator echoed. "Najak out."

The captain glanced at Leach, who was standing beside Simenon at the engineering console. "You've got the conn, Number One. Commander Picard, you're with me."

With that, he got up and made his way aft to the turbolift. As the second officer followed him, he saw the expression on Leach's face. If looks could have killed, Picard would have been torn atom from atom.

Ruhalter couldn't have failed to notice his exec's displeasure. However, he didn't comment on it as he and Picard entered the lift and watched the sliding doors close behind them.

Instead, he said, "I was really looking forward to beaming down and seeing that Kelvan colony."

Picard nodded. "So was I, sir."

"I guess we shouldn't complain. We'll no doubt be seeing plenty on the other side of the galactic barrier."

"No doubt," the second officer agreed.

Just then, the turbolift doors opened again. The captain exited ahead of Picard and led the way to the transporter room, where a woman named Vandermeer was working the control console.

"Anything yet?" Ruhalter asked her.

"No, sir," said the transporter operator, consulting her monitor. "Wait . . . I'm getting a message from the surface."

"The colony administrator's office?" asked the captain.

"Yes. They say they're ready to beam someone up."

Ruhalter nodded. "Contact the bridge and tell Mr. Leach I want the shields dropped. Then let the Kelvans know we're ready. But as soon as our visitor arrives, I want the shields back up again."

"Aye, sir," said Vandermeer, carrying out her orders.

Picard too felt uneasy when the *Stargazer*'s deflectors were lowered. After all, it left the ship vulnerable to all manner of mishaps. Unfortunately, they couldn't effect a transport with the shields in place.

"He's on his way," Vandermeer announced.

Picard turned to the raised, oval platform in the back of the room. A shaft of light appeared there, then slowly resolved itself into a humanoid form. A moment later, the light died, leaving a tall, fair-skinned man with unruly red hair and haunting, pale-blue eyes.

"You must be Jomar," Ruhalter observed. He smiled a craggy smile. "Welcome to the Federation *Starship Stargazer*. I'm Captain Ruhalter . . . and this is Commander Picard, my second officer."

The Kelvan stared at Ruhalter for a full second before he answered. "Thank you, Captain." He turned to Picard. "Commander."

Jomar's tone was flat and utterly devoid of enthusiasm. And his expression—or rather, his lack of one—would have been the envy of many a logical Vulcan.

"If you'll follow us," said the captain, "we'll show you to your quarters. I think you'll find them—"

"I have a great deal of work to do," the Kelvan declared, unceremoniously interrupting Ruhalter's invitation. "I would prefer to familiarize myself with your ship's tactical systems and subsystems before I give any thought to sleeping accommodations."

The captain appeared unoffended. "Of course," he told Jomar. "We can start in engineering, if you like."

"That would be satisfactory," said the Kelvan.

Ruhalter tapped the Starfleet insignia on his chest. "Captain to bridge. Break orbit, Mr. Leach. We've got our passenger."

"Acknowledged, sir," said Leach.

The captain turned to Jomar. "Next stop, engineering."

The Kelvan didn't respond. He just waited for Ruhalter and Picard to lead the way, then fell in behind them.

Charming, thought the second officer. But then, they hadn't enlisted Jomar's assistance because of his advanced social skills. If all went well, he would be their secret weapon against the Nuyyad.

Five

Picard sat in his usual place at the black oval table in the *Stargazer*'s lounge and watched Captain Ruhalter bring the meeting to order.

Unlike the last meeting the second officer had attended there, this one didn't call for the presence of the entire senior staff. The topic was a largely technical one, so all of the officers present—with the exceptions of Ruhalter, Commander Leach, and Picard himself—were from the weapons and engineering sections.

And then, of course, there was the Kelvan. He was sitting beside the captain with his bright red hair in disarray, a deadpan expression on his face that betrayed his lack of humanity.

"I called this meeting," said Ruhalter, "so you could all meet Jomar here and hear his plans for the *Stargazer*'s tactical systems." He turned to the Kelvan. "Go ahead."

Jomar inclined his head. "Thank you, Captain." He scanned the other faces at the table without a hint of emotion. "As you may have heard," he went on abruptly, "the Nuyyad are a formidable enemy, with a long list of conquests to their credit."

"So we've been given to understand," said Ruhalter.

"However," the Kelvan went on, "the Nuyyad's vessels are no faster or more maneuverable than this one. Their shields are no stronger than the *Stargazer's* shields. In fact, they may be a little weaker. Where the Nuyyad far outstrip Federation technology is in a single area . . ."

"Firepower?" Simenon suggested.

"Firepower," Jomar confirmed ominously. "More specifically, a quartet of vidrion particle cannons, any one of which could pierce your shields with a single high-intensity barrage."

It wasn't good news. For a moment, they pondered it from one end of the table to the other.

Then Picard spoke up. "Vidrion particles? I don't believe I've ever heard of them."

"That is because they have not been discovered on this side of the barrier," the Kelvan explained. "My people have known of them for centuries, though we always considered them too unstable to be harnessed as directed energy. The Nuyyad have apparently solved that problem."

Ruhalter leaned forward. "You've got our attention, Jomar. How can we defend ourselves against these vidrion cannons?"

"By fighting fire with fire," said the Kelvan, "as the human expression articulates. We have discovered that lacing a standard, graviton-based deflector shield with a certain percentage of vidrion particles renders it all but impermeable to the Nuyyad's beams."

"And that," observed Ruhalter, "will give us a chance to launch an offensive of our own."

Jomar regarded the captain with his strange, pale-blue eyes. As in the transporter room, he seemed to stare. "Yes," the Kelvan said finally, "that is the intention."

Suddenly, Picard realized something. Jomar wasn't staring after all. It was just that his eyes weren't blinking.

But then, when the second officer thought about it, that made sense. The Kelvan had only assumed this form for the sake of convenience. His "eyes" were ornaments, lacking function, created to make the humanoids on the *Stargazer* feel more comfortable in his presence.

As for his true sensory organs, the ones he used to see and hear and so on . . . where *they* were located was anybody's guess.

"However," Jomar went on in his monotone, "it will not be enough to merely defend ourselves. If we are to hold our own against the Nuyyad, we must increase the power of our own weapons."

"Increase it *how?*" asked Werber.

The Kelvan shrugged. "By routing your warp chamber's plasma flow to your emitter crystals in a more pure and unadulterated form."

The weapons chief's eyes narrowed warily. "Go on."

"As the system is currently configured," said Jomar, "electroplasma must pass through a flow regulator, a distribution manifold, and a prefire chamber before it reaches the crystal. I propose that we delete the flow regulator and distribution manifold in favor of a single device, which would do the work of both of them—and at the same time, facilitate a higher subatomic energy level at the end of the process."

For a moment, every technician in the room was silent. Picard could see them pondering the Kelvan's idea, turning it over in their minds. Then Simenon broke the silence.

"Where did you come up with this?" he asked.

"Actually," Jomar told him, "it is the approach we have taken in Kelvan vessels for the last seventy years."

Vigo, a Pandrilite officer in the weapons section, leaned forward in his chair. "I don't understand," he confessed. "How can you achieve higher energy levels in the crystals without—"

Werber cut Vigo off with a preemptive wave of his hand. "Without compromising the integrity of the conduit network?" he asked, finishing the Pandrilite's question himself.

As Picard watched, Vigo slumped back in his chair again and fell silent. However, he didn't look at all happy about it.

Meanwhile, the Kelvan answered Werber's question. "Starfleet Command has made available to me considerable data concerning the conduit network and its rated tolerances. As far as I can tell, it is somewhat less durable than the energy channels in my people's ships—but nonetheless strong enough to withstand even a substantial increase in subatomic activity."

Simenon shook his lizardlike head from side to side. "Not from where I stand, it's not."

"No question about it," Werber added. "That plasma will never reach the pre-fire chamber. It'll blow up in the conduits first."

"And send us all to kingdom come," Leach agreed.

For once, Picard found himself on the first officer's side. He turned to Ruhalter. "It would be imprudent to make the kind of changes that are being discussed without considerable study. I advise against it."

"As do *I*," Leach chimed in, obviously reluctant to let Picard receive the credit for anything.

Ruhalter addressed the Kelvan. "To be honest, Jomar, I'm not thrilled with the idea either. It seems too damned dangerous. But your strategy for beefing up the shields . . . that I like." He glanced at Simenon, then Werber. "I want you to get started on that as soon as possible."

"Aye, sir," said the weapons chief.

"As you wish," the engineer added.

If the Kelvan resented the rejection of his phaser idea, he didn't show it. His expression was as neutral as ever.

"What else?" asked the captain.

"*Nothing* else," Jomar told him. "I have discussed all the possibilities I meant to discusss."

Ruhalter nodded. "All right, then. Thank you all for attending. Now let's get to work."

And with that, the meeting ended.

As Pug Joseph approached the *Stargazer*'s brig, he was forced to admit something to himself.

He had guarded his share of prisoners in the course of his brief career. Every security officer had. But he had never actually looked forward to guarding one until now.

Garner, the officer on duty in the brig, acknowledged Joseph with a businesslike nod. "All quiet," she reported.

"Good," he replied.

Not that he had expected Garner to say anything else. After all, it wasn't exactly a Nausicaan slave-runner they were holding. It was just a woman, and a very cooperative woman at that.

He looked past the brig's translucent, yellow barrier and saw Santana sitting upright on the edge of her sleeping pallet, her eyes closed, her hands held out in front of her as if in supplication. She had told Joseph about the technique during his last shift—a form of meditation, it was used widely in her colony as a way of achieving calm . . .

And perspective. She certainly needed that right now.

"Go ahead," he told Garner. "I can take it from here."

His colleague smiled as she passed him on her way out. "I'll see you later," she said.

"Later," he echoed.

But his mind was already focused on Santana, who hadn't fluttered an eyelash since he arrived. He considered saying something to let her know he was there, but he didn't want to disturb her.

"Mr. Joseph," she said abruptly. "Nice of you to drop by."

The security officer chuckled. "As if I had a choice."

Santana opened her eyes, disappointment etched in her face. "You mean you only come to see me because you *have* to?"

For a moment, he felt the need to apologize. Then he realized that she was just joking with him . . . again.

"Funny," he said.

"I'm glad you think so," Santana replied. "After all, you *are* my only audience."

"You didn't get along so well with Garner?"

She rolled her eyes. "She's not the friendliest person around. So, tell me . . . have you met the Kelvan yet?"

Joseph shook his head. "I haven't even caught a glimpse of him."

The woman's expression turned sour. "Figures. He's the one you *really* ought to be watching."

"Why do you say that?" he asked.

Santana looked as if she were about to say something critical—then stopped herself. "Never mind. I don't want to start any controversies. This mission is too important to all of us."

But it was too late. She had roused the old Pug Joseph—the one who couldn't help seeing danger at every turn.

"Are you saying he poses some kind of threat?" Joseph asked.

"Not necessarily," Santana said. "My people have had some unpleasant experiences with Kelvans, that's all. It doesn't mean this particular one is going to be a problem."

He searched her eyes. "Do you really believe that?"

She smiled disarmingly. "Why would I lie?"

Why indeed? Joseph asked himself. He couldn't come up with a good answer. When Santana first came aboard, he had been as suspicious of her as anyone else. Now he knew better.

"So," he said, switching tacks, "where were we?"

She knew exactly what he meant. "Let's see . . . you were telling me about the place where you were raised. Boston, wasn't it? And there's a river there where your parents took you for picnics . . ."

Joseph was pleased that she remembered. "The Charles."

"Yes," she said, closing her eyes so she could pick the image from his brain. "The Charles." Her brow creased with concentration. "And you had a little brother named Matthew, who lost his sneaker somehow and put his foot in the potato salad . . ."

Suddenly, Santana began to laugh, and before he knew it he was laughing with her, both of them caught up helplessly in the memory of little Matt stepping where he shouldn't have. The brig rang with their hilarity.

Pug Joseph found that he liked Santana very much, no matter what Commander Leach or anyone else said about her. In fact, he wished he could have felt this way about *everyone* he guarded.

Vigo wasn't particularly enamored of Jefferies tubes. His Pandrilite musculature made crawling through the cylindrical, circuit-laden passageways a cramped and uncomfortable proposition at best.

Fortunately for him, Starfleet weapons officers seldom had to negotiate the tubes the way engineers did. Their maintenance and repair activities were typically restricted to one of the ship's weapons rooms, or on a rare occasion, the bridge.

But there were exceptions to every rule. And at the moment, Vigo was caught up in one.

For some political reason that escaped the Pandrilite, Lieutenant Werber wanted his section to be well represented in the effort to implement the Kelvan's shield strategy. As a result, Vigo and several of his fellow weapons officers had been asked to assist their counterparts from engineering in retrofitting field generators and distortion amplifiers from one end of the ship to the other.

And that meant crawling through one Jefferies tube after another, enduring muscle cramps and skin abrasions in the process.

"Pass the spanner," said Engineer First Class Pernell, a spare, fair-haired man lying just ahead of the Pandrilite in the passageway.

Vigo found the requisite tool and removed it from his equipment bag. "Here it is," he said, and handed it to Pernell.

They were busy installing new graviton relays in one of the *Stargazer*'s field generators. The relays, which had been fabricated only an hour earlier, were designed to expedite the passage of vidrion particles through the deflector system.

The Pandrilite wiped perspiration from his brow with the back of his hand. It was hot in the tube too, so hot that he had begun to wonder if something had gone wrong with the ventilation system.

But that wasn't the worst of it. His shoulders stung where he had rubbed them raw against the walls of the passage, his hip hurt where he was forced to press it against a circuit bundle, and his legs were so contorted he could barely feel his feet.

But Vigo wasn't going to complain. He was a Pandrilite. He had been given an assignment and he would carry it out.

Suddenly, the weapons officer saw something move into the tube from a perpendicular passageway far down the line. At first, he thought it was one of his fellow crewmen, on his way to an assignment much like his own.

Then he realized that it wasn't a crewman. It wasn't even humanoid. It was the kind of life-form one might have seen at the bottom of an alien ocean, slithering out from under a rock to snatch unsuspecting sea creatures with its long, dark tentacles.

As Vigo watched, anxious and fascinated at the same time, the thing pulled itself along the tube with chilling efficiency. His hand darted to his hip instinctively, but he wasn't wearing a phaser.

"What is that?" Pernell asked, his voice thick with consternation.

The Pandrilite shook his head, his eyes glued to the tentacled monstrosity. "I don't know. I—"

Before he could finish his sentence, before he could even think about getting out of the Jefferies tube and calling for security, the thing began to change. Right before his eyes, its tentacles grew shorter and the mass at its core lengthened, until it wasn't nearly as horrific.

In a matter of seconds, it became the kind of figure Vigo had expected all along: a black set of work togs accommodating two arms and two legs and—in this case—a head full of fiery red hair.

"Bloody hell," Pernell whispered, his skin pale and slick with perspiration. "It's the *Kelvan*."

The Pandrilite nodded. It *was* the Kelvan. And now that he thought about it, he had been warned that Jomar might return to his original shape on occasion. He just hadn't been prepared for what that shape might be.

The Kelvan continued to make his way toward Vigo and Pernell, though he seemed somewhat less adept at maneuvering a human body through the tube. Finally, he got close enough to speak with them.

"Any problems?" Jomar asked.

"None so far," the weapons officer managed.

"Good," said the Kelvan.

Apparently, he was just checking up on them. No doubt, he meant to do that with the other retrofit teams as well.

"Do not let me keep you," Jomar added.

Then he made his way back down the tube. Eventually, he came to another perpendicular passageway and vanished into it. Vigo was glad the Kelvan had opted to retain his human form until he was out of sight.

"What a nasty thing *he* is," Pernell observed.

The weapons officer looked at him. "He's our ally, remember?"

But deep down inside, Vigo had to admit, where his instincts were stronger than his intellect, he thought of Jomar exactly the same way.

As Stephen Leach negotiated the long, subtle curve of the corridor, casting blue shadows in the light of the overheads, he felt as if he were finally making some progress.

For months, ever since the *Stargazer* left Earth's solar system, the first officer had been forced to take a backseat to Commander Picard when it came to the important assignments around the ship—assignments that required knowledge and leadership and experience.

And there was no one but Picard to blame for it. The second officer had a way of ingratiating himself to Captain Ruhalter that Leach couldn't seem to get the hang of.

Things had been different on the *Merced*. Leach had been the fair-haired boy there, a second officer who could do no wrong. He had had the kind of relationship with Captain Osborne that sons have with their fathers, and only then if they're very lucky.

If not for Picard, he might have had the same kind of relationship with Captain Ruhalter. No . . . not *might* have, Leach assured himself. *Would* have, without question.

But right from the beginning, Picard had upstaged and undermined and sabotaged the first officer, to the point where Ruhalter didn't seem to feel he could trust Leach's instincts—and instincts were more important to the captain than anything else.

It was insulting. It was frustrating. And Leach had decided that he had taken all he was going to take of it. He had promised himself that he was going to confront Ruhalter the next time he gave Picard a job that should have been the exec's.

Then, as if he had read Leach's mind, the captain contacted him in his quarters and put him in charge of the Kelvan's deflector modifications. Finally, Leach had a task he could sink his teeth into—and an opportunity, as well, he was quick to note. If he could see the retrofit schedule completed quickly and efficiently, he would prove to Ruhalter that he was good for something more than meeting visitors at the transporter platform.

Smiling to himself for the first time in a long time, the first officer stopped in front of the lounge doors and tapped the metal padd set into the bulkhead. A moment later, the doors slid aside, revealing the room's long, oval table.

There were three figures seated around it—Simenon, Werber, and Jomar. The Kelvan sat apart from the two officers, his pale blue eyes glazed over as if he were deep in thought.

But he wasn't. Leach knew that. It was simply one of the flaws in Jomar's imitation of a human being.

The first officer pulled out a chair and took his seat. "Thanks for coming," he told the others. "I'm hoping we can keep this short, so we can attend to our respective duties. All I need is an update on how the deflector modifications are going."

"They are going well," the Kelvan answered, before anyone else could be consulted. "We should be done on schedule."

Werber frowned. "As our colleague says, we'll be finished on time . . . barring any unforeseen complications, of course."

"No snags, then?" Leach asked.

"None," Jomar blurted. "Neither with the field generators nor the distortion amplifiers. Everything is proceeding smoothly."

Simenon regarded the Kelvan with disdainfully slitted eyes. "So far, so good," the engineer agreed.

Given the climate of optimism, Leach didn't think anything else really needed to be said. "All right, then. We'll reconvene at this time tomorrow. Until then, you're all—"

"You do not like me," the Kelvan observed abruptly, cutting off the first officer's directive.

It took Leach a full second to recover from the remark—perhaps because it had some truth to it. "I beg your pardon?" he said.

"You do not like me," Jomar repeated.

The first officer shifted uncomfortably in his chair. "Why would you say something like that?"

The Kelvan shrugged his narrow shoulders. "I am different. I do not emote as you do. I lack social graces. Do not bother to tell me that these facts are irrelevant. I know differently."

Leach could feel his opportunity to impress the captain slipping away . . . and quickly. Hiding his anxiety behind a smile, he dismissed Jomar's statement with a wave of his hand.

"Listen," he said, "we're Starfleet officers. We've each had experience with dozens of sentient life-forms—hundreds, in some cases—and believe me, you're not as different as you might believe."

"Nonetheless," Jomar insisted, "you do not like me. You resent my being here. Perhaps you feel that my contributions are unnecessary."

The Kelvan leaned forward in his chair. His face was still devoid of expression, but his posture suggested a purposefulness Leach hadn't seen in Jomar to that point.

"It does not matter to me what you think," the Kelvan told them. "You have not witnessed Nuyyad atrocities. You have not seen my people writhing in agony. You have not seen them die. But I have. That is why I will go to any length to halt the Nuyyad's advance."

The first officer didn't quite know what to say to that. Fortunately, Simenon bailed him out.

"We all have the same purpose in mind," the Gnalish assured Jomar. "Let's not waste any time arguing over how to pursue it."

The Kelvan considered Simenon, then nodded. "I will take you at your word." He turned to Leach. "If you have no further need of me, Commander, I will return to my duties."

The first officer was only too happy to accommodate Jomar. "You're dismissed," he said, completing his earlier thought.

The Kelvan got up stiffly and left the room. As the doors slid closed behind him, Leach felt a wave of relief. Grinning, he glanced at his colleagues. "Now, *that* was interesting."

Werber grunted disparagingly. "I'll say."

"Give him credit," Simenon rasped. "He's got the courage of his convictions. We should be glad he's on our side."

The first officer knew that the Gnalish loved sarcasm. For a moment, he thought Simenon was demonstrating that love. Then he realized that his friend was serious.

"You really think so?" asked Werber.

"I do," the engineer told him.

"Maybe Phigus is right," Leach conceded, though in the privacy of his mind he sincerely doubted it.

"Maybe," said Werber. "And maybe not."

"Time will tell," the first officer noted diplomatically. "Come on. Let's get some lunch."

Six

The galactic barrier was like a gaping wound in the fabric of space . . . a raw, red chasm seething with waves of violent energy. At least, that was the way it appeared to Picard, as he stood beside Captain Ruhalter's chair and gazed at the forward viewscreen.

As far as the *Stargazer*'s instruments were concerned, it was a different story entirely.

"The barrier registers on optical scanners," said Gerda Asmund from her navigation console, "but that's it. I can't get anything from any other sensor modality. Wideband electromagnetic, quark resonance, thermal imaging, neutrino spectrometry . . . not so much as a blip on any of them."

"No gravimetric distortions either," Idun observed. "Subspace field stress is zero."

Ruhalter got up from his center seat and approached the viewscreen. "So as far as most of our expensive, state-of-the-art instruments are concerned, this thing doesn't exist."

Gerda glanced at him. "That would be one way of putting it, sir."

It was a remarkable state of affairs indeed—and it came as no surprise to any of them.

In the sixty-eight years since Captain Kirk's vessel plunged through the barrier, the Federation had sent out numerous expeditions to study the phenomenon. They all came back with the same results. In other words, none at all.

The barrier defied conventional analysis. It could be seen, certainly. It could be felt, once one got close enough. But for all other intents and purposes, it was a phantom.

"Helm, take us down to warp one," said Ruhalter. "Navigation, divert all available power to the shields."

"Done, sir," the Asmunds replied at virtually the same time.

Despite the reduction in speed, the barrier loomed closer. Patterns of light began to emerge in it, taking the shape of globules and then flares. Picard felt his jaw clench.

He knew, of course, that there wasn't really any cause for concern. Deflector shield technology had come a long way since Captain Kirk braved the barrier in the original *Starship Enterprise*. The chances of any ESPers being exposed to the phenomenon and metamorphosing into modern-day Gary Mitchells were ridiculously remote.

Nonetheless, the sight of the phenomenon strained the second officer's nerves. If the shields dropped at the wrong moment, or if some part of the barrier proved much fiercer than the others . . .

"Status?" Ruhalter demanded.

"There's some turbulence up ahead," Idun reported evenly, "but nothing we can't handle."

Just then, the turbolift doors opened and Leach emerged. He had been overseeing a last-minute diagnostic on Jomar's shield alterations.

The captain glanced at him. "Any problems, Commander?"

Leach frowned as he took in the spectacle on the viewscreen. "None, sir. Everything's functioning perfectly."

The first officer was still perturbed about the idea of taking Santana back to her side of the barrier. He hadn't made any secret of that. And the bizarre spectacle on the screen couldn't have made it any easier for him.

The captain turned back to Idun. "Steady as she goes," he said.

"Aye, sir," his helm officer responded.

"Five million kilometers and closing," Gerda Asmund announced. "Four million. Three million . . ."

Picard felt a shudder run through the deck beneath his feet. He put his hand on the back of Ruhalter's chair, just in case the shudder was a portent of something worse.

"Two million," the navigator continued.

The barrier loomed in front of them, bigger than anything Picard had ever seen. He could discern vast shadows of light twisting within it, testing the limits of the screen's illumination dampers.

Gerda Asmund looked up at the screen. "One million . . ."

As she spoke the words, the phenomenon engulfed them, closing its jaws on the *Stargazer* as if the ship was a helpless minnow and the barrier was a colossal, writhing serpent.

The deck shuddered again, then slid to the right. Picard tightened his grasp on the captain's chair.

"Report," Ruhalter snapped.

"Shields at eighty-eight percent," the navigator responded.

"Warp drive operating at peak capacity," her sister added.

The viewscreen was a confusion of ruby-red twisters, a maelstrom of heaving, burning lava. The *Stargazer* bucked once, twice, and again, and the second officer had to fight to keep his feet.

But it didn't get any worse than that. Even under immense pressure, the shields held. The control consoles on the bridge managed not to spark or explode. And most importantly, no one was caught in the spasm of light that had signaled the beginning of Gary Mitchell's transformation.

The *Stargazer* endured one last buffet from the barrier's unknown energies, one last surge of hull-shivering fury. Then it burst free of the phenomenon into normal if unfamiliar space.

Picard took a deep breath . . . and smiled.

Without question, their passage through the barrier had been tense and plagued with uncertainties. It had been a study in faith and humility. But in retrospect, it had also been a thing of wonder.

It was for just such experiences that the second officer had joined Starfleet. Looking around, he saw that he wasn't the only one who felt that way. Paxton, the Asmunds, Cariello . . . they all looked pleased.

Even Ruhalter seemed to have relished the experience, if the bright glint in the man's eyes was any indication. Only Commander Leach looked vaguely disapproving. But then, knowing the man as he did, Picard wouldn't have expected anything else.

"Shields at seventy-eight percent," Gerda Asmund observed.

"All systems operational," said Idun.

The captain nodded. "Excellent." Then he turned to his first and second officers. "You're with me, gentlemen."

Without any explanation, he rose and made his way to the turbolift. Picard saw Leach hurry to fall in behind Ruhalter, as if it made a difference who was behind the captain as he entered the lift. Sighing, the second officer followed Leach into the compartment.

The doors whispered closed behind them. "Ship's lounge," said Ruhalter, his voice echoing in the enclosure.

Apparently, the captain meant to conduct a meeting with his two senior officers. However, Picard had no idea what the meeting was about.

The lift's progress through the ship was imperceptible to its occupants, except for a tiny monitor that showed their location. They were halfway to their destination when Ruhalter did something surprising.

"Computer," he said, "stop turbolift."

Picard looked at him. So did Leach.

"It just occurred to me," said the captain, "that we don't have to go to the lounge to have this meeting. After all, there's only the three of us, and this shouldn't take long."

"As you wish, sir," Leach responded.

Ruhalter regarded each of them in turn. "I have one question, gentlemen—and that's whether Serenity Santana can be trusted."

The first officer smiled a lopsided smile. "Since you're asking, sir, I don't think the woman is even remotely trustworthy—and for the record, I've felt that way since we arrived at Starbase Two-oh-nine."

The captain nodded, then turned to Picard. "What about you, Jean-Luc? What do you think?"

The second officer took some time to consider the question. "As you know," he said finally, "I've had a chance to get to know Ms. Santana. However, I would have to know her a lot better before I could vouch for her with any assurance."

"Unfortunately," Ruhalter told him, "we don't have time for you to get to know her better. You'll have to give me your appraisal of her based on what you know *now.*"

Picard frowned, hating to be pinned down this way. "Based on that," he said, "I'm inclined to believe she *can* be trusted."

Leach didn't seem surprised. "It's clear," he pointed out, "that Commander Picard is quite taken with Ms. Santana. I don't think he's thinking as clearly as he should be."

"Perhaps not," the captain conceded.

Leach looked pleased with himself.

But the second officer felt betrayed. He was thinking as incisively as ever, he assured himself. If Ruhalter disagreed with his conclusion, that was one thing. But to question his clarity . . .

Suddenly, a mischievous smile broke out on the captain's face. "Then again, Number One, Commander Picard may be right on target."

Leach's mouth fell open. "Sir . . . ?"

"You see," said Ruhalter, "I agree with Picard one hundred percent. I too think Ms. Santana can be trusted—and like you, Mr. Leach, I formed my opinion the moment I met her."

The second officer understood. "You went with your instincts."

"Yes," said the captain, his eyes twinkling. "As always."

"But, sir," Leach began, "if you had already made your decision—"

"Why did I ask for your opinions? Simple, Commander. I wanted to make sure I hadn't missed something."

The first officer looked as if he had been slapped in the face. "I have to protest, sir. If necessary, through official means."

Ruhalter seemed unperturbed by the remark. "That's your option, Mr. Leach— as always. But I hope you'll refrain from exercising it until after we've completed our mission."

"By then," Leach said coldly, "it may be too late."

"We'll see," the captain rejoined. "In any case, Santana has given us two sets of coordinates. One describes the location of her colony. The other will lead us to a Nuyyad supply depot."

"We're going to head for the depot," Picard guessed.

"Absolutely right," Ruhalter confirmed. "Why waste time? If there's a threat, let's see it."

"And if it's a trap?" Leach suggested.

"Then we'll see that too," said the captain. "Though my instincts tell me that won't happen."

The first officer's nostrils flared, but he didn't say anything more.

"Thank you for your input," Ruhalter told them. "Both of you. Computer, return us to the bridge."

Again, the turbolift began to move.

Pug Joseph closed his eyes and concentrated. "Okay," he said. "See if you can picture this."

Santana answered from the other side of the translucent barrier. "Protruding brow ridge, bony forehead, a preference for facial hair. Strong, by the look of him. And fierce."

Opening his eyes, the security officer smiled at the woman's skill. "He's called a Klingon."

"Friend?" Santana guessed.

"Friend *now,*" Joseph told her.

"But not always?"

"Until fifty years ago," he said, "the Klingons were almost constantly at war with us. Then we signed a nonaggression treaty with them."

"Got it," she responded. "Who's next?"

Again, the security officer closed his eyes and conjured an image. "How about this one?"

"Let's see," said Santana. "Aristocratic bearing, pointed ears, painfully precise haircut. If not for the subtle ridges above the eyes, I'd be tempted to say he's Vulcan."

Joseph laughed softly. "Very good. He's called a Romulan. And his people are an offshoot of the Vulcan species."

"Enemy?" she suggested.

"I'll say. We haven't seen them in more than twenty years, but people still worry about them."

"Give me another one," Santana told him.

"All right," he said, picturing someone else. "Here's one."

"Hmmm. Mottled red skin, long jaw tusks like an elephant's, spiny scalp projections instead of hair."

Joseph opened his eyes and shook his head in admiration. "A Vobilite."

"An enemy?"

"A friend. In fact, the Vobilites were one of the first species to support the idea of a United Federation of Planets. I served with one of them on my previous assignment."

Santana nodded. "Now it's my turn."

The security officer felt a chill climb his spine. "I didn't know you could project your thoughts."

She smiled. "I can't. I meant I was going to describe them out loud."

Joseph blushed. "Oh."

The woman thought for a moment. "Here's one. Tall and thin, with jet black fur and silver eyes."

He tried to put the information together. What he came up with seemed pretty elegant. "Sounds easy on the eyes."

"I've always thought so. They're called the Yotaavo."

"Friend?" he ventured, playing the game.

"Friend. We've done quite a bit of trading with them over the years. Want another one?"

Joseph shrugged. "Sure."

Again, Santana took a moment to choose. "Small and muscular, with four arms, short legs, and scaly, yellow skin."

The security officer constructed an image in his head. "I think I've got it. What are they called?"

"The Caddis."

"I'll say . . . friend."

"Actually," said the prisoner, "they've been both. When we first established the colony, they were always making life difficult for us. In the last fifty or sixty years, they've gotten to know us better. As a result, things have improved."

"How about an enemy?" Joseph asked. "A current one, I mean."

She frowned. "We've only got one of those. Big and fleshy, with shiny, black eyes and a fringe of dark hair around their skulls."

"The Nuyyad?" he asked.

Santana nodded. "Not that we've ever had a run-in with them—but we consider them our enemy just the same."

"I can't wait to meet them," Joseph said, injecting a note of sarcasm into his voice.

The woman didn't seem to notice the irony. "Oh yes, you can, Mr. Joseph. *Believe* me, you can."

Picard sat down at the black, oval table in the *Stargazer*'s lounge and faced his captain. "You wanted to see me, sir?"

Ruhalter nodded from the other side of the table. "I do indeed, Commander." He paused, as if choosing his words more carefully than usual. "According to regulations, we shouldn't be having this conversation. Nonetheless, I feel it's necessary."

The second officer waited patiently. The captain wasn't the sort to need any prodding.

"As you've no doubt noticed," said Ruhalter, "Commander Leach and I don't often see eye to eye. Don't get me wrong—he's an efficient officer, with an impressive background and considerable skill in some areas. But he's not a *first* officer. At least, not in my book."

Picard was surprised. Captains didn't normally make such comments about their execs—especially to subordinate officers.

"It's unfortunate, really," Ruhalter went on. "Captain Osborne expressed every confidence in Leach, and I relied heavily on his recommendation. It was one of the few times since I became a captain that I *didn't* go with my instincts—and look what happened."

The second officer had wondered how Ruhalter could have made such an error in judgment. Now he understood.

"I wound up with a man I can't get along with," said the captain. "A man eminently capable of carrying out a project on his own, yet plainly incapable of leading others." He shook his head ruefully. "It's not a good situation, Jean-Luc. And I'd be remiss if I didn't do something about it."

Do something? Picard repeated to himself. Might that mean what he thought it meant?

"As soon as we come back from this mission," Ruhalter told him, "I'm going to arrange for Commander Leach to be transferred to another ship. Or, failing that, to some other Starfleet facility. Of course, that's going to leave me short a first officer . . ." He smiled. "And I can't think of anyone I'd rather have serving in that capacity than you."

The second officer was at a loss for words. Finally, he found a few. "I would be honored, sir," he replied graciously. "That is, when the appropriate time comes."

The captain nodded approvingly. "I'm glad to hear you say that, Commander. It'll give me something to look forward to when I'm wrangling with your predecessor over Serenity Santana."

"Commander Leach still insists it was a mistake to bring her along?"

"Yes," said Ruhalter, "he does. And at every opportunity, I might add. It's making my head spin."

Picard understood. The first officer made *his* head spin sometimes too.

"In the meantime," the captain told him, "we have an important mission on our hands—and frankly, I'm afraid that Leach will do something to muck it up. I want you to keep an eye on him for me. If he gives an order that you think will lead to trouble, you're to let me know immediately. Is that understood?"

"It is," the second officer assured him.

"Good," said Ruhalter. "I—"

Abruptly, the lounge filled with the voice of the very man they were talking about. "Captain," said Leach, his tone taut with concern, "we've got a situation up here."

Ruhalter's brow knit. "Elaborate."

"There's a vessel approaching on an intercept course," Leach reported. "Bearing two-four-four-mark two. I have to tell you, sir, it doesn't look like anything we've encountered before."

The captain frowned and got to his feet. "Go to red alert, Commander. I'm on my way."

Picard was right behind him as he headed for the doors. His stomach muscles clenched as he wondered what they were up against. And then, all of a sudden, it came to him.

The Nuyyad.

Seven

As Picard pelted along the corridor in pursuit of Captain Ruhalter, he turned the idea over in his mind. *The Nuyyad.*

It was just a hunch, of course. He had no proof to back it up, no information on which to build a case. For all he knew, they hadn't been detected by the Nuyyad at all, but rather by some other species—one that only meant to investigate the *Stargazer*'s unfamiliar presence here.

But his instincts—the kind his commanding officer always spoke about—were working overtime, and they had come to a conclusion on their own.

Ruhalter might have been thinking along the same lines, but he needed some corroboration. Slightly more than halfway to the turbolift, he tapped his communicator badge. "Jomar," he said, "this is the captain. I need you on the bridge immediately."

The Kelvan replied just as the lift compartment arrived. "Coming," he said over the intercom system, his voice as empty of inflection as ever.

Then Picard and his commanding officer were inside the lift, the doors closed, moving silently toward the *Stargazer*'s bridge. Ruhalter scowled, but he didn't say anything. There was no point in doing so, Picard recognized, until they could see the problem for themselves.

Finally, after what seemed like an eternity, the turbolift doors opened and they emerged onto the bridge. The place was bathed in the crimson light of a red alert. As the captain replaced Leach in the center seat, Picard took in the sight depicted on the viewscreen.

"You see?" Leach asked Ruhalter.

The captain saw, all right. And so did Picard.

He saw an almost flat, silver diamond—one so large that it seemed to dominate the dark spaces around it. The similarly diamond-shaped appendages on either side of it were probably its warp nacelles, or whatever analogous equipment the vessel's occupants used for propulsion.

A cold and efficient-looking ship, Picard reflected. No doubt, it had been built by a cold and efficient people.

Ruhalter turned to Gerda Asmund. "How much time do we have before our paths converge, Lieutenant?"

"At the alien vessel's current rate of speed," said the navigator, "she'll reach us in less than six minutes."

The muscles in the captain's jaw rippled uncomfortably. "Keep me posted," he told Gerda.

Just then, the lift doors hissed open again. Glancing over his shoulder, Picard saw Jomar come out onto the bridge. The Kelvan's pale-blue eyes were immediately drawn to the viewscreen.

He uttered a single, colorless word: "Nuyyad."

Ruhalter grunted. "I had a feeling you were going to say that."

Jomar turned to him. "Captain," he said, "we did not expect to encounter the enemy so quickly. The modifications to the deflector grid have not yet been completed."

Ruhalter swore under his breath. "How far along are we?"

"We have finished perhaps eighty percent of the job," said the Kelvan. "But it would take several hours to do the rest."

"And we don't *have* several hours," Leach reminded them.

Picard looked at the first officer. Leach's expression seemed to say "I told you so." He had predicted that they would run into trouble if they followed Santana's instructions—and now, it seemed, they had.

"Four minutes," Gerda announced.

The second officer moved to the navigator's console, planted the heel of his hand on its edge and leaned in to get a better look. He could see a green blip crawling across the black background of Gerda's monitor.

The blip seemed so abstract, so theoretical. But the ship it represented was making warp eight, if their sensors were correct, with no sign whatsoever of slowing down.

"Activate what we have," Ruhalter said, referring to the shields. "And keep working. Let's see if we can get some more capacity on-line."

"As you wish," Jomar responded dispassionately, and made his way back to the turbolift.

The captain eased himself back in his seat, his expression as grave as Picard had ever seen it. They were at a disadvantage, the second officer told himself, and the captain knew it.

On the other hand, the *Stargazer* was a fast, well-equipped ship, and her crew had been battle-tested on other Starfleet vessels. They could yet prevail, Picard told himself.

"Three minutes," said Gerda.

Ruhalter's eyes narrowed. "Battle stations. Raise shields where we have them. Power phasers and arm photon torpedoes."

"Done, sir," said Lieutenant Werber, working at his weapons console aft of the center seat.

The second officer looked around the bridge. In addition to the captain, Leach, and himself, there were four officers present—the Asmunds, Werber, and Paxton. Every one of them was going about his business coolly and methodically, as if this sort of thing happened all the time.

For a moment, he almost thought he saw Idun Asmund smiling. Then the moment passed and he chalked it up to his imagination.

"Two minutes," Gerda told them.

The captain glanced at his communications officer. "Hail them, Mr. Paxton. Let's see what they do."

"Aye, sir," said Paxton.

Everyone waited for the results of his efforts. Finally, the communications officer looked up from his console.

"Nothing," he told Ruhalter.

The captain nodded. "Can't say I'm surprised."

"One minute," said Gerda, "and closing. Fifty seconds. Forty . . ."

Picard latched onto the back of the navigator's chair with his free hand. It made him feel a trifle more secure.

"Thirty seconds," Gerda announced. "Twenty. Ten . . ."

"Weapons range," said Lieutenant Werber, sounding too eager by half for Picard's taste.

"They're firing!" Gerda announced.

A barrage of green witch-lights streamed from the Nuyyad's weapons ports and exploded to spectacular effect on the viewscreen. The Federation ship bucked under the impact of the vidrion assault, but not so badly that anyone was hurt.

"Shields down twenty-two percent!" Werber called out.

Not good, Picard reflected. But if not for the Kelvan's modifications, they might have been destroyed altogether.

Ruhalter leaned forward in his seat, a look of determination on his face. "Target and fire!"

A moment later, the *Stargazer* released a series of yellow-white photon torpedoes—packets of matter and antimatter bound together by magnetic forces. They found their target in quick succession, returning the enemy's attack blow for ponderous blow.

But the Federation vessel couldn't continue to trade punches with her adversary—not when the Nuyyad possessed a weapon as devastating as a vidrion cannon. She had to make her move—and quickly.

"Evasive maneuvers!" the captain barked. "Pattern Delta!"

Idun Asmund pulled the *Stargazer* into a tight upward turn, taking her out of the enemy's sights for a moment. The Nuyyad obviously hadn't expected such an action, because they sent an emerald-green vidrion volley slicing through empty space.

"Target and fire!" Ruhalter bellowed.

Again, Werber released a flight of photon torpedoes. Again, they found their mark, wreaking havoc with the enemy's shields.

Picard's heart leaped. They were winning. If they could keep it going, the battle would be over in short order.

Unfortunately, the Nuyyad seemed to have another outcome in mind. They pumped out yet another round of vidrion particles, hammering the *Stargazer* even harder than before.

An aft console erupted in flames, prompting the second officer to grab a fire extinguisher and douse the blaze with white spray. Before he was done, he heard Gerda's status report.

"Shields down forty-eight percent, sir! Damage to decks six, seven, eight, and eleven!"

"Dispatch repair crews!" the captain told her.

It was a setback, Picard told himself, but no more than that. If anything, the enemy had only evened the odds.

"Pattern Epsilon!" Ruhalter called out.

This time, Idun sent the ship veering to starboard—just as the Nuyyad hurled another barrage at them. For a heartbeat, the second officer thought the maneuver would do the trick.

Then he found out otherwise. The deck slipped out from under him, pitching him forcibly into an aft console.

"Shields down eighty-two percent!" Gerda thundered. "Damage to decks five, nine, and ten!"

She had just gotten the words out when the viewscreen flooded with bright green fury. Picard barely had time to brace himself before the ship staggered hard to starboard, jerking his fellow officers half out of their seats.

Ruhalter thrust himself to his feet and came forward to glare at the screen, as if he could stop the Nuyyad by force of will alone. "Pattern Omega!" he snarled.

Idun sent them plummeting in a tight spiral, vidrion bundles bursting savagely all around them. Somehow, they emerged unscathed—but the enemy didn't let them go far. The Nuyyad ship banked and dogged their trail, like a predator that had smelled its victim's blood.

"Pattern Omicron!" the captain cried out, trying desperately to give them some breathing room.

Idun coerced the ship into a sudden, excruciatingly tight loop, causing the hull to groan and shiver under the strain. But the maneuver worked. Unable to stop in time, the Nuyyad vessel shot past them.

"Maximum warp!" Ruhalter commanded.

The *Stargazer* tore through the void at a thousand times the speed of light, putting a hundred million kilometers between herself and the enemy with each passing second. Picard eyed the viewscreen, but he saw no sign of the Nuyyad. All he could see were the stars streaming by.

The tension on the bridge eased a notch. Commander Leach, who had lost all the color in his face, sighed and eased himself into a vacant seat by the forward engineering console.

"Report," breathed the captain.

Gerda consulted her monitor. "Hull breaches on decks twelve, thirteen, and fourteen. Repair teams have been deployed to all damaged areas. Sickbay reports nine injured."

"Dead?" asked Ruhalter.

"No one," the navigator replied.

The captain seemed relieved. "Well," he said, "that's something to be thankful for. What about our shields?"

Gerda glanced at him and shook her head. "There aren't any, sir. That last volley took out the last of them."

No shields, thought Picard. It was a good thing they had escaped when they did. Another barrage like the last one, and—

"Captain!" exclaimed Werber, his face caught in the ruddy glare of his control panel. "They're on our tail again!"

"Give me a visual," said Ruhalter.

Once again, the viewscreen showed them the Nuyyad ship. Picard felt his jaw clench. Though they were pushing the *Stargazer's* warp drive as hard as they dared, the enemy was slowly catching up to them.

"Weapons range," Werber told them.

"Stand by, helm," the captain told Idun. "If we can't outrun them, we'll have to outfight them."

Picard stared at him, wondering about the wisdom of Ruhalter's strategy. As if he sensed the younger man's scrutiny, Ruhalter looked back.

I know, Jean-Luc, his expression seemed to say. *Without shields, we don't stand much of a chance. But what choice do I have?*

Picard wished he had a good answer. *None,* he conceded silently.

"Target photon torpedoes," said the captain.

"Aye, sir," came Werber's response.

Ruhalter's eyes narrowed with resolve. "Pattern Alpha."

All at once, Idun swung them hard to port. The *Stargazer* wheeled more quickly and gracefully than she had a right to, coming about a full one hundred and eighty degrees. Before the second officer knew it, he found himself face-to-face with the Nuyyad.

And the enemy hadn't cut his speed one iota.

"Fire!" the captain roared.

A swarm of photon torpedoes took flight, illuminating the void between the two combatants. At the same time, the Nuyyad vessel unleashed its most devastating attack yet.

It was a glorious, breathtaking spectacle, emerald green mingling with gold, brilliance weaving its way through brilliance. Unfortunately, it lasted only a fraction of a second.

Then the *Stargazer* reeled under the hull-buckling onslaught, sending Picard crashing into a bulkhead. Pain shot through his ribs and the side of his head and blackness began to overwhelm him.

No, he told himself, fighting to regain his senses. I cannot give in. I need to know what has happened. The taste of blood strong in his mouth, he pulled himself up along a console and took stock of the bridge.

The air was full of smoke and sparks and fire. Unmanned consoles beeped frantically and open conduits hissed deadly plasma. The second officer blinked, trying to see through the haze with badly stinging eyes, and spied someone sprawled on the deck near the captain's chair.

It was Ruhalter—and he wasn't moving.

Darting to the captain's side, Picard saw why. Half the man's face had been burned away in the explosion of a still-sputtering plasma conduit.

The second officer shook his head. No, he thought, denying it as hard as he could. It cannot be. It is not possible.

But it *was*.

Daithan Ruhalter was dead.

Abruptly, he realized that someone was standing next to him. Looking up, he saw that it was Paxton.

"My god," said the communications officer, gaping at the captain's corpse in disbelief.

Picard saw the look on Paxton's face and imagined the same look on his own—and a feeling of shame welled up inside him. He had to accept the situation, he told himself. He had to move on.

After all, the ship was in deadly danger. Their shields were down and they had an enemy taking shots at them with impunity.

As Picard thought that, he felt another jolt run through the ship—but it wasn't nearly as bad as the last one. Obviously, Idun Asmund was still at the helm, doing her job.

They needed a leader, however. And with Ruhalter dead, that left Leach—whether the man was up to the task or not. Starfleet protocol wouldn't tolerate anything less.

"Commander Leach!" Picard hollered into the miasma of fireshot smoke.

There was no answer.

Leaving Ruhalter's side, the second officer made his way forward. He had last seen Leach at the engineering console. With luck, the man would still be there.

But when Picard reached the spot, he couldn't find any sign of the first officer.

He looked around, hoping to catch a glimpse of him—and instead saw Gerda Asmund hunched over near her navigation console.

His first thought was that the woman had been hurt. Then, as he got closer, he saw a body stretched out on the deck beyond her. Gerda turned and looked up at the second officer.

"It's Leach," she told him, her concern evident in the knot of flesh at the bridge of her nose.

Picard moved around her and saw the first officer. His eyes were closed, his features slack, and there was blood seeping from a gash in his smoke-blackened temple.

"Dead?" the second officer said numbly.

Gerda shook her head. "No. He still has a pulse."

"Get him to sickbay," Picard told her. "And send some hands up here to see to the captain."

"Aye, sir," said the navigator.

Picking Leach up with athletic ease, she headed for the turbolift. The second officer watched her go for a moment, open plasma conduits and flaming consoles illuminating her passage.

As the lift doors opened, Picard felt another impact. But like the last one, this one had been tolerable.

He looked at the officers still left to him. Idun, who was battling her controls to keep them in one piece. Paxton, who had returned to his post at communications. And Werber, who looked eager to fire again if only someone would give him the order.

With Ruhalter and Leach victims of the Nuyyad, Picard would have to be the one to do that. In fact, he would have to give *all* the orders.

"Mr. Paxton," he barked, "take over at navigation."

"Aye, sir," the communications officer replied, and moved forward to do as he was asked.

Picard turned and gazed at the viewscreen, where a reverse perspective showed the Nuyyad ship clinging to them in pursuit. It only took him a moment to realize that there was something curious about the sight—and another moment to figure out what it was.

The enemy vessel was slightly atilt as it sped through space, slightly off-line relative to the axis of its forward progress. Picard knew enough about propulsion systems to understand the reason for such an aberration.

One of the Nuyyad ship's warp nacelles was misfiring. The one on the port side, it seemed to him. That suggested a weakness of which his helm officer could take advantage.

"Lieutenant Asmund," he said, "the enemy will have difficulty turning to starboard. Reprise Pattern Epsilon on my mark."

"Aye, sir," the helm officer replied.

Next, the second officer turned to Werber. "Target photon torpedoes."

"I've been doing nothing *but* targeting," Werber told him.

Ignoring the man's tone, Picard eyed the screen again. "Lieutenant Asmund—execute your maneuver. Lieutenant Werber—fire when ready."

The words had barely left his mouth when the Nuyyad spewed another wave of green fire at them, trying to finish off the *Stargazer.* But by then, Idun had gone into her turn.

The vidrion assault shot harmlessly by them. And as the Federation vessel continued to perform her maneuver, the enemy shot by as well—much to Werber's delight. Cheering beneath his breath, the weapons officer released a hail of golden photon torpedoes.

The first wave ripped into the Nuyyad's flank, shredding what remained of her shields. The second wave clawed chunks out of the vessel's hull. And the third penetrated to the very heart of the ship, finding and obliterating critical power relays.

A moment later, Picard knew that at least one torpedo had reached the enemy's warp core—because the Nuyyad ship tore itself apart in a ragged spasm of bright yellow fire.

The second officer watched the fragments of the shattered craft pinwheel end over end through space, expanding outward from the point of the explosion. There was a macabre grace to the scene, a feeling of something strangely akin to serenity.

He looked back over his shoulder. Ruhalter's corpse was gone, having been spirited away while Picard was busy with the Nuyyad.

But his work wasn't done yet. They were still in unfamiliar territory, with wounds to lick and the ever-present threat of another attack—not to mention some serious questions to answer.

And his bridge was on fire.

As Werber, Paxton, and Idun Asmund watched him, Picard moved to the rear of the bridge and found the fire extinguisher he had used before. Then he began spraying down the ruined remnants of the nearest console.

Carter Greyhorse ran his sleek, palm-sized regeneration unit over the flesh of Lieutenant Cariello's bare shoulder, creating a few more healthy, new cells to replace the ones she had lost to a white-hot spurt of plasma.

The doctor took a moment to examine his work. Satisfied with it, he checked Cariello's vital signs on her biobed's overhead readouts. The lieutenant's systems were all stable, he observed. In a day or so, after she had gotten some rest, there would be no indication that she had been within minutes of losing her life.

Activating an electromagnetic barrier around Cariello to guard against infection, Greyhorse moved to the next bed in line. Lieutenant Kochman was lying there in a stasis field, outwardly unharmed but inwardly suffering from broken ribs, ruptured organs, and considerable hemorrhaging.

He would require a good deal more work than Cariello, the doctor reflected. But at least the man was alive.

Greyhorse glanced at the corpses laid out under metallic blankets in the corner of his sickbay. There were four of them in all. Barr, Janes, Harras . . . and, of course, Captain Ruhalter.

If the chief medical officer had had more than twelve biobeds at his disposal, he wouldn't have subjected the deceased to the indignity of lying on the floor. But to his chagrin, he didn't have more than twelve beds—and his priority had to be the living.

Greyhorse was on the verge of deactivating Kochman's stasis field when he heard the sickbay doors hiss open. Glancing in that direction, he fully expected to see someone bringing in another casualty.

But this time, it was different. It wasn't just anyone being brought in. It was *her.*

At least, that was the way it looked to the doctor for a split second. Then he realized he was mistaken, and a wave of relief washed over him. It wasn't Gerda Asmund who was being carried into sickbay. It was Gerda who was doing the carrying.

And it was Commander Leach wrapped up in the woman's arms, Greyhorse realized—Commander Leach who was lying as limp and pale as death. Clearly, the first officer's condition would have to take precedence over anyone else's for the time being.

Leaving Kochman's side, the doctor crossed the room to the bed containing Ensign Kotsakos, whose injuries weren't nearly as severe. Deactivating the protective field around the ensign, Greyhorse picked the woman up as gently as he could and deposited her on the floor beside the bed.

He would have preferred to give her the benefit of the field for the next several hours. That would have been the ideal approach. However, Kotsakos would survive without the field. He couldn't say the same for Leach.

"Put him down here," Greyhorse told Gerda.

She did as he said, easing the first officer onto the biobed.

The doctor looked up to study the bed's readouts. Clearly, Leach was in bad shape—even worse than the ragged gash in his temple suggested. His vital signs were badly depressed.

"What can I do?" asked Gerda.

Greyhorse looked at her with the same longing and admiration he had felt the other day, when he had checked her ESPer capacity. But this time, he wasn't tongue-tied in the least.

"Check the other beds, one at a time, and call out their readings to me." He pointed to Kochman. "Starting with that one."

"And Leach?" the navigator asked.

"I'll take care of him," the doctor assured her.

She hesitated for just a moment, as if there was something else she wanted to say to him. Then she left the first officer in his capable hands and went to see how Kochman was doing.

Greyhorse drew a deep breath and wiped sweat from his brow with the back of his hand. In that moment when he thought Gerda was injured, he had gone through an eternity of hell in a single second.

He didn't like the idea of people getting hurt. He was a physician, after all. But if it came down to the navigator or someone else . . . he was glad it hadn't been Gerda.

As the turbolift doors opened, Ben Zoma emerged from the compartment and made his way down the corridor—phaser in hand.

He had good reason for concern. The moment the battle with the Nuyyad had ended, he had tried to contact the officer on duty in the brig. But there hadn't been any response—not a promising sign by anyone's reckoning.

And with the battering the *Stargazer* had taken, power conduits had been compromised on every deck. There was no guarantee that the brig's electromagnetic force field was still in place.

Which meant Serenity Santana might be free to go wherever she wanted. *Do* whatever she wanted.

That made Ben Zoma nervous, given the fact that the woman's motivations were still in question—maybe more so now than ever, considering they had followed her directions straight into the sights of an enemy battleship.

He hadn't been particularly suspicious of Santana when Captain Ruhalter brought her aboard. He had believed they were doing the right thing by checking out her warning. And even now, he wasn't convinced that she was in on the Nuyyad attack.

But he was the ship's security chief. With hundreds of lives at stake, he had to believe the worst of everyone.

Striding purposefully, Ben Zoma negotiated a bend in the corridor and came in sight of the brig. The first thing he saw was a body laid out on the deck. He recognized it as Pug Joseph, Santana's guard.

Instantly, the security chief broke into a run. When he reached Joseph, he dropped at the man's side and saw the blood running from Joseph's nose and mouth. He also saw the burgeoning bruise over Joseph's right eye.

He felt for a pulse—and found one. Tapping his combadge, he said, "Security, this is Ben Zoma."

"Pfeffer here, sir."

"I'm at the brig," the chief told Pfeffer. "Joseph is down. I'll need help getting him to sickbay."

"Acknowledged," said the security officer. "What about Santana, sir? Is the field still in place?"

Ben Zoma cursed under his breath and glanced in the direction of Santana's enclosure. "Stand by."

He had been so concerned about Joseph, he hadn't taken the time to check on their guest yet. Getting to his feet, he approached the entrance to the brig cautiously, phaser at the ready. Stopping at the doorway, he craned his neck to get a look inside at Santana's cell.

The force field was still in place, all right. But Santana was crumpled in the corner.

"Ms. Santana?" he called out, his voice echoing.

The woman didn't answer. She just lay there.

The security chief sighed. "Santana looks like she's in a bad way," he told Pfeffer. "I'll need help with her as well."

"On its way, sir," the officer assured him.

Eight

Captain's log, supplemental, Second Officer Jean-Luc Picard reporting. Now that I have had a few hours to assess our situation, I find that it is even more troubling than I anticipated. Six brave members of our crew perished in the course of the battle with the Nuyyad. One of them was Captain Ruhalter, for whom I had a great deal of personal respect and affection. Fourteen others are recuperating from serious injuries—among them Commander Leach, who has lapsed into a deep coma. The Stargazer *did not fare much better. Her ability to travel at faster-than-light velocities has been significantly curtailed, her starboard phaser batteries are nearly useless and her supply of photon torpedoes has been all but depleted. However, it's the ship's deflector grid that sustained the greatest damage. At this point, it can barely protect us from spaceborne particles. Perhaps needless to say, the vidrion-generating enhancements endorsed by Jomar were completely and utterly destroyed in the clash with the Nuyyad. Unless and until we can secure replacement parts for our shield generators, we will remain vulnerable in the extreme. As for Serenity Santana, our mysterious advisor . . . like Commander Leach, she was rendered comatose in the melee. We are thus deprived of an opportunity to determine her role in what appears to have been a carefully calculated trap—if she indeed had any role in it at all.*

Picard gazed at Serenity Santana. She lay still and pale on the flat surface of the biobed, her raven hair spread around her head, her chest rising and falling mechanically.

The second officer wished the woman were awake—and not just because he hated to see her lying there like that, limp and helpless, when she had once been so charming and vibrant. Not just because she was, quite possibly, the most beautiful woman he had ever seen.

As Picard had indicated in the log he had filed only a few minutes earlier, there were questions he wished to ask Santana. Mainly, he wanted to know how the Nuyyad had discovered the *Stargazer*—because he didn't believe for a second that the enemy had just stumbled onto them.

Space was a vast place, on this side of the galactic barrier as much as on the other one. The odds of two ships sensing each other even with long-range instruments were so slim as to almost be absurd.

And yet, they had barely penetrated the galactic barrier when the Nuyyad descended on them. If Santana had something to do with that, if she had betrayed them as Leach feared she would—

"You see, Commander?" called a deep voice.

Picard turned and saw Greyhorse coming toward him, his huge frame looking out of place in his lab coat. The doctor had been attending to an injured crewman on the other side of sickbay.

"As I indicated," Greyhorse went on, "Ms. Santana has retreated into a deep coma. But at least she's stable."

The second officer gazed at the colonist again. Even in her debilitated state, she was a compelling sight.

"Will she come out of it?" he asked.

"That's difficult to say," Greyhorse told him.

"Because her brain is different from ours?"

"Among other reasons, yes." The doctor pointed to the bed's readouts. "I want to show you something. Do you see those lines, Commander? The two near the top?"

Picard nodded. "What about them?"

"Those are the patient's brain waves," Greyhorse explained. He pressed a keypad next to the readout and it changed instantly—the top two lines in particular. "And these were her brain waves when she first came aboard. Do you see the difference?"

He did—but he didn't know what conclusion he was supposed to draw from the observation. "I'm sorry. I don't see what—"

The medical officer held up a large, powerful-looking hand. "I didn't expect you to draw any real conclusions. Let me walk you through it."

Picard thought that would be a good idea.

"A woman in Ms. Santana's condition should exhibit precious little brain activity. For example, she should have a very quiet cerebral cortex. However," said

Greyhorse, pointing to the topmost line on the readout, "we see that her cerebral cortex is anything *but* quiet. In fact, it's busier now than when she was awake. The same goes for portions of her cerebellum."

Picard mulled over the information. "So . . . you're saying some parts of her brain are actually busier in her comatose condition than they were when she was conscious?"

"Exactly," the doctor confirmed.

"And what do you make of that?"

The doctor shrugged his massive shoulders. "Again, difficult to say. The patient's brain may have gone into some kind of healing mode. Or . . ." His voice trailed off.

"Or?" Picard nudged.

"If her brain works like those of other telepaths, the patient may have purposely emphasized certain functions at the expense of others—which would suggest the possibility that this is not a naturally occurring coma, but one she induced on her own."

On her own? Picard thought. He looked at Greyhorse. "I don't understand. Why would she do such a thing?"

The other man returned his glance. "You are in a better position to know that than I am, Commander."

Picard turned to Santana again, as if he hoped to find the answer written on her lips. Was it possible that she had shut herself down purposely, in order to avoid answering difficult questions?

Somehow, the second officer didn't think so. Or was it just that he didn't *want* to think so?

"Thank you," he told Greyhorse. "You've given me much to think about. If there's any change in her condition, even a small one—"

"I'll be sure to let you know," the doctor assured him.

Picard nodded. Then, with a last glance at Santana, he left sickbay and returned to the bridge.

Pug Joseph touched the itchy spot just above his right cheekbone and recalled Doctor Greyhorse's orders not to scratch it.

In a day or so, his regenerated flesh would complete the healing process. Then no one would ever know he had hit his head against a bulkhead hard enough to knock himself out.

Fortunately, the security officer thought, he had suffered nothing more serious than a concussion. Otherwise, he would still be in sickbay along with Kochman and the other worst cases.

And they were the lucky ones, he reminded himself. The captain and some of the others hadn't made it at all.

Removing his food from the replicator enclosure, Joseph placed it on his tray. First his meat, then his rice, then his vegetables, and finally his juice. Then he moved across the crowded mess hall in the direction of one of its few empty tables.

His crewmates, who were all working triple shifts on one repair crew or another, had gathered in clusters all around the room. They were obviously seeking comfort in numbers—taking the opportunity to vent their sorrows and air their concerns, of which they had many.

The *Stargazer* had been hobbled pretty badly in the battle with the Nuyyad.

With key systems on the blink, people were worried about what they would do if another vessel showed up.

Joseph had thought about that possibility too, of course—and he probably felt the need to talk about it as much as anyone. But there were certain things he wanted very much *not* to talk about just then, so he had decided he would keep to himself.

Arriving at his solitary destination, he put his tray down and deposited himself in a chair. Then he pushed himself into his table and began to eat, mindful of the fact that he had to get back to work soon.

He was halfway finished when some of his crewmates walked in and took a table next to his. He recognized them as Lieutenant Werber, Chief Engineer Simenon, and a couple of the men who worked for him.

They didn't acknowledge Joseph's presence. In fact, they didn't acknowledge anyone. They were too engrossed in their conversation.

Joseph didn't want to eavesdrop. He was the kind of person who respected the rights of others, the right of privacy in particular. However, Werber and his companions were speaking so loudly, it would have been difficult not to hear them.

"—upstart is taking the captain's place," said Simenon. His expression was a distinctly sour one.

"And he was the one who convinced Ruhalter to trust Santana," Werber pointed out.

"How do you know?" asked the chief engineer.

"Leach told me," said the weapons officer.

Simenon shook his scaly head in disbelief. "The way that woman twisted Picard around her finger . . . it was disgraceful. And now we're all going to pay the price for it."

"You think she led us into a trap?" asked one of the other engineers, a man named Pernell.

Werber chuckled bitterly. "Is there any doubt of it?"

Pug Joseph swallowed and pushed his tray away. Suddenly, he didn't feel like eating anymore.

It seemed to him that Werber was right. Santana *had* led the *Stargazer* into a trap. In fact, she must have begun plotting it long before she set foot on the ship.

But it wasn't just Commander Picard whom she had hoodwinked. She had pulled the wool over Joseph's eyes as well. If he had been his usual alert self, he might have figured the woman out in time and warned Captain Ruhalter not to trust her.

But he had allowed Santana to charm him, to draw him in. He had let his guard down. And as a result, they had lost their captain and their first officer, and come within inches of losing their ship.

Joseph promised himself that as long as he lived, he would never let someone like Santana fool him again.

Idun Asmund made a small course adjustment to avoid some space debris and watched the stars slide to starboard on the viewscreen.

Commander Picard, who was standing behind her, nodded approvingly. The hollows under his eyes gave him the look of a man sacrificing sleep and other creature comforts for the sake of doing what needed to be done.

But then, he was laboring under a great burden. He had already scoured the ship for survivors, gotten repairs underway on key systems, and moved the ship away from the coordinates of their battle in case other enemy vessels were on their way.

Truly, Picard was a warrior.

However, he seemed unequal to his task in one respect and one respect only—though he moved around the bridge like a caged *targ,* he refused to settle into the center seat.

Of course, the captain had perished less than fourteen hours ago. Quite likely, Picard still thought of the seat as Ruhalter's and avoided it out of respect.

On the other hand, a Klingon wouldn't have hesitated to sit down. In fact, Idun reflected with a secret smile, a Klingon might have put a dagger in his superior to secure such an opportunity.

The helm officer frowned, regaining her composure. She was a Starfleet officer, she reminded herself. She had sworn allegiance to the Federation and the ideals it held dear.

But she had been raised as a Klingon, and part of her still thought as Klingons did—which was why she couldn't find solace in a leader who shied from leadership.

No matter the reason.

For the next hour or so, Picard continued to haunt the bridge, checking on this console or that one, stealing glances at the viewscreen every now and then. Then, apparently satisfied that the ship's most critical needs had been met, he tapped his communicator badge.

"This is Commander Picard," he said. "I would like the following personnel to meet me in the main lounge." And he reeled off a list of names, which included all of the surviving senior officers.

A staff meeting, Idun mused. The commander was going to address the men and women working under him, just as Captain Ruhalter had addressed them when he was still alive.

Picard hadn't yet deposited himself in the captain's chair, the helm officer noted. He hadn't yet seized the reins that had been turned over to him by default.

But at least he had made a start.

Picard surveyed the personnel seated around the lounge's black, oval table, their faces turned to him with varying degrees of expectation.

There were eight of them there—Jomar, Ben Zoma, Simenon, Greyhorse, Cariello, Werber, Paxton, and Picard himself. Eight of them who would attempt to survive in an unknown part of space and salvage what they could from the embers of disaster.

Normally, Captain Ruhalter would have conducted this meeting, wringing the best out of each of them and making them more than the sum of their parts. But Captain Ruhalter, unbelievable as it seemed, was dead—and Commander Leach was in a coma from which he might never emerge. For better or worse, it was Picard's meeting to conduct . . . Picard's ship and crew to command.

The second officer hadn't asked for this. He hadn't imagined himself ensconced in a center seat until years later, when he would have had a good deal more experience under his belt. But the situation was what it was, and he was determined to do what it demanded of him.

"I called you here for two reasons," he began. "One is to announce that, effective immediately, Lieutenant Ben Zoma will assume the post of acting second-in-command. At the same time, Lieutenant Ang will take over Mr. Ben Zoma's duties in the security section."

There were nods around the table, though not from Werber, Simenon, or Jomar. No surprise there, Picard thought. Ben Zoma had never been a favorite of Commander Leach or his friends.

"The second reason for this meeting," the commander said, "is the difficult set of circumstances in which we find ourselves. As you all know, we have taken heavy damage to our primary systems. Still, it remains our duty to survive . . . and to warn the Federation that the Nuyyad are every inch the threat of which we were warned."

No one seemed inclined to argue the point. However, he did receive some wary looks—predictably, from Leach's camp.

"There are two options open to us," Picard went on. "Two choices. We can make a run for the galactic barrier in our diminished condition and hope we don't run into the Nuyyad again. Or, as an alternative, we can try to find Serenity Santana's colony and seek replacement parts there."

"Her *colony?*" Werber echoed, a look of disgust and disbelief crossing his face. "Are you insane, Picard?"

The second officer felt a spurt of anger. He swallowed it back. "You will address me as you would have addressed Captain Ruhalter," he said in a clipped tone, "or I will find a weapons officer who can."

Werber went dark with anger. "You want the respect accorded a commanding officer? Then exercise the *judgment* of a commanding officer. That Santana woman led us into a trap, Commander. She almost destroyed us. I wouldn't trust *anything* she told us."

Picard glared at the weapons officer. "Despite appearances, we do *not* know for certain that Ms. Santana engaged in any treachery."

Werber looked at him wide-eyed. "Are you blind? She led us to the slaughter like a fat, little lamb. She—"

The second officer tapped the Starfleet insignia on his chest. "Security," he said, "this is Commander Picard. I would like an officer posted outside the lounge immediately."

"Right away, sir," came the response.

The weapons chief drew in a breath, then let it out. Clearly, he didn't relish the idea of being led away by a security officer. "What I *meant* to say," he amended with an effort, "is that, under the circumstances, it would be imprudent to believe anything Santana told us."

"I agree," said Jomar, albeit without emotion. "Who knows? There may never have been any *Valiant* survivors in the first place. And even if this colony exists, Santana might not have divulged its true coordinates."

Werber looked at him. "Hang on a second. You mean to say you've never heard of this colony?"

"Never," the Kelvan confirmed.

The weapons chief seemed confused. "But aren't you from this side of the galactic barrier?"

"I am," Jomar told him. "However, space is as enormous here as it is in your galaxy, and I only became familiar with a small portion of it before I emigrated to Nalogen Four."

It was Paxton who dragged the discussion back on track. "Even if Santana's colony exists," he said, "and even if she gave us the right coordinates, her people may not be all that glad to see us."

"True," Jomar remarked without inflection. "Especially if we're right in our assumption that Santana led us into a trap."

"Plus," Simenon hissed, "our technologies may be incompatible—in which case their parts would be useless to us, even assuming they're generous enough to give them away."

"Then you're in favor of trying to reach the barrier instead," said Picard. "Is that correct?"

"It is," the engineer agreed.

"Unfortunately," Ben Zoma said, "heading for the barrier may put us in an even worse bind."

"How so?" asked Cariello.

"For one thing," the acting executive officer noted, "it's just what the Nuyyad would expect us to do—retreat and regroup. For another thing, our shields are in no shape to protect us from the barrier's energies. We would only be creating the kind of supermen that nearly destroyed the *Enterprise* and the *Valiant*."

They were good points, Picard reflected—especially the one about crossing the barrier without shields. Judging from their expressions, his officers agreed with him. Even Werber seemed a trifle less certain of himself than he had been before.

But in the final analysis, it was Picard's decision. He took a moment to mull what he had heard to that point.

"Well?" Jomar asked of him, making no effort to disguise his impatience. "What do you plan to do, Commander?"

The second officer frowned. "Like some of you, I prefer the idea of returning to the galactic barrier."

Werber nodded. "Now you're talking."

"However," Picard added, "I do not wish to create any additional threats to the Federation—nor do I relish the prospect of destroying my vessel in order to negate such threats. And as Commander Ben Zoma points out, retreating through the barrier without sufficient shielding could create some prodigious threats indeed."

Werber paled as he realized where Picard's comments were leading him. "Oh no. You're not—"

"I *am*," Picard insisted, his posture unyielding. "I am going to try to find the colony Ms. Santana described, in the hope that it will equip us to eventually make it through the barrier unscathed."

He eyed each of his companions in turn, gauging their reactions. They didn't all look happy about his decision.

"If we're to come through this crisis intact," Picard said, "and warn the Federation about the Nuyyad, I will need the help and cooperation of everyone aboard this vessel." He glanced at Werber. "Without exception."

The lounge fell silent. It wasn't exactly the vote of confidence he had been hoping for.

"I respectfully request that you reconsider," Werber said, his tone anything but respectful.

"So do I," Simenon rasped.

"You are leading us into disaster," Jomar added bluntly, undeterred by any need to observe Starfleet protocol.

Picard smiled a grim smile. Clearly, his stint as commanding officer would not be an easy one. "My decision stands. You are dismissed." He looked around the room. "All of you."

One by one, his officers and the Kelvan left the room. Ben Zoma was the last to depart. Finally, the second officer was alone.

"Navigation," he said out loud, activating the intercom system. "This is Commander Picard."

"Asmund here," came the response.

Picard licked his lips. "Chart a course for Ms. Santana's colony. I believe you have the coordinates."

"I do, sir," Asmund confirmed. If she was surprised, it wasn't reflected in her voice. "Course set."

"Helm," said the second officer, "best speed. Engage."

"Acknowledged," Idun Asmund replied.

Picard leaned back in his chair in the otherwise empty lounge. The die was cast, he told himself. Now he would see if he had made the right choice . . . or the wrong one.

Nine

Hans Werber had traveled each and every corridor of the *Stargazer* at one time or another. But he had never before traveled one so quietly or with such serious intent.

Werber wasn't alone, either. He was followed by three other officers—Chen and Ramirez of his weapons section and Pernell of engineering. And all four of them were armed with phaser pistols that Werber had lifted with the help of his security clearance.

The weapons chief knew they didn't have much time. Pausing at an intersection, he peeked into the perpendicular passageway to make sure it was empty. Then he made a left turn, his fellow conspirators in tow.

Their objective was the third set of doors on the right. As soon as he arrived there, Werber removed a small tool from his tunic and inserted the end of it into an aperture in the bulkhead.

A moment later, the doors slid apart, granting him access to a suite. Leaving Pernell to close the doors again, Werber and the others moved into the darkness within.

Reluctant to warn the suite's occupant, the weapons chief decided not to turn on the lights. Instead, his phaser held in front of him, he advanced to the sleeping quarters at the apartment's far end.

So far, he reflected, everything had gone smoothly. But their job wasn't over yet. Far from it.

The door to the bedroom was open. Taking a deep, slow breath, Werber made his way inside. Then he trained his weapon on the vague outline of the bed and reached for the light padd on the wall.

As he turned up the illumination, he fired his phaser. Its lurid, red beam slammed into the bedcovers with enough force to stun an ox—or in this case, the misguided commanding officer of a starship.

But as Werber's eyes adjusted to the light, he saw that something was wrong. Picard's bed was empty . . . except for a small, bronze object of some kind. He took a closer look—

—and saw that it was a combadge.

Suddenly, the weapons chief realized what he had stumbled into. His throat constricting, his blood pounding in his temples, he whirled and launched himself back through the doorway. But by then, the dimly lit anteroom was rife with ruby-red phaser bolts.

Before Werber could do anything about it, one of the beams caught Chen in the chest and drove him into the wall behind him. Then a second shaft slugged Ramirez in the jaw, spinning him around.

As Ramirez collapsed alongside Chen, Werber fired at one of the several cranberry-colored tunics in the room. What's more, he thought he hit one. But as he tried to squeeze off a second shot, he felt something kick him in the wrist and saw his weapon go flying out of his hand.

Cradling his injured wrist, Werber saw who had disarmed him. It was Picard, a phaser in his hand. And there were three other figures behind him—Pug Joseph and two of his fellow security officers.

"Picard to Ben Zoma," said the second officer, making use of the ship's intercom system since his combadge was elsewhere.

"Ben Zoma here," came the answer. "We've discovered a few rats in my quarters, but they won't bother us again. And you?"

"We've taken care of Werber," Picard replied soberly.

The weapons chief scowled at the byplay. "This wouldn't have been necessary if you'd made the right decision," he spat.

Picard didn't argue the point. Instead, he gestured with his phaser, indicating the corridor outside. "Take these mutineers to the brig," he told the security officers. "If they require medical attention, Dr. Greyhorse can see them there."

"Aye, sir," Joseph replied.

Rather than wait to be manhandled, Werber put his head down and made his way to the turbolift.

Picard wasn't sure how many times the chimes sounded outside his quarters before he woke enough to acknowledge them.

Glancing at the chronometer that sat alongside his bed, he saw that it was almost time for him to get up anyway. And if it had been any other morning, he wouldn't have minded doing so in the least.

However, he had been up the better part of the night laying in wait for Werber and his compatriots. And even after the second officer had sprung his trap, he had had trouble sleeping.

It was understandable, he told himself. Armed mutinies had a way of unsettling one.

Swinging his legs out of bed, Picard got to his feet and pulled a robe on. Just in case his visitor was a tardy mutineer, he picked up the phaser he had acquired and tucked it into the palm of his hand. Then he made his way to the next room.

"Come," he said.

The sliding doors whooshed open, revealing the lizardlike form of Phigus Simenon standing in the corridor outside. The Gnalish's eyes were slitted and even more fiery than usual.

"Are you crazy?" he demanded of Picard, gesticulating as he entered the room. "Have you lost your mind entirely?"

Perhaps it was his weariness. Perhaps it was the undeniable frustration in Simenon's voice. Either way, the second officer wasn't inclined to take umbrage at the way he was being addressed.

"I would have to say 'no' to both questions," he answered drily. "Why do you ask?"

"Why do I ask?" the engineer echoed. "Could it have something to do with the way you've treated Werber and half a dozen other officers—throwing them in the brig just for disagreeing with your decisions?" He waddled up to Picard and glowered at him nose-to-snout. "While you're at it, Commander, why don't you throw *me* in the brig as well?"

The second officer waved away the notion. "You misunderstand," he said. "I didn't have Mr. Werber and his friends incarcerated because they disagreed with me. I had them incarcerated because they invaded my quarters with phasers in their hands and mutiny on their minds."

Simenon looked at him askance. "Mutiny . . . ?" he rasped.

"Indeed," Picard confirmed. "And it would have succeeded had it not been for Lieutenant Vigo in the weapons section, who overheard Werber and two of his fellow officers making plans to neutralize me."

The Gnalish gaped at him, then shook his head. "You're lying."

"I assure you," said the second officer, "I am not. Werber led an attempt at mutiny last night. If you have any doubts, you can ask one of the security officers who helped capture the conspirators."

In all the weeks Picard had spent on the *Stargazer,* he had never seen Phigus Simenon at a loss for words . . . until that very moment. The engineer looked positively deflated.

"You know," Simenon grated after a while, "it's not in my nature to admit that I'm wrong."

"So I gather," said the second officer.

"That fact notwithstanding," the Gnalish continued, "it seems I may have misjudged you."

"Actually," Picard said generously, "I may have misjudged you as well."

Simenon's eyes narrowed. "How so?"

"Frankly," the second officer told him, "I expected to find you among the mutineers. In their forefront, in fact. I would say we're both capable of jumping to conclusions."

The engineer snorted. "Apparently."

Picard considered Simenon. He and the Gnalish hadn't ever spoken at length before, especially about personal matters. But now that they had, the second officer found himself liking the fellow.

"I think I'll slink off now," said Simenon. "I've got some friends in the brig who'll no doubt need cheering up." He hesitated. "That is, if it's all right with my commanding officer."

Picard nodded. "Go ahead. Just one request."

"What's that?" asked the Gnalish.

"Don't slip any of the prisoners a phaser. I don't think the guards I've posted would appreciate it."

Simenon chuckled. "You have my word." Then, dragging his scaly tail behind him, he left Picard's quarters.

The second officer watched his doors slide closed behind the engineer. Then he returned to his bedroom and put down his phaser.

Someone had once told him that something good comes out of even the worst circumstances. If he had established even a small bond of trust with Simenon, perhaps there was an upside to the mutiny attempt after all.

In all the months he had spent on the *Stargazer,* Lieutenant Vigo had never visited the captain's ready room.

He had seen plenty of other officers entering and leaving the place from his vantage point at the bridge's weapons console. Sometimes, he had even gotten a glimpse of what it looked like inside. It was just that he himself had never been summoned there.

Until just a couple of minutes ago.

Standing outside the ready room doors, Vigo waited for the internal sensors to recognize his presence and alert Picard to the fact. A moment later, Vigo knew that the sensors had done their job, because the doors whispered open and gave him access.

He could see the second officer standing near an observation port, to one side of the captain's sleek, black desk. Picard smiled. "Please, Lieutenant. Take a seat."

"Thank you, sir," Vigo replied. He pulled out a chair that stood across the desk from the captain's and tried to make himself comfortable—not an easy thing for a being of his bulk.

Picard regarded him for a moment. Then he said, "I take it you heard about Lieutenant Werber."

The Pandrilite nodded. "That he was caught. Yes, sir."

Vigo had been forced to carry out his regular assignments, pretending that he didn't know anything about the mutiny. Otherwise, Werber and his comrades might have suspected a leak and called it off.

Knowing what was taking place elsewhere on the ship, it was difficult for him to keep his mind on his work. Almost impossible, in fact. But somehow, he had managed.

Then, early that morning, while he and two other crewmen were repairing a phaser turret, Vigo had heard the news. Werber and his mutineers had been caught. Picard and Ben Zoma had prevailed.

It hadn't given him any special pleasure to know that he was the one who had scuttled the mutiny. He had only done his duty, after all. There was nothing personal in it—only a sense of relief.

"Obviously," said Picard, "I can't allow Lieutenant Werber to go free. Not after what he tried to do."

"Yes, sir," Vigo agreed.

"And if he's in the brig," the second officer continued, "he can hardly serve as weapons chief."

The Pandrilite began to see where the conversation was going. Why would Picard discuss this with *him* unless . . .

"Sir," he blurted, "I didn't expose Lieutenant Werber's plans so I could replace him as weapons chief."

Picard smiled understandingly. "I know that, Lieutenant. In point of fact, I have had my eye on you for some time. I can tell you that few crewmen in any section, weapons or otherwise, have demonstrated as much dedication to their work as you have."

The Pandrilite was surprised. As far as he had been able to tell, only Werber had had the chance to see how hard he was working—and for whatever reason, the weapons chief had refused to acknowledge it.

"That's kind of you, sir," said Vigo.

"You needn't be humble," Picard told him. "It's part of my job to identify personnel with the potential for advancement. And, I'm happy to say, you have such potential. Even if Mr. Werber hadn't acted as he did, you would still have been considered for a promotion."

The Pandrilite found himself smiling. "It's gratifying to hear you say that, sir."

"Then you'll accept a promotion to weapons chief?" Picard asked.

Vigo's conscience was clear. Under the circumstances, how could he refuse? "I will," he assured the second officer. "Thank you again, sir."

"No, Mr. Vigo. Thank *you*. And by the way, your promotion is effective immediately. I will inform Commander Ben Zoma."

"Yes, sir," said the Pandrilite.

As he left the lounge, he felt a little dazed. But more than that, he felt vindicated. He had acted honorably . . . and contrary to the expectations of his friends, his actions had been rewarded.

There was some justice in the universe after all.

It was part of Gerda Asmund's job to conduct periodic long-range sensor scans—even when they *weren't* in an unfamiliar and potentially hostile sector of space.

Since the attack by the Nuyyad ship, she had been inclined to conduct her scans three times as often as usual. For the first thirty-two hours, she hadn't turned up anything interesting—including the colony described by Serenity Santana. But then, at that point, the place's coordinates were still outside their sensor range.

In the thirty-third hour, one of Gerda's sweeps picked up a concentration of thermal and electromagnetic radiation on what appeared to be a M-Class planet. She knew the signs. This wasn't a natural phenomenon. It was an installation of some kind—manufactured by a sentient civilization.

Just to be certain, Gerda checked its coordinates. Then she examined its sensor profile a second time. It was then that she noticed a second energy concentration— one so close to the first that it was almost indistinguishable from it at this distance.

But the second concentration wasn't on the planet's surface. The navigator could see that now. Unless she was mistaken, it was marginally closer than the first concentration.

In orbit above it.

Gerda turned to Commander Picard. "Sir?"

Picard approached her. "Yes, Lieutenant?"

"I think you should see this," she told him.

* * *

Picard again found himself addressing a lounge full of officers. As before, he had convened them on the heels of a tumultuous event that had resulted in a new face among them.

But it wasn't Werber's mutiny that had spurred this meeting. It was something a good deal more ominous.

The second officer leaned forward in his chair. *The captain's chair,* he remarked inwardly, correcting himself. "I called you here to apprise you of our most recent long-range sensor report. Though I normally steer clear of glib remarks, I cannot help describing it as good news and bad news."

"First," he said, "the good news. It seems the colony described by Serenity Santana exists after all. Furthermore, it is located at the coordinates with which she provided us."

There were expressions of relief all around the table. If the long-range sensors hadn't found Santana's colony, their chances of survival would have been almost nil.

"You are certain of this?" asked Jomar.

"Quite certain," Picard assured him.

The Kelvan's pale blue eyes narrowed. "And how long will it take us to reach this colony?"

"Approximately nine days," said the second officer. "Unless, of course, we can find a way to go faster than warp five."

"Which isn't likely," Simenon interjected flatly.

"What's the bad news?" asked Greyhorse.

Picard frowned. "There is a ship in orbit around Santana's colony. We believe it is a Nuyyad vessel."

He could feel the air in the lounge turning sour as his news sank in. He wasn't surprised in the least. The *Stargazer* was in no shape to endure another battle with the Nuyyad.

And yet, the only way to make themselves battle-ready again was to go through the enemy. They were in a quandary, to say the least.

"Clearly," he said, "we need a plan."

Jomar shook his head scornfully. "What we need, Commander, are weapons. And we have very few of those."

"Then we'll make some," Vigo interjected.

The Kelvan turned to him, his features in repose but his posture one of skepticism. "Out of what, if I may ask?"

"That is the question," Picard agreed. He looked around the table. "Considering the ingenuity and expertise represented in this room, I was hoping to get some answers."

It was a challenge, nothing more. However, there was an unexpected edge in Jomar's normally neutral voice as he answered it.

"We could have had weapons specifically designed with the Nuyyad in mind," he reminded them. "However, you turned down my offer to make them for you. Now it is too late for that."

"With all due respect," Picard told him, "there were reasons we turned down your offer. And as you say, it's too late to contemplate making those weapons now, so let's discuss something we *can* accomplish."

He addressed the entire group again. "In nine days, we will reach Ms. Santana's colony. If by that time, we cannot come up with a way to neutralize the Nuyyad presence there, we will have failed in our duty to the Federation—and I, for one, will not accept such an outcome."

For a moment, no one said anything. Then Vigo spoke up again, his blue brow furrowed with concentration. "I think I have an idea, sir."

"By all means," Picard told him, "share it with us."

The Pandrilite described what he had in mind. It didn't involve any exotic technology. But before he was finished, everyone in the lounge was a little more hopeful. Even Jomar.

Ten

Picard stood in front of the captain's chair and gazed at the forward viewscreen, where he could clearly see a Nuyyad vessel in orbit around a blue, green, and white planet.

The enemy ship looked exactly like the first one they had encountered. It was immense, flat, diamond-shaped . . . and more than likely, equipped with the same powerful vidrion cannons that had inflicted so much punishment on the *Stargazer* already.

Picard tried not to contemplate how much more damage they could do without any shields to slow them down.

"There it is," said Ben Zoma, who had come over to stand beside him.

The second officer nodded. "Slow to half impulse, helm."

"Half impulse," Idun confirmed.

Picard turned to Vigo, who was sitting in Werber's spot behind the weapons console. "Are the shuttles ready?" he asked.

"They are, sir," came the Pandrilite's response.

The second officer turned back to the screen. "Release them."

"Aye, sir," said Vigo.

Picard watched the viewscreen. If the Nuyyad vessel had picked up the *Stargazer* on her sensors, she wasn't giving the least indication of it. She was just sitting there in orbit around Santana's planet, looking like a large, deadly blade.

Abruptly, a handful of smaller craft invaded the screen from its bottom edge—seven remote-controlled Starfleet shuttles hurtling through the void at full impulse, rapidly leaving the *Stargazer* behind. The shuttles, which ranged in size up to a Type-7 personnel carrier, looked dwarfed by the Nuyyad ship even though the latter was much more distant.

"Status?" Picard demanded.

Gerda answered him. "Eighty seconds to target."

The commander could feel his heart thud against his ribs. Eighty seconds. Five million kilometers. The difference between victory and defeat, life and death, survival and annihilation.

Ben Zoma cast him a look of confidence, a look that seemed to assure Picard that everything would be all right. Then he retreated to the engineering console and began monitoring ship's systems.

Each of the shuttles carried an antimatter payload big enough to punch a hole in the Nuyyad vessel's shields. But to accomplish that feat, they would have to reach the enemy unscathed—and that, Picard reflected, was easier said than done.

He had barely completed the thought when one of the shuttles became a flare of white light on the viewscreen. Cursing beneath his breath, he whirled on his weapons officer.

"What happened, Mr. Vigo?"

The Pandrilite shook his large blue head, obviously as confused by the premature explosion as Picard was. "I don't know, sir. I didn't trigger it, I can tell you that."

"I can confirm that," Ben Zoma interjected. "The payload seemed to go off on its own."

The second officer could feel his teeth grinding. If the other shuttles went off prematurely, they would be all but toothless. The Nuyyad vessel could pick them off at its leisure.

"Fifty seconds," Gerda announced.

It was time for the *Stargazer* to enter the fray. "Full impulse," Picard told Idun Asmund.

"Aye, sir," said the helm officer.

"Power phasers," the commander added.

"Powering phasers," Vigo replied, activating the batteries that could still generate a charge.

"Forty seconds," declared Gerda, her face caught in the glare of her navigation controls.

He glanced at Ben Zoma. His friend returned it—and even managed a jaunty smile. *I've still got confidence in you,* it seemed to say.

Suddenly, a green globe shot out from the Nuyyad ship and skewered one of the shuttles. Again, Picard saw a flash of brilliance. Then a second shuttle was hit. It too vanished in a splash of glory.

That left four of the smaller craft—a little more than half of what they had started out with. And they still hadn't gotten within two million kilometers of their target.

"Evasive maneuvers," said the second officer.

"Aye, sir," Vigo responded, implementing one of the patterns they had programmed in advance.

On the screen, the shuttles began banking and weaving, making the enemy's job that much more difficult. Unfortunately, it would get easier again as they got closer to the Nuyyad vessel.

"Thirty seconds," said the navigator.

Picard desperately wanted to accelerate the shuttles' progress. But he didn't dare have them drop in and out of warp speed so close to a planet, where gravity added a potentially disastrous layer of difficulty.

In the end, he had no choice. He would have to grit his teeth and hope the shuttles did their job.

The Nuyyad fired another series of green vidrion blasts. However, to Picard's relief, none of them found their marks. The four remaining shuttles went on, intact.

Gerda looked up from her controls, no doubt eager to see the drama with her own eyes. "Twenty seconds."

The enemy vessel unleashed yet another wave of vidrion splendor. For a moment, as the *Stargazer*'s shuttles passed through it, Picard lost sight of them. Then the emerald brilliance of the energy bursts faded and he was able to catch a glimpse of the smaller craft.

There were three left, it seemed. Part of that light display must have been one of them exploding.

One less shuttle meant one less shot at success. That was the inescapable reality of it. But they were getting close now to the enemy. With luck, Vigo's plan would pan out.

Again, Picard shot a look at Ben Zoma. As before, the man didn't seem to have a care in the world.

"Phaser range," the weapons officer announced.

"Fire on my mark," Picard barked.

The Nuyyad bombarded the shuttles again, lighting torches of pale green fire in the void. Picard squinted to see through them, to get an idea of whether any of his craft had made it through.

"Five seconds," said Gerda. "Four. Three . . ."

Then Picard spotted them—not just one of the shuttles, but all three. As his navigator counted down to zero, they smashed headlong into the Nuyyad's deflector shields.

And went off.

If the vidrion bursts had been showy, the shuttle explosions were positively magnificent, magnified by their reflection off the enemy's shields. But Picard didn't take any time to appreciate their glory. His sole interest was how much damage they could do.

"Fire!" he bellowed.

Instantly, the starboard phaser banks lashed out with everything they had, driving their crimson energy through each of the three spots where the shuttles had exploded.

Picard turned to Gerda. "Report!"

"We've penetrated their shields!" she told him. "Sensors show significant damage to their hull!"

He turned back to the viewscreen, smelling the victory they had been hoping for. "Fire again, Mr. Vigo!"

A second time, the *Stargazer*'s phaser beams slashed through the enemy's tattered shields, piercing the vessel's outer skin and setting off a string of small explosions.

But the Nuyyad wasn't ready to call it quits yet. A moment after Picard's ship fired, the enemy unleashed a salvo of its own.

"Brace yourselves!" the second officer called out.

Fortunately, Idun managed to slip past most of the barrage—but not all of it. The force of the vidrion assault drove Picard to the deck, his head missing the base of Ruhalter's chair by inches.

Consoles exploded aft of him, shooting geysers of white-hot sparks at the ceiling. As a cloud of smoke began to gather, he dragged himself up and glared at the viewscreen.

The enemy ship had suffered extensive damage, her hull plates twisted and blackened from stem to stern. Still, she was functioning—and if she was functioning, she was a threat.

Picard meant to put an end to it. "Mr. Vigo," he said, trying not to choke on the smoke filling his bridge, "fire again!"

On the screen, the Nuyyad vessel seemed to writhe under the impact of the *Stargazer*'s phaser beams. She was wracked by one internal explosion after another as the directed energy ripped into key systems. Finally, unable to endure the torment any longer, she flew apart in a splash of gold that blotted out the stars.

Picard wasn't a bloodthirsty man and never had been. However, he found himself nodding in approval as pieces of Nuyyad debris spun through space in an ever-expanding wave.

He glanced over his shoulder at the ruined aft consoles. Ben Zoma and a couple of other officers had gotten hold of fire extinguishers and were spraying foam over the flames, though the control panels themselves would require extensive repairs.

Ben Zoma seemed to sense that his friend was watching him. Returning the look, he smiled a big smile. You see? he seemed to say. I told you you could do it.

The second officer turned to Gerda. "Report."

The navigator consulted her monitor. "Damage to decks three, four, and six," she replied. "Photon torpedo launchers are off-line. Likewise, the starboard sensor array."

Picard grunted. They were shieldless and half-blind, and their once-powerful arsenal was limited to a couple of battered phaser banks. But it could have been worse.

Much worse.

"Casualties?" he asked.

Gerda paused for a moment, then looked up at him. "None, sir. Everyone made it through intact."

It was better than the second officer might have guessed—better even than he might have hoped. "Excellent," he said.

There was only one thing left to do. After all, they had come all this way for a reason. He regarded the forward screen, which now showed him an unobstructed view of the planet.

"Mr. Paxton," he said, "hail the colony."

"Aye, sir," came the response.

Almost a minute passed as Paxton tried one frequency after another. Finally, he seemed to hit on the right one.

"They're returning our hail," he told Picard.

The commander folded his arms across his chest. "On screen."

Abruptly, the image on the viewscreen was replaced by that of a long-faced, middle-aged man with thick eyebrows and dark, wavy hair. He seemed to stare at Picard for a moment, as if he couldn't believe his eyes.

Then he smiled.

"You're from Earth," he concluded. "So Daniels and Santana must have reached you."

"They did indeed," Picard confirmed. He identified himself as the commander of the *Stargazer*.

"My name is Shield Williamson," said the colonist. "I'm in charge here. Speaking for everyone, I have to tell you how grateful we are that you chose to help us."

"Especially after you led us into a trap," Picard expanded, hoping to nail down at least that bit of information.

Williamson's smile faded. But far from denying the charge, he nodded soberly. "Yes. After that."

"I trust the Nuyyad ship we destroyed had something to do with it?" the commander suggested.

The colonist sighed. "It had everything to do with it."

"I would like very much to hear the details," said Picard. "But first, I need to know if you will assist us. We have suffered considerable damage at the hands of the Nuyyad. We were hoping—"

"That we could help with repairs?" Williamson spread his hands out. "Absolutely—however we can. As I said, Commander, we're grateful for what you did for us—especially in light of what happened before."

"Thank you," said Picard.

"It's the least we can do," the colonist told him. "And if I may ask, how are our people—Daniels and Santana?"

The second officer frowned. "Daniels was detained for security reasons by our Starfleet. There were suspicions about him and Santana, as you seem to have anticipated."

"I'm sorry to hear that," said Williamson. "And what of Santana? Is she with you now?"

"She is," Picard told him. "However, she was severely injured in the Nuyyad's ambush."

The colonist looked devastated. "Is she alive?"

"Yes. But she seems to have withdrawn into some sort of coma. Our doctor is at a loss as to—"

"Our physicians will know how to treat her," Williamson assured him. "But we've got to hurry. Her condition sounds precarious."

Picard had no intention of hanging onto Santana if there was any chance her people could help her. She may have led the *Stargazer* into a deadly trap, but it wasn't his place to demand an eye for an eye.

"As you wish," he replied. "I'll notify my ship's surgeon." He tapped his combadge. "Picard to Greyhorse. We're going to beam Santana down to the colony."

"That's fine," came the medical officer's reply. "I'll prepare her for transport immediately. But I want to come along, Commander. The woman is my patient, remember."

Picard regarded Williamson. "Do you have a problem with Dr. Greyhorse beaming down as well?"

The colonist looked at him as if he had grown another head. "Beaming down?" he echoed.

The second officer had forgotten . . . Santana's people were descended from a crew that left Earth nearly three hundred years earlier. At that time, there were no such things as molecular imaging scanners, phase transition coils, and pattern buffers.

As Earth pushed out into the galaxy in the twenty-second century, there had been a need for a quick way to board and disembark from spacegoing vessels— and transporter systems had filled that need. However, the colonists might never have been impelled in that direction.

"It's a sophisticated procedure," he explained, "in which a subject is disassembled at the subatomic level, transmitted to another location and reassembled at the other end."

Williamson looked at him. "Impressive. And are there any . . . casualties when you employ this technology?"

"None when the equipment is working correctly," Picard assured him. "And without question, it would be the fastest way to convey Ms. Santana to your planet's surface."

The colonist hesitated—but only for a moment. "Very well. Where should we expect your medical officer and Santana to arrive?"

"Where would you *like* them to arrive?"

Williamson thought about it. "What about the plaza outside our central medical facility? It's shaped like a hexagon and it sits between two of our tallest towers."

Picard glanced at his communications officer. "Mr. Paxton?"

Paxton responded without looking up. "I'm relaying the information to Lieutenant Vandermeer now, sir."

"Actually," Williamson interjected, "you may want to consider accompanying your medical officer. At some point, Commander, you and I will need to speak in person. It might as well be now."

"Sir," said Paxton, before Picard could give the colonist an answer, "Lieutenant Vandermeer says she's located the hexagonal plaza."

"Acknowledged," the second officer responded.

Ben Zoma, who had returned to the engineering console, whispered, "You're not going down there without a security escort, are you?"

Picard glanced at him. It was the type of sentiment he might have expressed to Captain Ruhalter just a few days earlier. But somehow, it sounded less urgent when one was on the other side of the rail.

He turned back to the colonist. "I would like to take you up on that," he said diplomatically. "However, I am not the only one who would like to speak with you."

"Bring whomever you wish," Williamson responded. "Even a security team, if you feel you need one. But as you'll see, Commander, we no longer have any reason to deceive you."

After their experience with Santana, Picard had no business believing Williamson. But for some reason, he did.

Eleven

Evening had already fallen on the colonists' continent when Jean-Luc Picard and his entourage beamed down from the Stargazer.

The second officer could have accompanied Greyhorse and Santana to the medical facility as he originally intended. However, he had instead accepted Shield Williamson's invitation to meet him in his offices.

Picard was instantly pleased that he had made that choice. Looking out from a semicircular balcony, he found himself gazing at the most impressive city he had ever seen.

It was sleek, elegant, magnificent in scale . . . a titanic landscape of hundred-story-high buildings with proud, rounded shoulders and breathtaking, sky-spanning footbridges, cast in soft pinks and yellows by an abundance of tethered, softly glowing globes.

Hovercars of different sizes and shapes sailed effortlessly through the spired landscape, looking like graceful, exotic fish in the depths of an alien ocean. As for foliage . . . dark blue trees and shrubs were everywhere, defining spacious, ground-level plazas and overhanging public balconies, filling the air with a pleasant, slightly tart fragrance.

Picard had never been here before. And yet, it seemed to him that he *had* been here, or at least someplace very much like it.

And he knew why. As a cadet at Starfleet Academy, he had studied many things—archaeology, drama, and astrophysics, to name a few. He had also developed more than a passing interest in architecture.

In the year 2064, a year before the *S.S. Valiant* left Earth orbit, a Frenchman named Goimard had unveiled his vision for rebuilding a world that had been wracked by its third World War. Unfortunately—at least from Picard's point of view—that vision had only blossomed in dribs and drabs, a series of perhaps thirty buildings in nearly as many locations.

Evidently, he reflected, one of the *Valiant*'s survivors had been a Goimard aficionado—because here, on a planet a great many light-years from Earth, the Frenchman's dream had been realized in all its glory. Picard felt compelled to smile at the irony.

"Not bad for a ragtag band of survivors," Ben Zoma quipped.

"They've had almost three hundred years to build," Picard reminded him. "This place could be thirty years older than our colony on Mars."

"Welcome to Magnia," said Williamson.

The second officer turned and saw their host approaching them through a wide, arched set of sliding doors. In person, Williamson was considerably taller than he had appeared on the viewscreen. He was also alone—a clear demonstration of trust.

Picard smiled. "Magnia," he said, letting the word roll off his tongue. "Goimard's name for his perfect city."

The colonist's eyebrows shot up. "You know his work?"

"I do," said the second officer. "And frankly, I'm delighted to see it expressed here so faithfully. No doubt, Goimard himself would have been delighted as well."

"We like to think so," Williamson replied.

"How is Santana?" Picard inquired.

The colonist's expression sobered. "She suffered considerable damage. However, our physicians tell me she'll be all right."

"That's good to hear."

Williamson indicated the arched doorway with a gesture. "Shall we?" he said, and led the way.

His offices were expansive, with rounded, pastel-colored furniture, ornate moldings, and an entire wall full of oval monitors. Each screen showed them a repair effort in a particular part of the city.

Picard looked at their host. "Your defenses, I take it?"

"Yes," said Williamson. "I dispatched teams to our shield generators as soon as I knew that the Nuyyad were gone." He gazed critically at one screen in particular. "Unfortunately, they're not gone for good. The Nuyyad are eventually going to figure out what happened to their ship—and when they do, they'll be merciless."

Picard had no doubt of it. After all, he had experienced the Nuyyad's propensity for violence firsthand.

"I don't suppose you've had a chance to plan for that contingency?" the colonist asked him optimistically.

The second officer shook his head. "I must admit, I have not. However, I am of the mind that Magnia and the *Stargazer* can help each other out of this predicament . . . if they so choose."

"Rest assured," Williamson told him earnestly, "my people will do anything you require of them."

"I am glad to hear you say that. Mainly, we are in need of parts to replace those the Nuyyad destroyed. Though I realize your technologies and ours may have developed along different lines, I am hopeful that you either have the necessary parts on hand or can manufacture them for us."

The colonist shrugged. "I would be glad to have my engineers take a look at the specifications."

"And in return," said Picard, glancing at the oval screens, "we will see what we can do to expedite your repair schedule."

Williamson nodded. "That would be much appreciated."

"Are you familiar with the Kelvans?" Ben Zoma asked.

Unexpectedly, the other man's expression seemed to sour. "I am," he said. "Why do you ask?"

"We have a Kelvan on board," Ben Zoma explained, "an engineer named Jomar who seems to know Nuyyad tactical systems pretty well. You may want to consult with him."

Williamson didn't answer right away.

"Judging by your expression and your silence," Picard asked, "am I to infer that you've had conflicts with the Kelvans?"

The colonist frowned. "They're not the Nuyyad," he said, "I'll grant you that. But those few we've met have been arrogant and untrustworthy in their dealings with us."

Picard smiled. "Jomar *can* be arrogant at times. On the other hand, he's absolutely dedicated to stopping the Nuyyad from invading the Federation. If I were you, I would take advantage of that dedication."

Williamson thought for a moment, then nodded. "All right. In the interest of working together, we'll welcome this Jomar as well."

"Good," said Picard. "But before we work out the details, I would like to know more about the Nuyyad's interest in your world . . . as it may shape some of our tactical decisions."

"Of course."

"From what I have seen so far," the second officer went on, "the Nuyyad did not have any presence here on your planet's surface. They seemed content to remain on their vessel."

"That's true," the colonist responded.

"Then why bother to come here at all?" asked Ben Zoma.

Williamson smiled ruefully. "Actually," he said, "it was your fault. Your Federation's, I mean."

Picard was surprised. "The Federation's?"

"That's right," the colonist told him. "A short time ago, the Nuyyad got wind of your existence—apparently, from a species that routinely crosses the galactic barrier. They're known as the Liharon."

Picard nodded. "Yes . . . I am familiar with the Liharon. They are traders, for the most part."

"They trade, all right," said Williamson. "But not material goods. Their main business is information."

Again, the Earthman was surprised. "The Liharon are spies? No one in Starfleet has ever suspected . . ."

"Of course not," said the colonist. "If everyone knew the Liharon for what they are, they wouldn't be very effective."

"I guess not," Ben Zoma allowed.

Williamson continued. "Once the Nuyyad knew something about the Federation, they couldn't help seeing it as a potential conquest. But before they could launch a military offensive on the other side of the barrier, they needed to know more about your defensive capabilities."

The second officer began to understand. "And even the Liharon couldn't obtain that kind of data. Then someone pointed out the similarities between your people and the human species . . ."

"Exactly," said the colonist. "An intrusion into our database confirmed the connection. We were human, the Nuyyad discovered. Even better, we shared a common history with Federation humans. And if we sent a plea for help to the Federation, it would likely be answered."

Picard grunted thoughtfully. "So it *was* our fault that the Nuyyad were drawn to you."

Williamson smiled again. "As I said. Mind you, none of us wanted to cooperate with them. We had no desire to be part of their plans for conquest. However, we had little choice in the matter."

"Because the Nuyyad had taken your world hostage," Ben Zoma observed.

"Yes," said the colonist. "Once they had us where they wanted us, they went through our records. After a while, they selected two 'volunteers' on the basis of intelligence and resourcefulness."

"Daniels and Santana," said Picard.

"Daniels and Santana," Williamson confirmed. "They were to visit Federation territory and lure a Starfleet vessel out past the barrier."

"Judas goats," Ben Zoma noted.

"Yes," said the colonist. "Though quite unwillingly. After all, they hated the Nuyyad species and all it stood for. However, the alternative to cooperation was to see their families and friends tortured to death, and that was too bloody a scenario for either of them to contemplate."

Picard couldn't help sympathizing with Santana's plight. Had he been given the same choice by the Nuyyad, he would have had a difficult time deciding which road to take.

"I hope you understand," said Williamson, "how terrible we feel about this. We're a proud people. The notion of being forced to do something against our will is anathema to us."

Picard nodded. "And the fact that you were betraying your own species must have made it even more difficult."

The remark elicited an unexpected change in the colonist's demeanor. He seemed aloof for a moment, almost resentful. However, he continued to look the Starfleet officer in the eye.

"Clearly," he said, "we didn't warm to the prospect of deceiving anyone. But to be perfectly honest, Commander Picard . . . we feel no more kinship with Earth than we do with any other inhabited world."

At first, the second officer thought he might have heard incorrectly. Then he saw the boggled expression on Ben Zoma's face.

"And why is that?" Picard asked the colonist.

Williamson shrugged. "Put yourself in our ancestors' positions. You've risked your life to push out your people's boundaries, to further Earth's knowledge of the galaxy. And yet, when you fail to return, what does your homeworld do for you?

"Does it plan a rescue? Does it dispatch another vessel to go after you, to see if there were any survivors of your flight? Even after Federation technology allows your people to cross the barrier unscathed, does even one Earth ship come out here to determine your fate?"

"The *Valiant*'s captain sent out a message buoy," Picard noted. "It suggested that he was going to destroy his ship."

"And that was enough?" Williamson asked evenly. "Nobody cared enough to pursue the matter further?"

There was little the commander could say to that. "Apparently not," he conceded, feeling a twinge of shame on the Federation's behalf.

The colonist spread his hands out. "Then I ask you . . . is it any wonder we no longer feel any particular kinship with Earth? Is it a surprise that we've come to see ourselves as a separate civilization . . . even a separate species in some respects?"

Picard saw Williamson's point. As far as the Magnians were concerned, Earth and its people were a distant memory . . . and under the circumstances, not an especially sweet one.

Of course, he still didn't approve of what Santana had done. It was still an act of treachery that had cost some of his comrades their lives. However, he understood now why she was willing to contemplate it.

"I would like to return to my ship now," said Picard, "and put together the engineering teams that will help you."

"Excellent," Williamson told him. "And I will put some teams together to help *you.*"

It seemed like an arrangement from which both sides could only benefit. Picard hoped that it would actually work out that way.

Greyhorse peered through the oval window at Serenity Santana and her Magnian physicians. Then he turned to Law, the medical center's director, who stood beside him in a white lab coat.

"This is how you treat *all* your patients?" he asked.

Law, a small man with Asian features, shook his head. "Only those who *can* be treated this way. Direct mental stimulation is a valuable tool, make no mistake. But in many cases, we're still forced to resort to pharmaceuticals or even scalpels."

On the other side of the window, Santana was lying on a narrow bed under a set of low-hanging blue lights. None of the four doctors surrounding her was actually touching the woman. Instead, they seemed to be leaning over her, eyes closed, focusing on an invisible process.

"What's your success rate using this kind of procedure?" Greyhorse wondered aloud, his inquiry sounding more blunt than he had intended.

Law smiled. "Very high, I'm pleased to say. More than ninety-eight percent. And we are constantly trying to improve on that." He watched his colleagues work on Santana. "Of course, in the present case, the problem was a little more complicated, since the patient's injury took place days ago and had already been treated in other ways."

The ship's surgeon looked at the smaller man. "Are you saying I actually set you back?"

The colonist shrugged. "Just a little. The important thing is that Serenity will be fine."

"You sound as if you know her," Greyhorse observed.

"I do," said Law. "She was a playmate of my eldest daughter. But then, most people in Magnia know each other, if only by family or reputation. After all, Doctor, we're a small community. It's only recently that our population has begun to nudge a hundred thousand."

"In the city, you mean?"

The Magnian smiled again. "Very few people live *outside* the city. Despite the complications created by our telepathic abilities, we have come to enjoy the feeling of having others in close proximity."

Greyhorse didn't understand. "It seems to me that proximity would tend to preclude privacy."

"Not here," Law told him.

Picard saw Simenon's blood-red eyes narrow in disbelief. "You promised them *what?*" he spat.

The second officer, who was sitting on the other side of the lounge's black, oval table, frowned at the engineer's response. "I made available our technical expertise to help them repair their shield generators. It seemed like an eminently reasonable offer, given their willingness to come up with the parts we need."

Simenon harrumphed. "You call it reasonable to put your crew in the hands of the same people who led you into an ambush?"

Picard regarded the Gnalish, one of three individuals whom he had invited to this meeting. The other two were Jomar and Vigo, the acting weapons chief, who sat on either side of Simenon.

"It is true," said the second officer, "that we may be placing the fox in charge of the hen house. Nonetheless, I am inclined to trust the Magnians' intentions in this regard."

"After what they did to us?" the engineer asked.

Picard nodded. "Shield Williamson could have denied his people's role in the ambush, but he chose not to do so. He told me what they had done and why, without pulling any punches."

Simenon's eyes narrowed, but he didn't try to interrupt. The second officer took that as a good sign.

"Furthermore," he said, "Williamson could have refrained from mentioning his mixed feelings about the Federation—but again, he chose the path of honesty." He leaned forward in his seat. "I believe the Magnians will hold up their end of the bargain, Lieutenant. And I also believe that my people will be safe on the planet's surface."

The chief engineer folded his scaly arms across his chest, obviously still somewhat skeptical of the colonists' motives. "You're the one in command," he rasped, recognizing the fact if not quite approving of it.

Next, Picard turned to Vigo. "You have been sending data as to what parts we require to bring our weapons systems back up to snuff?"

The Pandrilite nodded. "I have, sir."

"And the Magnians' response?"

"They don't have anything like them on hand," said Vigo. "However, they're confident they can manufacture what we need in short order."

"Excellent," Picard replied. Last, he looked to the Kelvan. "I have not forgotten your concerns about dealing with the Magnians, Jomar. And as you are not technically a member of this crew, I am not in a position to give you orders. However, you are our expert in vidrion technology, which the colonists need desperately if they are to withstand the Nuyyad's next attack. With that in mind, I hope you will honor the agreement I made."

The Kelvan's stare was as blank as ever. For a moment, he remained silent. Then he said, "I will help."

It didn't quite answer Picard's question. But under the circumstances, he supposed it would have to do.

Twelve

"A spike?" Picard echoed. "In her brain waves?"

On the other side of Greyhorse's desk, the doctor nodded. "It was difficult to miss, believe me. And it began before we were hit with enemy fire, so it couldn't have been a reaction to the battle itself."

"What are you saying?" asked the second officer.

"It's just a theory, of course," Greyhorse noted. "But when I saw the spike, it occurred to me that Santana might have been communicating with the other colonists."

"Even in her comatose state?" Picard wondered.

The doctor nodded. "It's the most viable explanation. I would've mentioned it sooner, but there wasn't a chance to do so. I was too busy rushing my patient down to the planet's surface."

"I understand," said the second officer.

He considered the implications—and didn't like what he found himself thinking. "Doctor Greyhorse . . . you mentioned earlier that Ms. Santana's coma might have been self-induced."

"That's correct," Greyhorse confirmed.

"Is it also possible that she was never in a coma in the first place—and only gave the appearance of it?"

The doctor mulled it over. "According to my instruments, the woman was definitely in a coma. And just a little while ago, in the Magnians' medical center, I saw their doctors working on her—which wouldn't have been necessary if she were just faking it."

"What sort of work were they doing?"

Greyhorse shrugged. "They were using the power of their minds."

"Just standing there?"

"Yes," said the doctor.

"Which, if you were a suspicious person, you might have discounted as window dressing."

Greyhorse looked at Picard. "You're suggesting that their procedure was a sham, Commander? A show for my benefit?"

"I am not suggesting anything," said the second officer. "I am merely bringing up the question."

The doctor's dark eyes narrowed. "I don't understand. I thought you trusted the Magnians."

Picard sighed. "I am so inclined, yes. However, in the position I now occupy, I feel compelled to consider all the angles."

Including the angle that assumed he was wrong about Shield Williamson . . . and that he was placing his people in deadly danger.

Not for the first time, the commander wished he had the benefit of Captain Ruhalter's input. But the captain was in a long, coffinlike capsule in one of their cargo bays, pending their return to the Federation, and in no position to offer advice.

"Thank you for your input," he told Greyhorse.

"It's my job," the physician reminded him.

Yes, thought Picard. Just as it's my job to see to it we're not caught by surprise a second time.

Captain's log, supplemental. Despite the questions that have been raised concerning the Magnians in general and Serenity Santana in particular, I am still willing to trust them. Even as I speak, the colonists are manufacturing critical replacement parts for our propulsion system, phaser banks and shield generators. In exchange, we are applying our own expertise to the rebuilding of the several deflector stations that form a perimeter around Magnia, making those installations even more effective than before. I'm on my way to the planet's surface to see how the work is progressing.

Picard tapped his combadge, automatically ending his log entry, and entered the *Stargazer*'s main transporter room.

Vandermeer was the operator on duty. Nodding to the woman, the second officer crossed the floor to the transporter platform and took his place there. Then he turned back to Vandermeer and said, "Energize."

The next thing he knew, he was standing in a grassy valley full of rocky gray outcroppings, dwarfed by one of the Magnians' shield generators. Rising at least a hundred and fifty meters into the air, the device looked like a child's ice cream cone—minus the ice cream.

The nuclear reactor that powered the device was located several hundred meters underground, where the Starfleet officer couldn't see it. Fortunately, there wasn't a problem with the reactor; the problem was with the mechanism that converted the reactor's energy into a stream of polarized gravitons and projected them out into space.

A group of four was laboring at the squat, squared-off base of the generator, where an access panel had been removed. Three of the four were Magnians; the fourth was Simenon, who was showing the colonists how to alter their equipment to produce vidrion particles.

Teams were working on the city's five other shield generators as well. They hoped to have all six locations producing vidrions as well as gravitons by the time the Nuyyad returned.

As on the *Stargazer*, the retrofit process looked to be a tedious one. However, if it bought the colonists another few minutes in the upcoming confrontation, it would be well worth it.

Picard's hair lifted in the rising wind, a harbinger of the blue-gray storm clouds piling up behind the pastel skyline of Magnia. The birds that had circled the splendid towers in twos and threes earlier in the day were gone, having fled to more secure positions.

They knew a storm was coming, the second officer reflected. They just didn't know how fierce a storm it would be. But then, he had a storm of his own to worry about.

He approached Simenon without the engineer seeming to notice him. "How are we doing?" he asked, his voice echoing.

Simenon turned and stared at him blankly for a moment. Then he held up a scaly hand as if asking for Picard's forbearance, closed his eyes, and concentrated on something.

Never having seen him act that way before, Picard became concerned. Just as he was about to hike up the hill and try to rouse him, the Gnalish opened his eyes again.

The second officer studied him. "Are you all right?" he asked.

Simenon snorted. "I'm fine. I was just trying to show our friends here how to link a couple of EPS circuits."

Picard looked at him. "You were . . . *showing* them . . . ?"

The engineer scowled. "Telepathically, of course."

"Ah," said the second officer, as understanding dawned.

It made perfect sense, now that he thought about it. In a telepathic society, teamwork would bypass the spoken word. He was a little surprised that an alien mind fit in so well with the others, but he was hardly an expert on the subject.

"Come down here and bring me up to speed," said Picard.

Simenon seemed reluctant to abandon his work, but he made his way down the hillside nonetheless. When he reached the second officer, he said, "You don't really want to know how the work is going . . . do you?"

"I do," Picard told him. "But as you seem to have guessed, I also want to know about your coworkers. No doubt, you've gotten some insights into them by virtue of their telepathic contact."

The engineer looked back over his shoulder at the Magnians. "I've gotten some insights, all right. I've learned that they're a private bunch, as Eliopoulos told us. They don't like to expose any more of themselves than they have to. But I've seen enough of them to say they're also among the most courageous people I've ever met."

Picard looked at him. "Courageous . . . ?"

Simenon nodded his lizardlike head. "I know. Just a few hours ago, I was saying you were crazy to get involved with them, and now I'm extolling their virtues. But it's true about their courage. The Nuyyad may be on their way with an armada at this very moment, but these people don't let it faze them. They just go about their business as if they were fixing cooking equipment instead of shield projectors."

A glowing assessment, the second officer reflected. Perhaps *too* glowing. By the engineer's own admission, he was seldom inclined to admit that he had been in error. Yet here he was, admitting it—and with uncharacteristic enthusiasm, no less.

Simenon indicated the open access panel with a gesture. "If there's nothing else, I ought to get back to work."

"By all means," said Picard.

But as he watched the engineer climb the hillside, he had to wonder . . . was his crew really in danger of being influenced by the colonists? Was that something he needed to be concerned about? Or with an entire ship full of people to look after, was he just being a mother hen?

As he weighed the possibilities, his combadge beeped. Tapping it, he said, "Picard here."

"This is Ben Zoma, Commander. Shield Williamson just contacted us. He wants to know if we're ready to beam up his engineers."

The second officer had expected the call. After all, the Magnians couldn't supply the *Stargazer* with parts until they saw firsthand what kind of damage had been done.

He frowned, suddenly reluctant to give the colonists access to his ship. If his suspicions had any basis in reality . . .

But what was the alternative? To refuse the assistance they had risked so much to obtain? To spurn what they so desperately needed if they were to survive and warn the Federation?

"Inform Mr. Williamson that we're ready," Picard told his friend. "But see to it that his people are provided with an escort everywhere they go. And I mean *everywhere.*"

"Acknowledged," said Ben Zoma, in a tone that assured the second officer that his order would be taken seriously.

"And beam me back up as well," Picard added. He gazed at Simenon and his Magnian coworkers, who were still cooperating without the benefit of vocal expression. "I believe I've seen all I needed to see."

Pug Joseph watched the trio of colonists make their way past the brig, escorted by Ensign Montenegro. There were two men and a woman, all very human-looking, all dressed in the same green jumpsuit that Santana had worn.

And all curious enough to glance in the direction of the incarcerated mutineers as they walked by.

"He's making a mistake, you know," Werber announced with unconcealed disdain. "A big mistake."

Joseph glanced at the deposed weapons chief, who had walked up to the inner edge of his cell's translucent electromagnetic barrier. Werber's eyes looked hard with hatred and resentment.

"I beg your pardon?" said the security officer.

"Your friend Picard," the prisoner elaborated. "He's making a mistake. That Santana woman couldn't be trusted—we all know that now. And if her people are anything like her, they can't be trusted either."

Joseph frowned at Werber's remark. Since Santana had played him for a fool, he had come to resent her as much as the prisoner did—maybe more. However, he wasn't going to discuss his feelings with someone he was guarding. That was how he had gotten himself into trouble the last time.

From now on, the security officer promised himself, he was just going to do what was expected of him and leave the conversations to other people. "Whatever you say," he said.

Werber swore under his breath. "You know I'm right. And you know if I were free, I'd do something about it."

"But you're not," Joseph reminded him.

The prisoner paused for a moment. *"You* are," he said at last. "Free, I mean. You could stop these people . . . maybe even stop Picard."

"That would be mutiny," the security officer noted.

Pernell, who occupied the cell next to Werber's, laughed at the comment. Joseph frowned at him.

"Would it?" asked Werber. "Or would it be an act of heroism? You know what they say, Lieutenant . . . history is written by the victors."

Joseph didn't say anything in return. He just listened to the Magnians' footfalls recede in the distance.

"Admit it," said Werber. "Seeing those people gets under your skin the same way it gets under mine. We've been burned, both of us—and no matter what, we don't want to get burned again."

Still, the security officer didn't answer him.

It wasn't that he couldn't find a kernel of truth in what Werber was saying. It was just that Pug Joseph wasn't a mutineer.

At least, he didn't think he was.

Picard looked around the chamber into which he had materialized. It was high—at least two stories tall—with pale orange walls, a vaulted ceiling, a white marble floor, and fluted blue columns.

It was also the location, buried deep in the heart of Magnia, from which the city's half-dozen shield generators were operated.

In the center of the chamber was a steel-blue, hexagonal control device that was twice the second officer's height. Each of its six sides featured an oval screen, a keypad, and a sleek attached chair.

Five of the chairs were occupied by Magnians. The sixth was occupied by an equally human-looking figure, though his loose-fitting black togs and unruly red hair marked him as Jomar.

Some of the colonists glanced at Picard, then went back to their work. However, the Kelvan seemed not to notice him. He was too busy tapping data into his keypad.

Picard approached him. "Jomar?"

At the sound of his voice, the Kelvan turned. His pale eyes acknowledged the second officer without emotion. "Commander."

"I came down to see how you were doing," said Picard. "Mr. Williamson informs me that your work is proceeding more slowly than expected."

Jomar frowned ever so slightly. "It proceeds as it proceeds" was all the answer he seemed inclined to give. Then he returned his attention to his pale-green screen.

"Is there a problem?" asked the second officer. "Something I can help you with, perhaps?"

The Kelvan didn't look away from his work this time. "There is no problem," he stated.

Picard was far from satisfied with the response, but he nodded. "Carry on, then," he told Jomar.

He considered the Kelvan a moment longer as Jomar went about his labors. Something *was* wrong, it seemed to the second officer. Every now and then, a Magnian would frown in the alien's direction.

He decided to speak with Williamson again. With luck, the colonist could shed some light on the matter.

He had raised his hand to tap his combadge when someone said, "Commander?" The voice sounded awfully familiar.

Then he realized it wasn't a voice at all. It was just a word in his head, planted telepathically.

Turning, Picard saw Serenity Santana come through the control chamber's only doorway.

The colonist was as beautiful as when he first saw her. Her lips were full of color again, her eyes deep and searching, her long, black hair loosely cascading over one shoulder.

"Ms. Santana," Picard replied.

She feigned disapproval. "People generally use their first names here. Please . . . call me Serenity."

Remembering what she had done to the *Stargazer*, he kept his response to a single word. "Serenity."

Santana's eyes crinkled at the corners as she looked into his. It seemed to Picard that the woman was skimming the surface of his mind. "You're surprised to see me."

"I am," he admitted freely. "Apparently, your people's medical techniques are even more formidable than I was led to believe."

"To an outsider," she said, "I can see how they would appear that way." She paused. "I owe you an apology, don't I?"

The second officer shook his head from side to side. "Mr. Williamson has made your apologies for you. He spoke of the pressures the Nuyyad placed on you and Daniels."

The woman looked relieved. "Then you see I had no choice? I had to do as the Nuyyad demanded."

"So it would seem," he responded flatly, keeping his thoughts to himself as much as possible.

Santana studied him a little longer. Then she smiled wistfully. "You know," she said, "I thought we had the makings of an intriguing friendship. I hope what happened doesn't make that impossible."

Picard wanted very much to tell her that their friendship could still develop unimpeded. However, he couldn't allow himself the luxury. He held the fate of an entire crew in his hands, and he wasn't about to jeopardize it by giving rein to his emotions.

No matter how strong they might be.

Besides, Picard thought, Santana had caused the deaths of Captain Ruhalter and several other crewmen, and injured a great many more. It wasn't easy to forget that.

"I will try to keep an open mind," he told her, his tone as devoid of emotion as Jomar's.

The woman sighed. "Under the circumstances, I suppose that's the best answer I can hope to get."

Picard didn't know what to say to that. But as it turned out, he didn't have to say anything at all—because at that moment, an argument was breaking out on the other side of the shield control device.

"Are you out of your mind?" someone hollered.

"Insulting me will not mask your ineptitude," came the response.

Picard couldn't identify the first voice right off the bat, but he could certainly identify the second one. Quite clearly, it was Jomar, and his tone was an edgy one.

Circumnavigating the control device, the second officer saw what the dispute was about. The Kelvan was tapping away at one of the colonists' keypads, erasing work that had already been done.

"If you cannot follow directions properly," Jomar added, "do not participate in this activity."

The Magnian in question, a dark-haired man who had been introduced to Picard as Armor Brentano, looked around angrily at his fellow technicians. "Did you see what he did to my screen? He's insane!"

"No," said Jomar, looking up from the keypad. "I am meticulous. Perhaps it is you who are insane."

Brentano took a couple of steps toward the Kelvan. "Am I the one who just wrecked half a day's work?"

"Perhaps it was half a day's work," Jomar remarked coldly, "but it was not half a day's progress."

Picard had heard enough. "Calm down," he told the combatants, moving forward with the intention of getting between them.

Santana reinforced the commander's sentiments with her own. "Cut it out, both of you. We're not going to beat the Nuyyad by squabbling."

But Brentano and the Kelvan didn't seem to hear them—or if they did, they weren't inclined to take the advice to heart. The colonist planted a finger in Jomar's chest.

"You think you know everything," he shouted, "don't you? You slimy, tentacled son of a—"

Brentano never completed his invective.

One moment, he was standing nose-to-nose with the Kelvan, poking his forefinger into Jomar's sternum. The next, the colonist seemed to disappear, completely and utterly.

Picard couldn't believe his eyes—and he wasn't the only one shocked by what he had seen.

"What did you do to him?" demanded Santana.

The Kelvan turned to her with his customary lack of passion. "I did *this*," he replied calmly. And he pointed to a small, coarse-looking object sitting on the ground.

Picard took a closer look at the thing. It had four triangular faces, making it a perfect tetrahedron.

"What the blazes are you talking about?" snapped another of the Magnians. "Where's Brentano?"

"He is here," Jomar told her, unperturbed by the woman's display of emotion. "However, he has assumed a less disagreeable form."

The colonist still didn't understand. But Picard, to his horror, was beginning to. Kneeling, he picked up the tetrahedron and turned it over carefully in his hands.

"What he means," the commander said, "is that *this* is Brentano." He looked up at the Kelvan. "At least, it was."

The colonist screwed up her features in disbelief. "What are you talking about?" she asked Picard.

He didn't blame her for reacting that way. A hundred years earlier, Captain Kirk had to have doubted his own sanity when he discovered that his ship had been littered with tetrahedron-shaped blocks . . . and was told that they were distillations of his crew.

Just as the block in his hands, Picard surmised, was a distillation of Armor Brentano.

He put the tetrahedron back on the ground, then looked up at Jomar. "Change him back," he said.

The Kelvan's eyes narrowed, but he didn't answer.

"Change him *back.*"

"He was insolent," Jomar remarked.

"Nonetheless," Picard insisted, his tone unrelenting.

The Kelvan reached for one of the studs on his belt. A moment later, as if by magic, Brentano was standing in front of them again, looking a trifle dazed but otherwise unharmed.

"What happened . . . ?" he asked.

"That's what *I* would like to know," said Santana. She glared at Jomar with unconcealed animosity.

"A misunderstanding," Picard assured her. "Nothing more. Nor is it likely to happen again." He glanced at Jomar. "Isn't that right?"

The Kelvan shrugged. "It will not happen again," he agreed.

"It would be best," the second officer advised, "if we forgot about this and resumed our work."

Taking her cue from him, Santana managed to submerge her anger. "Commander Picard is right," she told the other Magnians. "Let's just get back to what we were doing."

Having done her part to smooth things over, she helped Brentano back to his seat. A moment later, Jomar and the other colonists returned to their workstations as well.

Nonetheless, the damage had been done. The second officer could see that with crystal clarity. None of the colonists would be comfortable working with Jomar after what they had just seen.

Nor could Picard blame them.

Unfortunately, the Kelvan was still the foremost authority on vidrion generation. Despite everything, he would have to remain in the control chamber for the foreseeable future.

But he wouldn't remain the *Stargazer*'s only representative there. The second officer resolved to dispatch one of his other engineers as well—perhaps Simenon himself, since he and the Kelvan seemed to have a good rapport.

As for Santana . . . she seemed inclined to remain alongside Brentano for the moment, helping him see what it was about his work that had produced the Kelvan's objection. A good idea, Picard reflected.

He had barely completed the thought when Santana glanced at him. *I'm glad you think so,* she replied.

The second officer acknowledged her remark with a nod. Then he tapped his communicator and asked Vandermeer to beam him up.

He would still speak with Williamson, to at least let the man know what had taken place. Despite Picard's concerns about the Magnians, this alliance was still important to the *Stargazer.*

And he didn't want Jomar's penchant for insensitivity to wreck it.

Thirteen

Picard watched Shield Williamson's reaction from across a large and ornate wooden desk.

"With luck," the man said, "what the Kelvan did was an isolated incident and we'll see no repeats of it."

"That is my hope as well," the Starfleet officer told him.

Williamson sat back in his chair. "Actually, Commander, I'm glad you're here. My engineers have pointed something out to me."

"Oh?" said Picard.

"They see an opportunity to not only repair your equipment, but to modify it— much as your people are modifying our shield technology to make use of the Kelvan's vidrion particles."

"Which systems are we talking about?" asked the second officer.

"Sensors and tractors," said Williamson. "However, I should tell you . . . for these modifications to be of any utility, you'll require Magnian operators." He paused. "And from what I gather, you're already uncomfortable with our presence aboard your ship."

Picard was surprised by the remark, but he absorbed it without flinching. "Am I to assume you've been reading our thoughts?"

The colonist smiled. "We haven't had to. It's apparent in the way your people look at us, the way they follow us wherever we go."

"As I instructed them," the second officer admitted.

"Because you don't trust us?"

Picard sighed. "Because I cannot afford to."

"An honest answer," Williamson observed.

"To an honest question," Picard replied.

They both fell silent for a moment.

"Consider this," Williamson said at last. "We're operating on faith as much as you are. Once we help you repair your warp drive and your weapons systems, what's to keep you from taking off for Federation space . . . and leaving us to defend ourselves against the Nuyyad?"

The second officer frowned. "Which could be why you want to place some of your people on the *Stargazer* . . . to keep us from reneging on our bargain when the attack comes."

The Magnian's eyes narrowed. "Touché."

Picard shrugged. "My apologies. It seemed to be the obvious response."

This time, the room seemed to echo with their silence.

"Any agreement," said Williamson, "is only as strong as the intentions of the parties involved in it. If there's some way I can convince you we mean only good . . ."

Unfortunately, Picard couldn't think of one.

"Mind you," he said, "I *want* to trust you. My instincts *tell* me to trust you. I just don't have the *luxury* of trusting you."

And his trust had been watered down by recent events, though he didn't feel compelled to mention that.

Williamson smiled a little sadly. "Does that mean that you're turning down our offer?"

The second officer couldn't deny the appeal of sensor and tractor enhancements, considering they didn't know how many Nuyyad vessels they might eventually be facing—or how powerful they might be.

He took a moment to weigh the benefits against the risks—and made his decision. "In the interest of defending Magnia as well as the *Stargazer*," he said, "I'll accept your operators."

Williamson nodded. "You've made the right choice, Commander."

I certainly hope so, thought Picard.

Lieutenant Vigo sat with his back against the curvature of a Jefferies tube and watched another piece of conduit casing go sailing past him.

A couple of colonists were waiting to receive the component farther down the line. Even from a distance, the acting weapons chief could see the concentration on their faces—a concentration that had been there since earlier that morning, when the *Stargazer* beamed up a supply of replacement parts from the planet's surface.

"How's it going?" asked Lieutenant Iulus, a curly-haired security officer, as he made his way toward Vigo from a perpendicular tube.

"Rather well, it seems," said the Pandrilite, watching the Magnians snatch the piece of casing out of the air and fit it into the conduit they were building. "These people have hauled more parts in the last hour than you and I could have lugged in a day."

Iulus nodded. "Amazing."

"Very much so," said Vigo. "And yet, separately, none of them can move one of these parts even an inch."

The security officer looked at him. "So how do they do it?"

"By working together," the weapons officer replied. "When they pool their efforts, they raise their effectiveness in leaps and bounds. At least, that's how it was explained to me."

"You know what?" said Iulus. "They can do it any way they want—as long as they're finished before the Nuyyad get here."

Vigo grunted softly. That was one way of looking at the situation.

Unfortunately, Picard had insisted that every colonist on the *Stargazer* have an escort. Clearly, the *commander* didn't want the Magnians to do their jobs any way they wanted.

It seemed like a shift from Picard's earlier stance, when he had been willing to place more trust in the colonists. But then, Vigo mused, even commanding officers were allowed to change their minds.

"Lieutenant?" called one of the colonists from his place at the end of the tube. "Could I see you for a moment?"

It was the first time any of the Magnians had asked for Vigo's help. He wondered what the man wanted.

"I'll see you later," he told Iulus.

"Sure," said the security officer.

Then the Pandrilite moved his bulk through the tube, wishing fervently that he could have glided through it like one of the casing components instead.

Jean-Luc Picard entered his quarters, sought out his bed and sank into it gratefully. It had been a long day.

All in all, the work had gone well—both on the *Stargazer* and on the planet's surface. Simenon had reported that the warp drive was almost functional again, and the colonists were on the verge of bringing their shield generators back on-line.

And having had a chance to look at Williamson's proposal regarding the *Stargazer*'s sensor and tractor systems, it appealed to him even more. If it meant having a few colonists on board during the impending battle, he could live with it.

After all, he had gotten this far taking chances. With luck, the same approach would get his ship home.

The only fly in the ointment was the incident with Jomar. However, there hadn't been any reprise of it, nor had Picard been forced to deal with any other instances of hostility.

He closed his eyes, knowing the work on his ship would continue unabated throughout the night. By morning, the second officer hoped, there would be even better things to report.

Abruptly, as if fate were intent on being cruel to him, he heard a beeping sound. Envisioning an emergency, he swung his legs out of bed and returned to his anteroom.

"Come," he said.

The doors to his quarters slid apart, revealing Lieutenant Vigo. The Pandrilite entered the room a little tentatively.

"What is it?" Picard asked wearily.

"I have some news for you, sir." Vigo looked apologetic. "News you are not going to like."

Picard ran his fingers through his hair. "Go ahead."

"Remember the shuttle that exploded prematurely? When we were trying to liberate the colony?"

The second officer nodded. "Of course."

"At the time," said the Pandrilite, "it appeared to be an accident. But just a little while ago, one of the Magnian engineers came across some evidence that indicates otherwise."

"You're saying it was sabotage?" Picard asked.

"Judge for yourself, sir," Vigo told him.

Crossing to the second officer's workstation, he brought up a red and blue diagram of a secondary command junction. "This is one of the switching points from my bridge console to the remote control node. During the battle, all my signals to the shuttles passed through it."

"All right," said Picard.

"Take a close look," Vigo advised. "What do you see?"

The second officer did as the Pandrilite suggested. After a moment, he realized what Vigo was talking about. The junction had been modified—purposely, it appeared.

A second data line had been spliced in, allowing the command junction to simultaneously accommodate two completely separate sets of signals. And since the first signal would go through unhindered, the change wouldn't show up on a routine diagnostic.

If someone had wished, they could have taken advantage of this situation to blow up one of the *Stargazer*'s shuttles without warning. In fact, they could have blown up *all* the shuttles.

Picard looked at the acting weapons chief. "It seems we have a saboteur on our hands."

"That was my conclusion too, sir."

"Do you have any idea who it might be?" the second officer asked.

Vigo shook his hairless, blue head. "No, sir. However, I believe there are ways to find out."

"See that you pursue them," Picard told him. "However, you must do so without letting anyone know what you're doing. We need to keep this privileged information for the time being."

"Yes, sir," said the weapons officer, and left the room with a laudable sense of urgency.

Picard watched the doors to his quarters slide closed, leaving him alone again. Dropping into a chair, he heaved a sigh.

Just when he thought the dawn might be in sight, the shadowy figure of a saboteur had appeared on the horizon.

He needed to think this through, he told himself. But he was too fatigued to do so on his own. Looking up at the intercom grid in the ceiling, he called upon the one man he felt he could trust implicitly.

"Mr. Ben Zoma," he said, "this is Commander Picard."

"Ben Zoma here," came the reply.

"Meet me in my quarters," the second officer told him. "I've learned something you may find interesting."

Gilaad Ben Zoma sat back in his chair and considered the problem with which his friend had presented him.

Finally, he spoke. "There were only two unknown quantities on the ship when we came up with the notion of using shuttles as tactical weapons. One of them was Jomar. The other was Serenity Santana."

"Ms. Santana was unconscious," Picard reminded him.

The second officer was seated on the other side of his quarters' anteroom, a cup of hot tea resting on a table beside him. He looked as if he would much rather have gone to bed than begun unraveling a mystery.

"True," Ben Zoma conceded. "But do you remember what you told me about her brain activity? How it remained elevated even when she was unconscious? For all we know, she could have been manipulating someone in order to sabotage that shuttle."

The second officer tilted his head. "You mean . . . one of us?"

"A crewman," Ben Zoma suggested. "You, me . . . anyone, really. They might not even have a recollection of having helped her."

"On the other hand," said Picard, "Santana has already admitted her treachery regarding the ambush. If she had used a pawn to sabotage the shuttle, why wouldn't she have admitted that as well?"

"Good point," Ben Zoma acknowledged. Suddenly, something occurred to him. "Unless she had two different agendas . . ."

"I beg your pardon?"

"What if Santana's role in the ambush was what she claimed it was—a response to the Nuyyad's threats—but her sabotage of the shuttle was for a different purpose entirely?"

Picard mulled it over. "That would explain why her fellow colonist didn't think twice about bringing our attention to the altered junction."

"On the other hand," said Ben Zoma, arguing with his own proposition, "what could she have gained by blowing up the shuttle?"

"The same as Jomar," said the second officer. "Nothing—except possibly the sacrifice of their own lives."

"We're lacking a motive," Ben Zoma noted.

"So it would seem," said his friend.

Ben Zoma looked at him. "You might want to confront one of them about this. Or maybe mention it to our friend Williamson. One of them is bound to tell you something interesting."

The commander considered it. After a while, he shook his head. "I don't think so, Gilaad. I want to identify the culprit before he or she realizes we have suspicions."

"Then we need to keep tabs on them around the clock. Follow their every move until they slip up."

"If you say so," said Picard.

"I'll volunteer to hound Jomar," Ben Zoma offered.

"And Santana?"

"I'll send Pug down to do that. He knows her as well as any of us. And after the way Santana humiliated him, he'll be that much more determined to catch her red-handed."

The second officer took a deep breath. "We need to unmask this saboteur—and quickly. Otherwise, there is no telling when a key system might betray us, repairs or no repairs."

Ben Zoma sympathized with his friend. Commanding a vessel was a difficult task at the best of times. In a situation where the ground kept shifting underfoot, it was nearly impossible.

"We'll catch your saboteur," he assured Picard.

The second officer grunted. "You sound rather certain."

Ben Zoma smiled. "I've never let you down before," he said, wishing he were even half as confident as he sounded.

It was early the next morning, as Picard was getting dressed, that he got a call from Shield Williamson.

Taking it in his quarters, he saw the Magnian's face appear on his monitor screen. "Is everything all right?" asked the second officer.

"That depends," said Williamson.

"On what?"

"On how you feel about having Serenity Santana board your ship again."

Picard looked at the colonist. "For what reason?"

"One of the technicians we planned to send up isn't feeling well. Santana is the only other Magnian who's qualified to do the job."

Troubled by the proposition, the second officer shook his head. "You must know how this looks."

"Like I'm trying to pull a fast one," Williamson conceded. "Of course, the decision is entirely yours."

Picard considered his options—and the old saying came to him: Keep your friends close and your enemies closer. And it would certainly be a simpler matter for Pug Joseph to keep an eye on Santana if she was working there on the *Stargazer.*

"Send her up," he told the Magnian.

But even as he extended the invitation, he could feel himself inching further out on the limb he had chosen.

Fourteen

Captain's log, supplemental. At last, we are ready. Magnia's defenses have been fully resurrected—and thanks to Jomar, they should be in a better position to withstand the Nuyyad now that their shields will be laced with vidrion particles. The Stargazer's *systems have been restored as well, from our warp drive to our deflector grid. What's more, the colonists have made use of their technical expertise and their inborn talents to provide us with a couple of tools we didn't have before—improved sensor and tractor functions. Unfortunately, we have made no discernible progress in our search for a saboteur, but we remain hopeful. After all, we have some of our best people on the case.*

Pug Joseph entered the tiny engineering support room on Deck 26 and spotted Serenity Santana among her colleagues.

The dark-haired woman was shoulder to shoulder with them on her knees, fitting the forward dorsal tractor control node with devices capable of marrying telekinetic energy to the attractive and repellant forces in a directed graviton stream. Every so often she would glance at one of her fellow colonists and receive a glance in return, then go back to work.

None of the Magnians said a word. However, they all seemed to know what to do with the equipment they had brought with them.

Ensign Montenegro, an engineer, was standing in the corner of the room, his arms folded across his chest. Like Joseph, Montenegro was just a spectator. Their guests were the ones applying all the elbow grease.

The security officer felt uncomfortable being in the same room as Santana. If it had been up to him, he would have left. But he was under orders, so he stayed and kept an eye on the woman.

After a few minutes, she seemed to sense his scrutiny and looked back over her shoulder at him. He didn't look away, but he didn't acknowledge her either. He just stood there and did his job.

Santana worked for another ten minutes or so. Then she got up, stretched her muscles and walked over to Joseph. He felt his jaw clench.

"Long time no see," said the colonist.

The security officer didn't utter a word in response. He just stood there, returning her scrutiny.

"I'm sorry for pulling the wool over your eyes," she said.

Joseph didn't give her the satisfaction of an answer.

"I mean it," Santana added. "I've already told Commander Picard, but I want to tell you as well."

Still, he remained silent.

"You've got to want to say *something* to me," the woman told him.

He did. But he didn't say it.

Santana looked at him a moment longer, her dark eyes full of what appeared to be pain. Then she returned to her work.

Joseph didn't like the idea of hurting her. However, as he had said to himself often enough, he was determined not to give the colonist an opportunity to fool him again.

Carter Greyhorse had been busy over the last few days, to say the least—busy with Santana and Leach and the less severely injured survivors of their encounter with the Nuyyad.

And with the exception of a few helpless moments, he hadn't spent any of that time thinking about Gerda Asmund.

But when the medical officer returned from Magnia, he hadn't had the option of burying himself in patient care any longer—and his preoccupation with the navigator had threatened to paralyze him in a duranium straitjacket of despair.

Despair, because he had no chance with her. He had come to accept that, at least on an intellectual level. They were too different. She was vibrant, vigorous, full of life. And he was . . . *not*.

So, in the absence of an urgent need for his medical skills, Greyhorse had come up with another project in which to immerse himself—a project he had begun even before he saw Gerda in the gym. He had renewed his interest in the creation of synthetic psilosynine.

The doctor had even gone so far as to replicate a batch of the neurotransmitter himself, following the guidelines of the Betazoid scientist who had pioneered the process. And now, having brought the stuff back to sickbay, he was testing its integrity at his office computer.

It was turning out to be a success, too. Not just the psilosynine itself, but its ability to take his mind off Gerda.

Just as Greyhorse acknowledged that, he caught a glimpse of someone walking into sickbay.

Turning away from his screen, he saw that it was Joseph from security. Under normal circumstances, the doctor would have completed his tests, then gone to see what Joseph wanted from him. However, their circumstances were anything but normal these days.

Getting up from his computer terminal, Greyhorse exited his office and emerged into the central triage area. "Something I can do for you?" he asked the security officer.

"I hope so," said Joseph. He looked around. "And I hope you'll keep this conversation confidential—as a matter of ship's security."

Ship's security? "All right," Greyhorse responded, wondering what the problem might be.

"You treated Serenity Santana while she was comatose?"

"I did," Greyhorse confirmed.

"And you told Commander Picard that you saw her brain waves spike when we were approaching her world?"

"That's correct," said the medical officer. Suddenly, it occurred to him where Joseph might be going with this. "Santana's all right, isn't she?"

The other man looked up at him, jolted from his line of questioning. "She's fine, as far as I can tell."

"Then this isn't about her health?" asked Greyhorse.

"No," Joseph assured him. "It's about an act of sabotage." And he went on to describe the way one of their command junctions had been tampered with.

"But what does this have to do with Ms. Santana?" asked the doctor.

"Obviously, she couldn't have sabotaged the shuttle herself. But Commander Picard and Lieutenant Ben Zoma think she might have manipulated someone else into doing it."

"Someone else?" Greyhorse echoed, considering the possibility for the first time. "You mean . . ."

"You," said Joseph. He looked disturbed by what he was saying. "Or me. Or anyone on the ship."

The doctor sat down on the edge of a biobed and thought about it. It was an eerie proposition at best. Unfortunately, he didn't know enough about Santana's abilities to confirm the theory or deny it.

"It's possible," he said at last. "But I can't say for certain."

The security officer looked disappointed. "Commander Picard thought you might say that."

Greyhorse had an idea. "Have you checked the internal sensor logs? They would tell you who might have approached that command junction."

Joseph smiled a tolerant smile. "That was the first thing we tried. But internal sensors aren't very dependable in the vicinity of the warp engines, which is where the junction was located. And whoever did the tampering was smart enough to take off his or her combadge so we wouldn't be able to track them that way either."

The doctor shrugged. "It was just a thought."

"Thanks anyway," said the security officer.

But he didn't leave. He just stood there, his eyes glazing over, as if he had fallen deep into thought.

"Lieutenant?" said Greyhorse.

Joseph looked at him as if he had woken from a dream. "Hmm?"

"Are you feeling all right?" the physician inquired.

"I'm okay. Just a little . . . preoccupied is all." The security officer hesitated. Then he said, "Can I level with you?"

Greyhorse nodded. "Certainly."

Joseph smiled again—a little sheepishly, this time. "To be honest, I don't have a whole lot of friends on the ship. It's always been that way for me, I don't know why. But when I was guarding Ms. Santana, I . . . well, I sort of came to like her."

"As a friend?" the doctor asked.

"That," said the security officer, "and maybe a little more. I know it sounds ridiculous, but I think I fell for her the first time I saw her—when she was sitting on her cot in the brig."

Even Greyhorse had to chuckle at that. "Quite an image," he conceded.

"I thought she liked me too," Joseph confided. "Maybe not the way I liked *her*, but at least a little. Then I found out that she was playing me for a chump, right from the start."

"Playing *all* of us," the doctor interjected.

"But me most of all," the security officer insisted. "I mean, I trusted her. I let a pretty face make me forget my training." He looked embarrassed. "I'll bet that never happened to *you*."

Greyhorse was about to agree with the man, at least inwardly—when a sequence of images flashed through his mind, coming one after the other with jolting familiarity.

Out of the corner of his eye, he saw someone carrying a wounded Gerda into sickbay. Then he took another look and realized that it was Gerda who was doing the carrying, and that it was Leach who had been hurt.

The doctor's heart began to pound as it had pounded then. Even if he managed to forget everything else about Gerda, he would never forget that sight as long as he lived.

Greyhorse regained his composure. "Never," he agreed, lying through his teeth. "But that doesn't mean you should be beating yourself up over it. We're people, Lieutenant, not machines. We have feelings. And sometimes, like it or not, those feelings get in the way of our jobs."

Joseph considered the advice. "Maybe you're right."

But Greyhorse knew the security officer didn't mean it. He would continue to berate himself, advice or no advice.

Well, he told himself, at least I tried.

"If you think of anything that might shed some light," said Joseph, "let me know, all right?"

"I will," the doctor promised him.

But as the security officer left, Greyhorse wasn't thinking about Joseph's problem. He wasn't thinking about psilosynine either. He was thinking about Gerda Asmund again.

Phigus Simenon looked up at the wedge of blue sky caught between the spires of Magnia's tallest towers.

He couldn't see the *Stargazer*. But then, he hadn't expected to. The ship was too far away even to be spotted at night, when the atmosphere of this world wasn't suffused with its sun's light.

Abruptly, the engineer heard his communicator beep. It was what he had been waiting for. Tapping it, he said, "Simenon here."

"This is Commander Picard. I'm taking us out of orbit."

"Acknowledged," said the engineer.

"Good luck," Picard told him.

"To you, too," Simenon replied.

"Picard out."

The Gnalish stared at the sky a little longer. Then he turned to Armor Brentano, who had been attending him patiently.

"Ready?" asked the colonist.

"Ready," said Simenon.

Then he followed Brentano across the plaza to the elegant pink building that housed the shield control center, where they would bide their time until the enemy arrived.

* * *

Less than seventeen hours after Picard removed the *Stargazer* from Magnia's sensor range, he heard Gerda Asmund announce the approach of two vessels she had spotted on her monitor.

The second officer had been leaning over Vigo's weapons panel, supervising some last-minute diagnostics. Moving to a position just in front of the captain's center seat, he gazed at the viewscreen.

"Can you give me a visual?" he asked.

Gerda worked for a moment. Then the screen filled with the sight of not one Nuyyad vessel but two, both of them as big and powerful-looking as the ones Picard had seen earlier. Obviously, the enemy believed that would be more than enough to put down the *Stargazer.*

We will have to show them the error of their ways, thought the second officer. "Red alert," he said. "All hands to battle stations. Raise shields and power up phasers."

"Raising shields," Gerda confirmed.

"Diverting power to phasers," said Vigo.

"Their speed?" asked Picard.

"Full impulse," Idun reported.

This was it, the second officer told himself, glaring at the enemy. This was the test of all their hard work. They would either turn the Nuyyad back or be destroyed in the attempt.

"Any sign that they see us?" he asked his navigator.

"None, sir," said Gerda, her hands darting over her control panel. "They're heading straight for the colony."

As we expected, thought Picard. But he couldn't help thinking of Simenon, whom he had left to help defend Magnia.

He hoped that he and the engineer would both be around to congratulate each other when the battle was over.

"Here they come," said Simenon, tracking the two yellow blips on his black sensor screen.

Brentano, who was seated to the engineer's left, cast a thought: *Shields are at full strength.*

Phasers powered and ready, replied Hilton-Smith, the blond woman to Simenon's right.

"Target phasers," intoned Shield Williamson, who had taken up a position behind the Gnalish.

Targeting, Hilton-Smith responded.

Range in thirty seconds, Brentano informed them.

On Simenon's screen, one of the yellow blips unleashed a series of green energy bursts. A moment later, the other blip followed suit. Apparently, the engineer reflected, the Nuyyad's weapons range was a little greater than that of the colonists.

Direct hits, said Brentano. *But no damage to report. Shields are holding at eighty-six percent.*

Range in fifteen seconds, thought Hilton-Smith.

Simenon watched the blips get closer. Again, they fired their vidrion cannons, and this time he thought he could feel a little tremor in the floor beneath him.

Shields down to seventy-two percent, Brentano told them.

Range in five seconds, Hilton-Smith reported, her eyes reflecting the light from her screen. *Four. Three. Two . . .*

"Fire!" Williamson commanded, his voice ripping through the chamber.

On Simenon's monitor, a half dozen red phaser beams reached out and pummeled the enemy vessels. Inwardly, the Gnalish cheered. After all, he had personally helped increase the force of those beams.

"Their shields are taking a beating," observed Brentano, pure excitement in his voice.

Of course, none of them expected to win this battle from the ground. If the Magnians were going to prevail, their allies in the heavens would have to take the lead.

Just as the engineer thought that, he saw a third blip enter the picture. *The Stargazer has arrived,* he announced silently, but not without a certain amount of pride.

Picard eyed the bright, diamond-shaped ships on his viewscreen. "Fire again!" he thundered.

A second time, the *Stargazer's* phasers stabbed at the enemy vessels, wreaking havoc with their shields. What's more, the Magnians' sensor enhancements allowed each beam to find its precise target.

Finally, the Nuyyad must have realized that something new had been added to the mix. Both ships peeled away, resorting to evasive maneuvers.

But Picard knew he had the enemy off-balance. The last thing he wanted to do was give them time to regroup.

"Stay on them," he told Idun Asmund.

"Aye, sir," said his helm officer, following one of the Nuyyad ships as it sped away.

"Get a lock on their aft shield generators," he told Vigo.

Again, they were able to benefit from the Magnians' participation in their sensor operations. The Pandrilite looked up. "Got them, sir."

"Fire!" barked Picard.

The *Stargazer's* phasers raked the enemy's hindquarters with a devastating barrage. Unfortunately, they could dog only one vessel at a time—and the second officer was wary of getting caught in a crossfire.

He turned to his navigator. "Where is the other one?"

"Bearing two-five-two-mark-six," Gerda told him. "But it's got its hands full with what the Magnians are throwing at it."

Picard nodded, satisfied with the way the battle was going. It was just the way they had planned it.

Suddenly, Gerda swiveled in her chair, her eyes wide with surprise and anger. "Shields are down!" she snarled.

The second officer didn't understand. "We haven't even been hit," he pointed out.

"Nonetheless," the navigator insisted, "shields are down!"

Picard cursed beneath his breath. "Fall back!" he told Idun, the words leaving a bitter taste in his mouth.

But as if the Nuyyad had sensed the *Stargazer's* untimely vulnerability, the enemy vessel wheeled and came after her. The second officer looked on helplessly as the Nuyyad's cannons belched vidrion fury.

"Brace yourselves!" he cried out.

A moment later, the deck slid out from under him and sparks shot across the bridge. No, Picard thought. This cannot be happening. We *had* them.

Hadn't the enemy been at a distinct tactical disadvantage? And hadn't they just reconstructed the *Stargazer*'s deflector grid unit by unit? How could it have failed again so quickly?

Abruptly, a chill climbed the rungs of the second officer's spine. *The saboteur,* he thought. It was the only explanation.

A second vidrion barrage pounded them, sending the *Stargazer* reeling to starboard. Flung into the side of the captain's chair, Picard heard the deckplates shriek like banshees.

"Evasive maneuvers," he told Idun. "Pattern Omega!"

As the helm officer sent them spiraling out of harm's way, Picard tried to take stock of his options. Shields or no shields, he told himself, he had to create an opportunity to strike back.

Then Vigo called out the best thing the second officer could have hoped to hear. "I've got the shields back on-line, sir!"

Uncertain as to how long they would *stay* on-line, Picard turned to the viewscreen. The Nuyyad vessel was bearing down on them, following up on the surprising damage done by its volleys. Quite possibly, the enemy commander expected to finish them off.

The fellow was going to be disappointed, the second officer thought. With the *Stargazer*'s shields restored, Picard had all his options in front of him again—and he knew which one he wanted to use.

"Divert power to tractor beam," he snapped. "Target a point on their shields in line with their main emitter."

Normally, a tractor beam was useless against an enemy's shields. However, this wasn't just any tractor beam. It was one that had the minds of more than a dozen Magnians to strengthen and manipulate it.

"Ready phasers and photon torpedoes!" the second officer called out.

But even as he gave the order, he saw the enemy release a volley of bright green vidrion packets. They loomed on the forward viewer, growing gigantic before Picard could do anything about them, finally filling the screen from edge to edge.

Then they tore into the *Stargazer* with all their savage, disruptive force. But Jomar's vidrion-laced deflectors seemed to hold against the Nuyyad assault, keeping its destructive potential at arm's length.

"Engage tractor!" the second officer told his navigator.

Gerda did as she was told—and used the ghostly beam to punch a hole through the enemy's shields. Seeing the aperture, Picard smiled a grim smile and glanced at Vigo.

"Fire!" he said.

Instantly, the weapons chief drove his phaser bolts through the gap created by the tractor beam, piercing the outer skin of the Nuyyad ship. Then he followed up with a couple of photon torpedoes.

With neither shields nor hull to stop them or even slow them down, the torpedoes entered the enemy vessel and vented their matter-antimatter payload in a massive outpouring of yellow-white splendor.

Even if he had wanted to watch the resulting debris spin off into space, the second officer didn't have the time. He had to turn his attention to his other adversary.

"Give me a visual of the other ship," he told Gerda.

The image on the viewscreen changed, showing him the lone surviving diamond shape. It was exchanging fire with the planet's surface, perhaps unaware that its sister vessel had been destroyed.

"Target their deflectors," said Picard, "just as we did before. Ready phasers and torpedoes."

"Ready, sir," came Vigo's reply.

The Nuyyad vessel began to come about, leaving Magnia alone for the moment. Obviously, its commander had recognized a more pressing concern.

"Engage tractor beam!" snapped the second officer. On the viewscreen, the pale, barely visible shaft of the tractor opened a window in the enemy's shields. "Fire!" he commanded.

The diamond shape didn't stand a chance. Before it could launch an offensive of its own, before it could try to get out of the *Stargazer*'s range, a pair of crimson phaser beams sliced through the opening in its defenses and penetrated its hull.

As before, Vigo followed the phaser attack with a pair of photon torpedoes. And as before, they exploded inside the enemy ship, blotting out the stars with a splash of deadly, yellow-white brilliance.

"Well done," said Picard. He turned to Gerda. "Damage?"

"Shields are down twenty-two percent," the navigator reported. "Otherwise, all systems are functioning at rated capacity."

The second officer was pleased beyond all expectation. "Well done indeed," he told his officers.

"Sir," said Paxton from his communications console, "Mr. Williamson is hailing us from the surface."

Picard smiled. "Put him on screen, Lieutenant."

A moment later, the Magnian's visage appeared. "Tell me our instruments are accurate, Commander. The Nuyyad . . . ?"

"Have been destroyed," the second officer confirmed.

Williamson looked relieved. "And the *Stargazer?*"

"Has not been," Picard said. "How is Magnia?"

"Unharmed as well," the colonist reported. "Our only casualty was a stand of old trees of which I was rather fond."

"It could have been worse," the second officer told him.

He glanced at Vigo, recalling their momentary shield failure, and contemplated the danger in which it had placed them. If the weapons chief hadn't managed to get the deflectors back on-line . . .

"Much worse," he added.

Fifteen

Picard sat behind Captain Ruhalter's desk and regarded his acting weapons chief. "What happened out there?" he asked.

Vigo frowned. "Honestly, sir . . . when we lost our shields, I was too surprised to even think for a moment. After all, nothing like that had ever happened to me. Then I thought of the saboteur."

"As did I," the second officer admitted.

"I remembered how he had run a parallel data line through that command junction, and I started thinking of which command junctions were involved in the deflector function. As it turned out, there were only four of them, so I began bypassing them one after the other. After I bypassed the third one, we regained shield control."

"And you brought the deflectors back up," Picard concluded.

The weapons officer nodded. "That's correct, sir."

Picard sat back in his chair. "I hope I don't have to tell you how critical that action was. If not for you, Lieutenant, our encounter with the Nuyyad might have had a very different conclusion."

Vigo looked a little embarrassed. "I was glad to be of help, sir."

"You can be of further help," the second officer told him. "I want you to examine this altered shield command junction. See if you can glean anything from it—perhaps in comparison to the first altered junction we discovered. Then report back to me."

"Aye, sir," said Vigo. But he didn't get up from his chair right away.

"What is it?" asked Picard.

The Pandrilite looked apologetic. "Begging your pardon, sir, but are we going to return to the Federation with the saboteur on board?"

The second officer was about to ask why that would be of particular concern to his weapons chief. Then it hit him with the impact of a directed energy beam: *the galactic barrier.*

If their shields dropped just before they went through it, they would be naked to the phenomenon. The crew would be completely and utterly exposed to the barrier's mysterious and volatile energies.

Kirk's ship had had some protection, primitive as it might be by contemporary standards, and Gary Mitchell had still become a being capable of enslaving his entire species. How much more monstrous an entity might be created on a vessel that had no shielding at all?

"I see your point," said Picard.

Clearly, they couldn't go back to the Federation as they had planned. Not yet, anyway. First, they would have to identify and neutralize the saboteur, then scour the ship for lingering signs of his or her handiwork.

"I will find the saboteur," the second officer promised. "I don't yet know how, but I will do it."

"I'm sure you will, sir," said Vigo, his expression an earnest one. "If there's anything I can do . . ."

"I'll let you know," Picard told him. "And Lieutenant . . ."

"Aye, sir?" said the weapons officer.

"As before, not a word of this to anyone."

"You can trust me, sir," Vigo assured him.

No doubt, Picard mused. He wished he could say that about *everyone* aboard the *Stargazer.*

Carter Greyhorse walked into the *Stargazer's* lounge, where Commander Picard was already seated at the black oval table.

"Doctor," said the second officer, by way of acknowledgment.

"You wanted to speak with me?" asked Greyhorse, pulling out a chair opposite Picard's and sitting down.

"I did," said the commander. "But I'd prefer to wait until the others arrive before I begin our discussion."

Others? Greyhorse wondered.

He had barely completed the thought when Ben Zoma, Simenon, Paxton, and Cariello walked into the room, one right after the other. Nodding to the doctor, they took their seats.

Greyhorse hadn't realized that this was to be a staff meeting. But then, he could easily have missed that part of Picard's summons.

Ever since his visit from Pug Joseph, the medical officer had been unable to keep from thinking about Gerda Asmund again. He was so preoccupied, so distracted, he hadn't even felt an urge to complete his tests on the psilosynine he had synthesized.

And with renewed longing had come a renewed sense of despair. Gerda was so forceful, so graceful, so vibrant . . . so unlike Greyhorse. What chance could he possibly have with her?

"Doctor Greyhorse?"

Greyhorse turned to Picard. "Yes?"

"I would like to get underway now," said the second officer.

The doctor looked around and saw that Vigo and Jomar had joined them without his realizing it. They were sitting at the table along with the others. My god, he told himself, it's worse than I thought.

"The reason I called this meeting," said Picard, "is to discuss what course of action we should adopt next."

Simenon looked at him. "I'm a little confused. Aren't we supposed to be going home?"

"Yes," said Cariello, "to warn the Federation about the Nuyyad?"

"Indeed," Picard replied, "that is the agenda I had intended to follow. However, it occurs to me there is something more we can accomplish here before we return."

"Explain," said the Kelvan.

"As you will recall," said Picard, "we were told about a supply depot that the enemy had set up on this side of the galactic barrier—one that seemed to be a critical part of their invasion plans."

Greyhorse thought he could see where the second officer was headed. "You want to scout out this depot?"

Picard shook his head from side to side. "No," he told his assembled officers and allies. "I want to destroy it."

The doctor looked at him, struck dumb by the audacity of his declaration. So, apparently, was everyone else sitting around the table.

"Are you sure that's wise, sir?" asked Paxton.

"I believe it is," said the second officer. "For one thing, you saw how easily we handled those two Nuyyad ships."

"But not without the help of the Magnians' phaser batteries," Ben Zoma reminded him.

"No question," Picard responded, "the colonists on the ground played a critical part in our victory. However, I believe we would have defeated the Nuyyad even without their assistance. Our enhanced sensor and tractor functions provided us with a much greater tactical advantage than I would ever have imagined possible."

"Let me understand this," said Simenon, his slitted eyes narrowing in his scaly face. "You want to attack an enemy installation—where we're liable to face a force considerably larger than two ships? And you want us to do it entirely on our own?"

The second officer leaned forward. "I want to take the Nuyyad by surprise—and they won't be expecting a countermaneuver so soon after their assault on Magnia. On the other hand, if we opt to alert the Federation and watch them put together a task force, the Nuyyad will have had time to increase the strength of their defenses."

"Are we even certain there *is* a depot?" asked Greyhorse. "Wasn't that just the bait in the Nuyyad's trap?"

"It exists," the second officer insisted. "Shield Williamson has given me the coordinates."

"Can we believe him this time?" asked Cariello.

"A fair question," Picard told her. "But since our arrival here, the colonists have made good on all their promises. I no longer feel compelled to question their sincerity."

"Nor do I," Simenon conceded.

"The elimination of the depot is a worthwhile goal," Vigo observed. "One worth taking a risk to achieve."

"Exactly right," said Picard. "We can vastly improve Starfleet's tactical position, giving Command the time it needs to prepare for an invasion . . . or perhaps even head it off."

"If we're successful," Simenon argued.

"Of course," the Pandrilite conceded. "However, we can send out a subspace message either way, so the Federation will be warned about the Nuyyad even if the *Stargazer* is destroyed."

"Well?" asked the second officer. "Do we go after the depot or not?"

Glances were exchanged as everyone present considered the question. It was Jomar who finally broke the silence.

"I am in favor of attacking the depot," he said.

Vigo turned to Picard. "So am I."

Ben Zoma shrugged. "I'm convinced."

"Same here," said Paxton, though without as much enthusiasm.

Simenon shook his head stubbornly. "I'll grant you, the Magnians give us an edge in a fight—and so do Jomar's vidrion-laced shields. But it's not *that* big an edge."

"I'm with Simenon," said Cariello. "I was on the receiving end of a Nuyyad advantage once. I don't look forward to being there again."

That left Greyhorse.

As the others looked to him, he frowned at the scrutiny. "I'm no tactician, you understand. However, I too have to agree with Mr. Simenon. Enhanced shields, sensors, and tractor beams don't inspire much confidence when stacked against an indeterminate number of enemy ships."

Picard nodded. "Thank you for your input." He swept the table with a glance. "All of you."

"You're welcome," said the engineer, his ruby eyes gleaming. "But what are you going to do?"

The second officer looked at him. "I have not been swayed from my original inclination," he noted. "We will break orbit and head for the depot as soon as I can coordinate the details with Mr. Williamson."

Simenon snorted. "Captain Ruhalter was the same way."

Picard turned to him, his eyes flashing with restrained emotion. "And what does that mean?"

The engineer returned his glare. "He had an opinion when he walked into a meeting, and he had an opinion when he walked out—and as I recall, they were always the same."

The second officer seemed to take the remark in stride. "I had a great deal of respect for Captain Ruhalter, as you are no doubt aware. However, he and I are by no means the same. When I come into a meeting, Mr. Simenon, it is with an open mind."

The Gnalish wasn't the type to let a matter go if he felt strongly about it. But to Greyhorse's surprise, he let *this* one go. "I guess I'll have to take your word for it," he said.

Picard nodded, clearly satisfied with Simenon's response. Then he turned to the others. "You are all dismissed," he told them.

As the doctor pushed his chair back and got up, he couldn't help wishing that the second officer had some secret weapon he hadn't informed them of. He was still wishing that as he left the room and returned to sickbay.

As the doors to his quarters whispered closed behind him, Picard made his way to his workstation, sat down and established contact with a terminal elsewhere on the ship.

A moment later, Ben Zoma's face appeared on the screen. "We've got to stop meeting like this," he quipped.

"Well?" asked Picard, ignoring his friend's remark. "What did you think of my performance?"

Ben Zoma shrugged. "I thought they bought it."

"You don't think any of them were suspicious?"

"Not at all. I think they believe that you're determined to attack the supply depot." Ben Zoma smiled. "For a moment, even I believed it, and I was in on the game from the start."

The second officer nodded. "So far, so good. Now let's hope the saboteur takes the bait."

In truth, he had no intention of attacking the supply depot. The only reason he had announced his desire to do so was to encourage the saboteur to rig another command junction.

That was what he or she had done the last two times a confrontation with the Nuyyad was imminent. With luck, the saboteur would be moved to give a repeat performance.

Except this time, Picard would have Vigo monitoring every command junction in the ship, looking for anyone who might want to crawl into a Jefferies tube when no one was looking. And when they found that person, they would have their saboteur.

Or so the theory went.

"The question," said Ben Zoma, "is how far are we willing to go with this charade? Halfway to the depot? Three quarters of the way?"

The second officer posed a question of his own. "And what will we do if no one has been tripped up by then?"

"You're the acting captain," his friend reminded him.

"So I am," Picard acknowledged, his demeanor as grave as the situation demanded. "And *as* the acting captain, I think I'll worry about it when the time comes."

Greyhorse sat at his desk and tried to focus on the results of his psilosynine research. But try as he might, he couldn't keep his mind on them. He was thinking about Gerda Asmund again.

The doctor wondered what she thought about the idea of their going into battle. Was the Klingon in her looking forward to the challenge? Or was she as concerned about the prospect of facing all those ships as Greyhorse himself was?

He wished he could come up with something to make it a more even battle—and not just for the positive effect it might have on the outcome of their mission. A contribution like that would make Gerda notice him. It might even earn him her respect.

The medical officer dismissed the notion with a deep-throated sound of disgust. Who am I kidding? he asked himself. He wasn't an engineer, as so many others had been in his family. He didn't have the expertise to add anything to the *Stargazer's* arsenal.

He was just a doctor. He could treat the wounded as they were brought into sickbay, but he couldn't do anything about the odds of their getting hurt in the first place.

The only battle he had ever won was on a chessboard, back in medical school. His first-year roommate, a gregarious and energetic man named Slattery, had taught him how to play the game—not the modern three-dimensional version, but the original.

At first, Slattery had beaten him every time. Then, little by little, Greyhorse had given him more of a run for his money. Finally, just before spring break, he managed to checkmate Slattery's king.

He remembered the man's reaction with crystal clarity. "Damn," Slattery had said with undisguised wonder and admiration, "when did you turn into a mindreader?"

The doctor's eyes were drawn to the series of chemical reactions represented on his computer screen, each of which played a part in the creation of psilosynine. If he had been born with such a neurotransmitter in his brain, he might have been a *real* mindreader.

Of course, back at the Academy, Greyhorse had never met a real mindreader. Now he could actually say he had treated one in his sickbay. What would Slattery have to say about . . .

He stopped himself, his brain suddenly ranging ahead of his recollection. He was making connections that he hadn't made before, connections that seemed so obvious now that he felt mortified.

A real mindreader, he repeated inwardly.

The medical officer studied the screen again, staring at the complex chains of molecules that had figured in his re-creation of psilosynine. *If he had been born with such a neurotransmitter . . .*

Greyhorse's heart was pounding. He had to speak with Commander Picard, he told himself, and he had to do it quickly.

* * *

Picard gazed across the captain's desk at the hulking, stony-featured form of Carter Greyhorse. "You made it sound as if this were a matter of some urgency," he told the doctor.

Greyhorse leaned forward in his chair. "It is. Or rather, it might be. All I need is a chance to find out."

The second officer wasn't in the mood for riddles. "Perhaps we should start at the beginning," he suggested.

"Of course," said the doctor. He drew a deep breath and let it out slowly. "Ever since we left Earth, I've been attempting to duplicate the work of a Betazoid scientist named Relanios."

Picard nodded. "I've heard of him."

Greyhorse looked at him, surprised. "You have?"

The commander smiled. "I have other interests beside beating the tar out of hostile aliens, Doctor. As I recall, Turan Relanios was synthesizing the neurotransmitter that gives Betazoids their—"

He stopped himself in midsentence, grasping the import of what Greyhorse must have done. "You've synthesized psilosynine?"

"Yes," said the doctor, his dark eyes bright beneath his jutting brow. "Then you see the possibilities? You see how important this substance might be to us?"

Picard nodded. "Indeed."

In a human being, the neurotransmitter might create a fleeting capacity for telepathic communication. But in a mind already developed along such lines . . . a mind like a Magnian's . . .

Then something occurred to him.

"There's a danger here," said the second officer.

"That the psilosynine might trigger a reaction in the colonists' brains," Greyhorse acknowledged, dismissing the idea in the same breath. "That they might develop even greater powers . . . along with the personality aberrations experienced by Gary Mitchell."

Picard regarded him. "You don't seem especially concerned."

"I *am* concerned," said the doctor. *"Deeply* concerned. However, I made a study of Serenity Santana's neurological profile before I came to see you. And on a preliminary basis, at least, I would have to say there isn't anything to worry about."

"But you cannot be certain?"

Greyhorse shook his massive head. "Not until I have had a chance to conduct clinical tests."

"Which would have to be conducted under the most closely monitored conditions," Picard maintained.

After all, he already had a faceless saboteur to contend with. He didn't need a burgeoning superman prowling his ship in the bargain.

"You mean guards," said the doctor. "In my sickbay."

"Yes," the second officer insisted, refusing to yield on this point. "Several of them. And all armed."

Greyhorse obviously didn't like the idea. But given what was at stake, he seemed willing to acquiesce. "All right," he told the second officer. "But we need to begin as quickly as possible."

"As quickly as we can find a Magnian who will agree to be your guinea pig," said Picard.

The doctor looked unperturbed. "Leave that to me."

The second officer knew that they were about to tread new ground in the field of biomedical research. They were about to go where no human scientist had gone before.

He just hoped they wouldn't end up regretting it.

Sixteen

Captain's log, supplemental. I have discussed Dr. Greyhorse's idea with Mr. Ben Zoma, the only other officer on this ship who knows every facet of my mind in these complicated times. Unfortunately, he is less sanguine about the doctor's scheme than I am. Ben Zoma had come to think of our attack on the Nuyyad supply depot strictly as a ruse to bring our saboteur to the surface, in keeping with our original intention. Now that I am suggesting we actually go through with the assault—providing the doctor's clinical studies pan out—Ben Zoma is like a man who thought he was playing Russian roulette with a toy phaser and has discovered his weapon is real. One thing is clear to me—if we are going to attack the depot, we need to put our saboteur problem behind us. I am not oblivious to the irony in this sort of thinking. Before, we pursued the depot strategy as a way of eliminating our saboteur. Now, in effect, we have to eliminate our saboteur in order to pursue our depot strategy.

As Picard walked down the corridor, he reflected on the charge Simenon had leveled against him: *Captain Ruhalter was the same way.*

As the second officer noted at the meeting, he had respected and admired Ruhalter. However, he realized now that he wasn't completely comfortable with the man's approach to command.

Ruhalter had indeed relied on his instincts, often to the exclusion of other potentially valuable information and opinions. For a long time, of course, that method had worked for him—but in the end it had produced a bloody disaster.

Picard wasn't spurning the value of instinct—quite the contrary. He had gone with his gut more than once since his captain's demise. But he preferred to poll his officers, to obtain their feedback and draw on their expertise before he made a decision on a major point of strategy.

And not *just* his officers. He was willing to solicit advice even from the most unlikely sources.

Like the one he was about to visit at that very moment.

Up ahead, the second officer saw the open entrance to the brig and caught a glimpse of Lieutenant Pierzynski, who was leaning against a bulkhead inside. The rangy, fair-haired Pierzynski was the security officer who had taken Pug Joseph's place on guard duty.

As Picard got closer, Pierzynski must have caught sight of him, because he straightened up suddenly. If his behavior wasn't enough of a clue, the ruddy color in his face gave away his embarrassment.

"Anything I can do for you, sir?" asked Pierzynski.

"There is indeed," said the second officer. As he entered the brig area, he spotted Werber sitting on his cot behind the electromagnetic barrier. "You can repair to the hallway for a moment, Lieutenant. I would like to speak with the chief in private."

The security officer hesitated, no doubt weighing the wisdom of leaving Picard alone with seven mutineers. In the end, however, Pierzynski must have thought it was all right, because he said, "Aye, sir. I'll be right outside if you need me."

"Thank you," the second officer replied.

As Pierzynski left the room, Picard pressed some studs on a nearby bulkhead panel and altered the polarity of six of the seven barriers—Werber's being the exception. The effect was to make those barriers impervious to sound as well as light. Then he pressed another stud and saw the doors to the corridor slide shut.

Finally, he turned to Werber and nodded. "Chief."

The weapons officer shot him a dirty look. "Nice of you to visit," he declared, his voice dripping with sarcasm. "I'd offer you a chair, but I don't seem to have any lying around."

The second officer didn't take the bait. "This isn't a social call," he replied. "I've come on ship's business."

The prisoner laughed bitterly. "What do I care about your ship, Picard? If you're in the center seat, she'll be debris soon anyway."

"That's certainly a possibility," the commander said.

Clearly, it wasn't the comeback Werber had expected. "And what's that supposed to mean?"

"Since I thwarted your mutiny attempt, the *Stargazer* has been the victim of sabotage," Picard explained. "Not once, but twice now. The third time, it might prove our undoing."

That seemed to get the prisoner's attention. However, he resisted the temptation to inquire about it.

"I thought a veteran weapons officer might have some interest in identifying the saboteur," Picard went on. "Especially when he's someone who took his oath as seriously as you did."

Werber scowled. "To hell with my oath. Look where it got me."

Ah, the commander mused. Progress.

"I'll be honest with you," he told the prisoner. "I need your help. I need to pick your brain the way Captain Ruhalter did."

Werber looked at him askance. "Is it my imagination, or are you telling me you want to cut a deal?"

Picard shook his head. "No deals."

The weapons chief lifted his chin, which had grown a golden brown stubble during the time of his incarceration. "Then why should I even think about helping you?"

"Perhaps you shouldn't," the commander answered. "Think about helping *me,* that is. But you might want to help this ship, or the crewmen who served so ably under you. Or you might want to get involved purely for the sake of your own preservation."

Werber stared at him for what seemed like a very long time. Then he said, "All right. Tell me what you've got."

Picard told him, holding nothing back.

He informed the prisoner of Vigo's findings concerning the shuttle explosion. He described the way the ship's shields had dropped without notice during the second battle for Magnia. And he spoke of Vigo's second discovery, which only served to corroborate the first.

The prisoner considered the information, his eyes narrowing as he turned it over and over in his mind, inspecting it from different angles. But after a while, he shook his hairless head.

"I need more to go on," he said.

The commander was disappointed, but he didn't show it. "Right now, I'm afraid I haven't got anything more. But if additional information turns up, you will have it as soon as I do."

Werber grunted. "I can't wait."

"I will speak with you soon, I hope," said Picard. "Until then, I hope you will keep what I've told you confidential—so as not to diminish our chances of catching the saboteur." And he reached for the control panel that would open the doors to the corridor again.

But before he could press the padd, he heard the mutineer call his name. Turning again, he said, "Yes?"

Werber was on his feet, approaching the barrier. "I'm not surprised that the ship was sabotaged," he remarked, "considering how trusting you are of people like Santana."

The second officer allowed himself an ironic smile. "Interesting that you should say that, Chief. Mr. Ben Zoma is of the opinion that I'm placing too much trust in *you.*"

And with that, Picard opened the doors and emerged from the brig, allowing Pierzynski to resume his lonely vigil.

Gerda Asmund entered the turbolift ahead of her sister and punched in her destination on the control panel. Then, as Idun joined her in the compartment, Gerda watched the doors begin to slide closed.

"The end of another shift," her sister commented.

"And an uneventful one," said Gerda, as the turbolift began to move.

Idun glanced at her, her lip curled in amusement. "Another three such shifts and we'll have reached the Nuyyad supply depot. That promises to be *far* from uneventful."

Gerda nodded. "True."

"And," her sister added, "we haven't exactly been idle for the last week and a half. We were hoping for just *one* battle, remember? And so far, we've gotten three of them."

"I know," said Gerda. "Still . . ."

"What?" asked Idun.

"I don't know," the navigator told her. "It still feels to me as if something is missing."

"Something?" her sister echoed.

Gerda shrugged. "I can't put my finger on it. It's just not as satisfying as I thought it would be . . . as I *wanted* it to be."

Idun rolled her eyes. "Some saber bears aren't happy until they've eaten the entire *targ.*"

Gerda looked at her. "You think I'm a glutton?"

"Honestly?" her sister asked. "Yes."

Gerda knew Idun was seldom wrong about her. "Maybe you're right," she said. "Maybe I ought to be grateful for what I've got."

And yet, she couldn't help feeling there should be *more*.

Pug Joseph stood at the entrance to sickbay's triage area and watched Greyhorse press a hypospray containing psilosynine against Serenity Santana's naked arm.

As far as the security officer was concerned, it was insanity. If Santana was the saboteur and wanted to see the *Stargazer* destroyed, why give her yet another tool to accomplish that?

But then, he told himself, if they didn't subject Santana to the same tests as the other Magnians on board, she might catch on to their suspicions about her. And Commander Picard didn't want that.

Besides, there were precautions in place. For one thing, Greyhorse was introducing his synthetic neurotransmitter gradually, bit by tiny bit. For another, Joseph and a half dozen of his fellow security officers were on hand in case anything went awry.

Santana stole a glance at him. She knew he was here, of course. And she knew also that he still didn't trust her, no matter what she had done in the most recent battle.

It made him the perfect choice to keep an eye on her. After all, Joseph's feelings of mistrust had begun with the ambush the woman had led them to, not the discoveries of sabotage. So even if she got close enough to reach into his mind, he wouldn't be giving anything away.

Eventually, he reflected, she would slip up. She would try to rig another command junction when she thought no one was looking. And when she did, he would be there to catch her.

That is, if anyone still could.

As Gilaad Ben Zoma entered the *Stargazer*'s spare and economical engineering section, he saw the unmistakable figure of Jomar standing in front of a sleek, black diagnostic console.

The Kelvan had spent much of the last two days at the console, checking and rechecking for flaws in his vidrion injectors. Ben Zoma knew that because he had monitored Jomar's computer activities from security.

The Kelvan hadn't given even a hint that he meant to damage anything or obstruct any aspect of the ship's operations. He had simply run the same program, over and over, as if he were searching for something.

Ben Zoma wanted to know what it was. And since he couldn't ask that question of his computer screen, he had come down to engineering to get an answer from the horse's mouth.

Taking up a position at the console to Jomar's right, the human went through the motions of initiating a diagnostic of his own. Then he turned to the Kelvan, as if he were just trying to be friendly.

"It must be hard," he said.

Jomar glanced back at him. "I beg your pardon?"

Ben Zoma smiled. "You know . . . having made your contribution already. All you can do is mark time until we reach the depot."

The Kelvan returned his attention to his screen. "Inactivity is not as distasteful to my species as it is to yours—so even if I *were* marking time, it would not be a problem. However, I am not merely keeping myself busy. I am seeking the source of the shield lapse we suffered during our most recent encounter with the Nuyyad."

"That's right," said Ben Zoma. "There *was* a lapse, wasn't there?"

Jomar turned to him again and scrutinized him with his unblinking, pale-blue eyes. "Let us be honest with each other, shall we?"

"What do you mean?"

"Despite your casual reference to the recent shield failure," the Kelvan continued, "I believe it was of grave concern to you and Commander Picard. The fact that you have not asked my advice in the matter, nor made any public efforts to keep it from happening again, tells me that you may suspect me of having caused it."

Ben Zoma laughed. "You've got quite an imagination."

"Do I?" asked Jomar. "Because I also imagine that the only reason you came to engineering is to see if I will say something incriminating. If that is the case, let me put your mind to rest—I did not tamper with your shields. Your time would be better spent spying on Serenity Santana and her fellow colonists. If there was indeed an incident of tampering, it is they you should hold accountable."

"Do you have any proof that they did anything?" asked Ben Zoma.

"Gathering proof is not my job," said Jomar. "It is yours." Then he went back to his diagnostic program.

The officer looked at the Kelvan a moment longer. Then he turned back to his own console, where he continued to run a diagnostic of his own.

Well, he thought, that could have gone better.

Carter Greyhorse sat back in his chair and tapped his combadge. "Commander Picard," he said, "this is Dr. Greyhorse."

"I've been meaning to speak with you," said Picard, his voice filling the physician's office. "Have you got something to report?"

"I do," Greyhorse told him. "I've completed my clinical work and I've come to a conclusion."

"Which is?" asked the second officer.

"That, as far as I'm concerned, there's no reason not to give the Magnians full doses of the synthetic psilosynine."

"They've shown no personality aberrations?"

"None that I have noticed. No erratic increases or reductions in their telekinetic or telepathic abilities either. In fact, nothing at all that we need to be concerned about."

"But their abilities can be amplified?" asked Picard.

"Significantly," said the doctor. "By fifty to seventy percent, depending on the individual. Enough, I imagine, to make a difference in the effectiveness of our enhanced tractor beam."

"To say the least," the second officer agreed. "Tell me . . . if you began administering full doses to the Magnians now, how long would it be before they took effect?"

"Two to three hours—again, depending on the individual."

"We will arrive at our target in approximately thirty-six hours," said Picard. "Plan accordingly."

"I will," Greyhorse assured him.

"Picard out."

His conversation with the second officer completed, the doctor got up from his desk to check on his last remaining patient. Bypassing the triage area, which was occupied wall to wall by Magnians, he proceeded to his sickbay's small critical care facility.

There, he saw Commander Leach.

The first officer was laid out on a biobed, a metallic blanket covering him from the neck down, a stasis field preventing his condition from deteriorating. But even with all that, Leach looked deathly pale, an unavoidable consequence of his coma.

Greyhorse used the control padd on the side of the first officer's bed to check his vital signs. They were stable, which was about all the doctor could hope for at the moment.

If and when they reached a Federation starbase, there were things that could be done for Leach—procedures that would give the man an opportunity for a full recovery. But on the *Stargazer*, with its limited equipment, Greyhorse had done all he possibly could.

More satisfying was his work with the colonists. His efforts there would give Picard and his tactical people an advantage—the edge they needed to achieve a victory, perhaps.

I should be pleased, the doctor thought.

Unfortunately, his accomplishment hadn't obtained the thing he wanted most—Gerda Asmund's attention. He had seen her on two occasions over the last couple of days, once in a corridor and once in the lounge, and she hadn't even acknowledged his presence.

She must have known about his work. It had to be the talk of everyone on the ship. But it hadn't fazed her.

In that respect, at least, Greyhorse's victory seemed a hollow one.

Lieutenant Vigo was sitting at the computer terminal in his quarters, running yet another time-consuming scan of the ship's myriad command junctions, when he heard his name called over the intercom system.

The voice was Commander Picard's. Having heard it every few hours for the last couple of days, the Pandrilite would quite likely have recognized it in his sleep.

"Aye, sir?" said Vigo.

"Anything?" asked Picard.

"Nothing at all," the weapons officer told him. "I haven't seen even a hint of impropriety."

The commander sighed audibly. "I wish I could say that no news is good news, Lieutenant. But in this instance, that is not the case."

"I'll keep at it, sir," Vigo promised. What else could he say?

"I have no doubt of it," said Picard. "And, of course, if anything *does* come up—"

"I'll contact you immediately," the Pandrilite told him.

There was a pause. "Someday," the commander said, "you and I will have more pleasant matters to talk about. But if it's all right with you, Lieutenant, we won't talk quite as often."

Vigo smiled. "I'll be sure to remind you, sir."

* * *

For the second time in seventy-two hours, Jean-Luc Picard found himself approaching the ship's brig.

This time, it was Lieutenant Garner who was standing inside the open doorway, keeping an eye on the mutineers. And she wasn't the least bit surprised by the second officer's appearance, because it was she who had communicated with him at Hans Werber's request.

As before, the weapons chief was sitting on his cot. When he saw that Picard had arrived, he stood up. His expression was more thoughtful than belligerent for a change.

"Leave us, please," said the second officer.

Garner did as she was instructed. Then Picard touched the bulkhead controls and saw to it that he and Werber had some privacy.

"Here I am," said the commander. "Have you thought of something?"

Werber nodded. "I think so."

Picard expected him to say Santana was the guilty party, and attempt to lay out some proof of it. But he didn't. In fact, the weapons officer was no longer quite so sure that the colonist was involved.

"Then who's the saboteur?" asked the commander.

"I don't know," said the prisoner. "But I know how to find him." And he went on to elaborate.

Picard considered the information. "I appreciate your help," he said at last. "If it leads us to the saboteur—"

The mutineer preempted him with a gesture. "Don't make me any promises, Commander. Just get the sonuvabitch."

Picard nodded. "I will certainly try."

Seventeen

Greyhorse pressed the hypospray against Armor Brentano's arm and released a full dose of psilosynine into the man's system.

The Magnian looked at him. "That's it?"

"That's it," the medical officer confirmed.

"When will I start feeling different?" Brentano asked.

"In the next two to three hours," said Greyhorse. "And you will continue to feel that way for anywhere from four to five hours."

"So we're not far from the depot?" the colonist concluded.

"So I've been told."

Reaching into the pocket of his lab coat, Greyhorse removed a metal disk about the size of his fingernail. Positioning it between thumb and forefinger, he placed it against Brentano's temple—where it remained.

"What's this?" his patient wanted to know.

"A monitoring device," he said. "If your brain waves start to change, I want to know about it."

"So you can shut me down?" asked Brentano.

"Exactly right," said the medical officer. "For the sake of everyone on this ship—you included."

"What if I snap and rip it off?" he asked, smiling.

Greyhorse didn't feel compelled to smile back. "Then I'll know it and the result will be the same."

"I'll remember that," Brentano promised him.

I assure you, the doctor added silently, at least one of us will.

Gerda Asmund had hoped that her mood would improve. However, it had gotten worse with each passing day.

Finally, as the *Stargazer* came within sensor range of her target, the navigator found herself looking forward to the battle ahead. However, the prospect wasn't the blood-roiling elixir it should have been.

What's more, her sister knew it. Idun had been watching her like a mother *s'tarahk* ever since their talk in the turbolift, trying her best to gain some insight into Gerda's feelings.

But how could Idun understand her lack of enthusiasm when Gerda herself didn't understand it?

Abruptly, she was drawn out of her reverie by a beeping sound—a sensor alarm she had set earlier. Looking down at her monitor, she saw that visual information was available on the depot.

Her sister, who had heard the alarm as well, turned to her. Idun, at least, was eager to engage the enemy, and had been for some time. Gerda could see it in her eyes.

The navigator glanced back over her shoulder at Commander Picard, who was discussing something with Lieutenant Ben Zoma in front of the captain's chair. "We're in visual range of the depot," she announced.

Picard regarded her. "On screen," he said.

Working at her controls, Gerda complied.

Pug Joseph was standing just inside the entrance to the engineering support room on Deck 26, watching Serenity Santana and her fellow colonists gather in an approximate semicircle and exert their influence on the *Stargazer*'s dorsal tractor node.

Not that the security officer could actually see the Magnians *doing* anything. After all, they were working solely with the power of their minds, their collective energy amplified by the neurotransmitter Dr. Greyhorse had concocted for them.

The only visible evidence of the colonists' efforts was the flock of triangular, palm-sized devices they had attached to the tractor node days earlier. The things were humming softly to themselves and throbbing with a bright yellow light.

They had hummed and throbbed the same way during the second battle for Magnia. At least, that was how Joseph remembered it. It frustrated him that the Magnians' activities were so foreign to him, so alien, and therefore so difficult to monitor.

How was he supposed to keep an eye on Santana if he couldn't tell what she was really doing? How did he know she was gearing up for the battle ahead and not plotting with her friends to cripple the ship?

The answer, of course, was he *didn't*.

Suddenly, Santana turned away from the tractor node and looked back over her shoulder at him. The expression on her face—one of anxiety—made the security officer wonder what the woman was up to.

Pug, he heard in his head, *something's wrong. We can sense someone tampering with a command junction.*

Joseph looked at her, wary of a trick. "Who's doing it?" he asked.

Santana didn't answer right away. Then she made a single word materialize in his brain: *Jomar.*

The security officer walked over to the nearest console and tapped into the *Stargazer*'s internal sensor net. However, there was no indication of any tampering. There wasn't anyone in the Jefferies tubes at all. And Jomar, apparently, was in his quarters.

He turned back to Santana, wondering what she was trying to pull *this* time. "No one is anywhere near a command junction."

She left the semicircle and came over to him. Gazing at the monitor, she saw what he had seen—in other words, nothing.

"He's there," Santana insisted. She looked up at Joseph. "Dammit, I can *feel* him."

Reacting to the woman's display of emotion, he put his hand on the phaser pistol dangling at his hip. "I'll have someone check Jomar's quarters. In the meantime, you can—"

"No!" she snapped, her dark eyes filled with dread—or so it seemed. "By then, it'll be too late!"

The security officer drew his phaser, leery of what Santana could do with the doctor's neurotransmitter flowing in her veins. "Move back," he told her. "Do it."

She looked at his weapon, then at him again. "You don't understand," she told him.

"Don't I?" he asked.

Then something happened—Joseph wasn't sure what. He seemed to lose control of his limbs, his body becoming a heavy and unresponsive mass of flesh. The phaser fell from his limp, paralyzed hand and hit the deck.

And a moment later, the security officer joined it, his mind spiraling down into darkness.

As Picard watched, Gerda Asmund manipulated her controls. A moment later, the viewscreen filled with the image he had been waiting for.

And what an image it was.

In the second officer's imagination, the depot had been an impressive thing—a large, sprawling facility surrounded by powerful-looking, diamond-shaped warships. It had been equipped with a multitude of cargo hatches and docking ports, everything it needed to facilitate the transfer of food and material goods.

Its reality was even more impressive—and a good deal more daunting. The depot looked more like a fortress than a supply facility, and more like the crown of an ancient king than either, with its circular configuration of diamond-shaped towers and its circlet of weapons ports and its flawless, almost luminescent surfaces.

As prodigious as the enemy's fighting ships were, the depot was bigger and better-armed by a factor of at least ten. It was perhaps the truest symbol of Nuyyad pride they had seen yet.

"Looks like this is the place," breathed Ben Zoma.

"You know what they say," Picard told him. "The bigger they are, the harder they fall."

"An interesting observation," the other man noted. "But given a choice, I'll take big anyday."

Picard shot him a disparaging glance.

"Except this one, of course," Ben Zoma added cheerfully.

"Of course," the second officer responded. He scanned for the number of Nuyyad vessels. "I'm reading four ships. Can you confirm that, Lieutenant Asmund?"

"I show four as well, sir."

"It could have been worse," Picard allowed.

Suddenly, an alert light on the captain's armrest began blinking red. Noticing it, Picard touched the padd beside it.

"Mr. Vigo?" he asked, feeling an adrenaline rush as he anticipated the weapons chief's response.

"Aye, sir. I've got a problem in the phaser line. Command junction twenty-eight, accessible from Deck Ten."

"Acknowledged," said the second officer. He straightened and glanced at his friend. "Let's go."

"I'm right behind you," Ben Zoma assured him.

Together, they entered the turbolift and punched in a destination. Then they removed the phasers they had hidden in their tunics.

When the turbolift stopped at Deck Ten, they got out and pelted down the corridor. Before long, they came to a ladder and a round door that would give them access to the network of Jefferies tubes that permeated the ship.

Picard went up the ladder first, pulled open the door and crawled into the tube. As Ben Zoma had promised, he wasn't far behind.

It wasn't easy making progress through the tube's cylindrical, circuit-studded confines, which forced the Starfleet officers to hunch over as they ran. However, they reached the first intersection more quickly than Picard would have believed possible.

It was then that they heard the clatter of a violent confrontation. Looking in every direction, Ben Zoma finally spotted it.

"There," he said, pointing.

Following his friend's gesture, the second officer saw two combatants. One appeared to be Santana. The other was a dark, many-tentacled thing that could only have been Jomar in his natural state.

The colonist was trying to hold the Kelvan off with her arms—the way any human might try to hold off something big and monstrous—and not having much luck. But to Picard's surprise and dismay, she was also launching a series of tiny, pink lightning bolts at her adversary.

The Kelvan recoiled wherever the tiny lightnings struck, but the rest of him remained unaffected. Flinging one slimy limb after another at his target, he tried to envelop her, to crush her in his powerful embrace. And no doubt, he would have, had it not been for the energy bolts Santana was able to marshal against him.

As Picard and Ben Zoma moved closer, neither Santana nor Jomar seemed able to gain an advantage. In short, their struggle was a standoff—an impassioned and violent one, certainly, but a standoff all the same.

Ben Zoma swore beneath his breath. "For heaven sakes, Jean-Luc, we've got to do something."

Picard nodded. "But to whom?"

Clearly, one of the combatants was the saboteur they had been looking for. But the other was an innocent bystander at worst, and at best a hero who had risked life and limb.

"We'll stun them both," Picard decided.

"Done," said his companion.

As Picard took aim at Santana, he saw her glance in his direction. Her eyes seemed to reach out to him, pleading for understanding.

It was all the distraction that Jomar needed. Lashing out at Santana, he snapped her head back. The colonist went limp. But before she could slump to the bottom of the tube, the Kelvan caught her up in his tentacles.

Picard still didn't know which of the two was the saboteur. However, he didn't want to see Santana hurt any worse than she was already.

"Let her go!" he barked at Jomar, his voice echoing raucously along the length of the Jefferies tube.

The Kelvan turned to him and underwent a transformation. He seemed to re-shape himself before Picard's eyes, his tentacles shrinking and consolidating and giving way to arms and legs. In a matter of seconds, Jomar had assumed his human form again.

With an unconscious Santana in his arms, he approached the Starfleet officer. "I have apprehended the saboteur," he said, his blue eyes steady and unblinking, his voice as flat as ever.

Picard didn't lower his weapon. After all, there was still a lot that had to be cleared up. "That's far enough," he told the Kelvan.

Jomar stopped in his tracks. "Is something wrong?"

Picard declined to answer the question. "Put Santana down and back away," he said.

The Kelvan hesitated for just a moment. Then he knelt, placed the colonist on the curved surface and retreated from the spot.

Picard pointed to Santana with his phaser. "Gilaad," he said, "make sure she's still alive."

Ben Zoma tucked his weapon away and moved to the woman's side. Then he felt her neck for a pulse and looked back at his friend.

"She's still with us, all right. I—"

Before he could get another word out, the tube filled with a hideous, high-pitched scream and Jomar began to change again. Faster than Picard would have thought possible, his human attributes melted away and a swarm of long, dark tentacles took their place.

Picard raised his phaser and aimed it at the center of the monstrosity. But before he could press the trigger, he felt something clammy close around his hand. With a twisting motion that nearly broke his wrist, it wrenched the weapon out of his grasp.

By then, Ben Zoma had drawn his phaser—but he wasn't quick enough either.

As Picard watched helplessly, Jomar snatched the man's phaser away with one tentacle and lashed him across the face with another.

Ben Zoma crumpled, stunned or worse. Picard started forward to help his friend, but a moist, black tentacle grabbed hold of his ankle and a half-dozen others knocked him off his feet.

Looking up, he saw a pair of tiny, gray orbs glaring at him above an obscenely pink maw. He tried to crawl away, but he was still held fast by the ankle. Unable to escape, he watched helplessly as a swarm of tentacles slithered toward his throat.

Picard fought some of them away, but he couldn't fight all of them. He felt a tentacle snare one of his wrists, then the other. And finally, as he growled out loud with the effort to free himself, he felt a third tentacle begin to close around his throat.

The Kelvan's grip tightened and Picard's breath was cut off. He tried to claw at the muscular piece of flesh around his windpipe, but his wrists were too well constrained. Deprived of oxygen while his exertions made his need for it even more urgent, he saw darkness closing in on him.

Ben Zoma, the second officer thought. His friend was his only chance now—if he was still alive.

Suddenly, there was a flash of red light. *Phaser light*—Picard was certain of it. But Jomar's tentacle didn't let go.

Then he saw the flash again, even brighter than before—and this time, it had some effect. The Kelvan seemed to stagger under the impact and lose his grip on his victim's wrists and ankle.

A third flash, and Jomar lost his stranglehold as well. Picard slumped to the floor and drew in a deep, rasping breath.

His instincts told him to run—to get out of range of the Kelvan's deadly tentacles. But he resisted the impulse and did something else entirely. He sought out his captor's face—if it could indeed be called a face—and drove his fist into it as hard as he could.

The yellow eyes blinked and the pink maw let out a blood-chilling scream—not out of pain, Picard thought, as much as surprise. Apparently, the last thing Jomar had expected was a punch in the nose.

It threw the Kelvan off-balance and made him that much more vulnerable to what followed—an intense, red stream of directed energy that got through the mess of dark tentacles and hammered Jomar's grotesque torso.

The Kelvan collapsed, his long, snakelike limbs flying in every direction. He looked disoriented, his maw opening and closing, his gray orbs half-lidded with dark flesh—but not yet out for the count.

Then yet another blast battered his slimy black head . . . and it lolled to the bottom of the tube, senseless.

Picard kicked away a tentacle that lay across his foot and turned to his rescuer. He was eager to thank his friend Ben Zoma for his dramatic and timely phaser assault.

Then he saw that it wasn't his friend at all. It was Pug Joseph, staring wide-eyed at Jomar with his weapon still in his hand.

Eighteen

"Mr. Joseph?" said Picard.

The security officer looked as much in need of an explanation as the second officer. "Sir?" he responded.

Before Picard could clear up any of the confusion, he had the Kelvan's other victims to think about. Locating Ben Zoma, he saw that his friend was trying to sit up—a good portent indeed.

Santana, on the other hand, was still stretched out on the bottom of the tube, a sweep of raven hair obscuring part of her face. Kneeling beside her, the second officer took her pulse.

Joseph knelt too, his brow knit at the sight of the stricken woman, his expression giving away his very genuine concern. "Is she . . . ?"

"Her pulse is strong," Picard assured the security officer. "I believe she will be all right."

But she wouldn't be participating in any battles anytime soon, he decided. And not just because of the beating she had taken.

Santana had never demonstrated the ability to create pink lightning bolts before—but Gary Mitchell had. Kirk reported that he had seen the man do it more than once. If the Magnian's newfound ability was a side effect of the doctor's psilosynine, the second officer was going to shut the experiment down as soon as possible.

Glancing at Jomar, he saw that the Kelvan was still unconscious. However, Picard was uncertain how long he would remain that way.

He tapped his combadge. "Picard to Lieutenant Ang. I need all the security officers you can spare, on the double."

"Aye, sir," said Ang. "Where shall I send them?"

"I'm in a Jefferies tube accessible from Deck Ten. Hurry, Lieutenant. I have injured to get to sickbay."

"On our way," Ang assured him.

"What happened?" asked Ben Zoma, holding the side of his mottled, swollen face as he staggered to his feet.

"We found our saboteur," said Picard.

Gilaad Ben Zoma sat on a biobed in sickbay and allowed Greyhorse to inject him with a hypospray full of painkiller.

Eventually, he would need oral surgery as a result of the blow Jomar had dealt him. But for now, he couldn't afford not to be up and about.

"How do you feel now?" asked the doctor.

"Much better," said Ben Zoma.

"Then you agree?" asked Picard, who was standing beside Greyhorse.

Greyhorse nodded. "Absolutely. We can't let the Magnians direct our tractor beam if even one of them is exhibiting unexpected side effects."

Ben Zoma looked across the triage area at Santana, who was lying on the same biobed she had occupied during her coma. The woman was awake, but dazed—the result of a severe concussion.

Pug Joseph was standing beside her, theoretically to guard against her doing anything rash. But in truth, the security officer looked more concerned than watchful.

As Ben Zoma understood it, Santana had knocked Joseph out in an effort to reach Jomar before he could carry out his latest act of sabotage. When she found herself unequal to the task, she roused the security officer telepathically—something she couldn't have done without the psilosynine amplifying her abilities—and summoned him to tip the balance.

Ben Zoma was glad she had. And he wasn't the only one.

"For the time being," said the doctor, "I'm going to get the other colonists down here and administer sedatives to them. But I can't make any promises as to the drugs' effectiveness—"

"So you'll need security personnel," Picard deduced. "I understand. Believe me, Doctor, I wouldn't have had it any other way."

The second officer had barely completed his statement when a handful of security officers, led by Lieutenant Ang, escorted Jomar into sickbay. The Kelvan had assumed human form again, Ben Zoma noticed, and didn't appear to be offering the officers any resistance.

"Bring him over here," Greyhorse instructed them, tilting his head to indicate an empty biobed.

Ang looked to Ben Zoma first.

"Do as the doctor says," Ben Zoma told him.

"I am not in need of medical attention," Jomar protested.

"I will be the judge of that," said Greyhorse.

As the Kelvan was brought to the bed, Picard put his hand on his friend's shoulder. "You *are* all right, aren't you?" he asked.

Ben Zoma shrugged. "I've been better. Fortunately, my body doesn't know that right now. How about you?"

"I'll live," the second officer told him. He glanced at Jomar. "If only long enough to find out our guest's motivation for sabotage."

"I'd be interested in that story myself," said Ben Zoma. "And now that we're not headed for the depot any longer, we'll have plenty of time to hear him tell it."

Picard looked at him questioningly. "Not headed for the depot . . . ?"

"Our secret weapon is kaput, remember? Without the Magnians manning our tractor beam, we don't stand a chance. And with our saboteur out in the open, there's no reason to even pretend we're going."

His friend frowned. "Perhaps you're r—"

"Commander Picard?" came a voice over the intercom, interrupting the second officer's remark.

Ben Zoma recognized the voice as Gerda Asmund's.

"Yes, Lieutenant?" Picard responded.

"Sir," said the navigator, "two of the Nuyyad ships have left the depot and are coming after us."

In the wake of the announcement, the security officers exchanged glances. Greyhorse looked disturbed as well.

The muscles rippled in the second officer's jaw. "Then again," he said, "perhaps we'll be having that battle after all."

Ben Zoma acknowledged the grim truth of Picard's statement. The depot was significantly closer to the galactic barrier than the *Stargazer* was. If they wanted to return to warn the Federation about the Nuyyad, they would at some point have to engage the enemy.

"We can't resort to the Magnians," Ben Zoma sighed. "But without them, we'll be outgunned."

His friend shook his head. "Two against one, Gilaad. It doesn't sound very promising, does it?"

"We can still beat them," someone said.

Tracing the comment to its source, Ben Zoma saw Jomar looking at them from his heavily guarded biobed. The Kelvan's pale-blue eyes glistened in the light from the overheads.

"I beg your pardon?" Picard replied.

"I said we can beat them," Jomar repeated without inflection. "That is, if you allow me to complete my work."

"And what work is that?" asked Ben Zoma.

The Kelvan continued to stare at them. "The work I did in an attempt to minimize the effects of your plasma flow regulator and distribution manifold on your phaser system."

Ang looked at him. "What . . . ?"

But Ben Zoma understood. "I get it now. That secondary command line you were laying in . . . you were trying to streamline our plasma delivery system and beef up phaser power."

"That is correct," Jomar confirmed. "The incidents you no doubt attributed to sabotage were inadvertent and . . . unfortunate."

Picard regarded the Kelvan with narrowed eyes. "You were expressly forbidden to tamper with the phaser system."

Jomar looked unimpressed. "The Nuyyad must be stopped, Commander. And I had every confidence that the *Stargazer*'s plasma conduits could tolerate the modifications."

The second officer turned ruddy with anger. "It wasn't your choice to make, Jomar. It was Captain Ruhalter's—and now it's mine. But at no time was it ever *yours.*"

"I stand corrected," Jomar replied evenly, though it was clear he didn't mean it in the least. "However, you now have an option that you would not have had otherwise."

He was right, of course, Ben Zoma reflected. And with a couple of Nuyyad warships on a collision course with the *Stargazer,* they needed all the options they could get.

Picard must have been thinking the same thing. No doubt, he was leery about working alongside someone who had been trying to choke him a short while earlier—and the Kelvan's scheme was still a dangerous one.

But the alternative was to take a chance on making Gary Mitchell–style monsters out of Santana's contingent. And that, in the long run, might be infinitely *more* dangerous.

The second officer looked at Ben Zoma. What do *you* think? Picard seemed to be asking.

"Let's do it," his friend said.

The commander thought about it a moment longer. Then he turned to Jomar again. "Very well. How much time do you need?"

"Not much," the Kelvan told him. "Twenty minutes, perhaps."

Picard nodded. "You've got it."

Once again, Ben Zoma thought, they were putting their trust in someone who had previously proven unworthy of it. In Santana's case, they had been fortunate enough to make the right choice.

Now they were shooting for double or nothing.

Captain's log, supplemental. Rather than wait for the enemy vessels to come to us, I have decided to go on the offensive and meet them head-on. I hope Jomar's phaser enhancement is everything he claims, or we will find ourselves with a great many regrets.

In the dusky scarlet illumination of a red alert, Picard eyed the pair of Nuyyad vessels on his viewscreen.

"Range?" he asked.

"Twenty-two billion kilometers," said Gerda, "and closing."

At warp seven, the *Stargazer* would cover fifty percent of that distance in the next minute and meet the enemy halfway. It didn't leave them much time to gird themselves for battle.

The second officer turned to Vigo. "Power up phasers and photon torpedoes," he said.

"Aye, sir," Vigo responded.

Picard looked to Gerda again. "Raise shields."

"Raising shields," she confirmed.

The commander took a deep breath and watched the Nuyyad ships loom larger on the screen. For the time being, they were content to fly parallel courses, though that would no doubt change in the next few seconds.

As if on cue, the enemy vessels peeled off in different directions, aiming to catch the Federation ship in a crossfire. Picard thought for a moment and turned to his helm officer.

"Go after the one to starboard," he commanded.

"Aye, sir," said Idun.

Abruptly, the *Stargazer* veered to the right, keeping one of the Nuyyad ships in sight while momentarily ignoring the other. It was the maneuver that had been recommended by all Picard's tactics instructors at the Academy—but not as a long-term solution.

It would buy him a few seconds, at best. But if luck was on his side, that would be all the time he needed.

"Lock on target," he told Vigo.

"Targeting," came the reply.

"Phaser range," said Gerda.

"Fire!" snapped Picard.

Twin phaser beams lanced through space and skewered the enemy ship. At normal strength, the commander would have expected them to weaken the diamond-shape's shields, perhaps even shake up the Nuyyad inside.

The crimson beams didn't do that. They did a lot *more*.

Instead of softening the enemy's defenses, they seared right through them and penetrated the Nuyyad's hull. Before Picard could give Vigo the order to fire again, his adversary suffered a vicious, blinding explosion amidships. With the second officer looking on in morbid fascination, the Nuyyad succumbed to a second explosion and then a third, and finally came apart in a white-hot burst of debris.

"Enemy vessel to port," Gerda reported.

"Bring us about," Picard told Idun.

As they swung hard to port, the viewscreen found their other antagonist. But at the same time, a string of vidrion bundles came slicing from the vessel's cannons, filling the screen with their fury.

The second officer braced himself, but the impact wasn't as bad as he had expected. Their vidrion-reinforced shields were holding up well—he could tell even without asking Gerda for the details.

"Target and fire!" he told Vigo.

A moment later, their phaser banks erupted again—gutting the enemy ship as they had gutted the other one, and with much the same results. The Nuyyad was ripped to shreds in a chain of spectacular explosions, one right after the other. The last of them left nothing in its wake but a languidly expanding wave of space junk.

Suddenly, the *Stargazer* was alone in the void, registering nothing on her forward viewscreen but the light of distant stars. Picard expelled a breath he hadn't known he was holding.

Ben Zoma appeared beside him. "Apparently," he said, "Jomar knew what he was talking about."

"Apparently so," the second officer replied.

But there was still the question they had brought up when Captain Ruhalter was still alive—as to whether the plasma conduits could tolerate the kind of stress Jomar's enhancement would place on them. With that in mind, Picard asked Vigo to run a diagnostic.

After a moment, the weapons officer made his report. "The stress appears to have been considerable, sir. But the conduits held. There's no sign of damage to them."

The commander nodded. "Thank you, Lieutenant."

Ben Zoma looked at him. "Now what?"

Picard frowned. There was really only one option, as far as he was concerned. "Now we go after the depot."

His colleague smiled a halfhearted smile. "I was afraid you were going to say that."

"If you were in my place," asked the second officer, "would you be turning back now?"

"If I were in your place," said Ben Zoma, "I wouldn't have come this far in the first place."

Picard shot him a disparaging look.

"You asked," his friend reminded him.

By the commander's estimate, they were still two hundred and fifty billion kilometers from their target—more than twenty minutes' travel at warp seven. With their pursuers out of the way, there was still plenty of time to change course and head for the barrier instead.

But Picard had undertaken a mission, and he was determined to see it through. "Resume course," he told Idun.

The helm officer seemed to approve of the decision. "Aye, sir," she said, and made a small adjustment in their heading.

Soon, the commander reflected, their struggles would be over—one way or the other.

Pug Joseph looked down at Serenity Santana, whose dark eyes were closed in recuperative repose.

She might have died in her fight with Jomar, he told himself. The Kelvan might have miscalculated and killed her. And then Joseph would never have had the chance to speak with Santana again . . .

And to tell her he was sorry.

Not for being vigilant, because it was a security officer's job to be vigilant. But for not accepting her apology when she tendered it to him in the engineering support room on Deck 26.

On the other side of the triage area, Dr. Greyhorse was puttering around with his instruments. He seemed distracted—as distracted as Joseph had been when he last visited sickbay. Or maybe, knowing how the security officer felt about Santana, the doctor was simply giving him some privacy.

Joseph gazed at the colonist again and resisted an impulse to straighten a lock of her hair. He had been so determined not to get fooled again, he had almost prevented her from going after Jomar.

If he had been successful, the Kelvan would have faced Picard and Ben Zoma alone, without any help from Santana. There was no telling what would have happened to the officers then.

Picard trusted her, Joseph thought. Maybe I should have trusted her too. He resolved to tell her that when she woke.

There's no need, said a voice in his head. *You've told me already.*

And Santana opened her eyes.

He felt his face flush with embarrassment. "You were reading my mind," he said accusingly.

"Are you upset with me?" she asked, her voice thin and reedy from the medication Greyhorse had administered.

The security officer started to say yes, started to protest that she had violated his privacy. Then he stopped himself. "Not anymore," he told her. "Not after what you risked to stop Jomar."

Santana smiled wearily. "I was afraid he would transform me into a tetrahedron," she murmured, "the way he transformed Brentano. That made me fight a little harder."

"So he wouldn't get the chance," Joseph deduced.

"Uh huh." The colonist drew a breath, then let it out. "I'm glad you're not angry at me."

So was he. He said so.

"I'm so tired," Santana told him, stumbling over the words. "Would you do me a favor, Lieutenant?"

"Anything," the security officer answered.

"Would you stand guard over me? Just for old times' sake?"

He nodded. "I'd be glad to."

A moment later, Santana was asleep.

*   *   *

Picard regarded the Nuyyad supply installation on his screen and counted the number of warships circling it.

"Is it my imagination," he asked Ben Zoma, "or are there four vessels defending the depot again?"

"There are four, all right," said his friend. "Apparently, the Nuyyad had other ships in the area."

"And maybe more on the way," the second officer noted. "All the more reason to act quickly."

Ben Zoma didn't respond to the statement, but his expression wasn't one of complete confidence. Then again, he hadn't been eager to go after the depot from the beginning.

Picard took another look at the depot and its fleet of defenders. Was his friend right? Were they out of their league? Or would their secret weapon be enough to pull off a victory?

There was only one way to find out.

"All hands to battle stations," he said.

All over the ship, he knew, crewmen were rushing to their predetermined posts. He remembered what it was like to respond to such an order, to know that a battle was imminent.

On the bridge, it was a different experience entirely. It was at once headier and more daunting. After all, he wasn't just responsible for one isolated job. He was responsible for *all* of them.

"Strafing run?" Ben Zoma suggested.

The second officer shook his head. He had already considered the idea and rejected it. "I would rather be in their midst, where they will have to worry about hitting each other with their vidrion bursts."

Just as the second officer expressed that sentiment, he saw two more of the enemy ships move out to meet him. Apparently, the choice of approach had been taken out of their hands.

"Phaser range?" he asked Vigo.

"In a few seconds, sir," the weapons officer told him.

"Target the foremost vessel," said Picard.

"Targeting," Vigo responded.

"Range," Gerda announced.

The commander eyed the viewscreen. "Fire!"

The Nuyyad tried to twist out of the way. But the *Stargazer*'s phaser beams punched through the vessel's shields, shearing off its nacelles on one side and cutting a deep furrow on the other.

A moment later, the enemy ship met its demise in a ball of yellow-white flame—a blast so prodigious that it licked at the extremities of the victim's sister vessels.

"Evasive maneuvers!" Picard called out. "Pattern Gamma!"

Accelerating, the *Stargazer* split the difference between the Nuyyad ships and blew right through the remnants of the vessel she had destroyed. The enemy must have been surprised, because it didn't even get off a volley.

"Pattern Alpha!" the second officer demanded. "I want them both in our sights again!"

Idun muscled the ship hard to port until the Nuyyad appeared on the viewscreen. Then she bore down on them.

"Target the starboard vessel and fire!" said Picard.

At close range, their enhanced phasers were even more effective. The beams rammed through one side of the Nuyyad ship and came out the other. And in the process, they started a series of savage explosions that gradually tore the vessel to pieces.

The third vessel raked them with a vidrion barrage, causing the *Stargazer* to jerk to port. But again, their shields kept them from serious harm. Then it was the Federation ship's turn again.

"Target and fire!" Picard told his weapons officer.

Once more, Vigo's aim was impeccable. Their phasers speared the Nuyyad vessel through its heart, causing it to tremble and writhe with plasma eruptions until it was claimed by a massive conflagration.

For the second time that day, the second officer found himself the winning combatant. But he wasn't done yet—not while the supply depot still lay ahead of them.

"Resume course?" asked Idun.

Picard nodded. "And give me a visual of the installation."

Instantly, an image of the depot leaped to the viewscreen. Up close, the thing was even more gigantic, even more daunting than before. It dwarfed its lone remaining defender.

The second officer focused himself on the task ahead. He hadn't forgotten that he chose this course over the objections of others. If it failed, he would have only himself to blame.

That is, if he was still in a position to blame anyone at all.

Abruptly, the last of the Nuyyad ships came after them. No doubt, its commanding officer knew the other vessels had failed miserably, and his was likely to do the same. But it didn't stop him.

"Phaser range," said Vigo.

Picard regarded the enemy. "Target and fire!"

This time, the enemy veered at just the right moment and eluded the *Stargazer*'s first volley. But her second assault nailed the Nuyyad ship. Pierced to its core, it shivered violently and succumbed to a frenzy of yellow-white brilliance.

That left only one target. The second officer considered its mighty sprawl of diamond-shaped plates on the viewscreen.

It hadn't fired a single shot. Maybe I was wrong about its firepower, Picard thought. Maybe it's a sitting duck after all.

"Aim for its center," he decided. "Fire when ready, Lieutenant."

"Aye, sir," said Vigo, his long, blue fingers skittering over the lower portion of his control panel.

But the supply depot struck first.

It sent out a stream of vidrion bundles that far surpassed anything the Nuyyad's ships had thrown at them. Seizing the captain's chair for support, the commander rode out one bone-jarring impact after the other.

"Status?" he called out, as Idun did her best to make them a more difficult target.

"Shields down twenty-six percent," Gerda responded crisply. "No hull breaches, no casualties."

"Sir!" said Vigo, his voice taut with urgency.

Picard turned to him. "Lieutenant?"

The Pandrilite looked stricken. "Sir, phasers are off-line!"

The second officer felt the blood rush from his face. Without the amplified phaser power Jomar had given them, they were all but toothless.

And the depot still hung defiantly in space, ready to serve as the key to a Nuyyad invasion of the Federation . . .

Nineteen

Another pale-green flight of vidrion packets blossomed on Picard's viewscreen, seeking to bludgeon his ship out of space.

Idun gave it the slip with a twisting pattern that tested the limits of the inertial dampers. However, she couldn't keep it up indefinitely. The installation's gunners were too accurate, their weapons too powerful.

And there was no telling how many more enemy vessels were on their way, eager to finish what the depot's vidrion cannons had started.

To this point, Picard had relied on the talents of the Magnians and a Kelvan to get him past the rough spots. Now he was on his own. If he was going to prevail, he was going to have to rely on *himself.*

But what could he do? The depot was significantly better armed than they were, better equipped . . .

Then he remembered something one of his professors had taught him back at the Academy, when he and his classmates were studying shield theory. *The larger and more complicated an object's shape, the more difficult it is to protect effectively.*

The depot was very large, very complicated. Its armor had to have some chinks in it. All the second officer had to do was find them.

"Mr. Vigo," he said, approaching the weapons console, "analyze the installation's shield structure. See if you can find a weak point."

He peered over the Pandrilite's shoulder as he called up a sensor-driven picture of the enemy's shields. Together, they pored over it, knowing that they might absorb a vidrion barrage at any moment.

"Here," said Vigo, pointing to a spot between two of the massive diamond shapes that encircled the depot. "There's a lower graviton concentration at each of these junctures. If we can get close enough, we might be able to penetrate one with a few well-placed photon torpedoes."

Picard agreed. "We will get close enough," he assured the weapons officer. Then he turned to Idun. "Aim for a juncture between two of the diamond shapes. We need to hit it with a torpedo barrage."

His helm officer did as she was instructed. Like a hawk stooping to take a field mouse, the *Stargazer* darted for the depot's weak spot.

The Nuyyad gunners must have seen them coming. But unlike a ship, the installation wasn't mobile. It couldn't evade their attack. All it could do was punish its enemy with all the firepower at its disposal.

Picard felt the bridge shiver as the first volley rammed into them. The viewscreen went dead for a second, then flickered back to life.

"Shields down forty-two percent," Gerda called out.

The second volley hit them even harder, rattling the second officer's teeth. An unmanned console went up in sparks and filled the air with the acrid smell of smoke.

"Shields down sixty-four percent," the navigator barked.

The third volley forced Picard to grab Vigo's chairback or be knocked off his feet. As he recovered, he saw that a plasma conduit had sprung a leak.

"Shields down ninety percent," Gerda reported dutifully.

They couldn't take another blast like the last one, the second officer told himself. But then, maybe they wouldn't have to.

"Now, Mr. Vigo!" he shouted over the hiss of seething plasma.

A string of golden photon torpedoes went hurtling toward the depot. Before the enemy could fire again, the torpedoes hit their target—and were rewarded with a titanic display of pyrotechnics.

But did they pierce the Nuyyad's shields? As Idun Asmund pulled them off their collision course, Picard peered at the weapons console and checked the depot's status.

For a moment, he couldn't believe his eyes. Then Vigo said it out loud, giving his discovery the weight of reality.

"We must have hit one of their primary shield generators, sir. They're defenseless from one end to the other."

As defenseless as the *Stargazer* had been after its initial encounter with the Nuyyad. As defenseless as the Magnians had been when the second officer found them.

Picard eyed the viewscreen, which was still tracking the enemy depot as Idun brought them about. The installation didn't look any different to the human eye, but to their sensors it was naked and unprotected.

He had a feeling the Nuyyad would remember this day. Certainly, he knew *he* would. "Target and fire," he told his weapons officer.

Vigo unleashed one torpedo assault after the other, pounding the installation in a half-dozen places. And everywhere the matter-antimatter packets landed, they blew something up.

Finally, the last remaining section erupted in a fit of expanding energy, painting the void with its glory. Then it faded, leaving an empty space where a Nuyyad presence had been.

"Serves them right," said Ben Zoma.

Picard looked at his friend and wished he could disagree.

Captain's log, supplemental. We have returned to Magnia to drop off the colonists who aided us with our tactical enhancements. Fortunately, none of them have shown any lasting effects from their exposure to psilosynine. Though I had reason to distrust these people when I first met them, I now see that they are as trustworthy as anyone I know. They are also what the name of their ancestors' ship proclaimed: valiant. In accordance with Shield Williamson's request, I recommend that Guard Daniels be returned to the colony and that its existence henceforth be kept a Federation secret—for our good as well as that of the colonists. After all, there are those who might try to tap into the Magnians' potential for their own ends. As for Jomar . . . I am grateful for his assistance in destroying the Nuyyad depot, which proved critical to our efforts. However, his arro-

*gance, penchant for violence and insistence on implementing his plans
over our objections mark him as someone the Federation should avoid in
the future. And while it pains me to paint all Kelvans with the same brush,
I find I must do exactly that—or fail in my service to the Federation. My
recommendation is that we encourage the Kelvans to remain an insular
society . . . indefinitely.*

Picard gazed at Serenity Santana, the sun of her world sinking through tall
trees into a deep, red-orange miasma behind her.

"Will you miss me?" she asked with a smile, the mountain wind lifting her
raven hair.

Torn between emotions, the second officer shrugged. "What can I say? I wish
we had met under different circumstances."

"Then . . . you *won't* miss me?"

He couldn't help chuckling a little at her cleverness. "I didn't say that," he told her.

Abruptly, his combadge beeped. He tapped it in response. "Picard here."

"We're ready to leave, sir," said Ben Zoma. "If you're ready to beam up . . . ?"

The second officer glanced at Santana again. "Give me a minute, Gilaad.
Picard out."

"You know," she said, "we Magnians like our privacy. But if you ever get the
urge to visit us . . ."

Picard nodded. "I'll know where to find you."

"I hope so," Santana told him, her eyes telling him she meant it with all her heart.

Then she and the mountain and the sunset were gone, and he found himself
standing on a transporter pad . . . feeling empty and terribly alone.

Carter Greyhorse was on his way to the mess hall to secure some lunch when
he saw Gerda Asmund turn into the corridor up ahead of him.

He would never have planned to confront Gerda with his feelings about her
in a million years. But something about the moment seemed to reek of opportunity.

"Miss Asmund?" the doctor said, his heart pounding as he hastened to catch up
with her.

It was only after he had gotten within a couple of meters of her that the navigator
cast a glance back over her shoulder. Her expression wasn't an especially inviting one.

"What do you want?" she asked, as blunt as any Klingon.

"I . . ." Greyhorse stumbled over the words. "I'd like to talk with you sometime.
Perhaps over a cup of coffee . . . ?"

"I don't drink coffee," Gerda told him in a peremptory tone. "Leave me alone."
And she kept on going.

"Wait," he said, grabbing her arm to hold her back. "Please. I really need to
speak with—"

Before he could finish what he was saying, Gerda lashed out at him with the
heel of her boot. It was one of the moves he had seen her make in the gymnasium,
one of the exercises he had watched in awe.

Without thinking, the doctor reacted—and before the navigator's foot could
reach the side of his head, he caught it in his hand.

Suddenly, Gerda's attitude changed. She looked surprised at his quickness—

but not *just* surprised. If he were compelled to describe her expression, he would have called it one of . . .

Admiration.

Unfortunately, it didn't last long. As she twisted, out of his grip, the woman's lips pulled back and she lashed out again—this time, with her fist. It hit him hard in his solar plexus, driving the wind out of his lungs.

As Greyhorse doubled over, she struck him in the chin with the heel of her hand. The blow drove his head up and back, sending him staggering into the bulkhead behind him.

For a moment, he thought she would come at him again. But she didn't. She just stood there in her martial stance, feet spread apart, hands raised in front of her, ready to dole out additional punishment if that was what she chose to do.

"I didn't mean to antagonize you," he told her, the taste of blood thick in his mouth.

"I told you to leave me alone," Gerda snarled.

The doctor took a step forward, knowing full well the risk he ran. But he didn't care. He had had her on his mind too long. Once and for all, he had to tell her how he felt.

"Just let me ex—"

As before, she attacked him before he could speak, landing an openhanded pile driver to his mouth. But he kept his balance somehow. And when she followed with another openhanded assault, he didn't just block it with his forearm. He slugged her back.

Either she hadn't expected Greyhorse to retaliate or he just got lucky, because the blow caught her sharply in the side of the head. In fact, it sent her reeling, clutching at the bulkhead for support.

He didn't anticipate that she would remain that way for long, so he spoke up while he had the chance. "You're all I can think of," the doctor told her. "All I *want* to think of. I can't go on like this. If I haven't got a chance, I need to hear you say it."

Gerda's eyes narrowed, giving her a vaguely wolflike expression. But she didn't say anything.

"Well?" he prodded miserably.

"You fight like a child," she told him, the disgust in her voice cutting him even more than the words.

Greyhorse drew a deep breath. That was it, then. Gerda couldn't make it any plainer than that.

He turned and retreated down the corridor, starting to feel bruises where the woman had struck him. But before the doctor could get very far, Gerda spoke again.

"Greyhorse."

He turned to look at her. There was something in the navigator's eyes, he thought, and it wasn't disdain or revulsion. It looked more like the admiration he had seen earlier.

"Meet me in the gym tomorrow morning at eight," she said. "Perhaps I can teach you to fight like a warrior."

The doctor had never been an emotional man. But he felt such joy then, such a rush of heady optimism, that he could barely find the voice to get out a response.

"I'll be there," he promised her.

* * *

Picard regarded the six officers whom he had summoned to the *Stargazer*'s observation lounge. Paxton, Cariello, Ben Zoma, Simenon, Greyhorse, and Vigo looked back at him from their places around the oval table.

"I called you here," he said, "because you have all had questions regarding the events of the last several days, during which time I have been forced to sometimes operate on a clandestine basis. I thought I would answer these questions all at once."

Then he proceeded to do just that. When he was done, not everyone was happy—Simenon least of all. But even the Gnalish understood the second officer's need for secrecy at various times.

Greyhorse, who had apparently bruised his chin during an accident in sickbay, didn't fully grasp Werber's contribution.

"Chief Werber," Picard explained, "was the one who predicted that the phaser junctions were likely to be tampered with next."

"But he didn't know *which* junction?" the doctor asked.

"That is correct," said the second officer. "We only found that out when Vigo detected a problem in the line. And it wasn't until we spoke to Jomar in sickbay that we understood his objective."

Greyhorse nodded. "I see."

Picard looked around the room. "If there are no further questions, I thank you for persevering in such trying circumstances . . . and commend you to your respective assignments."

He watched his command staff file out of the lounge, one by one. However, one of his officers declined to leave.

"You have something on your mind," Ben Zoma told him. "And it has nothing to do with flow regulators and distribution manifolds."

Picard nodded. "You're right, Gilaad. You see, my mother taught me that one can learn from every experience. I am trying to puzzle out what I can learn from this one."

The other man shrugged. "Not to listen to your fellow officers all the time—especially if they're as wrong as I was about attacking the depot?"

The commander smiled. "Perhaps. Or rather," he said, thinking out loud, "to draw on every resource available to you . . ."

"Even if it means taking the advice of a sworn enemy as seriously as that of a friend."

Picard mulled it over. "That was certainly the way it worked out."

"You know," said Ben Zoma, "I think your mother would have been proud of you right now."

"I hope so," the second officer replied earnestly.

"Captain Ruhalter would have been proud of you too."

Picard looked at him askance. "You think so?"

His friend smiled. "Don't you?"

The second officer wanted to believe that Ruhalter would have approved of his performance. However, he wasn't so sure that that would have been the case.

And he was even less certain of what they would have to say about it at Starfleet Headquarters.

* * *

As the *Stargazer* hung motionless in space, her computer running yet another shield diagnostic, Gerda Asmund gazed at the immense, rose-colored expanse of the galactic barrier.

Of course, she didn't blame Commander Picard for wanting to be thorough. The navigator wasn't eager to go through the phenomenon with a soft spot in their shields either.

Beside her, her sister waited with the patience of a hunter for the order to engage engines and send them soaring through the barrier. Until recently, Idun had known everything about her.

But she didn't know about Carter Greyhorse.

Life is funny, Gerda mused. Just when she discovered that battle was no longer enough for her, just when a hole had opened in her life, she found what she needed to fill it.

"Everything checks out," said Vigo, interrupting her reverie.

Gerda liked the Pandrilite. He had been raw and unproven at the time of Werber's mutiny, but no one could have done a better job at the weapons console than he had. In fact, he seemed to gain confidence with each passing day.

Picard turned to Vigo. "Thank you, Lieutenant." Looking to the viewscreen, he said, "Helm . . . warp six." Then, with a gesture that suggested forward motion, he added, "Engage."

And they sailed into the scarlet abyss of the barrier.

Twenty

Picard considered the pinched, dark-haired man in the admiral's uniform seated across the desk from him.

Admiral Mehdi was still studying the logs posted by the second officer in the wake of the Nuyyad's ambush. He looked grim as he read from his monitor screen, his wrinkled brow creased down the middle.

Finally, Mehdi looked up. "You had quite a struggle, I see."

Picard nodded. "Yes, sir."

"And a number of difficult choices to make."

Picard sighed. "Admiral," he said, "I am not certain I provided you with a full explanation of—"

Mehdi held a thin, almost spindly hand up for silence. "I can imagine what you're about to say, Commander. However, I believe I already possess all the information I require."

The second officer bit his lip and sat back in his chair. "Of course, sir," he replied.

The admiral's eyes seemed to reach into him. "To summarize, you pursued several rather unorthodox options. First, you advised Captain Ruhalter that Serenity Santana could be trusted . . . over the official protestations of First Officer Leach."

Picard swallowed. "Yes, sir."

"Second," said Mehdi, "you chose to take your vessel to the Magnians' colony instead of the galactic barrier, even though—as some of your officers were quick to point out—there was no proof the place even existed, much less that it could give you the assistance you needed."

Picard didn't like the way this was going. "That is correct, sir."

"And in so doing," the admiral continued, "you jeopardized not only the lives of your crew, but your ability to warn the Federation about the Nuyyad. Is this also correct?"

"It is."

"Then," said Mehdi, "knowing that the Magnians had already led you into an ambush, you beamed a number of them up to the *Stargazer* and gave them access to strategic systems. In addition, you allowed their mental powers to be amplified through the use of a synthetic neurotransmitter, thereby inviting the possibility of an enclave of Gary Mitchells running amok aboard your vessel."

"I did," Picard had to admit.

"And, finally, you removed the safeguards from your phaser technology in order to take out a single enemy installation—once again, wagering your ship and crew on a long shot. Is this true?"

Picard had only one answer. "It is, sir."

The admiral considered the younger man a moment longer. "In your estimate, Commander, are these the actions of a Starfleet second officer?"

Picard sighed. "I'm not in a position to say, sir."

"Then let me tell you," Mehdi remarked, "they're not. They're the actions of a Starfleet captain—and a damned remarkable one at that."

Picard wasn't certain he had heard the older man correctly. "I beg your pardon?" he said.

"What you did," Mehdi told him, "what you accomplished against staggering odds . . . shows me that you're more than ready to command. And since you've already won the admiration of the *Stargazer*'s crew, it stands to reason that you should remain with that vessel—as her captain."

Picard didn't know what to say. "Sir—"

Again, the admiral held up his hand. "You're grateful. I know. But between the two of us, I can't tolerate maudlin displays."

"Actually," said Picard, "I was going to ask about Commander Leach."

Mehdi frowned. "Fortunately, Commander Leach will make a full recovery from his injuries. But I don't believe he was ever qualified to serve as first officer on a starship. Command will find a posting for him that's more in line with his abilities."

"I see," said Picard.

It was almost exactly what Ruhalter had said about Leach. In that respect, at least, Ruhalter and Mehdi thought much alike.

"You're a brilliant fellow," the admiral informed him, "and a thoughtful commanding officer, who is obviously not afraid to take the unorthodox and even the unpopular path. I wish you, and those who serve under you, long and illustrious careers."

This time, Picard *did* want to thank the man. But to his chagrin, he didn't get the chance.

"Now get out of my office," said Mehdi, "and start showing me I made the right choice."

Captain Jean-Luc Picard smiled. "Yes, sir," he replied, and took his leave of the admiral.

* * *

Hans Werber had to admit that the accommodations in the Starfleet brig were a little better than in the *Stargazer*'s. But that didn't make him feel a whole lot better.

Hearing the sound of footsteps in the corridor outside his cell, he looked up—and saw a familiar if unexpected face through the barrier.

"Picard?" he said.

"In the flesh," said his visitor.

"I didn't think I'd ever see *you* again," Werber confessed.

Picard regarded him. "You mean because you tried to stun me in my sleep and take over a vessel under my command?"

"Well," said the weapons officer, "yeah."

The other man smiled a taut smile. "I don't believe I will forget that incident anytime soon. But neither will I forget that you helped me uncover Jomar's clandestine activities—or that, in the end, you put your resentment aside and did what your duty demanded."

Werber shrugged. "You didn't have to come here to tell me that."

"I also didn't have to put in a word on your behalf with the judge advocate general," said Picard. "Nonetheless, I did. Perhaps he'll take it into account when he tries your case."

The weapons officer couldn't believe it. "You did that for me? You've got to be kidding."

"I am not," his visitor assured him. "I wanted the court to have all the facts in front of it."

Werber didn't say anything. He couldn't.

"We'll see each other again," Picard told him. Then he turned and started down the corridor.

"Hey, Picard!" the prisoner called, getting to his feet and approaching the energy barrier.

The other man stopped and looked back. "Yes?"

"You know what?" said Werber. "I was wrong. You're going to make a hell of a captain someday."

Picard nodded. "I hope you're right."

EPILOGUE

United Space Probe Agency Escape Pods
<u>S.S. Valiant</u>
2069

One

Dennis Gardenhire checked his instruments. "Hold on," he said. "It could be a rough ride."

Activating the reverse thrusters, the navigator felt them slow the escape pod's descent. Then he made adjustments in the shape of their shields to minimize the stress of entry.

Gardenhire had piloted a pod prototype a dozen times before the *Valiant* left Earth orbit, and gone through escape simulations a hundred times more. But penetrating the atmosphere of an alien world with shield generators that hadn't been dependable for weeks and an inertial damper that hadn't worked correctly from the beginning . . .

That was a different story entirely.

Still, Gardenhire asked himself, what choice did they have? Their pod was low on fuel and even lower on nutritional packets and potable water, and this was the only habitable world they had come across.

Through the pod's observation portal, he could see the ragged white of dense clouds ripping past them. But they were high clouds—sixty-five thousand kilometers high. The pod still had a long way to go before it reached the planet's surface.

Gardenhire looked around at the other faces in the escape vehicle. They looked back at him with trust if not complete confidence, knowing he would do his best to land them safely despite the pod's limitations.

There was Coquillette, the little medic who had seen them through everything from seasickness to bedsores. And O'Shaugnessy, the craggy-faced assistant engineer who had nursed their engines as deftly as Coquillette had nursed the crew.

There was Santana, the stoic and uncomplaining security officer, and Daniels, the astrophysicist with the wicked sense of humor. And finally, Williamson, the balding supply officer who had bullied them into surviving one day after another, regardless of whether they wanted to or not.

By getting this far, they had already set themselves apart as the lucky ones, the ones on whom Fortune had smiled. Only twelve of the *Valiant*'s fourteen escape pods had cleared the explosion that destroyed the ship, and one of those twelve had fallen victim to a plasma breach days later.

The units that remained intact were packed with six or seven people each, with so little living space that only one person could move around at a time. But then, the pods hadn't been designed with an eye to creature comfort. They were survival tools, and survival was a grim business at best.

Gardenhire had always prided himself on his ability to stay cool, to perform calmly under pressure. But after just a month of such close confinement, his nerves had frayed to the breaking point. He was tense, irritable, ready to lash out at anyone who looked at him sideways.

Then came the change.

It was subtle at first, so subtle that the navigator had to wonder if he was losing his mind. But as it turned out, he wasn't losing anything. He was gaining something remarkable.

He could hear the thoughts of his fellow crewmen.

Not all of them, of course—just a stray reflection or two. But it distracted Gardenhire from his misery. It gave him something to think about as he lay prone in his padded shock bunk and waited for his appointed exercise period.

The navigator wasn't oblivious to the fact that telepathy had been one of Agnarsson's talents too. In the back of his mind, he knew he might become what the engineer had become.

But somehow, he felt confident that it wouldn't happen. After all, it had been weeks since the crew was exposed to the Big Red phenomenon. If Gardenhire was going to be altered to the same extent as Agnarsson, if he was going to mutate into a gray-haired, silver-eyed superman, it seemed likely that it would have happened already.

Besides, it was different when the individual undergoing the transformation was oneself. For obvious reasons, it made the prospect seem a lot less chilling.

Then, one day when the navigator was skimming Coquillette's thoughts, he felt an awareness there—a facility capable of not only recognizing his intrusion, but responding to it.

He was afraid that the medic would balk at his invasion of her privacy—for clearly, that was what it was. And in a tinderbox like the escape pod, that was the last thing they needed.

But as it happened, Coquillette didn't mind his trespass at all. In fact, she seemed to welcome it.

It made her feel less lonely, she told him—communicating not in spoken words, but in precise and evocative thoughts. It let her know she wasn't the only one who was experiencing some kind of transformation.

It made Gardenhire wonder . . . if he and Coquillette had changed, was it possible that some of the others were changing as well? And like the medic, were they too uneasy with the situation to speak of it?

Both of them wanted to discuss the matter with the group. However, they were concerned . . . if they were the only ones who had been affected, how would their companions look at them? Would they see Gardenhire and Coquillette as threats to the welfare of their miniature society—threats that had to be dealt with in a harsh and immediate manner?

Then, while they were wondering what to do, O'Shaugnessy responded to their telepathic intrusions as well. And a day later, Williamson did the same. It was Williamson who insisted that they let the others in on what was happening to them.

As Gardenhire had expected, the revelation didn't go very well. Santana didn't say much, but his thoughts were decidedly frightened ones. And though Daniels made a joke about it, it didn't take a telepath to see he was every bit as scared as Santana.

The atmosphere in the pod became taut and uneasy. No one said anything more about the transformations, but they were a subtext in every conversation, a stubborn and nettlesome ghost haunting them every hour of the artificially induced day and night.

Until Santana and Daniels found themselves with telepathic powers of their own, their discoveries coming less than a day apart. At that point, the air of suspicion went away. They were all equals again, working together toward a common goal.

But there were other surprises in store for them. One day, when Williamson was delving in a locker for a hard-to-reach nutritional packet, he saw the thing move obediently into his outstretched hand.

Apparently, he had developed a knack for telekinesis. Announcing his discovery to his podmates (as if he could have kept it secret from a bunch of telepaths), the supply officer challenged them to test their own talents in that regard.

At that juncture, only O'Shaugnessy and Santana exhibited rudimentary telekinetic abilities. But in the days that followed, the rest of them followed suit. Only Coquillette seemed to lag behind, never becoming anywhere near as adept as the rest of them.

They never figured out why. But then, they never figured out anything else about their powers either. Their newfound facilities were a mystery to them through and through.

Eventually, there was only one more step they had to take.

Since the destruction of the *Valiant,* the pods had maintained periodic radio contact—in the beginning, communicating as often as several times a day. Then, as tedium set in and there was less and less to say, their conversations had become correspondingly less frequent.

But in none of these give-and-takes had Gardenhire and his companions ever mentioned their transformations. The main reason for this restraint was simple—it seemed imprudent to give the crews of the other pods a reason to fear them.

Of course, Santana and Daniels could have sent a message to the other pods when they found out about their comrades' powers. At that juncture, they still appeared to be unaltered human beings, and they might have seen it as their duty to send out a warning.

Why had they hesitated? Not just out of fear that they might get caught, as they quite willingly revealed later. It was because they were explorers by nature, and they wanted to see where their podmates' transformations ultimately led them.

Such considerations notwithstanding, they all knew they would have to spill the beans someday. And that day arrived when the pods came within scanner range of a solar system.

By unanimous agreement, Gardenhire radioed McMillan and the other ranking officers and revealed everything that had happened. But far from exhibiting concern, the other pods appeared to be relieved.

Because they had been experiencing the same things.

It wasn't a possibility the navigator hadn't weighed in the back of his mind. The individuals in his group had been exposed to the same stimuli as the men and women in the other vehicles. It stood to reason that they might be changing too.

But it felt good to know for sure.

Especially when their scanners showed them a habitable planet in the solar system they had discovered. A planet with plenty of water and plant life. A planet where they might have a future.

The same planet toward which Gardenhire's pod was now dropping like a very large stone.

"We're falling too quickly," said Daniels, his brow uncharacteristically creased with concern.

"Much too quickly," agreed Coquillette.

Through the observation portal, the navigator could see a faint reddish hue—the play of friction about the shields. And as he had noted earlier, the shield generators had seen better days.

"Something's wrong with the thrusters," O'Shaugnessy said.

"Can you see that?" Gardenhire asked. "Or are you just guessing?"

"I can see it," the engineer assured him, his eyes glazing over as he focused his mind. "One of the release apertures is jammed shut."

The navigator knew that that was no small matter. There were only four apertures and they needed all of them to brake their descent.

"Can you *un*jam it?" asked Coquillette.

O'Shaugnessy shook his head. "This isn't a nutritional packet we're talking about. It's a machine part."

"What if we were to work *together?"* asked Williamson.

Daniels seemed to like the idea. "It's worth a shot—and we don't have too many other options."

Outside the pod, the heat was increasing. What had been a faint red glow was now a deep crimson. They were starting to vibrate as well, starting to experience the roughness Gardenhire had warned them about.

"How's this going to work?" asked Santana.

Gardenhire turned to O'Shaugnessy. "If you can picture the lever that opens the aperture, we can try to access it through you."

"Then we all put pressure on it at once," Daniels added.

"Exactly," said the navigator.

O'Shaugnessy nodded. "Let's do it."

Gardenhire concentrated on linking his thoughts to the engineer's, picturing what O'Shaugnessy was picturing. It turned out to be easier than he had imagined. He could see the lever in question, even feel the place where the thing was stuck.

If the navigator could have reached into the mechanism with his hand, he might have been able to free the offending lever. As it was, he focused on moving it with the power of his mind.

He sensed the others, vague presences all around him. They were pushing with their minds as well.

Come on, came a thought—O'Shaugnessy's. *We can do it.*

And the lever moved.

In fact, Gardenhire was surprised at how little resistance it offered them. It was like moving a feather.

But were they in time? The navigator looked out the observation portal and saw that the aura had become an actual flame. Their shields were rapidly losing their battle with the planet's atmosphere.

Turning to his instrument panel, he checked the pod's rate of descent. It was less than it had been, certainly, but still a good deal more than what safety demanded.

"What's the verdict?" asked Daniels.

"Not good," Gardenhire told him.

"We're still falling too fast," said Coquillette, "aren't we?"

The navigator nodded.

"Wait a minute," said Santana. "O'Shaugnessy couldn't move that lever at all—but when we worked together, it moved easily. Maybe we could slow the pod down the same way."

At first blush, it seemed like a crazy idea. But the more Gardenhire thought about it, the less crazy it sounded.

"Let's try it," said Williamson.

Outside, the flames of their descent had completely obscured their view of the alien sky. Soon, they would feel the temperature begin to rise inside the pod. And after that . . .

"O'Shaugnessy will be our point again," said the navigator, "since he did such a good job last time."

Without a moment's hesitation, the engineer closed his eyes. "All right . . . I'm picturing the underside of the pod. We need to push against it, to slow it down . . ."

Linking his mind to O'Shaugnessy's, Gardenhire could see the flat titanium surface. Surrounded by the four thruster apertures, he pushed up against it. He wasn't alone, either. He felt the others with him, around him and inside him, adding their strength to his own.

At first, he didn't perceive any difference. Then their efforts began to pay off. The pod began to slow down.

Breaking contact with O'Shaugnessy for a moment, the navigator darted a glance at his instruments. They confirmed it—the escape vehicle was falling at a slower rate than before.

Keep it up, Gardenhire told the others.

They did as he asked, continuing to toil against the pull of gravity with all the telekinetic power at their disposal. And little by little, the pod continued to decelerate.

He glanced at the observation portal. The shields were all but gone, but so were the flames that had blocked his view. He could see clouds again. And through them, patches of blue.

If he and the others had had enough time, they might have teamed up with the thrusters to stop their descent altogether. Unfortunately, they didn't have that much time. Gardenhire could see that all too clearly on his monitor, the harsh truth expressed in cold mathematical certainties.

The planet's surface was rushing up eagerly to meet them. And when it did, it would crack them open like an egg.

The injustice of it pierced the navigator's heart like a dagger. To have come this far, to have tried this hard, only to be crushed on a hard and unfeeling alien landscape . . .

Then he saw a way out.

"We need to do more than slow down," Gardenhire said. "We need to push ourselves *that* way." And he pointed to the bulkhead behind Daniels.

"What for?" asked Williamson.

"So we can splash down," the navigator explained. "Or would you prefer to crack up?"

"Let's *push*," said Daniels.

What Gardenhire was asking of them was a lot more complicated than what they had done before. They couldn't push in two directions at once; they had to find just the right vector.

Somehow, they managed it.

Then the six of them pushed for all they were worth. The mingling of their talents created an unexpected level of force, one that seemed to be more than the sum of their individual abilities.

The navigator moved closer to the window and looked down. He could see land through breaks in the cloud cover. He could make out a large, blue bowl of a bay, embraced by a hilly, green coastline.

It would be a good place for a settlement, he thought, a good place to make a future for themselves. That is, if they survived long enough to think about such things.

Push, he insisted.

They poured every last ounce of their energy into the effort, nudging the pod away from the land and out to sea. Gardenhire followed their progress on his instruments, cheering inwardly with each minute alteration in their angle of descent.

We're going to do it, he told the others.

It encouraged them to keep it up, to shove the pod as far out over the bay as they could. With a couple of kilometers to go, the navigator was certain of it—they had earned a water landing.

Brace yourselves, he thought.

They looked at each other as they slid into their shock bunks, needing no words—silent or otherwise—to communicate their feelings. Whether they survived or not, whether their temperamental dampers held or failed, they had fought the good fight. They had discovered a strength in themselves that few members of their species ever came to know.

Neither Gardenhire nor any of the others had a single regret.

Then they punched through the surface of the bay. The impact sent rattlings of pain through the navigator's skeleton, despite the gelatinous padding that lined his bunk. For a moment, he wondered if they might have hit something more than water—some submerged spine of land, perhaps.

Then he craned his neck to look out the observation portal and saw silver bubbles clustering around them like living seacreatures, enveloping them in an intricately woven cocoon of oxygen-rich atmosphere.

Slowly, feeling for injuries all the while, Gardenhire emerged from his bunk. One by one, the others did the same.

"Everyone all right?" asked Williamson, who looked a little dazed.

Santana felt his jaw. "Could have been worse."

Daniels kneaded his neck muscles. "You can say that again."

"How far down are we?" asked Coquillette.

The navigator checked his control panel, but his screen was blank. "I wish I could say. We must have lost external sensors when we hit."

O'Shaugnessy looked out the portal. "Who needs external sensors? I'd say we have five meters of water above us, tops."

"And we're rising," Williamson added, his eyes closed in concentration as he made the judgment.

Gardenhire concentrated as well and came to the same conclusion. Their mantle of bubbles was dissolving, abandoning them, and the waves above were getting closer. Finally, with an effervescent bounce, the pod broke the surface of the bay.

"Look!" said Santana, pointing to the portal.

The navigator looked through the transparent plate, which was dappled with prismatic droplets. In the distance, past a stretch of undulating blue water, he could see the rocky coastline they had managed to avoid. From here, it looked friendly, even inviting.

"I want to get out," Coquillette said suddenly.

Daniels grinned. "Me too."

Gardenhire considered it. There might be jagged rocks just under the surface, or a school of carnivorous sea monsters. But he knew how much the others wanted to leave the pod, because he wanted to leave it also.

"Let's get a little closer to shore first," he advised, running contrary to the current of enthusiasm.

Despite their urge to leave their artificial womb behind, the others agreed to do as the navigator asked. By then, working in concert had become almost second nature. They got the pod skidding through the waves rather easily and came within twenty meters of shore.

At that point, even Gardenhire couldn't stop them. They pried open the hatch cover and spilled out into the water—first Coquillette, then Daniels, then Williamson and Santana. Gardenhire was about to come out too when O'Shaugnessy gave him an unexpected shove.

As the navigator was immersed, he found that the water was warmer than it looked—so warm, in fact, that they were all inclined to linger in it. Gardenhire felt like a kid again, splashing and getting splashed, feeling the sun and the waves wash away weeks of tension and fear.

He wished Tarasco had lived to see this. He wished, at the very least, that the captain could have seen the fruits of his sacrifice.

Finally, the navigator and his comrades got too tired to splash anymore. They struck out for shore with long, easy strokes, tugging the pod along in their wake. That is, five of them did.

O'Shaugnessy chose to try to glide above the waves. But then, as Gardenhire had learned from weeks of sharing a pod with the man, O'Shaugnessy could be something of a showoff.

A Look Inside

Star Trek: The Next Generation—Reunion and
Star Trek: The Next Generation—The Valiant
with Michael Jan Friedman

by Kevin Dilmore

Kevin Dilmore: To put our conversation in perspective, *Reunion* was your fifth *Star Trek* novel, and it was written only a few years after your first.

Michael Jan Friedman: Yes. *Double, Double (Star Trek* No. 45) came out first, then came *A Call to Darkness (Star Trek: The Next Generation* No. 9). After that was *Doomsday World (ST: TNG* No. 12, written with Peter David, Robert Greenberger, and Carmen Carter), then *Fortune's Light (ST: TNG* No. 15).

KD: What started you on the *Star Trek* writing path? I'm assuming you were a fan of the original *Star Trek* series before deciding to write one of these novels.

MJF: I watched all of the original-series episodes as they came out—not in re-runs. I've hardly seen any of them in reruns, even up to today. But I never really thought I'd be writing a *Star Trek* novel. The few that I had read, I had enjoyed, including one by Howie Weinstein. I had written a couple of fantasy books for Warner (Books), and my agent at the time said that the people at Pocket (Books) were looking for new writers to write the *Star Trek* books. At the time, they were publishing only original-series books, and it was only six times a year. Dave Stern was the editor, and my agent hooked me up with him. I gave him a proposal, he liked it, and that became *Double, Double.*

KD: How long did it take for you to put that together?

MJF: Six or seven months, maybe. When I finished the manuscript of *Double, Double,* I said I wanted to write a *Next Generation* novel, because by that time the first season of *Next Generation* was under way on television. Dave Stern agreed, and I gave him a proposal, then started working on *A Call to Darkness.* It was just a quirk in the publishing schedule that they came out very close together.

KD: With *A Call to Darkness* coming out in the second season of the show, did you know ahead of time about the change in ship's doctors from Crusher to Pulaski or did you have to rewrite?

MJF: I think I started at least in the outline stage with Crusher, and then wound up with Pulaski.

KD: How did the collaborative *Doomsday World* take shape?

MJF: I forget whose idea it was, probably Bob Greenberger's. We were at a picnic on Long Island, and there were at least half a dozen *Star Trek* writers at the picnic. It was a great time. We talked about doing a collaborative novel. We weren't really sure what the structure would be, but we wound up with four commitments. Bob hadn't written a *Star Trek* novel, but he was involved in the conception of a lot of different *Trek* projects, so he was a valid contributor. The way we ended up doing it was that Bob did a detailed outline and we each wrote a section simultaneously, and when it was all over I polished everything. It was fun, and Bob, Peter, and I went on to do two other collaborations: *Disinherited (ST: TOS* No. 59) and *(Star Trek: Deep Space Nine* No. 20) *Wrath of the Prophets.*

KD: So we come to *Reunion,* which I understand was the first hardcover novel for *The Next Generation* crew. Who began discussion of that story?

MJF: I had heard or been told that *Next Generation* hardcovers were a possibility. Up to that time, there had only been the giant-sized paperbacks. To make a story worthwhile as a hardcover, it had to cut into a pretty decent-sized chunk of continuity. In *Double, Double* and beyond, I have been fascinated with the possibilities of crews other than the ones we have seen on TV and the movies. So, I thought, *Well, Picard had another crew. Maybe I could make up that crew.* I think there was some initial discussion of making it a *Stargazer* novel, and probably both Paramount and Dave Stern at the time preferred that it be a *Next Generation* book and that we flash back or otherwise discuss the original crew. And I've always kind of liked mysteries, so I made it a mystery. That was pretty much the genesis of it.

KD: *Reunion* remains one of the few straight-out "whodunits" in *Star Trek* fiction. I'm assuming that is something that appealed to your readers. Not only do they get some insight as to Picard's past, but they get a fun story as well.

MJF: I think so, yeah. At least that was the intent.

KD: With *Reunion,* you were working under these basic tenets: Jean-Luc Picard was a crew member and later the captain on a twenty-two-year mission to explore space. And that was about all you had with which to work, correct?

MJF: We knew that Jack Crusher was on the ship, and there was a crewman named Vigo. We knew that in "The Battle," one of the first-season *(ST:TNG)* episodes, where we first see the *Stargazer* as a hulk, Picard has sort of a flashback and someone is crying out "Vigo!" Later on, there was an episode in maybe the sixth season or so where we see Picard's supposed son, Jason Vigo ("Bloodlines").

I think that was an attempt to make that connection, but then somewhere along the line they kept the name but changed the character so there could not have been that connection. So I had Vigo to work with. I also knew how the *Stargazer*'s mission ended—in a clash with the Ferengi.

KD: So that was a pretty blank slate for you to work with, which I'm guessing made it that much more fun.

MJF: It was fun, but I wouldn't have minded a few other points to bounce off of. It makes for good ironies and so on. But it was fun in that respect. I was able to come up with a lot of characters I enjoyed.

KD: Regarding the core seven officers who show up in *Reunion,* you built that crew with Picard as captain, not Picard as a lower-ranks officer as he appears in *The Valiant.*

MJF: Right.

KD: Let's start with the first officer, Gilaad Ben Zoma. Where did you go to come up with him?

MJF: Without thinking about it too much, I went to my childhood. I have vivid memories of my father reciting the Passover service, and one of the rabbis that gets mentioned in that service is named Ben Zoma. There hadn't been any Jewish characters in *Star Trek* that I could remember, so I figured why not plunk one in there. And the visual I had for him was sort of Dean Martin. Dean Martin is kind of olive-skinned and has a ready sense of humor. And I remembered him fondly from my days of watching his variety shows as a kid. Not that I would build my life on Dean Martin's.

KD: And you didn't fill out the rest of the *Stargazer*'s crew with the Golddiggers.

MJF: (laughs) There you go. And that might not have been such a bad idea. But those were the things that kind of converged. And I wanted somebody who was different from Riker, but not so different that Picard would not be able to work with him.

KD: It definitely struck a different tone in relationship. Where Picard and Riker might resemble the teacher and student, Ben Zoma comes across as a contemporary to Picard.

MJF: Very much so. They work together, they confide in each other, there are no protocols separating them.

KD: How about a character who took a darker turn by the end of the book, Carter Greyhorse.

MJF: Yeah, Carter Greyhorse is an interesting character to me, still. In terms of how he looked, I was thinking of the Indian character in the film *One Flew Over the Cuckoo's Nest.*

KD: Chief.

MJF: Right. Big guy, kind of taciturn, and different in one regard in that Greyhorse is a little more intellectual than Chief. But I wanted someone unusual and, again, I couldn't remember any American Indians in *Star Trek,* so I wanted to put one in there.

KD: And other than in the comics, I don't know whether there was an approach to that type of character before Chakotay in *Star Trek: Voyager.*

MJF: When I started writing the book, I didn't . . . well, yeah, I guess I did know who the bad guy was going to be, Greyhorse. I wanted him to be different from the doctors we had seen at this point. I guess he had a little bit in common with Bashir in terms of his intellectual superiority, but Bashir had not shown up yet.

KD: The repartee between Greyhorse and Simenon seemed more playful rather than the sometimes antagonistic exchanges between Spock and McCoy. Was that something you were going for?

MJF: Yeah, exactly. I wanted a pair of guys who could snipe at each other and be in conflict and yet not be doing it in a petty way; it grows out of genuine mutual respect and affection. And that's how they are related to each other.

KD: And Simenon is from a reptilian species called the Gnalish? Tell me what you were thinking along those lines, as that was definitely an alien addition to a *Star Trek* crew.

MJF: The crews that we have seen on the screen, just because of the exigencies of the production process, had to be pretty humanoid. Now, with CGI, you can get away with a wider range of aliens. But at the time, we hadn't seen anyone like that on the screen. The closest we had come is the Gorn, and that was very stiff and awkward-looking. But I wanted to do something different. The thought of a sarcastic talking lizard kind of appealed to me.

KD: He is kind of a wise guy.

MJF: Yeah, but he has a heart of gold, of course, that he zealously conceals.

KD: The communications officer is an Aussie, which I thought was great.

MJF: Yeah, you'll see in all my books that *Star Trek* is very much an international thing. Even though at least some of our major characters are recognizably American, I wanted to provide a range of international flavor. I try to do it all over the place. I've even been criticized for using names that fans say are not *Star Trek* names.

KD: How do you have a name that is not *Star Trek?*

MJF: I don't know. I used some kind of French name once, and someone said, "Well, that's not a *Star Trek* name."

KD: And Picard is . . . ?

MJF: (laughs) Yeah, and Picard is okay, so go figure. But the international flavor is fun, and it's another way of distinguishing characters, especially when you're introducing a group all at once. But back to (Tricia) Cadwallader. I wanted her to be attractive and perky and an Aussie.

KD: She was fun in that she reminds me of what could have come of Yeoman Colt from the original *Star Trek* pilot, "The Cage."

MJF: And that was one of the things I thought about with her. Really, the only other crew that we really knew about at the time was Pike's. Shortly after *Reunion,* I did a book, *StarTrek: Legacy,* that had a lot of flashbacks to Pike's *Enterprise.* So Colt really was one of the influences on Cadwallader. Not the only one, I guess, but certainly the idea of a young, perky officer.

KD: And she's definitely one for whom being out in space remains a thrill.

MJF: Yes.

KD: Idun Asmund is one of the two *Stargazer* crew members who share space in the original cover artwork with Picard. Obviously, she is meant to be the alluring, exotic Starfleet officer in the bunch.

MJF: My idea for her started like this: Worf is a Klingon raised by humans. It didn't make sense for a Klingon to be on this ship, but I like Klingons and I wanted to have some influence from them, considering that is the other big race in terms of possibilities of people being on a starship. It was too early in the continuity for there to be a Klingon on the *Stargazer.* So I thought what if we turned it around and had humans raised by Klingons? At first, I got a little static over that. I showed the execution of the concept and it was okayed. But I wanted to turn Worf's paradigm around. And the fact that they turned out to be twins, well, it just struck me as being an interesting idea.

KD: There's always an idea when you're creating a crew that there are bridge stations you have got to fill. With Idun, did you create her character to fill the helmsman's slot, or did you create a great character and then decide later that she would be a good fit at the helm?

MJF: I probably started with the slot and filled it with her, and I'm not sure at what point I decided to make her twins. I guess I decided that when I realized what the plot of *Reunion* was going to be.

KD: I wondered whether that also was the case with Pug. To me, if I saw this guy walking down the hall, just from his physical description I'd pick him as a natural for security.

MJF: Yeah. Pug was named after a friend of mine, Peter Joseph, but they don't call my friend Pug. He looks nothing like Pug, and he's not in security. He doesn't even wear red shirts as far as I know. But I needed a guy, and I had a sense of who he would be and how he would fit in and where he would figure into the plot. I had to consider two things in a macro sense. One was an array of physical and social personalities who looked different and acted different to distinguish one from the other, with the exception of the twins, of course. The other thing was I needed suspects beyond the guy who actually did it.

KD: And some suspicion was loaded pretty quick, such as Guinan hinting that Pug may be an alcoholic with a temper. In this kind of story, I suppose that you have to put a dark shade on everyone.

MJF: But I like Pug a lot. He's just an earnest guy, especially in the *Stargazer* books. In *Reunion,* he was a little more seasoned and older.

KD: The interesting thing is that in this first story with the *Stargazer* crew, you are showing them at the end of their careers. But in the new books, you're showing them more at their fighting weights.

MJF: And that's very cool to me.

KD: So we're left with, and I almost can't say it with a straight face, Captain Morgen. As soon as I saw his name, I thought someone was mixing drinks.

MJF: (laughs) No, no, it was nothing like that. Actually, I conceived him as a very angular and hairless man, contrary to what you see on the original cover. And I came up with the Daa'Vit culture because it gave us the hook to bring them all together. It was just a plot device. While I was at it, I made Morgen someone that Worf could interact with. When these new guys are standing off by themselves, it's not nearly as interesting. I wanted as many different points of contact with the *Enterprise* crew as I could get. Wesley was able to interact with Simenon, Worf with Morgen, and so on. Interestingly enough, the one character besides Picard who should have interacted with this crew the most chose not to, and that was Beverly.

KD: For the reason that it was painful. It would be as if someone lost his wife and then went to her high-school reunion. And with that in mind, you had to create the character of Jack Crusher just so you could make sure to be true to him in his absence. The others have to refer to him consistently. So who is Jack Crusher?

MJF: Actually, in a book called *The First Virtue* (No. 6 in the *Double Helix* series, written with Christie Golden), I actually portray Jack in a buddy story with Tuvok. So what kind of guy is he? He's a nice guy, a good guy. He's not complicated. He's eager to do his job. You wouldn't call him devil-may-care, but he's willing to accept a little danger to do his job.

KD: With all this in the mix, it seems that the *Stargazer* crew is one with a lot of possibilities.

MJF: I agree. I like the crew. And the reason I added crew members in *Gauntlet* is that you already know what happens to these guys. In one sense, it's a good thing. You have the advantage of creating all of these ironies, but you also have the disadvantage of knowing they all survive except for the couple who don't. You want some sense of jeopardy, so I created the additional characters. They have something that the others do not have by virtue of our not knowing their fates.

KD: So it was eight years later that you revisited this crew for *The Valiant*.

MJF: Yes, but other things happened in between. I did a book with Kevin Ryan called *Requiem (ST:TNG* No. 42), in which some of the characters appeared in an extended prologue. Then I did *The First Virtue,* in which the crew appeared with Jack. In a three-issue arc of the comics, I did a story featuring Picard, Jack, and Ben Zoma, so there was a little whetting of the appetite along the way. But what happened was that my book *Starfleet: Year One* was supposed to be the first of an original book series. When official details about *Enterprise* started coming out, it was clear that my vision of the beginning of Starfleet was going to conflict with that vision. Rather than that series happening, we considered a *Stargazer* book series instead. But actually the decision to do *The Valiant* was independent of that. Originally, this was going to be a stand-alone book. When it became obvious that *Starfleet: Year One* was not going to be a series, we then switched gears and made *The Valiant* into essentially the first *Stargazer* book.

KD: Did that affect your plans for the story in any way?

MJF: To me, the seminal story in *Star Trek* is (the original-series episode) "Where No Man Has Gone Before." That may still be the best hour of *Star Trek* in my mind. The idea that Gary becomes superhuman has stuck in my mind and has surfaced in a few of the *Star Trek* books I have done and will continue to surface, as it did in the *My Brother's Keeper* trilogy. But I wasn't done with Gary Mitchell. I thought it would be cool to connect what happened on the *Valiant* to something later on in *Star Trek* continuity. Originally, I wasn't thinking of a *Stargazer* story for that. But I figured that I already had a crew that I could use again, and Kirk's already been connected to the old *Valiant.* So let's go ahead and connect Picard and do it in a way that also relates to another big element in continuity, which is how he got his command.

KD: And it was received well by readers.

MJF: I think its biggest virtue was that it connected all of these points. You have the Gary Mitchell back-story, the *Valiant,* the Kelvans from (the original-series episode) "By Any Other Name," and Picard's battlefield commission. That's a lot of interesting points.

KD: Tell me about what it's like to write Picard as a junior officer and captain on the *Stargazer* as opposed to writing him as commander of the *Enterprise.* To me, it might seem like writing the adventures of Superboy.

MJF: Yeah, it is. But it's very difficult, actually. If you go back to (the *ST:TNG* episode) "Tapestry," Picard's a hothead and he learns not to be one.

KD: But once you get your heart poked out by a Nausicaan, usually, it tones you down.

MJF: That's gonna happen. (laughs) So now he's toned down. But it sort of implies in "Tapestry" that once those events were over and he learned that lesson, he could have become a Milquetoast and never been a captain. So he's kind of forced into a middle ground, and that works very well for him in *The Next Generation* era, because he's an older guy. But in *Stargazer,* from that incident on, what is he like? Is he like the sixty-year-old Picard from the time he was twenty-five? What the hell is he like? It's always interesting to portray him in the *Stargazer* era. You don't want to portray him too much differently from where he ends up, but you don't want him too similar, either. He makes mistakes. It's difficult, and to tell you the truth, I'm not sure I always succeed. Really Picard is the most complex captain we have. I love Kirk, but Kirk was on for three years and I don't think he ever became as complex as Picard.

KD: So even though it initially was not meant to be, *The Valiant* was the introduction to your series of *Stargazer* novels, which are going strong today.

MJF: *The Valiant* very much sows the seeds for what happens later in the *Stargazer* series. And I am having fun with the new books.

KD: This is very interesting insight, Mike. Thanks for sharing it with your readers.

MJF: It was my pleasure.